TEESSIDE OUTSIDERS

To James

Cheers [signature]

TEESSIDE OUTSIDERS

JOHN NICHOLSON

Nick Guymer Series
No.13

Published by Head Publishing
Copyright © John Nicholson 2017

Edition edit by Robert Marcum

Printed by CMP

ISBN 978-0-9933817-6-8

http://www.johnnicholsonwriter.com

Thanks to my wonderful team:

Robert, my editor.
His insight, help and guidance was
invaluable in crafting this story.
Janet for proofreading and invaluable
scribbles in the margin.
Dawn for cover art and book design.

They all make me look better than I am.

"Sail away, away
Ripples never come back
Gone to the other side"

CHAPTER 1

The doorbell rang. Nick opened his front door. Standing there was Josh Jones, in a blue hoodie, t-shirt and loose, scruffy, worn-out jeans, his fair hair messy and ruffled.

'Hello, Josh! How are you doing?'

'How am I doing what?' asked Josh, with a blank look. 'No, don't bother explaining. There's no time. I need your help, Nick.'

That was classic Josh. His Asperger's could make him seem rude, but he wasn't. His brain just worked to alternative rules.

'OK, what's going on?'

'A boy that I know is going to kill himself.'

The lad said it with such a dry, flat voice that it was almost hard to take him seriously.

'What? Come in and explain.' He gestured for the lad to step inside.

Josh shook his head. 'No, I can't. He's going to do it very soon and I want you to stop him.'

Nick frowned. 'Well, who is he and why does he want to kill himself?'

Josh counted two points off on his fingers. 'First, he's called Paul Richardson; second, because he hates his body.'

'He what?'

Josh stared back at him. 'Is this one of those situations where I have to repeat myself, even though you've actually heard me?' he said, his face still expressionless. 'I suggest you just drive us down to Allens West station and stop him.'

Nick knew Josh wouldn't or couldn't joke about something like this, so he grabbed his leather jacket and keys, closing the door behind him.

'Why is he killing himself at Allens West?'

'Because it's one of the most unused, isolated stations on Teesside and somewhere that you can walk in front of a train without anyone seeing or trying to stop you.'

'Well, that's hard to argue with. Is he a friend of yours at 6th form?' He unlocked his old BMW.

'He's someone I know.'

'Is he an Aspie as well?'

'No. We are allowed to know people outside of our own kind, Nick. He's an NT like you, you fucking freak.'

Josh grinned suddenly and threw him a two-fingered peace sign, even despite the apparent seriousness of the moment. He used NT as an acronym for 'neuro-typical'. Nick doubted he was especially NT; in fact, as he learned more about it, he felt himself to be quite neuro-untypical.

'Don't swear, just explain the situation,' said Nick, knowing Josh liked short, simple questions and instructions.

They got into the car and he turned over the engine. It coughed and didn't start. He turned the key again. This time it fired. Nick stepped on the gas, revving the weak-sounding engine. Julie had said there was something badly knackered with it.

'Paul was going out with Connie McQueen. They broke up recently because she said he was fat and had a small penis, and her friends Emma West and Emily LeBron told everyone when we were in basketball training. They stood around him and taunted him by saying how he wasn't a real man. Afterwards he was so humiliated that he was even scared to change out of his gym clothes. He put his trousers on over his shorts. It wasn't nice and everyone else thought they were being nasty and tried to comfort Paul. But he already hated himself, and they knew that and still just tortured him for fun. That is why he is going to throw himself in front of a train.'

Nick drove away.

'That sounds horrible. But how do you know he's serious?' he said, glancing at Josh.

'Why would he not be serious?'

'People say things, Josh. They don't always mean them literally.'

Josh went quiet for a moment. 'But he's planned it all out. He's going to be killed by the train to Darlington at 1pm. It didn't occur to me that he'd be lying. Sorry. I took him at his word.'

'Well, let's hope he is lying. How old is he?'

'16. Same as me.'

'Is he mentally unwell?'

Josh made a funny noise with his lips. 'Well obviously he's mentally unwell, Nick. He's going to kill himself because of his body fat percentage and because of the size of one single part of his anatomy. That's a pretty good definition of mentally unwell, and I speak as a person who is often thought by stupid people to be mentally unwell.'

'Is he a good friend of yours?'

'I don't know what *good* means, in this context.' He said it flatly.

'Are you close mates? Friendly with each other, like?' When Josh asked you questions, it forced you to think about what you meant by common, everyday expressions, and sometimes it made you realise that you didn't even know what you meant by your own words.

'Well...sort of.'

'Why sort of?'

Josh frowned, knitting his light brown eyebrows together and focusing on his thoughts. Nick knew from his expression that he was about to go on one of his stream of consciousness rants, when words just fell out of him without pause or punctuation.

'We used to get on well and I enjoyed hanging around with him but now he watches pornography all the time and I don't like it and I've tried to like it but I don't or at least the stuff he watches is boring because sex is about what it makes you feel like with the person and you can't feel like that when you're just looking at people he thinks I'm prudish but I'm not anyway we fell out about it and he says it's great and I told him that it's not real and that it's not what real sex is like and I know that because you told me that ages ago and anyway it looks weird more like a biology lesson in fucking or something and the people look physically weird to me. I told him I reckon they're some sort of fucking fuck robots and OK so I've not actually had any sex in my 16 fucking years but I reckon I'm right but the way he goes on about it makes me think it's setting a bad example to kids and probably to adults as well and if you think about it it's like watching Scooby Doo and thinking your dog should be like Scooby and if it isn't it's not as a good a dog but Scooby isn't fucking real so you can't compare reality to fiction and it'll fucking do your head in if you even try do you get me?'

He took what seemed like his first breath in a minute, but hadn't finished yet.

'And that's one of the reasons he fucking hates his body. He looks at the men in those videos and doesn't see himself. He thinks he's no good and inadequate and that's just fucking stupid. I think it's messed with his head so badly and I've told him to stop looking it at but he won't listen to me 'cos I'm just an Aspie kid so what could I know?' He made a vibrating noise with his lips again, as though in contempt of the disregard his views had been shown.

Life around Josh could be a raw experience. He could throw you some curve balls, that was for sure, and he'd recently taken to swearing a lot, something Nick had admonished him for several times. He had no social inhibitions if he felt he was with friends and, from the introverted boy of 10 that he'd been when Nick had first met him, he'd grown into a confident, clever, vulgar 16-year-old, who could be a bit of a smart arse. However, when around strangers he'd learned to bite his tongue and consider his words more carefully, at least most of the time. But 16 is a difficult age for everyone; you're growing into the adult you'll become, and Nick was very much Josh's best adult friend, so he leaned on him for advice and guidance in social conventions, which he'd then try and remember and apply.

It was ironic that he should turn to him for such advice given Nick's own struggles in life, yet he found it easy to empathise with the lad, more so than he would for a regular boy of his age, and found himself being very protective towards him. It was unspoken between him and Julie, but nonetheless understood, that Josh had grown into being a kind of surrogate son for him, and as Nick had got more involved in his life in the last year or two, it gave him a lot of pleasure, and a unique sort of pleasure, at that. Josh's blunt honesty, free from politeness or inhibition, was refreshing. In a world which seemed to run on obfuscation, lying and pretence, Josh was incapable of sugar-coated platitudes and you always knew where you were with him. He could be funny, endearing and occasionally touchingly affectionate, but it was no use getting inhibited or embarrassed around him because of his forthright language, as he lacked any ability to intuit what was acceptable. He had to simply remember, rather than rely on instinct.

'OK, first, you're swearing far too much, Josh. You know it's a very bad habit, I've told you often enough. I don't mind it, but most people do when you swear as much as you just did there. Do you understand? Too much swearing puts people off you. It's not appropriate, it's vulgar and, what my mam would have called common.'

The lad scratched his scruffy head. ' "Common"? What's that mean?'

'To use my mother's language, "the sort of thing rough people would say". And you're not rough. So tone it down. Less use of the f-word.'

'Fuck. OK. I'm fucking sorry, Nick.' He looked at Nick and grinned. 'I did that on purpose.'

'I know you did, you cheeky fucker,' said Nick, with a wink.

Josh burst out laughing and threw his head back joyfully and slapped Nick on the leg. When he laughed, he really laughed. In such moments he looked so happy and so in love with life, that it could warm the coldest heart. His blue eyes shone with glee. Perhaps because so much of the time he said things in a blank, expressionless sort of way, when he did laugh it was all the more lovely to see.

Once the kid had settled down, Nick said, 'You do know there's no right or wrong size or shape of body, right? It's all about the person you are, not what your body is like, or any part of it.'

Josh turned to look at him. 'Of course. Remember, Nick, I am from Weirdsville. I know shit that kids my age don't normally know.'

'You like to think you do,' said Nick, keen to slap down Josh's growing smart-arse tendency. 'And sometimes you do, but not always. It's not like you're experienced in the matters of sex and stuff.'

'Sadly, no. But I very much would like to be. Preferably with Heather in my physics class. God I'd love to stuff my hard cock right up her.'

Nick snapped at him, clicked his fingers and jabbed a finger. 'Hey! You! I just told you, didn't I? Don't take liberties with me, Josh. I don't appreciate it. Less of that sort of talk. Right? I don't want to hear you talking like that. It's not right. Have some respect for her, for me and for yourself. I've told you this before, more than once.'

Josh suddenly wore the insolent expression of any teenager who had been told off but still felt he was in the right.

'But that is what I really, really want to do. It's not disrespectful. It's the opposite of that. I wouldn't say it in public. I've learned that you can't say that sort of thing. But I can in front of you because you know I'm a messed-up Aspie.'

'Don't use being an Aspie as an excuse, Josh. You know what's right and wrong. You're being vulgar and there's no need for it. Manners are important. I've told you that often enough, as well. Good manners help us all rub along together. So even when you're with me, keep those thoughts to yourself. I've told you about not sharing everything that's in your head, haven't I? There are some things you just don't voice and certainly not in such a crude way. I don't mind you talking about sexual things but it's important to do it in the right way. Alright?' He looked at Josh with a hard stare.

Josh knew he'd overstepped the mark. Nick tried to never admonish him unless he'd said or done something quite wrong, so that when he did, it had real impact.

He let out a sigh. 'Sorry, Nick. You have told me before. I just got carried away because I fancy her so much. She's gorgeous and I can't stop thinking about her.' He threw his head back. 'She's on my mind all the time. I can't stop imagining how she'd look naked. I love the way she smiles, the way she walks. Everything. Even the smell of her hair. It's all so intoxicating and completely and totally overwhelming. I've never felt anything like it before.'

He just stared straight ahead, clearly seeing her in his mind's eye, as he spoke, going through his first major teenage crush. Nick could easily remember just how incredible that was. It really was like being intoxicated. He'd fallen in and out of love what seemed like every other month from age 14, with an overwhelming intensity which, by and large, he'd always kept to himself. Somehow, the object of your crush always seemed so utterly perfect, and your love total and permanent, even though it often lasted little more than a few weeks.

'Look, man, I do understand. I was like that at your age. I often fell in love with girls who I just couldn't get out of my mind for a while. Everyone goes through it. And we all think extremely rude things about what we'd like to do with them. That's only natural. But I'll tell you this, right, if you treat girls as people and not as sex objects, you'll end up having a lot more sex. It's off-putting and not acceptable to refer to women in that way, even if you hear other lads doing it. You should have higher standards. It really isn't cool.'

'Yes, but I do get confused because finding someone so attractive is a compliment to them, so how can saying you want to...to do that to them be wrong?'

It wasn't an unreasonable question but it was the kind of distinction his condition meant he struggled with sometimes.

'Being sexually attracted to someone is perfectly natural, but how you express it matters. If all you do when Heather's name is mentioned is say how much you want to have sex with her, then it disregards all her other attributes. She's a fully rounded person, not merely a receptacle for your lust. And you don't "do it" to her, either, you do it *with* her. So get into the habit of having good manners around everyone. OK? Julie would want you to, as well. She'd call it objectifying women, and she really dislikes that. Right? It's nice to be cool, but it's much cooler to be nice.'

Josh said nothing but nodded in an exaggerated fashion. Nick felt like he'd made his point rather well.

'You're amazing,' said Josh, as they sat in a long queue of traffic, south of Stockton.

Nick grinned and a prickle went up and down his spine. 'Am I? Why?'

'You just say things to me that I don't hear anyone else say, and it all makes sense when you say it. Heather is intellectually brilliant, but my brain is dominated by thinking of her tits and arse and that's really unfair to her. I can see the logic of that. But I'd not have

7

thought of it if you hadn't just said it. See? Brilliant.'

Nick turned to him. 'Well, it's just common sense, really.'

'Sense, maybe. But not so common,' said Josh, suddenly sounding much older than his years.

Nick smiled to himself. The kid had no idea how much of a compliment that was.

They moved off along Darlington Road, sunlight casting dark, black shadows across the road.

'So this lad, Paul, does he have a troubled home life?'

Josh made a shrug. 'I don't know. I've met his parents. They seemed normal, whatever that means.'

'So he's not mentioned anything bad happening at home?'

He shook his head. 'No. Not to me, anyway. He doesn't talk about home at all.'

'And you're sure he's serious about killing himself?'

'Yes. In fact, when he told me, he was happier than usual.'

Nick looked at him. 'Really? What? Like it was a weight off his mind?'

Josh did his big exaggerated nod. 'Exactly. Which is weird. He's been depressed for months, and he'd started behaving in weird ways, sometimes, and talking dirty and stuff and getting on kids' nerves. And then he came in today with a smile on his face and told me what he was going to do. He seemed pleased about it.'

Nick stepped on the accelerator, overtook two cars and moved into some open road on Durham Lane.

That information made him extremely concerned, knowing as he did that being unusually happy was a common experience amongst people who had made their mind up to end it all. This clearly wasn't an error of understanding that Josh had made. It *was* going to happen.

They pulled into the station car park. Josh looked at his watch. 'It's 1.00pm exactly. Let's hope the train is, as usual, not on time.'

Nick sprinted onto the westbound platform and looked from side to side. There was no-one around. The train was just coming around a long arcing bend, a little way in the distance. Where was the kid?

There he was. Well beyond the platform, standing on the weed-strewn, ice-grey gravel to the side of the tracks was a thick-set boy. He was standing impassively, hands in a red hoodie, as though just waiting casually for the train. He had side-parted short, fair hair, and was dressed in the sort of modern jeans that are tight on the leg, but hang off the arse. He wasn't really, really fat, but he looked out of condition for a young lad, flabby and without muscle. He wasn't really going to throw himself in front the train, was he?

Yes, he bloody was.

He took his hands out of his pockets as the train approached.

'I'd suggest physical intervention at this point,' said Josh calmly in Nick's ear.

Nick sprinted down the platform.

The train had begun to slow down in order to stop at the station. On seeing the boy at the side of the track, the driver sounded a horn as a warning, but it clearly wasn't one that Paul Richardson wanted to heed.

The boy took two steps forward. That's all it took. Two steps from alive to dead.

Now he stood just looking at the train straight on, as though staring it down. The driver braked immediately, and a high-pitched screech rang out as Paul opened out his arms wide, with his head back in a kind of Jesus Christ pose, as though preparing to be crucified by the train.

The modest two-carriage train seemed huge compared to the boy and, even though it was rapidly slowing, it was going to hit him, it was going to knock the boy down, crush his bones and make human jam of him. God Almighty, what was going on in that poor boy's head? Clearly, he wanted to die. He really did. In that moment, that was his total desire. He'd had enough of this thing we call life. No more existence needed, he'd done his time on the chain gang, and didn't want to do any more breathing in, breathing out. No. This wasn't a cry for help, it wasn't a dare. It was just a simple, effective way to stop being alive.

The boy didn't hesitate or deliberate. He stood between the tracks, arms ready to embrace the tons of metal that would macerate him.

As Nick ran at top speed, years of watching football had taught him how to judge the distance between striker, defender, ball and goal. Every football fan has it. In an instant, you know if the ball is in that corridor of uncertainty between goalkeeper and defence, and you can tell in the blink of an eye who is going to get there first. As he flew towards the kid, he knew there was only a split second in it. He was ahead of the train, but only just. If the boy took a step away from him, it was all over, he'd never reach him in time.

But he didn't, he just stood stock still, arms wide.

Nick left the platform, feet plunging into the deep, crunching, chunky gravel, assessing as he ran how he was going to do this. Rugby tackle to take him out of danger, or a massive grab and pull back? He had to use his momentum. It was 51/49 but he felt he had the advantage. The lad could be saved, but only if he did this right. Do it wrong and they were both dead.

He was flying at top speed now, blood roaring in his ears as he tore towards the track, the train still braking hard and screeching, no more than nine feet away from the kid, eight feet, seven feet, six feet. Oh, fuck. The stink of burning brakes filled his nostrils.

It takes a special kind of brave or stupid to run out in front of a train, but Nick wasn't as attached to life as much as most people, and there was no way he wasn't going to give the upset boy a chance at life, even if it meant he was going to have to give up his own to do it. That's the deal. Kids come first.

So, recalling what Gary Hanrahan, his rugby and maths teacher at Ian Ramsey had taught him back in 1976 and 1977, during his largely unsuccessful stint as a winger on the school rugby team, without breaking stride he ran in front of the train and made a flying tackle, low and hard. He took the solidly set boy out with overwhelming power, grabbing him around the waist, his speed and strength lifting both of them off the ground as he did so, pushing hard with his shoulders and throwing him to one side, clear of the train. As he did so, he felt the front right side of the train clip his right foot as it screeched to a halt. The smell of diesel and the all-consuming noise of the halting train filled his ears as they landed on the hard, sharp gravel together. Nick's heart was in his throat as he gasped to get his breath back.

'Fucking hell! Why did you do that?! Don't you understand? I. Want. To. Be. Dead!!!!' screamed the boy from under him, shocked and angry, lashing out at him with his fists and feet. Nick stood up and looked down at him, breathless.

'You might hate yourself now, but you won't always. Trust me.' He heaved out the words in between big gulps of breath.

The boy let out a groan, rising to a growl and spat at him, still prone on his back, his eyes alight with anger and a crazed despair.

'Yes, I fucking will, you fucking idiot!! Death is the *only* way to escape yourself and everyone else!!'

CHAPTER 2

'Here you go, Superman,' said Julie, putting a glass of single malt in front of Nick in the Masham, in Hartburn Village. 'I'm very proud of you for saving that lad's life.'

'There wasn't any time to think about it, really. I knew I could get to him, if I was fast enough.' He took a sip of whisky. 'I just got to him in time.'

'Did the lad say anything to you afterwards?' She pushed a strand of blonde hair behind her ear and looked at him with her intense, turquoise eyes.

'He swore a lot at me, and at Josh as well, but the train driver had called the police and they were there almost straight away. They took my statement and then took him back to his parents, I think. It was upsetting to see a boy so determined to end it all. The way he shouted at me, he just wanted to not be alive. I hope he gets help. He seemed to be out of his mind, poor boy.'

She pushed her bottom lip out in sympathy. 'Social services will get involved, I would imagine, if he's not already in the system. How did Josh take it all?'

'In his typically pragmatic Josh way. Because he can't do empathy, he sees even the most dramatic things in a clinical, practical manner. He'd asked me to save the kid and I had, so when it was all over he just nodded and said, "That went well".'

Julie smiled and nodded. 'That's our Josh. The thing is, a boy of 16, who so clearly wanted to end it...well, that hasn't just come from nowhere. He must have been building up to it for a long time.'

'Josh reckoned he'd split up with a girlfriend after she and her friends had said he was fat and had a small dick. It seems as though that was what pushed him over the edge.'

Julie raised her eyebrows and rolled her eyes. 'That was very mean of her. Kids can be so nasty. Is he actually fat?'

Nick nodded. 'Well, he's not huge, but he's like a lot of kids these days, he has a thick tyre of fat around his waist and looks totally out of shape. No muscle at all. Flabby all over. In 10 years he will be very fat, if he doesn't do something about it. And he really took some shifting. I piled into him at top speed and it's just as well I did. He's about five foot seven and I'd guess getting on for at least 12 stone or more.'

She took a drink and shook her head, a frown on her brow. 'An insult from a girl doesn't just make a lad kill himself, not even one as intimate as that, which, by the way, someone needs to take her to one side and have a word with her about. There's no need to indulge in that sort of personal nastiness. She won't realise, but all it does is perpetuate the phallocentric nature of society. All hail the mighty penis.' She raised her hands as though in supplication to a God.

'The small dick insult is a classic of the genre, and must have been said by many a woman in order to try and hurt a bloke's feelings, or to get rid of him, but who knows, maybe he'd been horrible to her and had said similar things about her having small tits or something?'

She hummed agreement. 'Yeah, that could be true. Good point. And it's also quite typically teenagey and immature. Even so...'

'Have you ever said it as an insult?'

She puffed out her cheeks. 'No, I don't think so. I always tried to be nice when splitting up. In fact, sometimes I was nicer during the break-up than I had been during the relationship! Ha ha. Actually I was good at break-ups, because I had so much practise. I developed a nice routine which was basically the whole "it's not you, it's me" thing: "You're lovely, but I'm not interested in having a relationship". That sort of excuse. It almost always worked. Once, when I was at University, I had a clingy ex who wouldn't take no for an answer. I had to give him the hard word, in no uncertain terms. That happened a couple times over the years, but I wouldn't have gone to the sexual insult because that'd be to invest it with too much power and significance. Like I say, it's all too phallocentric. And anyway, I wouldn't have broken up with someone for that reason, not even aged 16. I'm not that shallow. I'd have at least pretended to myself that it was for a different reason, even if he had one that didn't touch the sides.' She snorted a laugh.

'That's very noble of you, Miss Wells.'

She wobbled her head in a silly way. 'Well, I'm a nice lass, me, aren't I? And I know how hung up you all are about those things between your legs, much more so than we women are. It's like your world revolves around it.'

'You can talk. You're the biggest cock-watcher I've ever known. You're always telling me which side a man dresses and guessing how well hung he is or isn't.'

She chortled her woody laugh. 'That's just a hobby. Every girl needs a hobby. And I'm good at it!' She laughed again. 'The lad behind the bar was dressing to the right - very niche is your right dresser. You don't see many of them.'

'I'll have to start going against nature then. I can't be in the dressing-to-the-left mainstream.'

'Wouldn't that be uncomfortable, or feel weird, the way writing with your other hand does?'

He looked from side to side to see if anyone was looking. 'Hang on, I'll let you know.' He put his hands down his pants and made the adjustment. Julie laughed.

'Oh, that's unhygienic. Go and wash your hands.'

'You're OK, I had a shower before coming out. Now, does that look any different?'

He stood up to show her.

'Oh no, I don't like that at all. It looks odd,' she said between gasps of laughter. 'It looks like you got a different one fitted.'

'It does feel odd. I think it'll find its way over to the other side soon enough. It won't be tamed. I've often thought it's the obvious part of the body to have interchangeable nozzles fitted. You'd carry around a range of shapes and sizes and fit the one your partner liked best.'

'Now that really would be a tool bag, wouldn't it? It'd be like a sexual ratchet set, you'd screw on the one which is the right size for the job in hand.'

'I can see you're attracted to the idea.'

She flashed her eyes at him. 'Fortunately, you came fitted with just the right-sized nozzle for me.'

14

'That was lucky for both of us, then.' He went to the bar and got two more drinks.

As he put the glasses down, Julie said, 'So this lass who was nasty to Paul Richardson was either just being a bitch, or has issues herself. She might have known he was vulnerable to that and just wanted to really upset him. Even if he'd been insulting, the better thing is to rise above it, not get down to their level. But then she's young, so...' she shrugged.

'Yeah, I'm tempted to just put it down to youth. According to Josh, he'd been watching a lot of porn online. Maybe his girlfriend said what she said because of that. Josh, in his rambling way, told me he'd told him to stop watching it because it was messing up his mind. He's not a fan of it himself.'

She took and drink and frowned. 'In what way did he think he was being messed up?'

'By the sounds of it, it had destroyed his self-worth, I think. Josh reckoned he was judging himself harshly against men in those videos and had worked up a huge degree of self-loathing, as a result. The girl, saying what she said, might have just been the last straw. That was his weak spot.'

'If a girl had been nasty to you at 16 about your doo-dah, would it have really upset you?'

'Oh god, yeah. Of course. I was sensitive lad, prone to overthink everything, so it'd have destroyed my confidence and I'd have been paranoid about it for ages.'

'A lad I fancied once took the piss out of me in 5th year for not having much in the breast department, and I stuffed my bra the next day, but mam told me off. I remember it clearly. She told me that if boys didn't like me how I was, I should tell them to sod off. She was right, the auld shitehawk.'

She winced as she sipped her wine. 'We're only going to see more of this, y'know. We see it at work with kids and young women. Porn is affecting absolutely everything in kids' lives - and in adults', too, for that matter - from how they feel they've got to behave in the bedroom, to what their partner might expect of them and how they should look in order to be thought sexy. It's an absolutely huge issue and y'know, I think it's hard for our generation to quite grasp, not just in how the porn aesthetic affects children, but just how ubiquitous it is. Porn was once an illicit, private thing, but for the younger generation, it's not. It's got a public currency to it. I had a 16-year-old girl as a service user last month who routinely watched hardcore porn with her boyfriend and let's just say, the outcome of this lifestyle choice was not a happy one. She was repeatedly raped in a manner that was directly inspired by those videos. In fact, we can usually tell the women whose partners routinely watch pornography, by what those men do to them sexually, and how they behave towards their partners.'

'Christ, how is it so obvious?'

She raised her eyebrows and looked at him with eyes wide.

'You don't want to know, luv. It's not nice.'

'No, you can tell me. I should know just in case it comes up with Josh.'

She shrugged. 'OK. Well, would you think it was right, respectful or desirable in any way to ejaculate in a woman's face?'

He flinched at her words, as though they gave him a little electric shock. 'What? No, of course not. Why would anyone want to do that? That's just awful. That seems really horribly abusive to me.' He blinked hard as though to try and wipe the image from his mind's eye.

She shrugged. 'I'm afraid it's a standard porn thing, man. It's become normalised. Some disagree with me, but I think it's all part of a way to keep women down, to humiliate and oppress and show them who's boss. If that makes you feel good, there's something wrong with you, in my book. The woman get's absolutely nothing out of it, except sore eyes, possibly. And that's just one typical thing, I won't put any more horrors in your brain, but there's plenty more such widespread, but common sexual abuse, all led and fed by pornography online.'

Nick made a growl in his throat and closed his eyes briefly. Sometimes the world felt like a vicious and depraved place. 'Bloody hell, times have changed. I once went to the Odeon with a girlfriend to see a Pink Panther film. The supporting feature was a vaguely bawdy film featuring Michelle Dotrice and at one point she was getting humped on a kitchen table. You couldn't see anything. There was possibly a flash of nipple and that was it. And I was mortified that I had to witness this with the girl I was dating. The idea of watching actual sex, good god, that'd have been off-the-scale embarrassing. I just couldn't have entertained that thought for a moment.'

'I know, but these are different days, kidda.' She smiled her warm smile and reached forward to pat him on the arm.

They sat for a moment and thought more about it.

'Do you think Paul, after getting dumped, went into one of those classic teenage strops where you scream, "you'll be sorry when I'm dead!", and has tried to kill himself to, well, to just show them?' asked Nick.

Julie thought about it, curling a loose strand of hair around her right index finger.

'Hmm, I think that's too simplistic. As a teenager you might do something impulsive when in that frame of mind - throw a brick through a window, or even cut yourself - but planning to kill yourself at 1pm and standing there calmly, waiting for the train, is a far, far deeper-rooted thing. He's planned it out and almost executed the plan. To me, that means there's a serious undiagnosed malaise at work, and when you talk about that stuff, you have to look at the family. Upset kids often means abuse at home, or from the extended family. Early sexualisation, too.'

'Hmm, Josh said he'd been talking dirty a lot as well. Probably got that from porn, too. Well, I hope he gets the help he needs. He was furious at me for stopping him.'

'Josh did a good job in coming to get you. It was very sensible of him to alert an adult.'

'He'd never have been able to push Paul out of the way, even if he'd tried and it *was* good of him, but honestly, Jules, he's getting a really foul mouth on him. He's clever and he knows it but I had to slap him down a couple of times while we were driving out to Allens West.'

'Why, what was he saying, like?' She turned her watch around on her wrist.

'Oh, he was just swearing a lot and being vulgar about a girl he fancies at 6th form, saying he wanted to stuff his hard cock right up her...'

Julie raised her eyebrows and shuddered briefly. 'Oh, fizz me, and what did you say to that?'

'I told him off. Told him to watch his language, and that if he treated girls with respect and not as sex objects, in the future, he'd get his end away a lot more.'

She burst out laughing. 'Very good advice. You missed your vocation as a counsellor.'

'It's right though, isn't it?'

She gave him a cynical look. 'Pfft! In an ideal world, maybe. But no, not really. The way to get the most sex is to identify emotionally vulnerable women and bully them into it. That or being good looking and playing drums or guitar in a rock band. But outside of sick relationships, yes, you were right, obviously. I'm glad you told him off, he looks up to you and he trusts you.'

'Yeah, I know he does. Puts a lot of pressure on me to get things right for him. But then, he's not getting much help anywhere else.'

'So he's still not got a girlfriend yet?'

'No, he's not had one so far. He'd have told me if he had. He's crazy about this girl Heather, who's in his class. He's got a proper big teenage crush on her.'

'Difficult for him to combine the standard teenage gaucheness with his Asperger's. I don't envy him,' said Julie.

'Totally, yeah. I'm going to have to have a long talk with him soon, I know it. He doesn't have any other male role model in his life. I worry he's going to get carried away and his lack of understanding of the subtext of relationships might get him into trouble. I don't want him forcing himself on some girl, or becoming a pest, creeping around lasses with his tongue hanging out. It's bad enough for any teenage kid, let alone one with his condition. He needs clear guidelines set out for him to remember and to follow.'

She took a sip of wine. 'Well, he's a very good-looking boy these days; very pretty, with those long eyelashes and shaggy fair hair.

And he's broad and fit. So I'm sure girls will be interested in him, but it'd be challenging to go out with him, I think.'

'Oh, totally, it'll be a special lass who takes him on. His lack of basic empathy can make him seem cold. But he's a very funny young lad and he's intelligent and interesting, and that's half the battle.'

'True, he does have good sense of humour at times, and that's always an attractive thing in anyone.'

'The thing is, he's older than his years in many ways, but he's also just a regular, bawdy, sex-obsessed teenage boy. Unusually, the older side of his make-up knows this and knows it's a cliché, but even so, his hormones are raging and like any 16-year-old lad, he's almost permanently horny and utterly fascinated by girls. At times he seems quite desperate to have some sort of sexual encounter, but his lack of social skills doesn't play in his favour. What he needs is a girlfriend who likes his bluntness and realises that he's not trying to be rude, he's just being open and honest. He'd never hide anything from you. You'd never have to worry about that. He wouldn't cheat on a girl, he'd just say, "I don't want to go out with you any more", and that'd be it.'

'I like his attitude to pornography. He got that from you, you know. If he's really holding out against that almost irresistible tide, you should take the credit.'

'Yeah, I think I've had a positive influence on him, but I'm not sure he's holding out against it exactly, he just seems to be able to see it for what it is. That's the older, cleverer part of his brain, at work. The 16-year-old boy is probably still knocking one out to pictures of naked women, and in some ways, I can't blame him for that. Your eyes can't get enough of nudity at his age. I've told him to keep it as a private thing, not to be in a rush about relationships and that he's got plenty of time for all that.'

She nodded. 'You're always in a rush at that age, though. It feels like everyone is copping off and you're the gooseberry, if you can't get anyone. I was obsessed with always having a boyfriend in my teens. It felt like you had to. Ridiculous, really.'

'Because I've said he can ask me anything about girls,

relationships and sex, he's been asking me all sorts of stuff, recently.'

'Has he? Sexual stuff? You've not said.'

'Oh, it's really not a big deal. I know why he's doing it.'

'What do you mean?'

'He's trying to get info out of me about you, isn't he? He's got a bit of a thing about you, so if I make a generalisation about something, he's been trying the "is that what Julie likes to do?" approach.'

Julie half-grimaced, half-laughed. She hunched her shoulders and wrinkled her nose.

'Eeurgh. I hope you don't tell him anything. I don't want him going home and, y'know...eeurgh.'

'Of course I don't. I've got quite good at not doing so, in fact. It's quite funny, he tries to be cool about it all, but you can see the blood pressure rising in his cheeks whenever he asks me anything.'

She laughed a little. 'What's he asked, then?'

He shook his head. 'Oh, you don't need to know, Jules, and I've told him it's confidential between me and him, so I better stick to that. It's just been a typical boy's things about his body, and what to do with girls. It's all just normal, healthy stuff. Nothing to worry about. It's the sort of thing he should be able to ask an elder brother or father about. But he doesn't have that option, so I'm there for him instead. I wish I'd had someone to guide me through my teenage years, but there was no way I could have ever talked to my parents about any of it. I've just told him that I'm there for him if he needs any help and he shouldn't be afraid or embarrassed to ask anything. That's as much as I can do, and I think he knows I'm on his side, if only because when he does say something out of order, and I tell him off, he looks embarrassed and apologetic. Bless 'im.'

'It's funny that so much of the time he's too emotionally disconnected to get embarrassed, but then with some people, on certain occasions, he's almost crippled by it.'

Nick nodded. 'That's the weird thing. Just when you think you've got him worked out, he can surprise you. It's not a fixed condition, I think. In different situations and with different people he can shift how he behaves quite markedly.'

She didn't say anything for a minute, then smiled and tipped her jaw up at him, so she was looking down her nose, a little. 'You know what?' She bit her bottom lip.

'What?'

'You'd have made such a good dad, if how you are with Josh is anything to go by.'

'Hmm, I've actually thought that a couple of times, and I enjoy it. It's nice to feel you can help. But then, it's a different gig just seeing a teenage boy every week or so, and having them under your feet 24/7.'

'Yeah, that is true. The teenage boy is a smelly, sticky, gross creature, it must be said. Mind you, teenage girls present as many, if not more challenges, not least to do with body image and appearance. And they're all getting sexualised so much younger. My dad's wife, Sheryl, was saying this to me last week when we went to Betty's in Northallerton for coffee. You know her granddaughters are 16 and 17?'

'Really? I suppose they must be. What relation are you to them, then?'

'Err...god knows. I dunno. They're my dad's grand-daughters, born to my half-sister. I think.'

'It's all very confusing. You've not met the girls, have you?'

She shook her head. 'But I will soon enough, with the whole family having moved over here from Australia.'

'I can't believe three generations have upped sticks and moved to the northeast from sunny Oz.'

She leaned on the table. 'They're a tight family. They didn't want to be far apart and dad really wanted to come back to the Northeast with Sheryl. When they said what they were going to do, their daughter, Carly, reckoned it'd be good for her two teenage girls to experience a different culture. But Sheryl was saying that one of the girls, Jade, is absolutely image obsessed and both of them spend half the day taking selfies of themselves.'

Nick rolled his eyes. 'That sounds almost mentally ill. We had a mirror in the hall and one in the bathroom and that was the only time I ever saw myself.'

'I was very image conscious, like all teenage kids, but the mirror in the hall was the only way I could look at myself, too. No full-length mirrors in the bedroom. Today they judge their appearances against pictures of models and film stars that have been Photoshopped, giving them unrealistic notions of what is supposed to be beautiful. And that's before we get back to porn. She says they obsess over tiny details like how big their earlobes are, or if they've got a thigh gap.'

'A what?'

'Thigh gap. It's a Thing.'

'How is a thigh gap, a Thing?'

She shrugged. 'I think it was a catwalk trend. These skinny models have matchstick legs, so their thighs don't touch in the middle. That's your thigh gap. The brainwashing is that such a thing is, for some reason, desireable.'

Nick rubbed his eyes in disbelief. 'But you don't have a thigh gap and you're pretty lean.'

'I know. I don't think I could have one unless I was anorexic. But then I play badminton and squash and we walk a lot, so I've got...'

'...well-developed thighs. I love your thighs...especially when they're wrapped around me. They're shaped like a couple of lovely parsnips.'

'Embraced by parsnips! Ha ha. I'm quite attached to them myself. And I like parsnips, especially honey roasted. Wouldn't like honey on my thighs, though. Not unless it's your special honey, anyway.' She grinned and gave him a saucy look.

'I think you'll find that is more accurately called Royal Jelly, my dear.'

She hooted a laugh. 'Is that what you're calling it now? Fair enough. Does it also have clinically unproven health benefits?'

'Do you feel healthy?'

'Yes, I do.'

'I rest my case, then.'

'Ha ha. Well, god knows I get a regular large dose, so you never know.'

'Well, I am a doctor of love.'

She laughed again and kicked him under the table. 'Well, I need you to fill my prescription.'

'That's a funny name for it.'

She wiped her eyes. 'Eee god, I could talk in double entendres with you all day.'

'But to get back to thigh gaps. Surely they're actually the product of starvation, which, call me old fashioned, should be thought of as a bad thing,' said Nick.

'Oh, yeah. I feel quite fortunate that when I was growing up, being a bit curvy of hip and arse was thought attractive.'

'Well, it's the defining thing about being a woman. Men don't have hips, women do. But, all of this must be a very difficult thing to see happening to your kids.'

'Totally. Carly is at her wits' end about it, apparently. She doesn't know how to counterbalance it with sanity. They get these weird ideas reinforced and endorsed all the time, just like Paul Richardson has. That's not to say they're not nice lasses, I think they probably are...but it's just kids are under so much pressure from all sides. We'll be meeting them soon enough. We're all going out for a meal.'

Nick visibly shrank in his seat.

'Aw, do I have to? How many will be there?'

She counted on her fingers. 'Dad, Sheryl, Carly and the two girls, Jade and Jenny. Five. And no, you don't have to come. I know you don't like big groups. Or you can just say hello, so you've met them.'

'Where are you eating?'

She pointed. 'Down the road in Big Meat.'

'Oh, Big Meat, eh,' he said, immediately feeling less hostile to the idea.

She laughed. 'Changed your mind now there's a chance of a platter of delish roast meat, haven't you?'

'I might be able to tolerate company, if I can eat some game birds and gravy.'

'Well I'm a game bird and you can eat me.'

'Another very good double entendre. You're a different sort of bird, that's a different sort of eating and a *very* different sort of gravy.'

She laughed. 'I'm sure most of the women you went out with only made moaning noises because you had them carrying heavy boxes of records.'

'The sad thing is that is almost certainly true.'

They laughed and took a drink, looking at each other with their usual mix of love spiced with lust.

Nick went on, 'I'm at least a couple of chapters ahead of Josh in the book of boy's life lessons. The problem is, and I've told him this, he's looking for absolutes all the time; what's the best way to talk to a girl, the best way to kiss, the best way to...well, you know. And I've told him that it's all subjective and beyond some basics, you have to make it up as you go along, depending on what you and her want. He doesn't like that. He needs rules to follow. Rights and wrongs. That suits his frame of mind. He's not a fan of variables. He likes statistics, logic and probability. He's got right into that in the last year. He sits working out probability equations. He reckons, for example, that the Boro have only a three per cent probability to go up this season. Even that seems high to me.'

She shook her head. 'We've no chance. Have you told him about contraception? I don't want him getting some lass up the duff the first time he does it, or thinking he can do it without using anything.'

'He knows about *all* of that.' He made a line in the air with an index finger. 'He's got an A grade in the biology. He knows where everything is, he just doesn't know how, or what to do with it, or when, for that matter.'

'More typically, that's known as being male, darlin'.' She gave him a sarcastic look.

'Who knows where everything is?' said Jeff, walking up behind her. '*Everything* is a lot of stuff to know the location of.' He grinned and sat down opposite them, tossing his long cloak of greying hair over his shoulders and tugging on his long beard.

'We were talking about young Josh,' said Nick.

'Ah. Right. He's a nice lad, him.'

'I was just saying he's got all the gear, but no idea,' said Nick. 'If you get me.'

'I should bloody hope so, he's only 16. I certainly don't want my

Argie being some sort of teenage Lothario, bedding girls left, right and centre. He'll only make me jealous.'

'Well, that's what we've been talking about: kids growing up too soon,' said Julie.

Jeff went on. 'Josh is a good lad. He's rockin' that early 90s Kurt Cobain look these days. All messy hair, lumberjack shirts and ripped jeans, which he really suits. He'll be fine, as long he mixes with kids who won't exploit the fact he's a bit wonky in the old bonce. You know, he's been in the shop a few times recently with a couple of girls, who I assume he goes to 6th form with. Him and Guru seem to get on well. I think they're from the same planet. He chats to Guru like he's a grown up, in order to impress the girls. Guru reckons he looks up stuff on Wikipedia and Discogs and then drops it into conversations to show off to the lasses.'

'Aw, bless him,' said Julie grinning. 'That would've impressed me. Not that he knew about obscure records, but rather that he'd made such an effort. I liked boys who tried to impress you with their intellect. Brains are attractive.'

'Only if they stay inside your head,' said Jeff, rapping on his skull with a knuckle. 'Messy otherwise. And painful. It's mostly cholesterol, your brain, y'know; mine is made out of butterflies and vodka, though.'

'He doesn't actually buy records, does he?' asked Julie.

'No, if he's on his own, he just hangs around, drinks green tea and looks at the Ohio Players covers, you know, the ones with naked women covered in honey, and in doing so is unwittingly carrying on one of our old traditions first performed by me and you in Debenham's US cut-off section in 1977.'

'I still have fantasies about that,' said Nick. 'Not the honied women, the cut-offs. Wish I'd bought all those Peanut Butter Conspiracy, Elephant's Memory and Guess Who records.'

Julie feigned a yawn. 'You're not going to start talking about obscure records, are you? If so I might as well go home.'

'Nah. I can't stop long, I just popped in to buy Batman here a drink,' said Jeff. 'What do you want?'

'I'll take a single malt off you, thanks man,' said Nick.

'How about you, Jules?'

'Same for me,' she said.

Jeff got the drinks and set them on the table. 'So tell us all about your life-saving mission,' he said.

Nick outlined what had happened.

'So this kid is a friend of Josh's at 6th form?' asked Jeff.

'Yeah. Well, as Josh says, he's someone he knows. Not sure he quite gets what *friend* means.'

'What was his name, again?' said Julie.

'Paul Richardson.'

She frowned. 'Does he live down The Avenue, off Bishopton Road West, by any chance?'

'Erm, yeah, I think he does. Josh said something about them always walking home together after college, and that's the way I used to go home from 6th form.'

She tugged at her bottom lip. 'I have a new service user called Richardson who lives on The Avenue. Hmm. I'll have to look into that. I can't quite recall off the top of my head what her issues are. She's new.'

Jeff raised his eyebrows. 'It's obvious to me. Gotta be child abuse going on there. Has to be. Especially if what Josh says is right. The lad's been messed up, poor kid. Wife is getting abused, kid is weird about his body, talking dirty and wants to die. God knows what's going on in the house. I mean, you almost flinch from even thinking about it, which isn't the right thing to do, obviously, but I reckon that's one of the reasons blokes get away with it. Nobody wants to think about that stuff, or confront how shite life is for some kids. It'll be an wicked Uncle Ernie job, you mark my words.'

'And, if you're right, he's been sent back to his abuser after his suicide bid, which would be entirely the wrong thing to do,' said Julie. She blew out her cheeks. 'Don't like that at all.'

'Hey, Jeff, do you want to come with us to Big Meat? When is it, Jules?'

'This Saturday evening.'

'I never turn down Big Meat. What's this all about?'

Julie explained.

'I've not actually met your dad since he's come back for good last year,' said Jeff.

'He's a nice bloke, I think,' said Nick. 'Quite a philosophical sort. But I've not met Sheryl, Carly and the girls, so I need you there to give me a conversational get out at all times.'

'And for my raw animal sex appeal, too,' said Jeff. 'Gotta show these Aussies what a real man looks like, rather than those tanned Bondi Beach types.'

'That goes without saying. But don't turn up in your swimming trunks.'

'OK, I'll park Arg with Mandy and I'll put me best bikini on.'

CHAPTER 3

Nick sat on their burgundy and gold silk patchwork bedspread, reading the *Gazette* while Julie dried her hair after a shower.

'I see our MP has unexpectedly carked it. Heart attack,' he said.

'Yeah, I heard that on BBC Tees. Teesside North and Central is a three-way marginal. Probably means loads of politicians will be sent up here to patronise us and pretend they have the first clue about Teesside, before scuttling back south after lying through their teeth. Does my head in.'

He finished reading the article. 'They reckon it'll be a dirty fight.'

'Oh, I've no doubt they'll spend a lot of time slagging each other off, instead of trying to understand the problems here. Then whoever gets elected will sod off to London and we'll never see them again. There's so much that could be done here, so many good people who we could draw on to help make Teesside a modern place and stop it being seen as a post-industrial wasteland.'

'What would you do, then?'

'Me? First thing, I'd make the town centre a place where people can live. Flats above all the shops. Make the old Swallow Hotel into affordable apartments. That'd stop the place becoming a wasteland after 5pm. It'd bring money into town. All the most vibrant towns have a mix of commercial and domestic at their heart. The trouble here is, town is purely commercial and everyone lives in the suburbs. Make the town vibrant and so many good things would flow from that. Then I'd reduce business rates so that small businesses can actually make a living and afford to have a shop on the High Street. And I'd put a rent cap on commercial buildings. There are far too many empty simply because they won't take a lower rent. I'd build new allotments because the ones we've got are oversubscribed. You'd save more money on improved health of the population from exercise and fresh food, than it would cost. And I'd set up a proper railway museum at Stockton Station. It was the first railway on earth, why the hell don't we celebrate it?' She cleared her throat.

'That'd just be for starters.'

He looked at her bare back. 'Every one of those is a brilliant idea.' After thinking about it for a moment, he added, 'Have you ever thought about standing for office? You're full of good ideas, you're passionate and articulate.'

'Oh, aye, many times. Everyone thought I'd leave University and go into politics because I was on every committee, and y'know, public speaking holds no fears for me, if I know what I'm talking about, anyway.'

'I think you should seriously consider it. I know you're supposed to be starting your OU degree later in the year, but you've got so much to offer and you could really make a difference.'

'But I'm not in a political party and I don't want to be. I don't want to have to toe anyone's line.'

'You don't have to. You could run as an Independent. The old tribal party thing is all bollocks these days. People don't like it anymore.'

She shook her head. 'Nah, I'm not sure. It'd be a lot of work and fizzin' intrusive, too. It's tempting but I love my job and that'd have to go out the window. Owee, let's get dressed for Big Meat.'

When he was going to be in public with a group of people, Nick knew he'd end up sweating heavily. He always did and always had done. He put it down to the subconscious stress of social situations, because even if he was enjoying himself and wasn't feeling consciously under pressure, at the end of the night he'd still be soaking wet under his armpits and down the centre of his back. He just never got away with it. Not once. He'd never met, nor even seen a man sweat as much as he did when in a group of people. One on one, he was fine. But anything more than that and he oozed like a used tea bag. As a teenage boy, having to wear a pale blue shirt for school, he'd take off his blazer at the end of the day with a sweat stain from his elbow to his waist. Even now it meant he pretty much had to choose black or white clothes for a night out like this one with Julie's extended family. Basically, anything that wouldn't show the sweat too much.

'Aw, you look proper smart in that, luv,' said Julie, messing with her hair in the bedroom dressing table mirror.

He brushed the shoulders of the black lightweight cashmere V-necked sweater and pulled it into shape. 'Yeah, is no t-shirt underneath OK? It gets hot in Big Meat.'

'Yeah, of course. You're OK with cashmere. No matter how much fluid oozes out of you, it won't show. You've still got a bit of tan left from our week in Spain last month, so you're giving it the full gorgeous. I'm amazed I've not sat on your face by now.' She chuckled to herself. That was one of her classic little charges to his psychic feel-good battery.

'What are you wearing, then?' he asked.

'I thought I'd go like this,' she said, standing up and opening her arms wide, resting her weight on one hip.

He looked her up and down. 'It's a strong look, Jules. It'll certainly turn heads if you arrive at Big Meat in a small pair of red knickers, red football socks and absolutely nothing else. It might be illegal to look so sexy in public. I tell you what. You'd get elected MP if you turned up to the hustings like that. Vote Wells for nudity and knickers.'

She shrugged, absentmindedly tweaked one of her small pink nipples and said, 'Oh, alright then, I'll put trousers and a top on, just for the sake of convention. But I'm only going in my blue jeans and my checky shirt. Can't be arsed to dress up.' She went to the wardrobe and pulled out her favourite green, blue and white plaid shirt and began getting dressed.

'So what do you think this Carly woman and her kids are going to be like?' asked Nick, looking at himself in the mirror.

'Well you've seen the photos on Facebook, they're all teeth and hair and eyebrows. Probably the sort of glamorous alpha females who'll think I'm a lesbian because I don't wear makeup or heels.'

'I hope not. I find those sort of women a bit intimidating. I don't know why, really. It's like they're the female equivalent of the rugby club sort of alpha male. All lippy and lashes, it's like the make-up is a shield between me and them, which is probably the whole point, I guess.' He sat down on the edge of the bed. 'The kids actually look quite like you, I think. At least in those Facebook pictures. Blonde hair, blue eyes, long legs.'

'I've not got long legs. I've got parsnip legs, so you reckon, anyway, remember? Hairy parsnips, presumably. And I've no thigh gap, either.'

'Aye, but you've got a substantial gap at the top of the inside of your thighs, and that's the most important gap of all.'

She gave him a mock shocked look and threw her long-toothed comb at him. 'A *substantial* gap, sir?! Well, that's your fault, isn't it? You've ruined me with that thing of yours! Me fanny's elastic band has snapped, like!' she said, lapsing into her thickest Teesside accent.

Half an hour later, as they travelled to Hartburn Village in the back of a minicab, Nick talked about Julie's dad.

'I like Robbie, he's very quiet, isn't he? Quite hard to get to know. That's not a criticism.'

She looked out of the window as the cab turned onto Yarm Lane. 'It's weird, because all I remember is him fighting with the lads and shouting at mother and being an argumentative drunk. It's like he's a different man and in some ways it's like he's not my dad at all. I have wondered if it's really him and not just someone pretending to be him. Though quite why anyone would do that, I can't imagine.'

'You can't imagine it, because he's quite obviously your dad. You look so like him. I wonder what he thinks of us? I mean, leaving a life in the sunshine for a life in an old farmhouse in rural North Yorkshire, outside of Northallerton, strikes me as a bit odd.'

'Why don't you ask him about it tonight? Might give you something to chat about.'

'Yeah, maybe I will. I don't think I'll be able to talk to two teenage girls.'

She looked at him. 'God, I know what you mean. You know what I worry about? I worry I'll seem like I'm being some trendy liberal oldie trying to be hip with the kids, when, the truth is, they think we're really, really old and have no idea what their lives are like.'

'Yeah, a 16-year-old will think we're both older than god. But the weird thing is, for our generation, that *was* true. My parents had no idea what it was like to be a kid in the 70s. But *we* really do know what it's like to be young, culturally. By and large, we get it, or we have some understanding. That must be quite annoying for kids

31

today.'

'Maybe it's quite good for them. I'm going to do a module for my Social Services degree called "Feminist Transgenerational Empathy".'

'Sounds like a progressive rock band to me.'

'I can't imagine my mother ever having any feminist transgenerational empathy towards me. She just used to tell me to find a rich posh husband, settle down and sprog some kids.'

He leaned into her and kissed her on the lips.

The cab pulled up outside the restaurant. They paid the driver. It was a dry, cool, late March night, with a hint of frost in the air. Jeff was just approaching as they did so, dressed in his usual denim shirt, black t-shirt and old jeans. It was less than a three-minute walk from his house. He waved.

'Ahoy hoy! My glamorous sexy friends!'

'Hey, man. Ready to eat a lot of meat and almost no vegetables?' said Nick.

'At all times, brother and sister. At all times.'

He grinned at both in turn, and, towering over them by nearly half a foot, put a hand on each of their shoulders. 'Thanks for inviting me to this animal protein feast.'

'Remember, you're sitting next to me. If things get boring we can discuss how many albums open on the left and not the right.'

Jeff stopped in his tracks, put his index finger on his nose, pulled an imaginary klaxon and made a honking noise. 'To kick that one off I give you Richie Haven's 1972 live album.'

'Nice. In return, I offer you Canned Heat *Live at Topanga Corral*, the US release.'

Jeff made an orgasmic face. 'Sweet. We will not say anything as interesting as that all night. To be continued...'

Robbie, Sheryl and the rest of the family were already seated at a large round table. They all stood up to greet them like a blonde and white-haired army.

'Nice to see you, darlin'. You look great,' said her father, giving Julie a light hug. He pointed in turn to the assembled women. 'Sheryl, Carly, Jenny and Jade.' Julie gave them a little wave as they all sat down.

'And I'm Jeff, and this man dressed as a cat burglar, is Nick, or Mrs Wells, to give him his proper name,' said Jeff, getting a big laugh in doing so. He was always good value in a large group. For the millionth time in his life, Nick felt envious of him for that.

The three men sat next to each other, as Julie began chattering to Sheryl, who was in her mid 60s and dressed, like her husband, in smart jeans and a white shirt. They weren't old hippies, but they could've passed for them. Right away, Nick noticed the two teenage girls were both glued to their phones, typing out messages at speed with their thumbs, so much so that apart from standing up and smiling nicely when their grandfather introduced them, they had almost totally ignored everything and everyone. Was this typical? To his generation, such behaviour seemed plain rude, but then, at least it meant you didn't have to be in the room, and he could see the attraction in that. Even so, it seemed like they were not experiencing life fully, almost wishing to be somewhere else, no matter where they were or what was happening.

They were both very good-looking girls, in different ways, though both had a perfect white teeth, tanned skin, outdoors Australian sort of look. Jenny had a square jaw, swimming-pool blue and porcelain white eyes and full lips. Her hair was cut short and bleached from blonde to platinum white, parted on the left. At not much short of six feet tall and with broad shoulders, she looked older than 16. Jade wasn't quite as tall, and had more delicate features, and wore scarlet lippy and a lot of make-up. She had fiercely shaped her eyebrows, so they looked drawn on with a stencil. Her shoulder-length, naturally blonde hair was tied back into a ponytail. They booth oozed an attractive self-confident air, even just sitting there, bolt upright, looking at their phones.

'Now then, Nick,' said Robbie, turning to him, speaking in an accent that was 75 per cent Aussie and 25 per cent Teesside, 'I finally got around to reading your novel, *Kidda*. I really enjoyed it.'

'Oh, that's good,' said Nick, looking into his bright turquoise eyes that Julie had so obviously inherited. As the result of years spent working outdoors and in the sun, his skin had a leathery, almost indelibly tanned look to it. He didn't really look in his late 60s in some ways, but he did have a tired aspect to him, as though he'd worked hard and long for many decades.

'I enjoyed the story and the twist at the end.' He went quiet, as he considered his words. Nick liked that in him. There was no rush. He'd rather someone took time over words, instead of just talking loud and saying nothing. Just filling silence was a terrible modern affliction.

'Listen, more than anything, I just enjoyed how you gave the reader a sense of Teesside. It was very evocative. I don't mind telling you, I had a tear in my eye on a couple of occasions. I told Jules and she said you've got a poet's soul. I reckon she's right, mate.'

He glanced at Julie, who was listening to Sheryl talking. She'd never said that to him. It was nice to hear. 'She's probably right. She's right about most things, is Jules.'

'Yeah, mate, I dunno what the right word is, romantic, I guess.'

'I do have that in my locker, and my writing can be quite sentimental, when I want it to be.'

'Yeah mate, it really struck a chord with me, perhaps because I'm so new back to the Northeast. I see the beauty of the place everywhere.'

'Beauty? Are you on powerful drugs, Robbie?' said Jeff, leaning over and pulling a face. Robbie laughed.

'It's great to be home, Jeff. You've no idea. And it is home. Oz is great. I owe the place everything. But home is where the heart is and now it's where my family is. I couldn't be happier.'

'So where are you living?' asked Jeff.

'We bought a ramshackle old farmhouse, a mile or two outside of Northallerton. I'm going to do it up. It's pretty run down, mate.'

'Nice. If you ever need a hand with labouring, I'm up for it. I'm rubbish at interior decor, painting and grouting, but I can push a mean wheelbarrow,' said Jeff.

'Nice one, mate, I'll take you up on that.'

Nick smiled. There was Jeff's easy way with strangers, again.

'So it was all about coming back to your roots?' asked Nick.

'Yeah.' Robbie paused, took a drink from a bottle of lager and composed his thoughts again. 'Listen, here's the thing, right? I'm 68. I've got anything from 5 to 15 years left, realistically. I wanted to come back to the place that shaped me and find some...' he stopped talking, took another drink and weighed up how to express himself '...find some understanding of myself.' He spoke with the Aussie rising inflective, like it was a question. 'And I wanted to lay to rest a lot of old ghosts.'

How had this man ever been married to Jackie Wells? A less philosophical, nuanced woman you'd never meet. He'd left her in 1977, 36 years ago. The life he'd lived in the council house in Hardwick seemed a life that had to have belonged to someone else.

'Robbie, can I ask you something quite personal?' said Nick.

He nodded. 'Sure, mate.'

'Why exactly did you leave Jackie, all those years ago?'

Without a pause, he answered. 'Oh, that's easy, mate. I've told Jules this. Look, with hindsight, I can see I felt trapped into being someone I wasn't. I had no idea what I was. But I felt pinned down like a butterfly on a board in a museum. I couldn't cope with it, so I drank, then came the problems as a result of that. I went totally tonto for a while, mate. But all I wanted was to be free of who I was supposed to be. When I went to Oz, I became who I really was. I worked at a market garden for years and eventually bought the business. I'm all about growing things and working with nature, not with steel, which was supposed to be my career.'

'Interesting. You got away, but came back,' said Jeff.

Robbie nodded. 'On my own terms, though. And it's great to see the kids, Jules, Kev and Ricky...well, maybe not Ricky. He's a total piss-head drongo. But Jules is such a great girl. I always knew she would be, y'know? Even when she was little, she was brainy and smart. Even aged four, she'd be forever asking me questions and was always at the central or local branch library. It's a blessing to see her again. Makes me so happy to have reconnected after all these years and to find you guys, too.'

'It's like you've lived two lives, Robbie,' said Jeff.

'You're not wrong, mate. That's just how it feels.'

'Bringing everyone over is a big deal, though,' said Jeff,

smoothing out his beard.

'Yeah, they were all really up for it. We're a close family and hate to be apart.'

'Where are the girls going to school?' asked Jeff.

'They're already at Stockton Sixth Form, mate. Jenny is first year, Jade is second. They did exams to match up their education in Australia to the curriculum here. Carly is working at Barclaycard in Stockton and has bought a place off Durham Road, so it makes sense for them to go there.'

'Oh, yeah, Julie mentioned that. Life must be very different in Stockton from what they were used to in Australia,' said Nick.

'It's not so different, apart from the weather. It's not like any of us lived the high life over there. We just lived in the cheap end of town.'

'Where was that?' asked Jeff.

'A place called Ballarat, 70 miles from Melbourne. It's not on the coast, so it's not like the girls will miss the beach lifestyle. They hardly ever went to the beach, in fact. And it can get stinking hot in the summer. Too hot, really. They miss their friends, but you know what? They soon made new friends.'

Nick glanced them both. They were whispering conspiratorially, the way teenagers do, clearly talking about himself, Jeff and Julie.

'I suppose it's so easy to keep in touch via Skype, and the like, even if you're 12,000 miles away,' said Nick.

Robbie nodded. 'Exactly. And as Carly worked for Barclaycard in Melbourne, she was able to get a transfer to their headquarters in Stockton. It all worked out well.'

'Where's the kids' dad?' said Nick. No-one had ever mentioned him.

Robbie shrugged indifferently, in just the same way Julie did. 'Ah, who knows? The guy walked out eight or nine years ago and never came back. Something I know a little bit about myself. Anyway, we tried to find him, but without luck. Luckily the business was doing well, so we could support Carly in bringing them up.'

'Well they look in fine fettle, Robbie,' said Jeff. 'Very Australian, like.'

He nodded. 'Yeah, I get you. Even I can see that. I'm afraid they'll be courted by all the local lads...'

For the first time Jade interrupted her grandfather.

'Don't start all that again, purrleeze. It's embarrassing.' She spoke in a broad Melbourne accent, which was a lot of treble and almost no bass.

'I'm just saying you'll look kinda exotic over here.'

'Exotic? Us?' questioned Jenny in a deeper, richer tone. 'You're kidding me. We're working-class Aussies from Ballarat, which is an unflushed toilet at the arse end of nowhere.'

Everyone around the table laughed at her colourful expression.

'With language like that, you'll have fitted right in,' said Jeff, approvingly.

'It's not that bad, Jen,' said her mother. 'It gets a lot of tourists these days. In fact it's got a lot of nice Victorian architecture.'

'That, mother, is a matter of opinion,' said Jenny, acerbically. 'I'm sticking with toilet.'

'Well, that's better than sticking *to* a toilet, Jen,' said her sister, dryly. 'And don't forget we've got the Welcome Nugget. A replica of the second biggest nugget of gold ever found. I mean, guys, that's awesome!' She exclaimed it in a mocking way.

'That figures. There's a lot of nuggets in Ballarat. I should know, you've dated a few of them, Jade,' said Jenny, with a cheeky, but nice, grin at her.

'That's true. It's been no better over here so far, either,' said her sister.

'That's because boys are the same all over the world: gross.' Jenny mimed putting her finger down her throat.

Once they'd put their phones down and actually began to interact, it was obvious that these were two sparky, intelligent young women and Nick caught himself thinking that they were exactly how he'd imagined Julie was at that age. A little precocious and smart, but also attractive and funny. They also had the classic teenage condition of thinking they were older and more worldly wise than they really were, in exactly the same way Josh did. He found himself instinctively liking both.

As there were eight of them, they ordered a huge rib of beef which was carved at the table. It was easy to see why the teenagers looked so broad, powerful and strong; they could eat a lot of top-notch protein and as a result, thankfully, would never have a thigh gap. It was so delicious and tender, served with lashings of onion gravy and mustard sauce, that you'd have had to have the willpower of a saint to resist gorging yourself on it.

Nick largely just listened and drank doubles, while everyone else talked, and that was how he liked it best. It was very noticeable how, as a family, they clearly got on really well and were happy in each other's company, talking across and to each other, the girls laughing and joking with their parents in a relaxed and natural way. There wasn't an ounce of sulky nastiness, nor any attitude. When the opposite was true of your own upbringing, it was very striking to see and it made Nick feel rather envious. It was obvious that was why they'd moved to England as a unit - to keep near to each other. It had to be such a contrast for Robbie to the family he'd had in Hardwick, which had been in an almost permanent state of war. These were decent, kind people, just being decent and kind with each other, and, in a harsh world, it was a pleasure to witness.

After the meal, they all stood outside the restaurant in the relative darkness of Hartburn Village.

'Nice to meet you guys,' said Sheryl. 'We must do this again soon.'

'This is a great restaurant,' added Carly. 'We must come here again.'

'See you, Jeff, that's some cool hair you've got on you, dude,' said Jenny, as they went their separate ways.

Jeff wafted it up and down, like two big dog's ears. 'Right back atcha, lady,' he replied with a big smile, and then put both thumbs up.

'Hey, Jen. Do you know a lad called Josh Jones?' asked Nick.

She nodded firmly. 'Yeah, he's in my form class. He's an Aspie kid.'

'Yeah, he's a friend of ours. We look out for him.'

She opened the palms of her hands out. 'He's, like, some kind of genius. But I don't really speak much to him.'

'How about Paul Richardson? Do you know him?'

She pulled a face. 'Ricco? Yeah, I know him, mate. He's a dirty bastard. Talks nasty all the time. They tell me he used to be a nice kid but he's gone freako this year.' She shuddered and made her retching gesture again.

'OK, thanks, Jen,' said Nick.

'No worries, mate. Nice to have met you two.'

Julie and Nick walked with Jeff back to his house, just along the road.

'That was a cracking feed. Thanks for asking me along,' said Jeff. 'Such bloody nice people. You don't meet families that are so happy together very often. It must be weird for you, Jules. You've suddenly acquired this new, really close family. They're obviously very tight.'

'It freaks me out a bit. And you're right, they're really nice. I feel jealous of them, to tell the truth. That's actually the family I wanted to grow up in. It makes me wonder if mam hasn't actually been a dark force in my life, because once dad was freed of her, he's flourished and was clearly capable of being a great dad and now a great granddad. Maybe I'd have done the same without her influence.'

'Maybe you'd be Prime Minister by now,' said Jeff. 'And I'm not even joking.'

Nick nudged her. 'See. Jeff thinks you should be Teesside North and Central's next MP as well.'

'What's this? Oh, aye, our MP bit the big one today, didn't he? Are you going to run for election, Jules? That'd be bloody ace,' he said, without hesitation adding, 'You'd win. You bloody would.'

'Gettaway with you. Why do you say that?'

They stopped outside Jeff's front gate. He held an index finger aloft at 45 degrees. 'Because I've never known or seen anyone as good as you at winning an argument. I've seen you tear people apart with a couple of sentences. You're brilliant at turning people's own words against themselves, which seems to be a useful weapon in politics and you've got the perfect blend of altruism and common sense.'

'You should try living with that talent,' said Nick. 'I think I've only ever won one argument with you. I've even lost arguments when I was definitely in the right!'

She laughed. 'Alright, that's enough flattery, lads. I'm not about to become an MP.'

After saying their goodbyes, Nick and Julie walked home slowly, arm in arm, talking about her new relations.

'When you think about it, it's all worked out quite well,' said Nick. 'Jackie and Con get on nicely, and seem OK about Robbie and his family. You're dealing with it, too, and have got some lovely new relations. Everyone seems to get on.'

'Hmm. I've been surprised at mam, really. She's basically said "live and let live". They're all too old to hold grudges, even though dad just walking out really messed her life up. She's every reason to feel bitter towards him, but credit to her, she's just waved it all away. I don't often admire mam, but I do over this. Mind, I also think that she's happier with Con than she ever was with dad, except perhaps in the early days.'

'What about you? You were affected so badly by his disappearance. You were 13, that's a really impressionable time. Don't you feel bitter, too?'

She pulled her lips together and nodded. 'I could do, but then, I did alright. I ended up married to a lovely bloke and doing a job I love. I did well at school and college. That's how I've chosen to look at it. I do genuinely feel aggrieved that he never got in touch. That was easily the worst thing about it. For years we thought he'd died. Maybe he had got drunk and fallen into the river, or whatever. That was an awful torture to have to go through and I have told him as much. He admits he was a coward and just wanted to put his head in the sand and pretend we didn't exist.'

Nick thought about it a little more. 'What I find hard to accept is that he abdicated his responsibilities as a father to all of you.'

'I agree. It's unforgivable. He's told me why he did what he did and I do understand, but I don't accept it, to be honest. I really don't and I never will.' She shook her head. 'I'm still a bit arm's length with him, due to that, and I think I always will be.'

'One big tick in the plus column for him is that he eventually came back and held up his hands.'

She nodded again, as they walked. 'Yeah, he didn't need to do that, and that speaks to the fact he felt guilty all these years. But y'know, guilty men seeking forgiveness from those he wronged is a bit of a classic in the abuse industry. They fuck you over for years, then realise they've been a twat and want you to wipe their slate clean, just like that.' She clicked her fingers. 'I'm not going to do that and I've told him that in no uncertain terms.'

'But you clearly don't feel bitter or angry enough not to have anything to do with him.'

She shook her head a little. 'No. Maybe I should, but I don't think it'd make me happier to take that position. And I do believe in redemption, but...and it's a big but...you have to prove it over months and years. It's like our Kev. He's reinventing himself as a sober, peaceful bloke. Fine. Fair play to him. But we'll see, y'know? The proof of the pudding is in the eating. So far so good. He's walking the walk and talking the talk. But I've earned the right to be cynical. Same with dad.'

'I do quite like Robbie. It strikes me that one of the hard things about life is that sometimes you like people who have done bad things. I want my bad people to be 100 per cent bad, not 33 per cent bad, 33 per cent intelligent, 34 per cent regular bloke.'

'Yeah, we all make mistakes, and are inadequate. Dad, I reckon, thinks he did the right thing for himself, and I think it's obvious that he did...but my moral compass says he did a very, very bad thing and handled it even worse.'

'Yeah, but it all made you the woman you became. And I love her,' said Nick, stopping to quickly kiss her, emotion rising in his chest.

She put the flat of her hand to his cheek. 'Aw, luv. Aw. Are you trying to get in my knickers, or what?'

'Ha, I don't usually have to *try*...'

She laughed and pushed at him. '...no, you don't. I wonder why that is, you gorgeous man?' She brushed hair off his forehead. 'You did really well tonight.'

'Did I? I didn't say much.'

'Well, you didn't have to. You just sat there oozing sexiness. Did you break out in a big sweat?' She put her hands inside his jacket and felt his armpits. 'Eee god, you're wringing wet, lad. What are you like?'

'Did you find out anything about the Richardson family?' he said, just as they reached Stockton High Street.

'Oh, yeah. The mother came to us two weeks ago. Said she felt depressed, alone and alienated from her husband, David, but felt obligated to stay with him for the sake of the kid. She's only been to us that once. Hard to get a proper picture just yet. It often takes time to find out exactly why the woman has come to us. People don't always open up immediately and say they've been suffering from domestic abuse. Sometimes they're not even sure what domestic abuse really is. You have to get their trust. She didn't mention social services being involved with the family, so if abuse is happening, it doesn't appear to have been reported. But she might not return to us, so it's all a bit up in the air. It's possible that she isn't being abused, but is just upset and needs a shoulder to cry on.'

Nick stopped outside of what used to be the Odeon cinema and thought for a moment. Julie put her arms around his waist and cuddled into him.

'You know what? It feels odd for me to have saved a lad's life and then for that act to be all but ignored by everyone. I don't want to be thanked for it, or anything, but if I was his parents, I'd have asked the police who saved their son, and they know it was me, and they know where we live, and have all our contact details. It's three days ago now.'

'That's a good point. Yeah. You'd come round or ring, to say thank you. Yeah, the fact that neither of them has done that doesn't exactly suggest a happy little family, does it?'

'No, it doesn't. I'm worried for the boy. How can we make sure he's OK? What are the procedures?'

She cleared her throat. 'It's not as straightforward as you might think. His doctor might get involved, social services will be alerted, but all these things often take a lot of time. In the meantime, he's vulnerable.'

'So there's no...' he thought a moment '...no...no collective hug from society? No-one saying, "don't kill yourself, better days are ahead"? Because I think there should be.'

She shook her head. 'No, there's nothing. If you're a vulnerable kid, whose parents are not proactive, you're on your own until the official wheels are in motion. There's nowhere for a boy like him to go to and say, "I feel like life is hopeless", and there should be somewhere on every High Street in every town that could help. The biggest killer of men under the age of 49 is suicide. We need to do something about that. That'd be another thing on my manifesto. I hope he calls the Samaritans. The police will have given him their information.'

They walked on. 'I'm going to go round to his house tomorrow morning and see if he's OK. It's not being nosey or intrusive to want to check on the health of a lad whose life you've saved, is it?'

'No, of course it isn't. Depending on what they're like, his parents might see it differently, perhaps, but...yeah, you should do that. I can't see what harm it would do. It'd be kind.'

CHAPTER 4

Sunday dawned clear blue and with the sort of glamorous hoar frost that the northeast of England does very well, where all of nature seems coated in magical ice diamonds. Nick took a fillet of smoked salmon out of the fridge for Julie's breakfast, made some scrambled eggs, wilted some spinach and called her down as the fish cooked.

She came in, fastening her hair up with a black plastic clip.

'Thanks, luv. I don't know what I'd do without your fab breakfasts.'

'Seems funny you working on a Sunday.'

'I know, but as I campaigned for us to be open on Sunday, because the breaking point for many women is another Saturday night of boozed-up abuse, I can hardly protest.'

'Fair enough. It's not like Sunday is a special day for us.'

'We used to enjoy a bit of Sunday morning nookie.'

'Saturday night's nookie was pretty damn good. You got very wild.'

'I know.' She laughed. 'I was going to say, I don't know what came over me. But I do know!'

'Indeed. I'll have to put some washing on.'

'Well, we can have Sunday night nookie as well,' she said.

'Sunday night nookie sounds holy...or holey, perhaps.'

'I love a bit of holy holey. Book me in for some later.' She tucked into her food as he poured her some coffee. 'How come you never ever overcook fish?' she said. 'This is perfect.'

'It's usually done quicker than you think, so just turn it down and give it a squeeze. If it's too soft, leave it until it firms up.'

He paused and waited for her to make a dirty joke.

'I hope you're impressed that I've made no response to that,' she said, pulling an innocent look.

'Very mature. You must have your sensible knickers on.'

'Of course I have. Can't go to work on a Sunday in sex pants, not

44

after what you did to them last night, anyway, you naughty boy.' A fast eater, she soon pushed her clean plate away and stood up. 'That was ace, luv. Right, I'm off.'

Once she'd left and he'd made his own breakfast, he got into the old BMW to drive down to The Avenue. Turning over the ignition, the engine coughed and wheezed, started and then died. He tried it several times, but it just wouldn't start. It was well over 25 years old and Julie had kept it going way beyond its natural life by replacing bits that were worn out, but it was only going one way and there was always going to be a time when it was too much trouble and expense to keep on fixing.

Cars go from being attractive, useful machines to being annoying, useless, heavy lumps of metal and rubber when they won't go. He kicked at the tyre and set off on foot to walk it, texting Julie to let her know. She sent a text back within a minute.

'When you're done at the Richardsons', come and see me. I can drive you home on my lunch break. Car shopping ahoy! Yay! I'll get something that suits you.'

It was a nice crisp March morning as he sauntered from their house in Norton, a couple of miles to The Avenue in Fairfield. When he was a kid, in the mid 1970s, he'd taken over his dad's pools round and The Avenue was part of that. He'd always thought of it as a rather leafy, posh road, full of detached houses, but in the Spring of 2013, as he turned and walked down it, it seemed much less so. The Richardsons' house was a modest semi-detached 1930s villa, and one he remembered collecting the pools coupon from inside the front porch. The owners back then left the coupon and money on a shelf and he would just open the porch door and pick it up. That was quite commonplace. He'd even open front doors, unannounced, and take the coupon and money from a hall table. Nobody seemed to think it would get stolen, and as far as he knew, it never did. Man, those were such different days.

He pressed the doorbell and heard it ding-dong inside. No reply. He rang it again. Still nothing. They were obviously out, even though there was a car parked outside. Walking down a path to the side of the house to a small back garden, he took a look around.

Everything was neat and tidy; the garden well-maintained. He knocked on the back door and waited, but no-one answered. There was a small shed in the far corner of the garden. He went to it and pulled open the unlocked door. Inside were a range of clean, well-kept gardening tools, a couple of saws and a few other tools. On the back of the door were two wire brackets. Nick recognised them immediately as he had the exact same ones in their own small shed at home. They were for hanging a bike on to keep up and out of the way. He hung the bike he had found at the back of the Zetland flats, and had since had fixed, on their shed door. There was no bike but there obviously usually was, as the muddy tyres had left marks on the door. Closing it again he noted not only the fact it was unlocked, but also that there was no key in the lock. He walked to the back window of the house, which looked out onto the garden, and tried to see inside.

His heart leapt with a hard, painful jab of electricity. What the fuck?!

The first thing he saw were the soles of a pair of small bare feet. He looked twice, his eyes not registering what they were actually staring at. Someone was lying flat out on the floor. Was it the boy? He looked again, and blinked. No. There were two people lying there, at an angle to each other, making a 'T' shape. Jesus Christ. Two adults. One male, one female. And they weren't moving. He knocked on the window as though to wake them up. But they weren't asleep. Of course they weren't.

They were both dead.

They had to be Paul Richardson's parents. Oh, god. Where was Paul? Was he dead, somewhere else in the house? Had he killed them? Had they killed him?

With a dry mouth and shaking hand he called 999, explained where he was and what he was looking at. He'd have called Mandy Beale directly, if she hadn't been in Canada, at a global anti-terrorism policing conference.

This was now a crime scene, so he told himself not to touch anything. Lord knows what had happened, he just hoped Paul was alive. The death of adults is bad enough, but at least they had a decent run and these two looked like they were in their mid 40s; the death of a child seems all the more tragic for cutting a life and all that potential so short.

As he waited for the police to come, he put his hands together, raised them to his lips and stared at the bodies. There was no blood visible. Both were on their backs, the woman barefooted, the man wearing checked woollen slippers. It all seemed so innocuous. The room wasn't trashed. There was no sign of a struggle. No furniture overturned. Nothing smashed. It looked like they'd just chosen to lie on their backs on the floor, arms by their side, close their eyes and go to sleep. Perhaps they had been poisoned or drugged. That had to be it. Maybe carbon monoxide poisoning from a faulty boiler? Staring at their motionless bodies, he looked hard to see if either of them was breathing. But there was not a sign of a breath. Also, having seen his fair share of expired bodies, he knew death had a special quality to it. Bodies don't look asleep, they look 'other'. They hold themselves differently to an unconscious but living person. The dead look heavier and more profoundly inert, in the way someone alive just can't.

Soon, police cars began to arrive and the house was sealed off. The Detective Inspector was a man called Vic Bowes, who Nick had come across a few times, none of them positive. He was nearing retirement and wore the tired expression of a man who had missed out on the important promotions and still felt bitter about it. The sort of copper who had seen so many bodies that death was only a tragedy because it meant he had to leave the station and stop eating biscuits. Nick didn't like him. Would never like him. What's more, the feeling was obviously mutual. To Bowes, Nick was a PC liberal hand-wringer who was under the thumb of his wife. To Nick, Bowes was an outdated, fat, macho idiot.

Bowes walked around the back of the house, hands in his pockets, heavy belly hanging over a pair of overly worn blue pants, face a high-blood-pressure pink and sagging heavily, shirt too tight to fasten the top button. Nick's heart sank as he saw him.

As he saw Nick, he gave him an equally weary sneer.

'Oh, there you are Mr Guymer. More dead people is it? Have you killed them?' It was his sarcastic idea of a joke.

'Bloody hell,' said Nick, scowling, 'have some respect, mate. There are two dead people in there. It's nothing to joke about.'

Bowes pushed a big fleshy pink hand through what was left of his hair. 'You've got to admit it, you find a lot of dead people on Teesside, you do. Maybe you're a serial killer, Mr Guymer.' He laughed a little at his pathetic attempt at humour.

Nick stood and looked at him, expressionless, then licked his lips and said, 'Being a comedian is harder than you thought, eh, Bowes?'

Bowes raised his eyebrows and let out groan of air. 'So what's gone on here then?' Several officers now stood by the back door.

Nick pointed at the house. 'There are two dead adults in there. The Richardsons. They have a son, Paul. I suggest you see if he's dead somewhere else in the house. If he's not, then he's probably left here on his bike. Here's a tip for you Vic, don't tread on evidence, follow PACE, always wear gloves, have an open mind and remember that at some point you might have to justify your actions in a court, so do it all by the book, right? I know it goes against your principles.'

He knew Bowes would hate him lecturing him in the way he'd heard Mandy lecture her underlings, largely because he hated Mandy Beale getting the big job, over a longer-serving man such as himself.

'Yeah yeah yeah, don't be a smart arse with me, Mr Guymer. I know police procedure, thank you very much.'

Nick didn't respond. The police were a weird mix of plodders, stupids and altruistic big brains. Bowes was the former. He went with one of his men into the house.

An officer stepped forward to take a statement from Nick. That didn't take long because there was so little to say. After that he texted Julie to update her.

'There's no-one else in the house,' said Vic Bowes, soon returning. 'Any idea where the son is?'

'No. How did they die?'

'Not obvious yet. My guess is they're druggies and OD'd.'

'Yeah, well, with all due respect, you've got that wrong,' said Nick, hands on his hips.

'How do you know?' said Bowes, indignant.

'There's no drug paraphernalia beside them. They'd need a needle or a spoon. You don't use them then put them away, before you lay down to die. And the house is too tidy. No-one who is mad for drugs lives in a neat, tidy house like that. They've not met their death by shooting up something. They might have had something administered to them, though. I'll give you that.'

Vic was annoyed and very tired. 'I know you like playing at policeman, Mr Guymer, but that's my job. Leave the detective work to the professionals. Now if you want to be helpful, tell me anything you know about Paul, the son. You must know something about him or his parents, or you'd not even be here, would you?'

That was annoying. Bowes was an experienced copper and not a total moron. Nick, knowing there was no way out of this, stuffed his hands in his pockets and looked at the ground. 'I saved his life on Wednesday. He was about to jump in front of a train and kill himself. I knocked him out of the way. I'd just come round to see if he was OK.'

Bowes raised his eyebrows again and passed a hand over his bald head. 'I heard about that. I didn't know that was you. Always one for the superhero shit, you, aren't you, eh?'

Why did he feel it necessary to say that? Nick looked up from the ground, stared into Vic Bowes's grey eyes surrounded by black dark rings and sagging eyelids, a surge of fury rising from his gut to his heart. 'I saved a boy's life. That's not nothing. Don't be a twat about it. Leave your chippy bullshit at the door, eh?!'

Bowes laughed in his face, presumably because he'd got a rise out of him. Shit. Nick hated giving him even that.

'So, how did you know where the boy lived?'

'Because his mother is a service user of my wife's women's domestic abuse organisation and she had her address.'

Bowes took this information as just another example of annoying do-gooders and gave him an expression that suggested disdain. 'You really are the amateur detective, aren't you?' He said like it was a bad thing. 'So where is he now?'

'How the hell should I know?' said Nick, incredulous at even being asked.

Bowes stared at him right in the eyes. Was he trying to intimidate him? Well, that wasn't going to happen. Nick knew he could render a flabby useless shite like Bowes unconscious with one punch. Or was he trying to suss out if he was guilty of doing something to the boy himself?

'Right. Well, you can get along now, while we go to work. I know where you live if we need to ask you any more questions.' He made a small patronizing dismissive gesture with his fingers, as if he was a small dog to be got rid of.

Nick walked to the policeman. Stopped. Put his hand on the copper's neck with a creepy delicacy, said nothing, stared for maybe three seconds and left. He'd picked that one up from Jeff's alter ego as a crazy person, an alter ego he occasionally liked to deploy to intimidate people.

He walked back to the front of the house, just as the low rumble of Julie's blue 1975 Porsche arrived.

'What on earth has happened here?' she said, getting out and standing, a hand on her hip.

'Lord knows. Paul's parents are dead. The lad isn't in there.'

'Has he killed his own mother and father?' She looked at the house, forehead wrinkled in a heavy frown.

'I have to say, that was one my first thoughts.'

'Was there any blood? How were they killed?'

He explained what he'd seen.

'How strange. Which DI is on the job?'

'Vic Bowes.'

She curled her top lip. 'Oh. Him. You know he doesn't like us because we're mates with Mandy.'

'Yeah, he was being very sarky with me. He winds me up, I'm afraid.'

She put her hand on the small of his back. 'Come on, I'll drive you home. No point in hanging around here.'

As they travelled, Julie said, 'Have you told Josh yet?'

'No.'

'Did you tell them about Josh being the boy's friend?'

'No.'

'Why not?'

'I don't want them hassling him. Paul probably has other friends, too. I don't want to single out Josh.'

Julie didn't respond, which Nick knew meant she disagreed with his choice and was just framing a response.

'Yeah, I appreciate that, especially with Bowes being involved, but that being said, Josh is an important element in Paul's life, this week. They're going to have to speak to him. I mean, he might know where he is, for all we know.'

'Yeah, I do know that. I'd like to be there if they do question him. I know how to handle him. If they go about it the wrong way, he'll get upset and hit the roof and get a fit of screaming habdabs, and his mother will just let it happen. She's always been too hands off, for my liking. I'll set up a meeting with him to tell him about Paul and to prepare him for the police.'

'Good idea. Invite him round our house this evening. On other matters, so the BMW is buggered?'

'As dead as the Richardsons. I think the time has come to get a new car.'

'That Beamer has been held together with knicker elastic and Sellotape for years. It needs serious money spending on it to get it through its next MOT. I think it's reached the point where fixing it will cost more in time and effort than just trading it in for scrap and getting something else.'

'Yup, you're right.'

She took her hands off the wheel and did a fast clap. 'Oooh, new car. What do you fancy, then?'

He blew out air in a half groan. 'Cars are not my thing, Jules. You know that. I'll let you choose, you're going to have to maintain it.'

'One of us should have a car that can hold four or five, but you want something with a bit of poke in her.'

'Are cars always female?'

'Of course, I'm not having the patriarchy owning cars as well.'

'Fair enough. It's just I tend to dislike car blokes. I don't mind if men like cars, it's just that if they do, so often they're such macho arse biscuits and I'm traditionally against macho arse biscuits.'

She cocked her head to one side. 'Aren't we all, darlin'? What you need is something reliable, solid but fast.'

'That's why I got the BMW. The single and only reason I bought it in Harrogate in the early 90s was that they go on forever, and so it has proved.'

'OK, well, I reckon we should get you a high-mileage Merc that's about six or seven years old. I used to be good on Mercs, 'cos I had one myself for the second half of the 90s, and if we're careful, you'll get 10 years out of it.'

'Yeah, whatever. I genuinely don't care. Cars are purely functional to me.'

'You say that, but you love this car.' She patted the old Porsche's steering wheel.

'I do like you driving me around in it, that's true, but that's not quite the same thing.'

'I bloody love this car. It may be older than your BMW, but it's the best car I've *ever* had. Not for anything mechanical, though that's special, but I just feel like it fits me like a glove. Me and her have got it locked down tight.'

'Yeah, I get that. You do totally suit it. And it does still have some serious poke and I know you love a bit of serious poke.'

She slapped him on his thigh.

'So will you keep an eye open for a decent car that we can afford?'

'Yeah. We'll get a bit of scrappage for the Beamer. I'll put some feelers out and see if we can't get you an old Merc. Are you sure you don't want something sporty?'

'Nah. It's just not me, that, is it?'

She shook her head. 'No, it's not and I'm pleased you're not a jacket 'n' jeans, middle-aged man desperately trying to compensate for his withered little winkie with a phallic symbol. Those men are sooo creepy. Eeurgh.'

He laughed. 'Thankfully that's one of the few neuroses that's not in my messed-up head.'

She pulled up outside their house on Norton High Street. He

leaned over and kissed her on the lips. 'You better get back to work. Thanks for giving me a lift.'

She put her hand on his arm with momentary concern. 'Are you OK? I mean, you just saw two dead bodies.'

He nodded and smiled. 'I'm fine. Dead bodies don't upset me. It's when they're alive that the trouble starts.'

CHAPTER 5

He went to the kitchen and put the kettle on. As it boiled, he texted Josh.

'*Fancy coming to ours for your tea? There's something I want to talk to you about. Are you busy?*'

Soon he texted back. '*Great. I've got basketball practice until 4.30. I'm at 6th form. Is that OK?*'

'*Fine. I'll tell Jules to pick you up at the gates at 4.45.*'

He sent a message to Julie to let her know, and then one to Josh's mother. Josh would love being picked up in her car outside 6th form. Even though Julie was old enough to be his mother, or even grandmother, the lad went a bit wobbly at the knees around her, and seemed fascinated by her, possibly because she was so old in his eyes and yet he found her so attractive. Nick understood it, if only because he'd been equally fascinated to the point of drooling about Sophia Loren, when he was 16 and she in her mid 40s. Not that Sophia Loren ever picked him up from outside of Stockton Sixth Form College in an old Porsche. Though god knows, he would have very much have loved that to happen.

He lost himself in his writing during the afternoon, and, as it often did when he was living in his head, time just drifted away. Soon it was 4.30. He went to the fridge and took out some fresh haddock fillets, sliced them into long thick strips, coated them in a little cornflour, then beat an egg in a bowl. After seasoning some rice crumb, he dipped the fish in the egg and then in the crumb.

After firing up his deep-fat fryer, watching the beef dripping dissolve in the rising heat, he dressed some salad leaves and shreds of beetroot and rolled some cold pieces of boiled potato in a little semolina, just as Julie's car rumbled to a halt outside.

'Hello, luv! Oooh, do I smell hot fat?' said Julie as she came in, with Josh behind her, quite blatantly staring at her backside, seemingly forgetting that he could be seen doing so. Clearly, a boy after his own heart. Nick grinned to himself.

'What are we having?' said Julie, putting her bag on the floor.

'Posh fish fingers and crunchy chips.'

Josh cheered and held his arms aloft. 'My favourite! And I'm starving.'

'How was the basketball?' Nick asked.

'Alright. It'd help if I was 6 foot 10 and not 5 foot 10. I've asked Miss Coates for stilts but she was not open to the idea for some reason. Fucking idiot.'

'Hey! Language. There's no call for that,' said Nick, pointing at him. 'Remember - be a nice lad.'

'Sorry. If you don't swear at school, the rough boys think you're a wimp. Then it becomes a regrettable habit and one appears to be a shitmuncher, like the rough lads, even when one isn't.'

'Yeah, I know, but you're not at school now, lad. I didn't realise you did training on a Sunday.'

'Miss Coates introduced it. It's good. It gives us more time to practice moves.'

Julie ruffled Josh's hair, winked at him and went upstairs to get changed, while Nick fried the potatoes.

'Wash your hands and set the table,' said Nick, as he lifted the potatoes out of the fat and onto a plate in and put it in the warm oven, then dropped the fish fingers into the dripping. Josh, as usual, did as he was asked.

'So what did you want to talk to me about?' said Josh, getting knives and forks out of the drawer.

'I'll tell you after we've eaten.'

'OK,' he said, happily. 'Are we having wine?' He put his hands on Nick's shoulders and leaned into him.

'Does your mother let you drink wine with a meal?'

Josh gave one of his exaggerated, rather childlike nods. 'I'm allowed it with fizzy water added. Not that she adds fizzy water to her own wine, I have noted.' He said it rather disapprovingly.

'I'll ask Jules if you're allowed a glass. I don't want to have to take you home drunk.'

'Cool. Did you drink at 16?' he asked.

'I did. Yeah. Quite heavily. But not at home. And I wasn't well, not that I knew that at the time.'

'You were ill?' The boy frowned at him, quizzically.

'I was upset and I drank to cope with the upset. But, like I say, I didn't know that at the time. I didn't understand because I was just a kid and I had no adult to help me.'

'Oh, yes. You've told me about that. You should have had a Nick to talk to, like me.'

Nick smiled at him, suddenly feeling tears rise behind his eyes. Josh smiled back in his unaffected, slightly daft way, which was the nearest he seemed to get to empathy.

Julie came back in, now dressed in army pants and white capped-sleeve t-shirt, her hair tied up in a colourful silk scarf.

'Can Josh have a glass of wine with his dinner?' said Nick.

She turned to Josh and looked him up and down. 'Yeah, I don't see why not. Just a small one.'

'Yay! Thanks, Jules. I love you in the army clothes. You're Captain Wells of the Teesside Desert Rats!'

'Back in line, Jones.'

She patted him on the shoulder, making the lad flush into a full pink blush, then got a bottle of Chardonnay out of the fridge, took a glass from the cupboard and poured it half full. 'There you go. I hope you like Chardo, it's all we've got in.'

The boy picked it up, sniffed at it, like an expert and took a sip. His eyes winced slightly, the way you do when you taste something you don't like, but he soon recovered his composure.

'Lovely, thanks Jules.' She had to laugh.

Nick served up the food, and put a bowl of homemade mayonnaise in the centre of the table along with a bottle of tomato sauce.

'Right, dig in,' he said.

'Have you always cooked?' said Josh, eating his food at high pace.

'Yeah, since I was a teenager. I really like it and it's a good skill to learn. Don't you ever cook?'

He shook his head as he scoffed some fish.

'It still isn't a thing at school?'

'No. Quite how we're all supposed to look after ourselves once we leave home does not seem to have occurred to anyone. Fucking idiots...sorry! Sorry for swearing! Sorry.'

'Apology accepted,' said Nick. 'I'll teach you how to cook, if you like.'

'It'll make you attractive to girls,' said Julie, raising an eyebrow at him.

'Will it?' That got his interest, so much so that he stopped eating.

'Oh, yeah. Women love a bloke who can feed them well. It's a primal thing,' said Julie. 'And it shows you're not a sexist idiot, who thinks a woman's place is in the kitchen.'

Josh nodded again. 'I'd like that, Nick. I'm not interested in being a chef, but I like eating and girls. The fish is excellent and I like the crunchy potatoes. My mother just heats food up, she doesn't cook anything. Heating is different from cooking.'

Nick liked his precise insight.

'He cooks me amazing breakfasts,' said Julie. 'If you can cook a good breakfast you're a bit of a star in most women's books, so you should learn.'

'The good thing is that it's not that difficult and you get praise for cooking, even if it's simple and easy. It's weird really,' said Nick.

'It's because food is vital for life,' said Josh, picking up a fish finger and dipping it into the mayo. 'So if someone gives you nice food, you're naturally going to feel they're a good person and someone you want to know. It's like you said, Jules, it's primal. We're built to ally ourselves to people who can help keep us alive.'

Nick and Julie glanced at each other. That was the older Josh; the Aspie who was at least 20 years in advance of 16; insightful and mature. What a fascinating lad.

'Have you seen Paul Richardson since the Allens West thing, Josh?' said Julie, biting into a potato.

'No, he wasn't at school on Thursday and Friday. I suppose the "why are you such a fucking loony?" people have got hold of him. Sorry I swore again. Sorry. I've had the loony people up my arse over the years. Sorry, is arse a swear? It's not, is it?'

'No, you're OK with arse. It's just fuck and cunt you need to avoid,' said Nick.

Josh burst into a paroxysm of laughter at the coarse language. The 16-year-old had returned to laugh at dirty words, delighted to have heard a grown up swear.

They finished their food. Josh took a drink of wine and winced again as he swallowed it. Julie put her right hand on the boy's arm and let it rest there, and in doing so, made the colour rise in his cheeks again.

'Josh. Something bad has happened that we've got to talk to you about. OK?'

'Bad? What?' He said it in his flat, wide-eyed way.

'Well, Nick found Paul's parents dead at their home in The Avenue today, but Paul wasn't there and we don't know where he's gone. Have you any idea where he might be?'

Josh's condition meant he responded to these facts without much emotion. He just looked at her with his pretty, almond-shaped, long-eyelashed eyes.

'That's an unusual thing to hear. I met his parents. They were called Terri and David Richardson. How did they die?'

'We don't know what happened, but we're concerned for Paul's welfare. Have you any idea where he might be?' asked Nick.

Josh shook his head. 'No. He hasn't responded to my texts since you saved him on Wednesday. He must want to be left alone. I know how that feels. Do you think he's killed himself? He really wanted to do that.' Josh never beat about the bush.

'Well, it's crossed my mind, obviously.'

'Do you think he killed his parents?' asked Josh, drinking more wine.

'We just don't know. Did he say anything about them or how they were treating him?' said Nick.

Josh thought about it and when he did that, he just sat perfectly still staring into the middle-distance. Finally, he spoke again. 'He said they didn't like him and that they were horrible to him. But all teenagers say that about their parents, I assume. It is all part of the game of growing up.'

And there was the older Josh again. Wise beyond his years.

'He's been going mad for months. I told my form teacher Mr

McGregor about it, but he didn't do anything, other than put it into Paul's notes.'

'How do you mean, "going mad"?' asked Julie.

Josh sipped a little wine again, perhaps getting a taste for it now. 'He started to behave in a way that wasn't commonplace. In an odd way compared to the norm.'

'What sort of odd behaviour?' asked Julie.

The boy wouldn't look her in the eye, his gaze flicking from side to side, as if to avoid seeing her.

'I can't tell you. I mean, I can tell you, but I don't want to because it involves saying something about...about something embarrassing,' said Josh, as he looked at his hands, clearly feeling awkward, now flushing pink.

It was strange to see him crippled by social embarrassment in front of her, if only because he was usually the absolute opposite with people he trusted. It meant it had to be a sexual thing.

Julie picked up on it. 'OK, well, if I leave the room, can you tell Nick?'

Josh nodded and watched as Julie stood up, once again staring at her backside as she left.

Nick touched him on the arm. 'You don't have to look at it every single time.' He winked to indicate he wasn't vexed, but was giving him a survival tip.

'Sorry, Nick.' He dropped his voice to a whisper. 'I don't think she noticed.'

'Now tell me about Paul. What was so odd about his behaviour? Was it sexual?'

'Sometimes. As I told you the other day, he became obsessed with his body.'

'With his genitals?'

Josh ruffled his fair hair so it all stuck up at wild angles. 'Yes, but with everything else as well. Feet, hands, nose, his weight; everything. He would talk about it all the time. I didn't like it. Something was going wrong with him. A year or so ago he was sharp and bright and really clever, but he changed a lot.'

'What is he good at?'

59

'Chemistry, physics and maths. We sat together in maths all through Ian Ramsey School and in 6th form, too. As long as I've known him, he never got less than an A in any exam for any science.'

'OK, but that changed earlier this year?'

'He's taking his A-levels a year early because he's so brilliant and they gave him a mock exam before Christmas and he got a C. He went mental, Nick. I mean really...' he made his vibrating noise with his lips and accompanied it with a high-pitched noise. 'He really changed. He became angry and said loads of rude words and was just obsessed with sex. I mean, I know I am as well. All kids are at 16. It is very distracting and it messes with your head. But Paul took it to an extreme I never heard anyone else take it to.'

'And that was because of the porn?'

'It seemed to coincide with his increased intake of that, yes. I told him I'd heard you say it messed with your head and my head is sooo messed with already, so I don't need any more messing. But after I said that to him, he got angry. Not with me. But with himself.'

'Angry?'

'Yes. He began to hit himself as we walked home.'

'Really? Where did he hit himself?'

Josh mimed punching himself on the cheekbone. 'He did it hard, as well. Then another day, on the way home...this is the rude bit...he showed me his dick and asked me if it was normal.'

Nick leaned forward, frowning, not liking what he was hearing at all. 'What? Where did this happen?'

'On Bishopton Road West.'

'What?! Outside? In public?'

Josh nodded. 'I told you he was behaving unconventionally.'

'So, let me get this right. You're walking along, on your way home from school, when he unzips, pulls it out and says, "Is this normal?"
'

'Exactly.' He nodded.

'Did anyone else see this?'

'Cars passed by, so someone must have. We didn't walk past anyone on foot.'

'And what happened next? What did you say?'

'I told him he was being weird and he had to stop it. I told him doing that was wrong. I mean, two years ago you gave me a long list of things you can't do in public, and that was one of them. Even if you hadn't, you don't see anyone else doing it, so it's obviously not allowed. Even I worked that out. But he just kept on at me. "What do you think? Is it any good?" and all of that sort of thing. I wouldn't look. I didn't want to look. How do I know what is normal, anyway? There probably isn't a normal. It's like asking if your ears are normal. There are loads of different shapes and sizes to ears...there is no normal.'

You couldn't argue with his logic. But Nick was shocked at what Josh was telling him.

'Did he do anything else to himself?'

Josh paused and stared at Nick, then nodded. 'Another time, we were walking home and he just punched himself in the balls, really hard. Out of nowhere.'

Nick recoiled in horror.

'Good god, Josh, why didn't you tell me this before now?'

He looked back at him. 'Well, I want to be able to deal with things on my own. I can't document every incident in my life for you. I did tell you he had been behaving oddly when we went to Allens West.'

'True. So he punched himself. He did it hard?'

'Yes. He really hurt himself.'

'Did he say anything before doing it?'

'He said "I'm shit", then squatted and punched himself, making sure he hit himself really hard in the balls. He was on his knees for a few minutes, while he recovered. I didn't know what to do. He just told me to fuck off, so I did. I couldn't think what else to do. It was confusing. I saw him at school the next day and I asked him if he was alright, because that's what you do when people have been hurt. But he just laughed it all off, like it wasn't a big thing. But hitting yourself in the balls is obviously not normal, so that day I went to Mr McGregor, my form teacher, and said Paul was behaving weird.'

'That was really good of you. Well done. Did you say exactly what he did?'

'I just said he was punching himself and hurting himself.'

'No more details than that?'

Josh shook his head. 'I felt like I couldn't say the dirty words to him. Like in front of Julie. I felt too embarrassed. I don't know why. I'm not normally bothered, just in some circumstances with some people. But I don't feel it with you. I can say anything to you.'

'Good. And because of that, I want you to tell me if anything like this happens again. I understand you want to stand on your own two feet, but this was quite a big thing...'

'...it wasn't a big thing at all,' said Josh, shaking his head.

'I beg to differ, Josh. And it's something you shouldn't keep to yourself, because Paul needs help, and it must have been disturbing for you to witness, as well.'

'No, I meant his dick wasn't a big thing. It was small, I think, by the typical 16-year-old standards, recorded in various medical journals that I've researched. But that doesn't mean it's not normal.'

At first, Nick thought he was making a joke, but quickly realised he wasn't. He was serious and just saying it in his matter-of-fact way.

'I think that's why he decided he hated himself,' said Josh. 'He really thinks there's something wrong with him. I tried to tell him he was being stupid because there is great variance in the size of all body parts, and that's just the way humans are, but I am not one of life's great diplomats and I probably just made things worse, I don't know. Then two days later, after Connie had dumped him, saying he was fat and had a small cock in the gym, he tried to kill himself. And he would have been successful if he hadn't told me before trying, and if you hadn't done what you did.'

It all sounded terribly like a boy who was undergoing sexual abuse at home or somewhere else, and who was seriously disturbed as a result.

'Ok, so where could he have gone? Does he have friends or relations elsewhere? Somewhere he could have gone on his bike?'

'I don't know.'

Julie put her head around the door. 'Is it all clear?'

'Yeah, all cool,' said Nick. 'We're just trying to think where Paul might have gone.'

'Good idea. Did he play for any school teams?' said Julie, picking up the wine she'd left.

Josh shook his head.

'Did he have any other friends, other than you?' said Nick.

'He did, but they all drifted away once he started going mad. I can't do being a friend. I find some people interesting, but that's not what you mean, I know.' He nodded to himself. 'I have come to the conclusion that friends are just something you neuro-typicals have.'

'Well, I think of you as my friend,' said Nick.

'So do I,' said Julie.

'Oh. That's good.'

Emotional reciprocation really wasn't in Josh's make-up.

'Oh, I should have said you are my friends, there, shouldn't I? Sorry. And now it's too late for it to sound sincere,' he said and clicked his fingers in a 'darn it' sort of gesture. When you conducted your life by a lot of learned responses, rather than by emotional intuition, such moments often occurred with the lad, but you got used to it. Josh didn't have an extreme form of Asperger's and was very aware of his condition, but even so, more often than not, he couldn't put himself into the shoes of the person he was talking to, or about.

'So what hobbies does Paul have?' said Nick.

'Drones. He's big on drones.'

'You mean drones as in little planes and things that you fly?' said Julie.

'Yes. Our physics teacher does an after-school class on how to build and maintain them. Paul goes to that. So do I. So does Heather. She's an expert droner and has built this amazing small machine, about the size of a bumble bee. She's amazing. She's an Aspie, too.'

'So were you good at making them?' said Nick.

'Not as good as Heather, I'm more into the data and computing side of things. The idea she's got is to go into surveillance and spying and then sell her inventions to the military. Well, her dad does anyway. She's not in it for money. She's ace. I get distracted in class by looking at Heather. She does my head in.'

'I hope you've been following my notes about that behaviour. About not staring and not getting into people's personal space, not touching yourself or saying rude things out loud. I know it's hard for you,' said Nick.

'It fucking is when I look at her. Rock hard.' He said it in his flat monotone.

Wearily, Nick sighed. 'What have I told you?' He jabbed his index finger at him sternly.

Josh put his hands up, then groaned and slumped into himself. 'But it's the truth, though. I can't understand how saying the truth in one situation is the right thing to do, and how saying it in another is totally wrong. It's stupid, why can't we just have one rule for every situation?' Nick felt sorry for him. It was exhausting dealing with him at times, but much more so for Josh himself.

It was important not to overstress the boy or he could have a meltdown and Nick sensed he was getting a bit wound up, so knew it was time to pull back and leave him be.

'You're a good lad and you do really well. I think you're a bit of a star,' said Julie. 'You just need to think twice before saying something rude like that. It might be factually true, but that doesn't matter when it's something sexual or intimate or private. Right? You keep those thoughts to yourself, just to be on the safe side.'

This made him blush again.

'Thank you, Julie. I will try to think twice.' The fact was, he'd never get it right all the time, it just wasn't possible for him. Then again, Nick sometimes felt the same way, often unsure how to respond in social situations.

'Now look, Josh. I had to tell the police about you getting me to save Paul's life with that train. They will certainly want to speak to his friends about how his parents died and where he might have been at the time. When that happens, you can call me to sit in with you during the interview, just so you've got someone who understands you present. The police can be very blunt and they can bombard you with questions. So you need someone there with you. Your mam isn't too good at that sort of thing. So, please Josh, if or when this happens, call me. Ok?'

'What will they ask me?' He frowned.

'I don't know, probably about his state of mind. You'll have to tell them about his self-harming and body dysmorphia.'

'I love dysmorphia. The word, not the condition. Diss-more-fear. Excellent.'

Julie smiled at him. 'C'mon then, mister, I'll run you home.' They stood up.

'Thank you for my dinner, Nick.' He held out his hand. Nick laughed. 'This isn't really a handshake thank-you situation, man.'

He shrugged. 'See - mad - how can anyone know that?'

CHAPTER 6

When Julie returned, he poured her a large glass of white wine, got himself a big vodka and tonic and they repaired to the living room, Nick clutching a few records he'd picked off the shelves.

'What are we listening to?' she asked, flopping down on the sofa and putting her feet up with a groan.

'Humble Pie's *As Safe As Yesterday Is* if that's OK.'

'Steve Marriott, eh? What a voice that lad had.'

'Yeah, I love this record.' He held it up to her. 'Pink Immediate label, first pressing.'

'Is that rare?'

'Yeah. Worth about £60, this.'

'Amazing. Where did you acquire it?'

'I can't remember. Had it 20 years or more.'

He dropped the needle.

'I feel like I really need this drink. Stressful day. I love Josh, but he does wear you out. I worry about him, y'know? How's his life going to work out? I'm not sure he's able to have a loving long-term relationship; in fact, right now I'm worried he's going to force his attentions on this Heather girl, not on purpose, but...well...you know what he's like. And if she's an Aspie as well, that could be problematic.'

She yawned. 'I do know what you mean. You've done a great job with him. I can see him remembering your life lessons and applying them. He was very obviously, ahem, shall we say "excited" in the car, if you know what I mean. But he is mad about that Heather girl. He was talking about her and he seems to know every detail of her. He can see her in his mind's eye like a photograph. It's a bit creepy really, if I'm honest.'

'I've told him about not being creepy.'

'And he looks at me like he's seeing me naked. He keeps looking me up and down, All wide eyes and tongue almost hanging out.'

'I've told him about that, as well. I've encouraged him to take sneaky looks and not just stare. I mean, we all do that. Makes the world go around, but he can just stare too long. He knows not to, but occasionally it seems to escape him. '

'Occasionally, Asperger's people have very high sex drives. He might be one of those. I just sense sex is dominating his every waking moment, at least right now.'

Nick rubbed his eyes. 'Oh, god. Obviously, being 16, that's a fairly natural state for any lad, but even so, he does seem almost overwhelmed by it all. Should I have another talk with him?'

'Well, you already have, often enough. It's not like he's your boy.'

'But his mother has taken her hands off the wheel. He doesn't even see his father. He goes back to that house in Palm Grove, gets himself something to eat and goes to that back bedroom and just sits on his own all night with Stanley. If she's not out, which she often is, she'll look in on him at 10ish and then say goodnight. He sits up into the night, and no-one knows what he's doing. He could be up to anything.'

'But he does need time on his own to maintain his peace of mind. Like you, he's happy in his own company,' she said.

'Yeah, and that's why I know how that can lead you to dwell in the isolation of your own mind. And that's where you get things out of shape and a bit weird.' He filled her in on everything Josh had told him about Paul after she'd left the kitchen.

'This poor lad, Paul. I mean, hitting himself like that, I fear for him, I really do,' Julie said. 'That's a proper bonkers episode. It's a different version of being a cutter and wanting to hurt yourself to exorcise the pain of your life.'

Nick thought about it for a few moments. 'Seems worse than that, and way more violent. Punching yourself hard in the balls is not just a statement of self-loathing, it's about hating that part of yourself He seems to have been stressing about it all. I mean, lobbing it out on Bishopton Road West. Dear me.'

She sat and thought for a quiet moment as the record came to an end. 'I imagine teenage boys are always a bit obsessed with that part of themselves and compare themselves with their mates.'

'Some lads did, though usually at a younger age. I didn't. But I was a bit over-focused on it at 16. You can't help it because it changes and...well...you use it for pleasure all the time.'

She said nothing for a minute, just shook her head and closed her eyes. 'I feel so sorry for kids today, they're under so much pressure from all sides.'

'What I think is rather weird about this is that he chose Josh to show himself to. Josh is not a sympathetic person. Anyone who knows him, knows that. That makes me think the lad is just out of control. He's not thinking. He's, for want of a better expression, lost his mind. And maybe if you've lost your mind, murdering your parents is also very easy.'

Nick's phone buzzed. It was Jeff.

'Greetings from Strangesville, Arizona. Just bought a dead hippie collection. Mucho vinyl of toppo de la qualitio (as they say in Billingham).'

Nick smiled.

'Found something that you will recognise. Come to the shop tomorrow to learn more.'

Nick replied a quick affirmative.

'Does Josh ever lie?' asked Julie, taking a drink.

'Good question. Not really. He can obfuscate when he doesn't want to tell you something, but doesn't seem to make up outright lies. Then again, maybe he could if he had to, but just never has to. So if he says this thing with Paul happened, I'm sure it did.'

'I wonder what his form teacher did about it?'

'Not much, by the sound of it. I hope the lad is alright, but...I dunno...I suspect he isn't. I've never heard of someone punching themselves in the face and in the balls. In a way, it's easier to imagine someone shooting or stabbing themselves. Somehow it seems much easier to do than punching yourself. Punching is more intimate, in a way. You have to touch yourself. It's yourself that is administering the violence to yourself, whereas a weapon is a kind of intermediary between your intent and the injury.'

She looked at him thoughtfully, but said nothing for some time.

'I know this is a horrible question, but it might be important. When you've felt suicidal, would the manner of your death be in any way important?'

That wasn't something he could answer quickly.

'God, I need time to think about that.'

'Take as long as you want, luv.' She flipped the record over, picked up the inner sleeve of the album and read the lyrics, as he dwelt on it, putting himself back in time to his lowest moments, as the music played.

'If I'd had a gun I would have shot myself in the head.' His eyes filled with tears as he said it. 'Because it would be guaranteed death. If I'd had a gun that time in Harrogate, I know I would have shot myself. But I didn't. I almost let myself fall out of the window instead.'

'What stopped you?'

He let out a trembling sigh and rested his fingertips on his forehead. 'There was a small boy walking by, with his dad. I couldn't let him see such a terrible thing as my body hitting the pavement. It'd be so unfair to him. So I slammed the window shut.'

'That suggests even at the point of total despair, you had concern for others.'

'Yeah, I did. I've never wanted to make a fuss about my death. I just wanted it to be over, and over quietly, without any big deal. The last thing I wanted was for it to impact on anyone else.'

'Over without pain?'

'Preferably. Though as long as death happened, I'd have taken a moment or three of pain. It's impossible to express just how little you care about yourself when you're consumed with depression.'

She got off the sofa, kneeled in front of him, took both of his hands and looked into his face with her beautiful, crystal clear eyes. She spoke softly but firmly.

'I think you're such a beautiful man, so full of compassion, intelligence, love and lust. I love you with all my heart. Please never forget that. And if you ever feel that bad again, please hold onto that thought.'

He smiled but didn't say anything for a while. 'Thanks, luv. It does give me a rubber ring to hang onto when swimming in baths of depression. I just thank God I don't feel like that today.'

'Today. Is that a significant qualification?'

'I don't take the future for granted, do I? All I can do is be alright today. That's my basic approach.'

She blinked slowly at him. 'You don't talk to me about this stuff much. You should, you know.'

'There's not much to be gained by talking about it.'

'I disagree. We should talk about it from time to time.'

'I don't want to upset you, or me.'

'You wouldn't. And now I need to physically show you how much I love you, so it sits front and centre of your brain, no matter what your mood is. Right?'

She sat on his lap, put her hands either side of his head and kissed him with a raw passion, then began to seduce him in her slow erotic, wonderfully uninhibited way, trying to make this a bookmark of pleasure in the novel of his life, for him to go back, take off the shelf and re-read whenever he needed to.

In the morning, he'd finished making Julie breakfast and seen her off to work, and was just settling down to eat some eggs and bacon when his phone buzzed. He didn't recognise the number.

'Hello?'

'Hello, is that Nick Guymer?' said a firm male voice.

'Yeah, who's this?'

'Mr Guymer, my name is Mike McGregor. I'm Josh Jones's form master. Is this a good time to talk?'

'Oh, hi. Yeah, of course. What can I do for you? Is Josh OK?'

'Err...he's in class, as usual.' That seemed to avoid a proper response to his question.

'Is something wrong?'

'You gave the school your consent to be Josh's first point of adult contact because, as the notes tell me, his mother works in York now, and has a significant commute if needed at the school during weekdays.'

'Yeah, that's right. Are you sure he's OK?' Nick was worried now.

'It'd probably be better if you could come into school to discuss things. There have been some significant developments this morning that might affect him.'

'Ok, I'll come down now. What sort of developments are you talking about?'

McGregor blew air into the phone, making it distort.

'I'm afraid his friend Paul Richardson has been found dead.'

CHAPTER 7

Nick got on his bike and cycled to the Sixth Form college. He turned down the drive, heading to a bike stand, seeing the whole place crawling with police officers and cars. There was yellow police tape at one side of the campus, sectioning off the right-hand side. He stood for a moment and looked at the scene. He now only had scattered fragments of memories of the place, mostly of girls he'd fallen in and out of love with, and playing records at lunchtime with Jeff. But it had all changed a lot. It was a much bigger college now, with additional buildings on all sides.

He expected to get stopped by an officer and asked what his business was, but they seemed to be more concerned with other things. Maybe they didn't want to overly disrupt normal college life. No point in upsetting the kids. As he pushed the entrance door open, it had to be the first time he'd been there since July 1979. Oh good god, where did the time go? He'd left as a lusty 18-year-old virgin, with undiagnosed episodes of depression, a fondness for drinking as a result, and a deep passion for music, records and writing. He half smiled to himself; well, at least one of those things had changed in the intervening years.

He went to the office and was greeted by a short woman about his own age, little more than 5 foot 3 inches tall, with curvy hips and substantial round breasts. She had small hands and features. With a straight fringe and shoulder-length brown hair framing her face, she had kind pale blue eyes and a mouth that curved upwards, even when not smiling, as though in anticipation of future amusement. Julie had that, too.

'Hi, there. Mr McGregor asked me to come and see him.'

She glanced up at him, but was distracted by the phone ringing.

'Sorry, I'll just get that. Can you just sign in. Thanks.' She took the call. It sounded like it was the press or TV. 'No, we've no comment. Thank you. No...no...no...I said we've no comment.' She raised her voice. 'Exactly which of the two words "no" and "comment" do you not understand?' She turned the phone to her, so she was looking directly at it, as though it was the person on the other end and barked, 'Go away!', then swore under her breath as she slammed the phone down. A shiver ran down Nick's spine from his neck to his coccyx. He loved stroppy, assertive women, with a propensity to swear, especially women with nice eyes like hers.

He wrote his name in the visitor book and handed it back to her, with a smile.

'I used to go here in the late 70s,' said Nick, making small talk.

'Did you? So did I,' she said. She smiled with a half-familiar look.

'When were you here?' she asked, getting to her feet.

'77 to 79.'

'Good god, that's my year. Do we know each other?' She leaned forward and squinted at him, taking off a pair of expensive, round frameless glasses to do so.

'I don't know. You look quite...'

She looked at his name in the visitor book. 'Eee, Nick Guymer, of course it is! Eee, remember me? I'm Janey James.' She pointed to herself, laughed and gave him a little stand-off hug. He looked once, twice and the third time she clicked into place. Janey James, my god.

'Hello, you. My, my, my, it's been a long time, Janey.'

'Well what a terrible, awful day to see you for the first time since 1979. I can't believe it. I really can't.' She bit her bottom lip and shook her head. 'Eee, remember the 5th year disco?' she said, with a light in her eyes.

'Of course. Glory days.' He had to laugh a little, because one thing came immediately to his mind, but it wasn't something that he could possibly tell her.

They'd sat together in English for two years in 4th and 5th year and then at an end-of-year disco, danced cheek to cheek, done a bit of groping and he'd walked her home and they'd kissed. And that was pretty much the full extent of their intimacy. She'd been a well-developed teenage girl, not that this made her especially attractive to him, per se. He didn't really get the big breasts thing, being largely indifferent to their size and shape. But they'd always been friendly and had got on well. Trouble was, he had been obsessed with Shawn Yeadon at the time, so probably didn't give her the attention she may have wanted and deserved from him. Jeff had told him often enough that she was sweet on him, but he'd never taken it that seriously, largely because she was always there. Smiley Janey James.

At the time, girls he was attracted to seemed unattainable, indeed, that seemed to be inevitable, but Janey was the opposite. She was always there with a nice grin and a joke, when they went into English class. He'd liked her but back then you didn't have girls as friends, for some reason. Yet, briefly casting his mind back now, what he thought was friendship had probably been a proper bond of affection between them, but one he was too immature to have realised existed, even if she had. They'd both gone to 6th form, but drifted away into different social groups, and he'd not thought of her since, really.

She stood hands on hips, still smiling. 'Eee, god. Well, I waited for two years for you to ask me out, Nick Guymer. I'm still waitin', by the way!!'

Nick made a shrugging gesture. 'Sorry. You should've asked me. I'd have said yes. I was just useless at being proactive with girls and terrified of rejection.'

She laughed again, seemingly very happy to see him again, despite the unfolding Paul Richardson tragedy. 'I wish I had, but girls never asked lads out back then, did they?'

'So how long have you worked here, Janey?'

'Oooh, must be nearly 20 years now.' She put her arms out wide. 'I'm the secretary. I run the place, effectively. It probably looks very different to you, but I've been here so long I can't tell.' She looked him up and down. 'You've aged really well, Nick. You look in great shape. Well done. I'm afraid I'm all heading south.' She pulled a silly face.

She looked really lovely. For a moment he felt a bit like Josh trying to remember the right words to say. He could hear his mother's voice: *"Just be a nice lad and have good manners."*

'I'm not sure about that, but you look great, Janey. As lovely as ever. Do you have kids?'

74

'Yeah, two boys. Well, I say boys but they're both in their 20s now. They fled the nest, of course; so did their dad, for that matter.' She tutted, then shrugged. 'How about you?'

'No kids. I married Julie Wells, she was three years behind us at Ian Ramsey.'

She pointed at him as she recalled the name. 'Oh, was she the sister of the Wells brothers? The hard lads?'

'That's her.'

'I remember her. She was pretty and blondish wasn't she? And, oh yeah, she always used to freak out at discos when they put on a rock song. Shaking her head and all that.'

'Yeah, she still does that. Still can't dance to save her life.'

They were interrupted by a worried man coming into the office at a brisk pace, holding his hand out as he entered.

'Mr Guymer. Michael McGregor, thank you for coming down. Shall we go to my office?'

Nick turned to Janey James, smiled and she responded likewise as he left. Ah, this place was really stirring up some ghosts. She seemed really nice. She always had. Why the hell hadn't he asked her out? Another of life's many, many regrets. Oh, the road not taken - it was a constant torture.

McGregor led him down a corridor and opened a cheap plywood door into his office. It was a windowless room with a desk, a computer, and an enormous bin full of waste paper. It also contained two padded office chairs, which he pulled around so they faced each other, so that he wasn't sitting behind his desk.

'Take a seat. Can I call you Nick?'

'Yeah, of course.' They sat down.

'Can I get you a coffee?'

'No. I'm fine, thanks.'

McGregor, an unremarkable sort of bloke, five nine, 150 pounds, late 30s, pushed at his short, cropped, greying dark hair and looked up at him with dark brown eyes.

'I had the police call me and the Head at 6.00am. They told me that the body of one of our 16-year-old boys, Paul Richardson, had been found.' He sniffed aggressively and shook his head. 'Poor lad.'

He sat, very tense, hands clamped between his knees.

'You won't know this, but the police have told me Paul's parents were also found dead yesterday.'

Nick interrupted. 'I do know. As weird as this might seem, it was actually me who found them and called the police.'

His face dropped into a heavy and puzzled frown. 'What?'

Nick explained how he'd saved Paul's life the previous Wednesday and then gone to the house on Sunday.

McGregor rubbed his eyes. 'Well, that's quite amazing, Nick. We weren't even told about his suicide attempt. Paul was last in school on Wednesday morning. The police should have told us, but they didn't. Bloody hell.' He shook his head. 'His mother called the day after and said Paul wasn't well, and that he'd be off for the rest of the week. So we thought nothing more of it. It's terrible to say this, but we were almost glad, so as not to have to deal with any of his more disruptive behaviour. I've been worried about him for a few months. You see, the thing is, he was, or used to be, a good boy. But this year he changed and became difficult. He was suspended in January for two weeks after being exceptionally vulgar towards me.'

'What did he say?'

McGregor raised his eyebrows, as though flinching from the memory. 'I gave him detention for swearing at me in class. Can I use very blunt language with you?'

'Of course.'

'Well, during the detention he said, "You just want to fuck me up the arse, you dirty bastard". We can't have kids talking like that to us. Then later, Josh came and told me that Paul had been hurting himself.'

'Was anything done to help him?'

'What Josh told me was written into Paul's school file. His parents were informed both times, of course. He had sessions with a counsellor, here, on college premises. But nothing did any good. He got worse, if anything. He often took days off and I have no idea where he was going or doing. No-one knew what to do. His parents were...well...I shouldn't speak ill of the dead, but they were the worst kind of liberal parents. You know? Hippy types who...oh, god...well...you know.' The poor bloke looked at the end of his tether. 'In your view was he losing his mind, in some way? He was desperate to die when I saved him.'

McGregor closed his eyes and scratched at an eyebrow. 'I'm not a doctor, but yes, he was obviously having a protracted breakdown, the like of which I've not seen before. Some days he was OK, but then he'd turn up with a look in his eye and he was gone again. It was like whatever was troubling him, took him over, like a demonic possession. I know that sounds dramatic and I'm not saying it was supernatural or anything, but it was like you were suddenly dealing with a different person.'

That sounded all too familiar to Nick. It sounded exactly how his mother was, when she began her descent into paranoid schizophrenia.

'Where was he found?'

'They found him on the roof, Nick. On the roof!'

'On the roof of the college?' Nick pointed upwards with his index finger. 'So that's why there are so many coppers outside. That's weird. Why was he up there?'

McGregor, clearly stressed out, shook his head again. 'He was on the gym roof. God knows why. The officer advised me the initial medical assessment was that he'd been up there for less than 24 hours.'

'Shit. That sounds like he died around the same time his parents died.'

'He was spotted early this morning by a cleaner at St Bede's school, next door. It's just awful. Anyway, the reason I called you is because my concern is that Josh will take this badly and be very upset. With Asperger's kids we have to pay them special attention. They sat together in mornings for registration and I'm told they were quite tight at Ian Ramsey.'

Nick shook his head. 'He'll be alright. He doesn't feel those destructive sorts of emotions. He'll just accept it as a fact. That's how he was with the suicide bid. How did Paul die, do you know?'

'They said it wasn't immediately obvious, but that there was no trauma on the body.'

'Is he still up there?'

'No they took him down before school opened, but obviously it's potentially a crime scene, so the police are all over that side.'

'Is it hard to get up there?'

'I wouldn't have thought so, but I've never tried. The rubbish skips and bins are all out that way. I think you could use one of those as a stepping stone and get onto the lower roof and then up higher on the gym. His bike was beside the bins. He must have arrived on it. Anyway, I thought it best to tell Josh when you were here. Is that OK? I may have overreacted and misjudged this, but I thought it best, given Josh's condition.'

'Sure. I think that's probably for the best.'

There was a knock at the door and a man put his head around. 'Sorry to interrupt, Michael. The press have got hold of it, Janey is fighting them off as best she can. I need to do a piece for them and local news. Can you make sure anyone who needs to know, knows before it goes out on the lunchtime news? I don't want friends and family finding out from the TV.' McGregor nodded.

'That's Ewan Davis, the Headmaster,' he said as the door closed. 'Right, I'll go and get Josh.'

Feeling agitated, Nick stood up and paced around the room, stopping to look at various documents pinned to a cork drawing board, mostly internal memos and admin along with holidays blocked out on a calendar poster. There was a photo of an older black-haired woman tucked into the frame, and another of a black labrador. On McGregor's desk was a card folder, the flap open, a pile of photos printed onto A4 paper spilling out. On the top was one of Jenny Wells, a full-length shot taken of her playing basketball in an American-style long vest and shorts, all long tanned legs and powerful shoulders, holding the ball in her hands. She was an awesome physical specimen for a 16-year-old kid. It was low resolution and a bit blurred, not professionally taken. Picking up the rest of the photos, he skimmed through them and they were all likewise. All girls, all playing some sort of sport, caught mid-action, except for one of a girl holding something. They looked like they were all taken without the girl being aware, taken surreptitiously, perhaps. He put the file down and closed it as he heard footsteps approaching. McGregor opened the door and came in, followed by Josh.

'Sit down, please, Josh,' said the teacher, pointing to a chair. Josh did so. Nick sat along from him, McGregor resting his hip on the edge of his desk.

Josh spoke quickly and without punctuation, clearly excited. 'Hello Nick it's odd seeing you in this context I bet something has happened and they've asked you to tell me about it because they think an Aspie kid is going to go bonkers because they don't understand what I'm really like and my guess is that Paul Richardson has been found dead and that's why there's a load of police around the place, am I right?'

At times, Josh could be an extraordinary boy, his combination of straight talking and perception almost unnerving.

'You've got it 100 per cent right,' said Nick.

'Yes! I knew it.' Josh punched the air and then gripped a fist. 'One nil.'

Nick looked at him through narrowed eyes. It was an odd reaction to death. But then, Josh could pull an odd reaction at any time.

'He was found on the roof of the gym. Mr McGregor thought it'd be better that you heard it from me, what with you two having been friends.'

Josh stared blankly. 'I don't understand why it'd be better from you. Sorry,' he said, looking between Nick and McGregor.

'Because upsetting news is best heard from friends, Josh,' said his form master. 'How do you feel about it?'

Josh blinked at him. 'How do I feel about it? Let's see now.' His face went blank and he stared into the middle distance. 'I don't know the answer to that. I thought it was very likely, given how he'd been behaving. How did he die?'

'They've not said yet,' said Nick.

'Did he kill himself?' asked Josh.

'We don't know that.'

Josh lapsed into another outburst. In such moments, he could seem very unsympathetic, because sympathy relies on some degree of empathy and emotional intelligence, two things he rarely had access to.

'I think he must have because he wanted to be dead and now he is so maybe now he's happy if you believe there's an afterlife to be happy in which I don't because it's clearly all made up by humans who are just scared of dying.'

He looked at Nick and shrugged. 'Is that it then?'

'Are you OK? Would you like counselling?' said McGregor, but Nick knew the response to that before Josh even uttered it.

'No, thank you. I will miss the nice Paul. I won't miss the horrible Paul of the last few months. That kid was...' he made his buzzing noise with his lips and a gesture with his hand held to his forehead, as though to indicate madness.

And that was that. Josh could get upset when he felt hassled, or was in an unpredictable situation with a lot of loud noise and crowds of people, but incidents like this didn't faze him at all. Even when he and Nick had been caught up in the barn fire at Flynn's farm that almost killed them both, he hadn't panicked and had been quickly resigned to whatever their fate was to be. On the whole, to Nick, it seemed to be a largely positive attribute. Paul was dead, no point in worrying about it now, because there was nothing he could do. In a way, it was a form of extreme sensibility.

'Thanks, Josh,' said his teacher.

Nick patted Josh on the top of his arm and smiled. 'I'll see you soon.'

'OK, Nick.' He turned to leave the room, stopped and turned to look back at him. 'Have you considered a serial killer has murdered both Paul and his parents?'

'Well, until we find out how they all died, we don't even know if it was murder, as opposed to suicide,' said Nick.

'True. Good point, Sherlock,' said Josh, then pulled a cross-eyed face at him, as a joke. It was, of course, inappropriate. But that was Josh.

After he'd left, Nick turned to McGregor. 'He takes things in his stride. He's very self-contained.'

'Yes. It's quite impressive. Maybe having Asperger's helps you deal with this heavy stuff.'

'How is Josh performing academically in his first year at 6th form?'

'Oh, he's excellent. If he continues on this path, he'll get straight A grades in maths, computer science and in physics, too, I've no doubt. He should apply to Oxford or Cambridge. There's only one thing concerns me...'

'...is it his swearing?'

'Well, yes. That's not so unusual, boys are always effin' and jeffin' but I'm more concerned about a streak of vulgar sexual language that seems to have developed in recent months. Again, we wouldn't normally worry too much, and would just admonish when necessary, but in Josh's case it's quite out of character. It's become quite aggressive. It may be nothing, but we are trained to try and spot over-sexualisation, or abuse manifesting itself.'

McGregor seemed over-trained and everything was delivered via that training, making him seem a bit robotic; a spouter of auto-response, rather than just being himself and deploying natural perception.

Nick ran his hand through his hair. 'I have spoken to him about this, because I've noticed it as well. I'm sure he's not at risk of abuse, or is currently experiencing it. If he was, he'd tell me. He's smitten with a girl called Heather...'

'...Heather Leary, yes. I've noticed this. They have been reported as occasionally being a little inappropriate.'

This sort of use of language annoyed Nick. It was imprecise.

'What does that mean?'

'What?'

'The words you just used.'

McGregor looked surprised to be subjected to a forensic analysis of his language.

'Err...well...'

'What does "inappropriate" mean?' said Nick, trying to help him.

'Oh, you know.'

'No. I don't know. Tell me.'

McGregor swallowed hard. 'Some...err...touching and closeness.'

'Mutual?'

'What?'

'Oh come on, Mike! Bloody hell! This is ridiculous. We both know the way kids are, we were both kids. Just say what you mean in normal words.'

He looked at Nick, sucked in a breath and went to his desk drawer, took out a flimsy card file and opened it. 'They were reported by his physics teacher as "touching each other inappropriately" during a drone club session. It's not serious, but it was noted by the teacher.'

Nick was annoyed. 'This is ridiculous. Why aren't details provided? That could just be holding hands or it could be mutual masturbation.'

McGregor looked very embarrassed. 'Yeah, well...' he looked at the sheet of paper. 'It doesn't give any more detail. We're required to report these things.'

'You're reporting that as though it's a bad thing. It's just kids finding out about themselves. You're all so PC, so scared of missing abuse, that you've lost sight of normal life - meanwhile Paul Richardson lost his mind and you did nothing to stop him killing himself! You're all so wide of the mark. Kids being mildly sexual with each other is the most normal thing. Yes, Josh is a little over-focused on sex, but then, we all were at 16. His problem is that he can't always think how his words might affect someone. That's part of his condition. He's not been hassling her, has he?'

He looked at the file. 'No. Not that I know of. She's a quite brilliant student. Exceptional, in fact. In my view she could pass a degree course in physics, even now. She's especially obsessed with electronics, A.I. and robotics.'

'She builds drones, I think.'

'That's it. She's not a very worldly girl, hasn't had boyfriends and such.'

'She's an Aspie as well, Josh says.'

'Yes. I mean, I can see why Josh is attracted to her. She's very pretty. Very well-developed. A real stunner. But I'd hate for him to get carried away and do something inappropriate which would mean we'd have to suspend him or worse. And sometimes, his language suggests that isn't that unlikely.'

Nick looked into McGregor's brown eyes. He didn't like the words "pretty", "well-developed" and "stunner", when used by an adult about a child. It made him feel uncomfortable. Was that an appropriate comment for a teacher to make? No. He was sure it wasn't. Julie had told him often enough to trust his gut instinct on such matters.

McGregor fell into a different light, in that moment. There was something dodgy about him.

'I'll have a sit down with him soon, and I'll go over everything with him again.'

'Thanks, Nick. Considering you're not his dad, that's very good of you.'

'Josh's welfare is close to my heart. He doesn't have a lot of parental guidance and he's at a classically difficult time in life. I'm happy to be there for him and hold his hand through it all, if I can.'

There was a knock at the door and the headmaster came in again. 'Mike, I need you for this press statement.'

Nick shook hands and left the office as the two men hurried away. He stood and watched them go, then went back into the office to look at the file of photos. Names were printed on the back along with a # number. He skimmed through them. One was tagged 'Heather Leary #11'.

She was certainly striking. Copper hair and eyelashes, with alabaster white skin. She was in a field in a white t-shirt, blue jeans and jumper, with a box under her arm, presumably used for flying the drones she built. She was obviously an early developer and already had the in-and-out body of a grown woman. He took a picture of her photograph with his phone, put the photos back in the file and went back to Janey James and signed out. 'Nice to see you again after all these years, Janey,' he said. 'I wish it could have been in happier circumstances.'

'Yeah, I do too, Nick.'

He took one of his cards out and put it on her desk. 'I'm a bit worried about Josh. I look out for him when his mother is at work...well...I look out for him all the time, really. If you ever see or hear anything of concern about his behaviour, will you let me know?'

'Of course. He was a friend of Paul's, I think. It's terrible what has happened to that boy and his family.'

'It is. Just awful.'

She was quick to stand up, move out from behind her desk and give him a tight hug. A very tight hug. Too tight, really. It really caught him by surprise and it felt a little inappropriate. He'd told her he was married, after all. As he was unsure if he was reading the situation correctly, he didn't resist, but didn't reciprocate, either.

'It's been lovely seeing you again,' she said.

'Yeah, you too, Janey,' he said, still surprised by her pulling such a move on him and so quickly.

He cycled into town, deep in thought. As he went into Jeff's shop, the sound of Tesla's *Mechanical Resonance* album met his ears.

'I've not heard this for 20 years,' he said, pointing at the speakers. 'Bloody hell, look at you.'

Jeff looked up from the computer. He was wearing a stars and stripes bandana, his long hair tied back in a pony tail.

'You've got a hanky on your head.'

'Have I?' He patted at it. 'Oh, yeah, so I have. Don't take the piss, I like it. It gives me a Sons of Anarchy, biker gang look.'

'It's normally a look adopted by the balding, aging rock star.'

'The Miami Steve look, aye. But people look to me for fashion tips. I have a responsibility to my community.'

'What do you reckon to it, Nick?' said Alisha, bringing over a mug of tea for Jeff. 'I think he looks good.'

'Yeah, you suit it, big man.'

'I've got a tie-dye one as well for the full 1967 look.'

'What does Mandy reckon?'

'She's not seen it yet. She's away, isn't she?'

'Do you want tea as well, Nick?' asked Alisha.

'Yeah, thanks Alisha, that's good of you.'

He perched himself on a stool beside the counter. 'I've just been at our old 6th-form college.'

'Oh, yeah? I wonder if they've upgraded the sound system since

1979. We shagged those speakers with Van Halen's first album. And I bet they don't have a smoking room any more!'

Nick took a deep breath. 'You're probably right. But I'm sad to say, the police found Paul Richardson's body this morning.'

Jeff stopped what he was doing and bowed his head. 'Oh, the poor lad. Bloody hell, what's gone on at that house? Three deaths in the same family, that seems very weird. Have they said how he died? Did he kill himself?'

Nick shook his head and took a mug of green tea from Alisha. 'They don't know. They found him early doors on the roof of the gym! Hasn't Mandy mentioned it? I know she's in Canada, but they'll surely keep her in touch.'

'I was talking to her last night. They're waiting on the post mortems on the parents. Reports from the scene are that there were no wounds, no bruising, no struggle. Obviously that was before Paul was found.'

'Must have been an OD suicide, then. It was the same with Paul, apparently. Not a mark on him.'

'That's what I said, but there was no note found in the house,' said Jeff.

'None on him, either. But that means nothing. Well, I suppose they'll find out what's happened when they do all the tests.'

'Maybe. I'll speak to her again tonight.'

'OK, let me know what she says. Josh's form master called me in because he wanted me there when Josh was told of Paul's death. He was worried he might go radge.'

'I bet he just shrugged and accepted it.'

'That's exactly what he did. I didn't much like Michael McGregor, the form master, though.'

'Oh, aye? Why not?' said Jeff, now tapping at his computer, answering email enquiries about records.

Nick took a drink of tea. 'Lots of reasons. Mostly because he referred to a girl as "a stunner", "well-developed" and "very pretty." What do you think of that?'

'A girl? A pupil? No way. He shouldn't be saying that.' Jeff made a gesture as though to cut his own throat. 'That's my gut instinct.

Sounds like he's perving on her. How old is she? 16? No. That is 100 per cent wrong. You've got to leave that shit at the door when you're a teacher.'

'Yeah, that was my feeling. It was about Heather Leary, the lass Josh is obsessed with.' He got his phone out and showed Jeff the photo he'd taken of her photo.

'Oh, yeah, I know her, she comes in here with another girl. She's the one Josh tries to impress. She's good looking, I suppose, but I'm not even comfortable saying that as a man in his 50s about a 16-year-old, and I'm not a teacher who is talking to a total stranger.' He looked past Nick as footsteps clattered on the wooden floor. 'Ah, Guru, my man!'

Nick turned to see Guru, Jeff's employee, coming in for the 12 till 8 shift. He was dressed in a black suit, with a black t-shirt underneath. The suit was very closely tailored. With no body fat to speak of, and a tanned bald head, he looked at least 15 years younger than his 60. There was something very physically attractive about him. He had a virile and vital aspect. That being said, Guru was odd. Odd like Josh was odd. Odder, if anything, as 50 per cent of what he said was aphorisms and song quotes.

'Hello G. How are you?' said Nick.

'Existing, nothing but existing,' said Guru, in his deep, Northallerton voice, quoting Jimi Hendrix. 'I like the bandana. A touch of "Turn on Your Lovelight", Ron "Pigpen" McKernan, Grateful Dead, 1969.'

'I'll take that.' Jeff held Nick's phone to him. 'Recognise her, G?'

He took it and looked closely. 'Indeed I do. She's a freak out in a moonage daydream. A Bowie collector, has all the albums, buys mainly singles, especially picture sleeves. Also loves Metallica. Says she won't buy online because it's cheating. I like her for that. Got some grinning lady soul about her.'

Jeff grinned and jerked his thumb at Guru. 'He's so good, isn't he? Knows all the punters and what they're interested in.'

'Last time she came in, she asked me for a recommendation, which I take as a great character quality...' he took off his jacket, hung it behind the counter and cracked his knuckles '...I suggested

Cockney Rebel's *The Psychomodo* and played it for her. She loved it and bought it. That is a girl with a touch of we are stardust, we are golden about her.'

'She's called Heather Leary,' said Nick.

'Ah, well, we're all called something,' said Guru. 'Your boy Josh, he's working out the meaning of the verb to love, in relation to her. Nice boy, but very much a case of you're either on the bus, or off the bus, with him. I bought the ticket and I'm happy to ride with him, but not everyone will feel the same.'

Nick grinned. He could listen to Guru talk all day long, if only to pick out the quotes from songs, poems and books. It seemed to come so naturally to him.

'Do you remember all customers' choices and preferences?' he said.

Guru lifted what would have been an eyebrow, if he had any body hair. 'Not consciously, but like sticky buds on a sweater, these things stay with me. Heather comes in with a girl who loves Iron Maiden. Buys picture discs. Scottish. Likes cheese and onion crisps, mother works in an accountant's office. She doesn't like Darren in her English class, wants to go out with Mohammed, whom she is very enamoured with.'

'Has Heather said anything about Josh?'

'She's an A-Grade too.'

'An A-Grade?' queried Nick.

'That's G's term for Asperger's,' said Jeff.

'It was just normal chit-chat. Last time they were in together, she said she'd like to go to his house to see his record collection. But, I'm sure he does not have a record collection.'

'He doesn't. So what did he say to that?'

'Not much other than to agree it would be a good idea, but in an abstract sort of way. Which was an error, because that was her invitation to start a relationship. But the boy is younger than yesterday. His time with her will come if he keeps his eyes on the road and his hands upon the wheel. Shall I start uploading all that new stock to the website, Amazon and Discogs?'

'Upload away, G,' said Jeff, stepping out from behind the counter.

'So what's this amazing thing you've found that you texted me about last night?' said Nick.

Jeff held an index finger up. 'Yes. I forgot. You know I have lodged bids on records at virtually every auction room from Berwick to Hull and across to Carlisle, don't you?'

'Yeah, a great way to acquire a lot of Leo Sayer and Jim Reeves records.'

'Indeed, but sometimes you get some gold.' He bent down and picked up a plastic box of records and put them on the counter. 'Now, does this look familiar?'

He thrust a record into his hands. Nick looked at it. 'Oh, my God, I've not seen this since the 80s.'

'Thought you'd like it.'

'*Open Road* by Windy Daze on the Greenwich label. How much?'

'It's worth £25 but you can have it for free.'

'For free? That's really good of you.'

'Not really because, in a way, you already own it. Look inside the sleeve.' Jeff was laughing, a wide smile above his big beard.

Nick slid the record out and peered inside the card sleeve.

'NG' was written in his distinctive messy lettering.

'Good god, this is my old copy from the 80s!'

Jeff nodded sagely and stroked his beard. 'I know.'

'Jesus Christ. You know what? I sold this in Whitehaven in 1989...don't ask why...how has it ended up back here?'

'Who knows?'

'That's just totally amazing,to me.'

'Yeah, it's a spooky coincidence, alright. But then it'd be weird if spooky coincidences didn't occasionally happen, I suppose. Thousands of records have passed through the shops since I started in Harrogate 22 years ago, so the law of averages dictates eventually one you've had before will pop up.'

Jeff looked through another box and pulled out another record. 'This lot came in from the Auction House in the Boro.' He held up a copy of the Beatles' *Revolver* album.

'Is it a rare pressing or something?'

'No, it's a bog-standard 70s copy but...' he took the record out '...I know you like this sort of thing.'

The white inner sleeve was covered in writing and doodles done in a rainbow of felt tip colours. There were bands names and musicians listed neatly with arrows and brackets connecting them together.

'Aw, I love it. I genuinely think this sort of thing is a kind of folk art. I bet this was a teenage kid, writing all their favourites down as they listened to this record.'

'It is a good example of the art form. Thought you'd like it.' He grinned beatifically at him and held his arms wide.

'Fantastic. Anyway, look, I was telling you about this teacher.'

'Oh, yeah, McGregor. What were the words he used, again?'

'He described Heather Leary as a very pretty, well-developed stunner. Are they appropriate words for a teacher to use? What do you think, G?'

The hairless man looked up from the computer screen. 'That sounds a little bit too, good morning little schoolgirl, can I come home with you?, to me.'

'Yeah, good reference, I agree,' said Jeff. 'I'm amazed he said it, even if he thinks it. In the current climate, you wouldn't even risk saying that. Classic sleaze, if you ask me.'

Nick tugged at his stubble. 'Yeah, and if that slipped out, I wonder what other even worse language he uses when he's not trying to be on his guard.'

Jeff nodded and smoothed out his beard. 'What's he like as a bloke?'

'Just a regular type of man. Mid 30s. Nothing exceptional about him, in any way.'

'Not creepy?' asked Jeff.

'Not until he said that about the girl, no.'

Jeff shrugged. 'Maybe it was just a slip of the tongue.'

Nick didn't reply, but as a man fascinated by the power of words, and the reasons behind the ones we choose to use, he felt very ill at ease about McGregor. And why did he have a pile of photos of only female pupils, and all of them seemingly taken without their knowing?

89

'Remember when we used to have our photo taken at school?' said Nick.

'Oh, yeah. That was always a big event. Funny really, when you look back at it. Photos were a rare thing back then. Loads of people didn't even have a camera. Photos were exotic.'

'Do they still do those head shots?'

'I don't know. I mean, there's no demand, surely.'

He explained what he'd seen in the files.

Guru looked up from entering data into the computer.

'Photos of teenage girls are very much in the young girl, my love for you is way out of line, territory. Might even be illegal, if taken without consent on school premises.'

'You should ask Jules, she'll have a better idea,' said Jeff. 'But he can't be a serious perv, can he? You'd never get away with it in a school. Not these days. There'll be an explanation for the photos.'

Nick rubbed his forehead with his fingertips. 'Yeah, I'm probably just being paranoid. Jules will give me the right perspective.'

CHAPTER 8

'Photos of girls playing sport at school? That's absolutely bang out of order,' said Julie, later that afternoon. 'How big were they?'

'They were printed on A4 paper. Not professionally, just on an inkjet printer. They weren't sexual, in any way. It's not like they were in the swimming baths, or anything. But they'd been taken on a phone and probably unbeknownst to the girl. The reason I say that is because they were all action shots of them in motion and apparently at some distance, then zoomed in. Though the one of Heather Leary wasn't of her playing sport; she was flying one of her drones, I think.'

Julie puffed out her cheeks. 'Pfft, don't like it. It's not necessary, is it? What purpose does it serve? The school would likely have one formal photo of every pupil on its records, I think that's fine, but there's no need for anything else. And there was one of Jenny?'

'Yeah. Looking very athletic, playing basketball.'

'I don't know what to say or do about it. We can hardly go marching down there and ask if he's a pervert. I suppose it's possible that there's an innocent explanation. We can't just go throwing serious accusations like that around.'

She dug her hands into the pockets of her jade-green hoodie and went on. 'All we can do is monitor the situation as best as we can. Both Jade and Jenny struck me as confident girls that would tell someone if they thought anything inappropriate was going on.'

'Yeah, I thought that, too. Aussies are not usually backwards at coming forwards, and they were certainly very self-assured in Big Meat, that evening.'

She nodded. 'It might be different if it was a boyfriend, though. Girls all too often forgive or overlook awful male behaviour, in the belief that they're in love. But with a teacher, at a new school, I think they'd stand up for themselves.'

Nick took his hand blender out of a drawer and used it to break down the mushroom soup he'd been cooking, poured in some cream and seasoned it, then toasted homemade oatcakes under the grill with cheddar cheese on them.

'That smells lovely,' said Julie, sitting down at the kitchen table. 'This is looking dangerously like a vegetarian meal.'

'It's OK, I used the chicken stock I made for the base.'

She sat down heavily and held her face in her hands.

'It's so sad about Paul. I keep thinking about you saving his life, but then a few days later, he's dead anyway. And him being on the roof, maybe just dying there on his own, at his own hand. It's bizarre and tragic. What the hell happened to him and his parents? It all sounds strange. For there to be no mark on them means they must have been drugged, doesn't it?'

'Yeah, I guess so. Whether suicide, or against their will.'

He served the soup, ladling it into large bowls, put a dollop of plain yoghurt in the centre and added parsley as a garnish and a crack of pepper.

'If you've finished faffing around, Delia Smith, can I gerrit in me gob now, like?' she said, in a broad Teesside accent. 'Mmm, this is lovely, very comforting. It's been cold today for March. Oh, I looked up my notes on Terri Richardson's solitary visit to TW.'

'Anything significant?'

'Not really. She said she was depressed, that things weren't good at home. The three of them were always arguing these days. She took away some leaflets on the Freedom Programme. She didn't present as an extreme case. There was no specific talk of abuse. Afterwards I made a note that she probably just wanted someone to talk to and was a bit isolated.'

Later that evening they'd just put their feet up to watch the Monday night football when Nick's phone rang.

'Now then, Jeff.'

'Now then. Just had a call from Mandy.'

'Have they found out the cause of death?'

'It wasn't about that.' His tone was sombre. Something was wrong.

'Oh, OK. What's up?'

'They've just found another body. A girl from Stockton Sixth Form called Connie McQueen. No marks on her, same as Paul and his parents.'

Nick sat bolt upright. 'Good god! Bloody hell fire. She was Paul's ex-girlfriend. Where was she found?'

'A place you and me know well: Greens Beck, just off Upsall Grove. She was found at 5.00pm today. Not long dead, apparently, probably killed on her way home from school, they think.'

'Really? Christ, we spent a lot of our teenage years around there, especially summer holidays. It always felt so safe and quiet, almost rural.'

'Yeah. Shocking, isn't it? Four unexplained deaths in quick succession. Tomorrow morning they're sending police into the 6th form to question the staff and to try and get a handle on what's happened.'

As he talked, Julie's phone vibrated with a text message. She picked it off the table and began reading.

Jeff continued. 'Both Paul and Connie are in Josh's form, both had McGregor as their form master. I told Mandy about your concerns about him. They've been noted. But they don't know for a fact any of these deaths are murders yet. They all could be suicide.'

Julie pointed to her phone and pulled a shocked face.

'But there must be 25 in that form. How on earth can they keep them all safe, if it is a killer?'

'Well, it's more about knowing how to keep themselves safe, I reckon,' said Jeff.

'Four deaths, all seemingly in the same way, that can't be suicide.'

'Seems unlikely, I agree. But all four were known to each other. Maybe they had a suicide pact or something.'

'Nah, no way. No-one has a suicide pact with their ex-boyfriend's parents. It's murder. It's a serial killer.'

'Shit. That's frightening. Hopefully there'll be no more and Connie is the last, poor lass.'

'Hopefully. But realistically, I don't see why it would be,' said Nick. 'More likely this is just the start.'

'That's just terrible,' said Julie, as Nick rang off from Jeff. 'Martha from TW just texted me. A few of us have been asked by the police to go into 6th form tomorrow to talk to the kids about keeping themselves safe, policing each other and spotting abuse danger signals. Basically, they want us to encourage them to report any suspicious activity by adults to us. Which is a very good idea as a lot of kids won't talk to the police, because they're worried they might get the abuser into trouble, as mad as that sounds.'

'It's bloody worrying, Jules. That form includes Josh and Jenny, for a start.'

She looked at him, her face creased in a deep frown, biting on her bottom lip. 'Shit. It's one thing to be in danger. It's another to just have a nameless, invisible threat. What's going on? What ties the Richardsons to this Connie McQueen girl? Is it just that she went out with Paul and insulted him?'

They sat in silence. Nick massaged his temples to try and squeeze some answers out of his brain.

'One question is, was Paul killed at the same time as his mam and dad, and then moved to the roof? Or was he killed, or did he kill himself, later? There's been no reported sighting of him after I found his parents. Nothing since his mother called the college on Thursday to say he wasn't well. But there's one thing we can be sure of.'

'What's that?'

'We speculated that Paul had killed his parents and then himself, but even if he did, he simply can't have killed Connie because she was alive after his body was found, and as she seems to have died in the same way, that points to it being one man, or some men, doing it all.'

'Or woman or women. In any case, it's the act of a crazy person. The first thing is to keep the kids safe,' said Julie.

'Totally. Y'know, I'd quite like to get back into McGregor's office and look in more detail at those photos in the file. There was a name on the back of each and a number too, but I didn't have time to write them all down. I'm still unhappy about his choice of words about Heather.'

'Come on, surely he's not a paedophile or a mass murderer.'

'Isn't he? He just might be. Think about it. He's the form master of the two dead children. He will probably have known Paul's parents from PTA meetings, or whatever. He might have been abusing Paul, and that's why Paul was so messed up. Then there's the photos of girls. It looks bad for him, I think.'

'OK, but a quadruple murderer? That's a rare and special sort of evil.' She gave him a cynical look.

Nick went to his computer and entered McGregor's name into Google. He was a social studies teacher, as well as deputy Head.

'What does "social studies" mean, Jules?'

'God knows. It was always a doss course at college with an impossible-to-fail degree.'

'There's an interview with him in the *Chronicle*, a couple of years ago. He was doing a marathon to raise money for Red Nose Day. Says he was born in Corby.'

'I bet his dad was a Scottish steelworker sent down south.'

'Yup. Spot on. Ah, here we go...got a degree in chemistry from Brunel University and a post grad in biology.'

'Interesting. How does that qualify you for being a social studies teacher?'

Nick kept reading. 'It says on the Stockton Sixth Form College website that social studies "provides coordinated, systematic study drawing upon such disciplines as anthropology, archaeology, economics, geography, history, jurisprudence, philosophy, political science, psychology, religion, and sociology, as well as appropriate content from the humanities, mathematics, and natural sciences". That's a hellishly broad brief. I reckon I could teach that.'

'So you're thinking that degrees in chemistry and biology give someone knowledge of how to poison people without leaving any trace.'

'Well, it bloody does. I think it's him. He's fucking murderer. The bastard.'

She put the palms of her hands towards him. 'Come on, we can't just say things like that without evidence. You're jumping to way too many conclusions, too quickly.'

'Maybe, but I don't think so. I'm going to nail him.'

Tuesday morning dawned damp, grey and cold.

'What does a woman wear to talk to 16- and 17-year-old kids?'

said Julie, sipping at her Sencha green tea in bed at 7.13am.

'You need to have authority, so you can't be too casual, but you want to be accepted by them, so you can't be too uptight or old fashioned.'

She looked at him and laughed. 'Getting fashion tips from you is like getting cycling lessons from a fish.'

'I know I'm hardly a dandy, but I'm right, aren't I? You should wear your black jeans, black boots with a grey hoodie. You'll look a bit like a plain-clothes copper. Neutral, relaxed but dark enough to be authoritative.'

She smiled and squeezed his leg. 'Sounds good to me. Your rehabilitation from dysfunctional loony to sensitive New Man is almost complete.'

He sipped at his tea, watching as she got out of bed and pulled clothes from drawers.

'As you've got your fashion goggles on, what sort of underwear do I choose for today?'

'You need confidence to stand up in front of a load of 16 and 17 year olds. They can smell weakness or uncertainty. So wear what makes you feel most confident.'

She rested her weight on one hip and thought for a moment.

'The sex pants always make me feel outgoing and self-confident, even though no-one knows I'm wearing them, obviously.' She rolled her eyes. 'God, I'm so messed up in the head, me.'

'Nah, that's not so weird. You should hear what's inside my head sometimes.'

'Ha. I'm assuming a lot of it is X-rated.'

'It is when you've got the sex pants on.'

She held three pairs up. 'OK, next choice, do I go black, white or red?'

'Gotta be red hot, baby.'

She pulled them over her head. 'Red it is.'

'Ha ha, I dare you to go like that!'

She went to the bathroom to get a shower, and when she returned, drying herself, he said, 'Are you going straight there, or are you going from work?'

'We're meeting there.'

'OK, well, I'm going to come in with you. I'll just text McGregor and say I need to speak to him about Josh again.'

'But what can you hope to find out?'

'I don't know. I can ask him about those photos for a start. Something is going on. No way is it a random coincidence that both kids are from his form class. No way.' He tapped at his phone. *'Need to talk to you this morning about Josh, re: the latest death. 9.15am OK?'*

By the time he had showered and dressed, McGregor had texted him back. *'I can only give you 10 minutes. Busy day.'*

As soon as they got the college, Julie had to meet up with her co-workers and plan the morning's events. Nick went back to the office to sign in. Janey James was there in a black suit and white top, looking worried.

'Hello again, Janey,' he said, signing the visitors book. She looked up and broke into her wide smile, albeit briefly.

'Hello, Nick. Can't keep you away from us.'

'I've got to see Mr McGregor again. The news of Connie McQueen's death is so shocking, isn't it?'

She shook her head in disbelief. 'I don't know what's going on, Nick. To be honest, I'm scared. We've got the police here, Teesside Women are going to advise the kids on staying safe. I mean, where's it all going to end? I'm all of a tizzy about it. It makes no sense.'

'It's a strange business, especially as Paul and Connie were both in the same form class. What was Connie like?' he asked.

'Well I don't want to speak ill of the dead, bless her, but she was a proper little madam. Very pretty and pouty. The sort of flirty girl who leads boys on and thinks she's very grown up, when she's just a girl really.'

'Promiscuous, do you think?'

She nodded firmly. 'I'd have been amazed if she wasn't. Paul was out of his depth with her, though. Or at least, I thought so.'

'Did you hear why they split up?'

'No. I just noticed they weren't holding hands any more at break.'

He explained what Josh had told him.

Janey curled her top lip and shook her head a little. 'Well I have to say that is very much the sort of thing she *would* say. I know people always make out a child whose died was a lovely kid, but I'd be lying to you if I said Connie was. She could be rude and bitchy and so could her friends Emma and Emily. They were a proper little gang. I feel sorry for Paul, it sounds like he was quite fragile as it was. Sorry for Connie too, she was just kid, for all her faults.'

She reached out and picked up a sheet of paper from a plastic tray.

'You look at a list of the names in that form and you can't help but wonder who is going to be next. You just can't not wonder that. It's very stressful.'

'Can I see that?'

She passed the list to him. There were 20 names on it, 11 girls and 9 boys. The girls' names seemed to match the names he'd seen on the back of the photos.

He closed the office door behind him and lowered his voice. 'Janey, I noticed when I was in Michael's office that he had photos of the girls in his form in a folder, often playing a sport. Is that school policy to have an informal photo of each pupil?'

Her phone rang. She made a face at him and picked it up. 'Hello? No. We've nothing to say. Goodbye.' No sooner had she put it down when it rang again. 'Hello? No. We've nothing to say. Oh shut up, you're not that important.' She rang off, leaned behind her and took the phone jack out of the wall.

'Fuck me,' she said, only just under her breath but still audible. 'Sorry, Nick, it's the only way to get a minute's peace.'

She stood up, smoothed out her trousers, and looked at him with a puzzled expression.

'Sorry, I think I must have misunderstood you. Every pupil has a formal photo of them for reference...but that's it. Nothing else.'

She moved out from behind her desk. She was about seven inches shorter than him, so was looking directly at his neck.

'Tell me again what you saw, Nick.'

He explained what he'd seen in the office. 'He had a brown card file and inside were photos, printed out onto paper.' He hesitated. 'Can I be honest with you, Janey? I know I'm a bit odd...not like

98

normal people...'

She interrupted him. 'You always were an odd lad and that's why I liked you, all those years ago. You can say whatever you like to me.'

'Thank you.' He went back to the door and closed it more firmly. 'This is just between you and me, but is McGregor alright? I mean, those photos of the girls playing sport were clearly taken informally. That seems weird to me. I'm worried about him. I think he might be the killer.'

She pulled her lips together into an annoyed pout. 'Those photos aren't right. Not only that, it's against school policy. Actually, it's illegal, I think.' She stood and thought for a moment. 'I should report them to the Head.'

'It's really illegal?'

'It's an invasion of privacy, at the very least. Photography of pupils by adults is absolutely not allowed on school premises.'

'OK, but are there any bad vibes around McGregor, Janey? Any rumours of him being interested in the girls? There were always one or two when we were both at Ian Ramsey.'

She shrugged. 'It's not like back in our day when we all knew the gym teacher was shagging Nicole Dennis in the fourth year. A teacher just couldn't get away with that now, thank god. No-one turns a blind eye, the way they once did. That being said...' she paused and looked away '...he is, what I call, "a watcher".'

'Meaning...?'

'Meaning he stands and watches the girls; follows them with his eyes when there's no reason to.'

He nodded. 'I know exactly what you mean. Well, I've arranged to meet him this morning. Should I ask him why he's got those photos?'

She looked at him with the large eyes he now remembered so liking as a teenager.

'Yes. You should. These are extraordinary times. There are two children dead, Nick. I'll have to tell the Head.'

'OK. I will. Can you wait until I've seen him before telling the Head, I want to get copies of the photos, in case they mysteriously disappear.'

'No problem. Now I'd better plug the phone in. Oh, good god, look at all these police cars arriving.' She nodded out of the window.

He squeezed her small hot, hand, just as Michael McGregor passed by the office window. Spotting Nick, he leaned in through the doorway.

'Hello, Nick. I'll be right with you. Make your way to my office, if you like.'

Nick winked at Janey and strode out.

How to deal with this? He mulled it over as he walked down the corridor to McGregor's office. There seemed absolutely nothing to be gained by pussyfooting around the issue. Go in hard. Like Souey under Big Jack in '74. Yeah. Metaphorically leave some blood on your boots.

He tried the door to his office but it was locked. He stood and waited, his mind rolling around ideas. Then McGregor approached.

'Sorry. Another crazy and upsetting morning,' he said, unlocking the office and putting the lights on.

Shit, he had to come up with a reason why he was here, in relation to Josh. Or did he? No. Have it out with him. These were dangerous days.

Nick strode in behind McGregor and closed the door.

'You've heard about the death of Connie McQueen...the whole place is in an uproar...'

He turned to look at Nick. They stood face to face.

'Yeah. She was one of the girls in your pile of photos that I saw here yesterday, on your desk. Photos of girls playing sport, all clearly taken surreptitiously, one of whom is now dead.'

Now felt like the right time to get serious.

He stepped up to McGregor, so he was right in his face and stared unblinking at him.

'Care to explain to me exactly why you had those photos, before you have to explain it to the police, because I'm sure you know it's illegal to take pictures of minors on school premises?'

McGregor was immediately defensive, but also looked confused.

'What? How come you saw those?'

'They were just sat there on your desk, man,' said Nick, pointing at it.

McGregor clearly understood immediately what Nick was suggesting and began protesting. 'Well, that shows I wasn't trying to hide them then, doesn't it? I can't believe...my god...you've got some bloody nerve, you have. What the hell are you accusing me of?'

'You still haven't answered my question.'

'Look. It's not what it seems.'

'Isn't it? What is it, then?'

McGregor looked very stressed, his eyes bloodshot. His face set in a deep frown. 'Look, I came in yesterday morning and on this desk were photos of 9 of the 11 girls in my form. I don't know who took them, or where they came from. They'd clearly been printed out on an inkjet. I assumed it was part of a project being run by the sports or art department. Then we had the news of Paul's death. I put them in a file, thinking that was the safest place for them. In fact, I assumed that's why they'd been put on the desk in the first place; for me to file. I'd have got to the bottom of what they were all about yesterday, if it had been a normal day.' He ran a hand over the top of his head. 'The world has been turned upside down. I don't bloody know what's going on! There's a killer on the loose, I think. Paul and now poor Connie. Jesus man, these are kids I know...or knew...I'm distraught at their deaths.'

Nick kept staring at him. He seemed very plausible. He seemed distraught and upset. It was a good answer and he'd come up with it without pausing or stuttering. He could just be a good liar, though. He knew himself that if you believed your own lies as you said them, you could seem very sincere.

'So you don't know who took them?'

'No idea, nor why.'

'OK, let's go with that.'

'Hang on, hang on - that's the truth. There's no just going with it. It's what happened!'

'Alright, there's no need to shout.'

'Why are you here? What's this about Josh?'

Nick hadn't got a story ready, he needed to buy a bit of time to come up with something.

'Can we look at those photos again?'

'Why? I'm sure they'll just be for a photography or media project.'

'So why the girls and not the boys?'

He shrugged his shoulders, frustrated. 'I don't know. Maybe it's a feminist project. Now about Josh, please.'

'Josh won't be able to cope with a lot of questions asked by the police. He needs careful handling or he'll have a meltdown. I'd like to sit in on any interviews he has, just as a calming presence.'

'Well, we don't know how the police are going to handle this yet. Everyone is concerned about the pupils' safety first and foremost.'

'Sure. Well, as soon as he has to do any interviews, can I be informed?'

'I daresay, yes. Now, look, I can't stay any longer talking to you about this. As deputy Head I've got to organise a lot this morning.'

He sighed, opened his desk, pulled out the file, almost threw it down on the desk. 'Put them back when you're done, Mr Guymer, I've really got to go.' He marched out, slamming the door behind him, his body language weary and somewhat defeated.

Nick allowed himself a small smile. He'd got what he wanted for now.

Pulling up the chair, he took out the photos and found the one with Connie McQueen's name on the back. She stood hands on hips, possibly playing netball or volleyball. Dressed in sportswear, and Lycra leggings, she was skinny, blonde and had her hair styled in the manner of Taylor Swift. He kissed his right index finger and placed it on her head. Bless her. It was awful to think of this girl's life being snuffed out. Nick flipped it over. In the top right her name was written, in the left corner, in light pencil was written #3.

What did that mean? He looked at the back of each sheet. They all had a different number. He put them into order. Emma West #4, Emily LeBron #5, Jenny Wells #6, Mary Bright #7, Gayle Framlington #8, Kelly-Anne Forest #9, Eileen McCourt #10, and Josh's favourite, Heather Leary, #11. Nine girls. Was that all the girls in the form? Why was there no #1 or #2?

If the numbers were to do with the deaths, Connie was actually the fourth to die, not the third, if you added in Paul and his parents. If you excluded them, she was the first, not third. But she was second if the numbers related to the deaths in the class. In fact, she was anything other than #3. No, the numbers were surely irrelevant to the deaths. He was looking for connections where none existed.

He took out his phone and photographed each of the photos of the girls in order of the number on the back. He took one of the back of Connie's photo to record that she was #3. As he finished, a bell rang. What did that mean?'

Putting the file away, he walked out of the office. A teacher ran down the corridor, followed by another man, and a youngish woman. What the hell was going on?

He walked down to the office. Janey was on the phone, putting it down, just as he walked in.

'Another girl's been found dead!' she shouted at him, her eyes glazed with tears, her voice cracking with shock and emotion. 'She's just been found by the side of the cycle track.'

'Christ almighty. What?' He looked at his phone. #4 was Emma West, a long-faced girl with a spiky haircut. 'Is it Emma West, Janey?'

'Yes! Yes is bloody well is! How did you know?' She ran out and down to the Head's office. Outside, there were a lot of sirens both in the distance and closer. Police officers swarmed out of the building, heading up Bishopton Road West on foot and in cars. Nick texted Julie to tell her what had happened.

His brain was in a whirl. Josh had said it was a serial killer, and now it clearly had to be. Someone who had something against a class of kids, for some reason. The numbers on the pictures really were the order the girls were to be killed in.

He leaned against Janey's desk. Something wasn't right about this. Why have an agenda against a class of pupils, and give the form master photos of the girls that would be killed and the order they'd be murdered in? If McGregor himself had taken and numbered them, why be so careless as to leave them around the school knowing you'd be killing the girls, and then give them to him? These deaths must have involved meticulous planning to avoid detection, anyone capable of that wouldn't just leave evidence like the photos on his desk, let alone give him access to them again that very morning.

Sirens blared out down Bishopton Road West as police closed off the whole area near to the cycle path, which had once been a railway track before the Beeching cuts of 1963. Nick wandered around without anyone noticing or caring. The place was in some state of uproar. He soon found the large classroom in which Julie was standing and talking to a group of kids. He looked in the small glass window and watched her working. She was very expressive, using her arms to make big gestures, sometimes bringing her hands together, sometimes opening her arms wide. The kids sat and watched her with fixed expressions. She was certainly keeping their attention.

Then she obviously began taking questions, pointing at kids with their hands up. She'd obviously said something funny, as the whole class burst into laughter. Good old Jules. What a star. She really would make a great MP. Did that class know that the absent Emma West was dead? They can't have, the police must have just found her, meaning she'd have been killed on her way to college.

He scanned the photos on his phone and found #5, Emily LeBron. A mixed-race girl with scraped-back hair, she was pictured playing basketball, having just thrown the ball.

And there she was, front and centre of the class. Well that was a relief. No-one could kill her here and now. Christ, she was next. The third of the girls who had taunted Paul. Was the lad murdering them from beyond the grave?

He stood for a couple of minutes watching Julie working. She would've been the sort of teacher kids always like; quite strict, but really fair and occasionally extremely rude.

Another class began to queue outside of the classroom, chattering excitedly amongst themselves. As the first class filed out, Julie emerged, winked at him and stood at the front of the line of kids.

'OK you lot, in you come.'

Once they'd all got inside, he had a quick word with her.

'Everything going alright?' he said.

'Good. They seem to be taking it all in. What's going on? What was that bell?'

She clearly had not read his text. He whispered into her ear. 'Emma West's body has been found by the cycle track.'

The colour dropped from her face.

'Oh, my god. Oh, no. I can't believe it. Another one?'

'Police are everywhere. Listen, McGregor says he found the photos of the girls on his desk, thought they were part of a project and just filed them. I think I believe him. But he doesn't know who put them there, or who took the photos.'

'OK. I've got to go and do this.'

'One other thing, there's a number in pencil on the back of each photo, Connie was 3, Emma 4. Next is Emily LeBron, she's was sitting in the front row in the middle. I don't know if you should say something...'

'...I can't say anything about that. It's not my job. The police will handle it. I've really got to go...'

Nick went back to the office to see Janey. She was standing talking to the man he recognised as the Head, Ewan Davis. He was clearly under severe stress, his face a picture of worry and strain, a vein standing out on his forehead, nodding his head at Janey's words. He glanced at Nick, said 'leave it with me' and strode out and into the path of DI Vic Bowes, who had just arrived.

Nick saw Bowes first and turned away, not wanting to attract his attention.

'I've told him about the photos,' said Janey. He leaned into her ear and quietly told her about the names and numbers on the back. She was horrified and looked at him with tears in her eyes.

'This just gets worse and worse. It feels like we're all under attack. Why Paul, Connie and Emma? What have they done?'

'Something must link them together, other than being in that form class. There are two girls not photographed. Possibly they were #1 and #2.'

'Usha Underwood and Lynne Smith have been off sick for, err, for two weeks in Usha's case and a month for Lynne. She's in hospital, actually.'

A glance told him that Bowes had gone off with the Head. Time to get out. He didn't want to be interviewed about why he was there. 'Contact me if anything just feels odd about anyone or anything. Where's your house?'

'Aiskew Grove.' She wrote down her address and mobile number. 'I'm not far from Palm Grove, where you grew up.'

'Great, well, stay in touch.' He squeezed her hand, feeling like she was the most upset of all in this. A school secretary is the hub around which the whole school revolves. They know the teachers, the admin, the kids and they connect each to the other. They are the oil in the system and without them, it all grinds to a halt.

He walked out of the college and down Bishopton Road into town.

It was 11.55am as he walked into Jeff's shop. The big man was behind the counter, as ever, squinting at a record.

'Hey, big man!'

'Ah, it's crazy sexy thighs dude.'

'Fancy a drink?'

Jeff looked at his watch.

'Aye. Go on. I've been up since 3am. Argie was being a total weepy, wailing nightmare half the night. The lad has got toothache. So I loaded him on painkillers and then couldn't get back sleep. I'm thinking of drugging him up for the next year, just to shut the wee shite up.'

'You do look a bit bleary.'

'Why are you up for an early drink, then?'

Nick shook his head. 'Heavy shit going down at Stockton Sixth Form College. I've just come from there.'

'Yeah? Well, Guru will be here in a minute...and indeed less than a minute. Here's the dude himself. Hey G!'

Guru came in wearing a poncho. 'Greetings to all sentient lifeforms, as well as any single-cell forms of existence present.'

'Me and Nick are going next door to the Royal Oak. We may be some time,' said Jeff.

'Enjoy your altered states, my friends. You've got to get in to get out.'

Nick pushed open the doors to the pub, feeling like only a big shot of something strong would sort his brain out.

'Whatcha drinkin'?' said Jeff.

'Gotta be a double voddy and tonic.'

'I'll ride that horse with you...sadly, no actual horse will be involved, though I am often mistaken for one when I remove my trousers.'

Nick took their usual table by the window, and looked out at the High Street.

Jeff soon returned with the drinks. 'Here we go. A couple of Mindbenders, but no Wayne Fontana. He once poured petrol over a bailiff's car and set it alight, y'know?'

'Did he? Good old Wayne. I don't blame him. Mind I hated those singles of his in the 60s.'

'Who didn't? Tommo has got them all. He loves him. Mind, he also loves Ken Dodd's many many 7-inch waxings. Terrible taste, has Tommo. Loves all the Working Men's Club greats. Cheers.'

They clinked glasses.

'So what's going down at the 6th form, booby cat?' said Jeff.

Nick sank the drink in one, and let out sharp breath as the heat of the vodka hit his throat, then began to explain about the latest death.

'Bloody hell. Who's killing these kids and why?' said Jeff. 'It's bloody awful. We've never had anything like this on Teesside, I mean, ever. A serial killer. Good grief. This bastard needs stopping.'

Nick took out his phone and showed him the photos of the girls. Jeff took the phone off him and held it close to his eyes.

'Their name and a number is written on the back of each photo...this is the one on Connie's...'

'...hold on. I've seen this number 3 before,' said Jeff, tapping at the phone.

'What do you mean?'

'On the back of the photos. The number. I've seen it before. It's very distinctive. Very cursive. Guru will know. Hold on...'

He went next door and came back two minutes later holding a piece of paper, his face set in a heavy frown.

'You're not going to like this, man,' said Jeff, pushing his hair back behind his ears. 'I don't even know what it means...shit...oh, bloody hell...it is not good...'

'...what? What are you talking about?' Nick leaned forward, worried.

'I knew I'd seen that 3 before.' He passed him the piece of paper, on which was written in black felt tip, a telephone number with three 3's. It was very obviously the same handwriting, the number 3 given a looping tail.

'OK, so where has this come from?'

'A customer left it with Guru.'

'One of your regulars?'

Jeff nodded, flicked his hair over his shoulders and took a drink. 'Yeah. Sort of.'

'So who is it?'

Jeff paused, took another drink, put the glass down and looked into Nick's eyes.

'It's Josh, Nick. It's Josh.'

CHAPTER 9

'What? How is it Josh?' said Nick, confused but with worry building in his guts.

'Remember, I told you he's been coming in the shop with those girls and has been trying to show off about knowing Guru. He gave G his phone number in the course of one of these little performances.'

Nick was shocked and puzzled and deep inside him something stirred, something he'd kept deep down and didn't want to address.

Jeff looked at the photos on Nick's phone and held the paper alongside.

'I suppose it's possible that it's someone else's handwriting, but...I mean, I've never seen a 3 written like that with the curly bottom end. That's really distinctive. Question is, of course, did he take these photos as well as write the numbers, and what do the numbers actually mean?'

'Connie was #3 and Emma #4. They've been killed in that order. That's what it means. Jesus.'

Nick went to the bar for another round.

'C'mon, Josh isn't a serial killer,' said Jeff as he returned. 'And anyway, what happened to #1 and #2 then?'

'Paul's parents were #1, Paul #2?'

Jeff held his nose, as if the idea stank. 'Nah, I'm not 'avin' that. If you're listing who you're going to kill, you have a system and stick to it. The parents would be one and two, Paul three, Emma four, and Connie five. It doesn't make sense otherwise. Also, why kill two adults and a boy and only then start on the nine girls? There's no method in that.'

Nick tugged at his lower lip, worried, then took the phone back, looking at each photo in turn.

'What's the lass called who he's mad on, again?' said Jeff.

'Heather Leary.' He flicked through and found her picture with the drone box in her hands. 'She's #11, the last.'

Jeff looked at her. 'Ah, yeah. OK. Let's just stretch our trousers a little and think about this. We both know Josh wouldn't harm a fly, but let's ignore that, say he's a serial killer, just for the sake of it, right? The last girl you'd kill *would* be the one you fancied the most wouldn't it? And being #11 means she *would* be the last.'

Nick folded his arms across his chest, trying to find an innocent excuse for Josh, but horribly, he couldn't.

'When will Mandy get back from Canada?'

'This evening. She's cut her trip short. Can't be away when there's a serial killer on the loose.'

Nick took a drink and pushed his hair off his forehead.

'I'm now really worried Josh is involved in this. Really worried. Jeff, man, I'm only going to say this to you but he's been swearing a lot recently, and being sexually vulgar, saying he wants to stick his hard cock up this Heather girl. I'm concerned he's developed some weird attitude to girls and...oh, sod it, I just don't know...I mean, why is his handwriting on those photos? Why?!'

He'd raised his voice. Two old women each with a half of Guinness turned to look at him.

Jeff raised his eyebrows, and lowered his voice. 'Before you go over the top, can I remind you of how we used to talk about Gillian Kerr when we were 16? Remember? And not just her, but pretty much every other girl we fancied. We were as foul-mouthed, as you like. I mean, "stick my hard cock up her" - that was nothing. Totally nothing. I'd be embarrassed to repeat what we used to say about Gillian to you now. We were mad about her. We used to imagine what her vagina looked and felt like, for god's sake. I mean, I don't recall the exact details of our language but I'm telling you this, it was sodding dirty and totally sex obsessed. We thought she was the most beautiful, sexy lass we'd ever seen, so what Josh said about Heather is relatively tame and unexceptional. Us wanting to do that to Gillian was a given.'

Nick reflected for a moment. They had been incredibly graphic in what they used to say. Good grief, yeah. 'Yeah, yeah, I know. You're right. He's 16 and horny, that's all.'

'Why don't you just ask him about the photos? He's rubbish at hiding anything. He couldn't lie to save his life, it's just not in his make-up. He reminds me of Data in *Star Trek* when he's got to say something that isn't true. He has to totally overthink it and thus it looks so unnatural and is an obvious lie.'

'That's true. Whether he took those photos or not, he's clearly had access to them.'

Jeff raised his index finger to 45 degrees. 'Can I just caution you on one thing: Don't forget you don't know those pictures are anything at all to do with the deaths of the kids. It could just be a coincidence that the two girls are #3 and #4. If we get a #5 and #6 then it's a different matter, but that's not happened. Emily LeBron is alive. As far as we know, at least.'

Jeff's words calmed Nick's nerves a little. He was getting carried away with the story, getting totally ahead of himself. First thing was to talk to Josh.

'The lad will be on his lunch break in 20 minutes. I'll text him and take him for a burger.'

He tapped at his phone.

'Were the police all over the place?' asked Jeff.

'Yeah, Julie and three of her co-workers were talking to the kids about staying safe and reporting any concerns. They're all trained in that. I think the feeling was that the advice was better coming from them, than from the police.'

'Getting experts in makes sense, not least because so many coppers speak in that weird stilted police language, making it hard to take them seriously.' Jeff folded his arms across his chest and thought for a moment. 'You know when you saw Paul Richardson's parents lying on their back-room floor?'

'Yeah?'

'How where the lying, exactly?'

'Both on their backs.'

Jeff closed his eyes and shook his head, briefly. 'No, I don't mean that. I mean if you collapse, you don't do it neatly. You crumple to the ground. It's like when you see someone passed out drunk, they have legs and arms all over the place, don't they? Similarly, when someone drops dead from a standing position, they stay where they fall, and it is almost impossible to fall neatly flat on your back.'

Nick went to his mind's eye to re-see the scenario. 'They were both lying with arms by their sides, legs together. Heads just turned a little to one side. The man at a right angle to the woman.'

'If they'd died in writhing agony, they'd have very messed-up clothing and hair.'

'They definitely didn't have that. I wish I'd thought to take a photo of them.'

Jeff spread out his hands on the table.

'OK. So, however they died, there are two options to consider. One is that they took something together, lay down together, and died.'

'I wondered that, but why do it on the back-room floor? A suicide pact is carefully planned out. You'd do it on your bed or in a significant place. You'd also hold hands, I think, as you went to the other side. It'd be a holy thing. You'd find a comfortable place and expire.'

'Good thinking. In that case we're left with the possibility that they were killed, or killed and laid out for some reason, in which case, given it'd take at least two people to carry an adult from one spot to another, it means we've got a conspiracy on our hands.'

Nick nodded. 'That all makes sense. But good luck proving who it is.'

'We know Paul was messed up and very upset, to the point of being very serious about killing himself. That can't have gone unnoticed at home. In fact, it just has to be something to do with his home life. At the very least, they must have ignored his change in character. But Mandy's said the early investigations hadn't revealed any criminal history, and no suspicions about either of the parents.'

'Julie's report on Terri said there was no mention of abuse. Just that the family had been arguing a lot and she was depressed. Julie thought she just wanted a shoulder to cry on.'

His phone buzzed with a text from Josh.

'See you at the gates at 12.30pm.'

Nick knocked his drink. 'Right, I'd better go and meet the boy.'

He walked back to the college. There were still police cars everywhere, but Julie's Porsche had gone. The TW women must have finished their work.

'To what do I owe this pleasure?' said Josh, walking up to him, dressed in a red-and-white checked shirt, with a grey t-shirt underneath and faded, raggy jeans. His long-ish floppy hair was uncombed and messy.

'I was just in the area and I wanted to get something to eat. Also, I heard about yet another girl being found dead. Are you feeling OK?'

But Josh was obviously a little excited, his eyes bright. 'Yes. It's been *very* interesting this morning. Julie came into the school, I hear. Some boys were talking about her. Sadly, I didn't get a talk from her, it was an older, ugly fat woman who talked to us about making sure we were safe, and how we should go to and from school in pairs. I'm going to use it as an excuse to walk home with Heather. Yes! Get in!' He punched the air.

'They told you about Emma West?'

'Yes. I didn't like her. She was one of the girls who was horrible to Paul, along with Emily LeBron. Bit of a bitch really. No need for that. I hate bitches, even if they have nice tits.'

Nick wanted to close his ears to this talk, not wanting to have to consider Josh was...no...no...he wasn't even going to think that.

'Language, Josh! Right? C'mon, let's get something to eat. Do you want a burger, or fish and chips?'

'Burger.'

'Right, let's go to that cafe across the road in the precinct.' They crossed the road. 'So what did they tell you about what's happened?'

'The headmaster called us all together and said Emma had been found dead this morning and that the police were investigating her, Connie's and Paul's deaths. That was it. They told us to be vigilant and to not talk to strangers...all the usual shite, even though it's pretty obvious that the person doing the killing isn't a stranger to any of us.'

'Why do you say that?'

'Because it's obvious.'

'Why is it obvious?'

The boy stopped and looked at Nick, square in the face. 'Because my form class is being slaughtered one by one. It's not random, it's deliberate, and a stranger doesn't do that. A stranger kills whoever they feel like killing. There'd be no pattern. I like patterns. I like order and structure and this is an ordered and structured series of killings.'

'And what's the gossip going around school about it all?'

Josh ruffled his hair. 'No-one knows what's going on. I have resisted saying much about it for fear of saying an entirely inappropriate thing, as I am prone to do, as you know. So I shut up and nod a lot.'

'Good lad, that's a thoughtful thing to do.'

'When people die, everyone loses their shit, even though death is entirely normal. We all die. It's a fact. We all know people get ill and die, get killed, get run over or have accidents. It's as natural as breathing. But no no no it's a big deal. Oh oh oh so shocking. But it's really not. We only have two states of being: alive or dead. So what's the big deal? No-one is surprised to be alive, so why is anyone surprised at death? But I know I can't say that to anyone so it's time for Aspie to shut up and wait until it's over.' He made a zipping gesture across his lips, being in a very animated mood.

It was a hell of an outburst, one which Nick, for all his worries, found himself agreeing with. Even so, tell that to the police and they'd suspect you were a cold-hearted killer. They went into the small cafe, set beside a supermarket. Nick ordered two burgers, one without a bun, chips and two teas, as Josh took a table by the window.

The brilliant thing about cheap cafes is that you don't have to wait. They had a big hot plate with meat frying on it, they flipped the burger, scooped chips out of their hot resting place and poured the tea, hoyed it onto warm plates and that was you done. Brilliant. He put the food and tea down.

'There you go. Are you sure you don't want something else?'

'This is fine, thank you, Nick. Very kind of you to buy it for me.'

Nick found himself wishing he wasn't going to have to ask him, what he knew he was going to have to ask him.

Josh was a fast eater, faster even than Julie and she could inhale food at a tremendous speed. So he soon demolished the burger.

'Here, you can have this one, too. I'll get something when I get home,' said Nick, pushing the remaining 75 per cent of his burger to Josh.

'I shall gladly hoover that into my capacious gob. Thank you,' said Josh, delightedly finishing it in two big bites and washing it down with tea, then cleaning his hands and mouth on a napkin.

'So when are you going to ask me what you came to ask me?' said the lad, annoyingly perceptive.

Nick cleared his throat, took his phone out and flicked at the screen until he found the photos of the girls.

'I was in Mr McGregor's office earlier and I noticed he had these photos in a file. Do you recognise them?'

He turned the phone to Josh. He looked at them and immediately flushed bright pink. Nick flicked through the images.

'Is there something you need to tell me about these, Josh? They all have your handwriting on the back, don't they?'

Josh was now very uncomfortable. His head bowed, his eyes twitching a little. Then he closed them, so as not to have to look at Nick, as he spoke. 'I took those and I printed them out. They were in my locker. And then they disappeared. Someone took them. I don't know who or how. They must have had a copy of my locker key or the master key. How did they get in McGregor's office?'

Nick was glad that at least he hadn't even tried to lie.

'He says he just found them on his desk. He thought they were part of a project or something.'

'So he doesn't know I took them?'

'No. But the thing is, Josh, you've numbered each picture from #3 to #11. Connie was #3 and Emma was #4. Tell me why. Who were #2 and #1?'

Josh lifted up his head, his eyes flicking from side to side, the way they often did when he was working something out. 'Teachers. One was Miss Trimble, two was Miss Coates. My two female teachers.'

'OK. Explain your numbering system to me.'

The boy leaned forward and spoke in a quiet voice.

'It was meant to be a private thing, Nick. Not for public consumption. You know how I like to order things, to rate them. I hate things not being orderly, it really troubles me.'

'Oh, right...I get it. So Heather is #11 and the highest score is the best; the most attractive?'

Josh raised his eyes to meet Nick's and nodded and still spoke in a whisper.

'Yes. The pictures were of the females in my daily school life. Two are missing due to being off sick. All I wanted to do was be able to look at them, without being a nuisance. I like to stare and really focus on things, but in real life you can't stare because it upsets people, but you *can* stare at photos. So I took them without them knowing. Was that wrong, Nick? I was trying to be respectful and not upset anyone.'

He looked at him earnestly.

Nick let out a tense sigh and took a drink from the mug of tea.

'Put it this way. If no-one had ever known, and they were just for your "private" use, then there's not really a problem, though it is a bit odd, but then you're a bit odd. But if it gets out into the wider world, it could seem the act of a stalker.'

Josh looked at him with indignation.

'But it's not like I took them in their bedroom, though obviously I would have loved to do that.'

'OK, so when did you take them?'

'Ten to twelve days ago.'

'And then what did you do with them?'

Josh stared at him silently. Nick knew that meant he didn't really understand.

'You want to know what I did with them?'

'Yeah.'

Josh went quiet and then said, 'I looked at some of them while masturbating.'

Nick groaned and closed his eyes. 'Yeah, I had assumed that, Josh. Thank you. I meant, apart from that. You brought them into school. Why?'

'Yes. That was my mistake. I wanted to be able to look at them in break-time. So I put them in my locker. They disappeared. Someone clearly took them and gave them to McGregor. Or put them in his office, for some reason. But they left the two of the teachers behind, also for some reason.'

'I wonder why they did that?' said Nick. 'That suggests a conspiracy to present you in a certain light.'

'Kids play jokes on other kids, all the time. Not even jokes, really, more like little cruelties. Doing things that they know will upset the other kid. It's easily the worst thing about school. It happens less in 6th form, but it still happens. Maybe that's why.'

'Yeah, I had my Ten Years After *Recorded Live* album stolen from the top of my locker in 6th form, rotten twats. I loved that album. That someone would do that, really hurt me at the time. Have you any idea at all who might have taken them and put them in McGregor's office?'

Josh shook his head.

'They must have been trying to achieve something other than to just deprive you of them. If they'd wanted to do that, they'd just have binned them, or made a show of you with them.'

'Maybe McGregor himself found them and is lying to you. Either that or he really does know where they came from and is simply not telling you the truth.'

'But two girls, your #3 and #4, have been killed. If the next one is your #5 then someone is using your numbers as a running order for the deaths.'

'I would suggest it is most probable that they're trying to make it look like I'm doing the killings. I will run some probability equations to try and get some insight.'

'What are they?'

'A way to assess how probable something is to happen given all other variables.'

Nick drained the dregs of the tea, and looked at Josh out of the top of his eyes.

'You're not killing them, are you, Josh? You can tell me if you are. I'll still love you.'

Josh burst out laughing and quickly clamped his hand over his mouth, then said, 'I did wonder how long it might be before you asked me that. I think the police should be asking me that as well, sooner or later.'

'You've got alibis for when the murders happened, though?'

Still amused, he stared back at Nick. 'I spend a lot of time on my own. I prefer it that way, you know that. So who knows what I might be getting up to? My mother certainly wouldn't have a clue. But as I don't know when or where the girls were killed, I don't know if I do have an alibi. But as I didn't kill them, it shouldn't matter whether I do or not.'

'That's true. Have you any idea who might have killed Connie and Emma, and Paul for that matter? If indeed they were murdered and it's not mass suicide.'

Josh didn't respond immediately, looking out of the window for a moment. 'No, but whoever it is must be insane, but they mustn't seem insane because if they seemed insane, it'd be obvious that they were the ones who'd done it. I think whoever it is, is somehow invisible. I also think Paul killed himself, that's all he wanted to do. When you saved him, he was furious you'd denied him the ability to die.'

'That's a good point. We should have a better idea soon because the post mortem should be out later today. How well did you know Connie and Emma?'

'Not very well. They were just there in my form class for 20 minutes each morning. They hadn't come with us from Ian Ramsey. As you know, they were nasty to Paul, along with Emily LeBron, and I really hated them for that. That's why they were the lowest-ranked girls. That being said, they are nice looking and have nice bodies, but they were horrible to Paul and they paid for that.'

Nick ignored how that sounded. 'So are you upset by the deaths?'

Josh stared blankly. 'I just accept them as having happened.'

'So losing Paul doesn't make you feel sad?'

The kid shook his head and picked up the laminated menu, as though perusing it. 'Sorry. I know I'm supposed to dine from the NT menu of sorrow and grief, but my head feels none of that and I don't really know what the word "sad" might mean, in the same way you obviously do. I just get on with things, while everyone else goes mental. I know Asperger's makes me different, but I really think my default is better. They're dead, what's the point in going on and on about it, or getting emotional? It won't change anything.'

He was right, course. But humans don't run on pure logic. Life is fuelled by emotions.

'Right, you better get back to your classes, lunchtime is nearly over.'

They stood up.

'Thanks for the food, Nick. I like seeing you.'

Nick hugged him, patting the boy on his back. 'Good to see you again. And take care. I won't tell McGregor about your photos just yet. I don't want you getting in trouble over it. But if anything else happens, it might have to come out.'

They walked outside. 'I consider what I did as harmless voyeurism. No-one noticed and the shots were taken in public situations. I didn't invade anyone's privacy. And anyway, every teenage boy needs his wanking material, Nick. Surely any adult can understand that?'

Nick laughed. 'I daresay you're right, Josh. But take a tip from me, that stuff is better sourced from your imagination than from photos.'

He went home and wrote some notes about everything he knew about the deaths so far, just so he had a record of it all. Nick liked taking notes and making lists. It helped him bring some order to the chaos of life. Maybe he wasn't that different to Josh, in some ways.

Afterwards, he took two ox cheeks that he'd been marinating in red wine out of the fridge, browned them in some beef fat, fried off some shallots and garlic and placed it all into his slow cooker, along with carrots, celery, the marinade and two spoonfuls of beef stock, then added enough water to cover them and put it on to cook for four hours, so it'd be ready around the time Jules got in from work.

The *Gazette* website was reporting the deaths as 'unexplained' but there was obviously very little for them to go on, other than to relate the barest of facts known. The words 'serial killer' were, significantly, not used. It all had the feel of a Mandy Beale clamp down. She disliked and was suspicious of the press, fearing it got in the way of her work, a lot more than it ever helped. Even at a distance of several thousand miles, she had wielded her power.

He groaned out loud and shook his head. Poor kids. This was all too often a terrible world, so terrible sometimes he caught himself almost being glad that they'd lost Joni to a miscarriage. She'd be walking now and wondering what the world was all about. And what did you tell them? That it's a world of people who want to hurt you, abuse you, or kill you?

How must the poor parents of the two girls who had died be feeling now? They'd loved their kids all the way from a night of lust, love and passion, through pregnancy to birth, through childhood and school, seen them grow into people with character and personality, gone through hours of laughter and tears together...and then, BAM! It all ended in an instant and without warning. No more. Gone. Taken from them on the cusp of adulthood. All their potential stolen. Everything their parents loved, snuffed out. It had to be unbearable. How could you ever live your life after such a trauma? It had to make life feel worthless. God bless them.

He bowed his head, put his hands together and said a short prayer, though quite why he could not have explained to anyone, not even to his vicar friend, Don Preston.

His phone vibrated, making him stir from his sorrowful reverie.

It was Jeff.

'Post mortem is in. Mandy's been in touch. Paul and both parents, "cause of death inconclusive".'

Nick typed his response. *'What does that mean?'*

Jeff replied, *'It means they'll have to do more tests but they all seemed to have died the same way. Meet in the Royal Oak 9.00pm? Mandy due back.'*

'We'll be there.'

CHAPTER 10

Julie took her wallet out of her old blue jeans and extracted a £20 note. 'Whatcha havin'?' she said, as they walked into the Royal Oak at 8.45pm.

'Can I have double vod and fizzy water?'

'After that delicious dinner, you can have a triple.'

'It was nice, wasn't it?'

'I'm still stuffed. When it's so lovely, it's hard to stop eating. God knows how much beef is now lodged in my colon.'

He put his arm around her shoulders. 'Do you want me to call Dyno-rod?'

'Oh, is that what you're calling it now? she said, with an eyebrow raised, then laughed.

She ordered them each the same drink and they took a seat by the window.

'Well, today has been quite a day, one way or another,' said Nick. 'My brain is in a whirl.'

'You're telling me. It's so stressful having to stand up in front of those classes, with all their eyes on you. It's not like doing anything else. At least when you do a book talk, people have volunteered to come, so they're on your side, in a way. A class of kids is compelled to be there, so if they don't like you or don't want to listen, they just won't and you can't make them. I was sweating buckets. It was trickling down my back at one point.'

'I thought you looked like a natural teacher when I watched you through the glass. You seemed to have a rapport with the kids.'

'I just resorted to a couple of double entendres and a single swear to endear myself to them and they were well behaved, because they all knew this was serious stuff.'

'How had they taken the deaths?'

She looked out of the window at the bright street lights of the High Street as a bus pulled up at the nearby stop. 'Hard to say. Upset and scared, but at the same time, kids are all about themselves and about what's going in their life. They all move on pretty quickly. And they didn't know about Emma's death at the time, only Connie and Paul. But it's obviously a big worry for them.'

'Yeah, I knew a lad who was killed in a car crash. I remember hearing about it, and it being a big shock for about an hour, but I was going to a school disco later and it wasn't long before I was more concerned with how to cop off with Janey James, who, funnily enough, is now the secretary at Stockton Sixth Form.'

'Oh, the short, busty lass in the office?'

'Yeah, that's her.'

'Aw, she was very nice, her. Nice eyes. So she was an ex-girlfriend of yours?' She patted his leg. 'She was a good 'un.'

'She wasn't really a girlfriend. We just groped each other in the darkness of the disco for an hour or two. But we'd sat together in English for two years and had always got on well.'

She rubbed her hands together.

'Oooh, I used to love a good grope in my teens. Get your hands on the merchandise before you buy to see if it's good quality. Always seemed a good strategy to me.'

'And there was plenty to get hold of on Janey, even back then. She was very chesty. I only have two memories...'

'...I only have two mammaries!'

'Well, thank the lord for that, Jules.'

She leaned forward and pecked him on the lips. 'What two filthy memories do you have, then?'

'First, that she smelled of Charlie perfume, if you remember that? It was very distinctive and sweet and had a touch of Agent Orange about it, which made your nostrils sting. Mind, it was the 70s and the air on Teesside was often a funny yellow colour and smelled of ammonia, so you needed a powerful perfume to cut through the smog.'

She took a drink. 'That was a classic teenage perfume for girls. We all went through a phase of wanting to be a "Charlie Girl" in the same way we all wanted to throw our hat in the air like Mary Tyler Moore.'

'I never liked her. I loved her sister, Rhoda, though. She was cool and lived in an apartment with a set-down floor - like a sunken living room, remember? Seemed so modern and cool.'

'Oh, aye, but in real life it'd be an absolutely death trap. You'd come home pissed, miss your step, fall and break your neck, wouldn't you?'

'I certainly would, it's a twisted ankle waiting to happen, at the very least.'

'So Janey smelt of Charlie...' she gestured for him to continue, always enjoying his tales of girlfriends past.

'...yeah, and if I smelt it now, it'd put me right back in that moment. But secondly, I remember I had my right hand between her legs, but from behind, as we were smooching and snogging.' He mimed where his hands were. 'You know how it goes. Hands on buttocks, slide down, underneath and to the centre. Bullseye!'

Julie laughed. 'Why does this not surprise me in the slightest, Guymer? You've not changed that move in 35 years, have you?'

'No, because it's still a big hit single.'

'True. You always did have perceptive fingers.'

'Anyway, as I did this, I encountered the thickest gusset seam ever in the history of underwear. I think her underwear must've been made of asbestos, or possibly tarpaulin. I could not believe it. Previous such encounters had discovered more flexible, soft fabric through which one could discern some anatomy, but this was locked down tight, as though welded in place with a steel rod. I remember tapping on it with my right index finger and it was rigid.'

She hooted a laughed and threw her head back. 'Oh, my god. Underwear in the 70s was somewhat primitive, but even I never had tarpaulin pants. More usually they were made of 100 per cent nylon and crackled with static when you took them off. It's a wonder I never set my fru-fru on fire, especially if you slept in them on brushed nylon bed sheets. They all but turned your fanny into a Van de Graaf generator.'

Nick looked at her quizzically. 'Turned your fanny into an early 70s progressive rock band? I like the sound of that. You'd have to have sex in an obscure time signature, though.'

She pulled a face. 'Oh no, that'd be no good. You want a good hard, four-on-the-floor for shagging, not some off beat jazz 7/13 time which ends with someone hitting a gong.'

'True. Sex should never involve banging a gong,' said Nick, just as Jeff walked in.

'That's your trouble, Guymer. You've no imagination,' Jeff said, slapping him on the shoulders from behind. 'Evening, Jules.' He pointed. 'I like the t-shirt of Joni Mitchell's *Ladies of the Canyon* album. You are so hip.'

She tugged at it. 'I love it. Got it online from DJTees. I bought the one of *Blue* as well.'

Mandy followed Jeff in and looked around, as though checking the place for villains. She looked windswept and pink cheeked.

'Now then, kids. Jeffrey: bar. Stella. Two.' She held up two fingers.

Jeff backed away, bowing and scraping. 'Yes my lady, very good my lady, anything you want my lady.'

'Piss off, you daft bugger,' she said, laughing. 'And get these two whatever they want.'

She sat down heavily and yawned. 'God, it feels like I've been travelling for a week.'

'Have you literally just got back from Canada?' asked Nick.

'I flew into Edinburgh and then got the train to Darlo, where Jeff picked me up.'

'So what's Toronto like?' said Julie.

She pushed at her mop of messy, curled hair. 'Lovely place from what I saw of it. I spent most of the days in a conference centre and most of the nights in a Holiday Inn, so I didn't get much sight-seeing done. It's smart, though. Makes this place look small and a bit pokey, really.'

'It always feels like that when we come back from Los Angeles, doesn't it?' said Julie.

'Yeah it's like going from a 150-watt bulb to a 20 watt.'

Jeff put two pints of lager on the table in front of Mandy.

'Your golden medicine, madam.'

'Cheers. By god I need this.' She sank half a pint in four swallows. 'Oh god, that's good. I swear this place does the best Stella. I know that must be rubbish. Billions of gallons of the stuff are brewed in massive factories, but it always seems to taste best in here.' She ran the back of her hand over her lips. 'And I've come back into a bloody murder spree. That's all I sodding need.'

'Well actually it might not be murder,' said Nick. 'We don't know for sure it is.'

Mandy was a dismissive gesture. 'Of course it is. Five deaths in three days. Three kids from the same class and one of those kid's parents. That's a mix of murder and suicide. I've looked at the notes. Alright it's not proven. Yet. But it is.'

'Are you going to take charge of the case, then, Mand?' asked Julie.

'Vic Bowes is the DI. But I'll be hands on. We'll be throwing a shit tonne of resources at it. We've got to. I mean, five deaths. Jesus.' She shook her head, as though dazed.

Jeff put the rest of the drinks on the table and sat down with a big grin on his face. 'So here we are again.'

'How's Argie?' asked Julie.

Jeff grinned and tugged at his beard. 'He's magnificent. He's learned that if you eat loads of baked beans, your bottom makes funny noises.'

They all laughed. 'Aw, bless 'im. He's got a lifetime of bum fun ahead of him,' said Mandy, sinking the remainder of the pint with a smooth technique. She was a hell of a drinker. Sometimes she just seemed to pour it into herself without it touching the sides.

'So how come the post mortem on the Richardsons was inconclusive?' said Nick.

Mandy shrugged. 'It just means it's not obvious why they carked it. It often happens. They just need to do more work. But I'll tell you this...' she held her forefinger at 45 degrees, in just the same way Jeff so often did. They really were a proper couple these days. '...given all the circs, it has to be poisoning. All of them the same way. No trauma to any of the bodies. No struggle. Nothing. As far as anyone knows, the vics just laid down and passed away.'

'But there are differences. The two girls were by the path network, Paul on the roof, his parents at home,' said Nick.

Mandy nodded. 'Any good theories as to why?'

Nick remembered what Josh had said, that Paul killed himself.

'How were the girls found? I mean where they just lying flat on their backs, like the parents?' he asked.

She nodded.

'And was Paul the same?'

'Not exactly, he was sort of on his side. But then he was on a sloping roof.' She took out her phone and showed him a photo of the deceased boy, taken by SOCO. Nick took a photo of the photo and looked at it. 'Poor lad. He was suicidal, though. He was furious at me for stopping him.'

'Have we had many child murders in the region? You don't hear about many,' said Julie.

Mandy took a big drink of her second pint of lager. 'Statistically, killing kids aged 18 and under is very rare. You don't get many. I've only had a handful over the years. And it's always a total nutter. Goes without saying, I suppose. And I don't recall any multiple murders. And the end isn't in sight. Why would they stop now? Something has gone off in their head. That's what worries me. We need to nick the perp, or perps, and nick them quick, or we'll have a lot more bodies on our hands.'

'How did things go with Josh?' asked Jeff. 'Did he explain why he'd put numbers on the back of the photos?'

Mandy took a drink of lager. 'Tell me about these photos.'

'It might seem a bit odd, but if you know Josh, it's not that odd for him. And he's going through a very horny teenage phase, right now. I'm 100 per cent sure his story is 100 per cent true. He just wanted to study the girls in the quiet of his own room or at break-time. To be honest, I totally get where he's coming from. I wasn't much different when I was his age. And I liked his reasoning that taking covert photos was much more polite than just staring at the girls.'

In contemplation, Mandy pulled her lips together in a big pink pucker and thought about it.

'For now, I totally accept what you say, Nick. OK, maybe you think he's not our perp, but if you ask me, the perp or perps and him are interwoven, because the killer is deliberately following his numbering.'

Nick shook his head. 'But the perp isn't doing that. Connie was #3 on Josh's list, but was the fourth to be killed if you include both Paul's parents, and even if you exclude them, she was the second from the class to die, not the third.'

Mandy grinned. 'For a daft lad, you've got a good brain, but you're overlooking one possibility. The parents are being classed as one death. Parents. Paul. Connie. Three. Emma. Four.' She counted them off on her fingers.

'But why would they be counted as one?' said Julie, eyebrows knitted together as she sipped at her drink.

'Who knows? Not me. So who were #1 and #2?'

'His two female teachers, Coates and Trimble,' said Nick.

Many belched a little, and took another drink. 'Interesting.'

'The only two photos missing were of the teachers. That suggests whoever put them on McGregor's desk excluded them on purpose,' said Jeff.

'We're interviewing all the staff and looking into their backgrounds,' said Mandy.

'Fizzin' hell, maybe those two women are the killers. There could be two involved, or even more if they moved the bodies to where they were found, rather than being killed where they were discovered,' said Julie.

'You're gerrin' ahead of yourself there, lady,' said Mandy with a shake of her head.

'And that doesn't even make any sense. Why leave any sort of clue as to who was going to be killed and in what order?' said Nick. 'They brought Josh's private matter into the public domain. The only reason to do that is surely to frame him for the murders. They could quite easily have done the killings without doing that.'

'I agree and I reckon Coates and Trimble's pictures not being taken from his locker is significant somehow,' said Mandy. 'Someone is trying to throw us off the scent.'

'Mandy, I'm worried about Vic interviewing Josh, which I know he's going to have to do. He's such a thoughtless klutz, he'll get the lad upset and you really don't want to get Josh upset. He goes ballistic and often won't come out of it for hours, or days, even,' said Nick. 'Can I just be there when the interview happens, just to keep an eye on the lad?'

'I'll see. I can't say more than that. I can't be seen to be doing you special favours.'

As she spoke, Jeff was looking at his phone. 'Interesting info ahoy. This Miss Trimble, is Karen Trimble. Teaches maths. It's all on the college website. Miss Coates is new to the college in September and does sports and PE. She must take Josh for his basketball training. Came from being a PE instructor in the army. Josh was right to put them on the bottom of his list. Judging by these photos of them. Both look like they could stop a cheap clock. Coates has got fierce green eyes.'

Mandy took his phone. 'Christ, you're not wrong. Dear me, Methuselah's ugly sisters.'

'How they look doesn't dictate how good they are at their job,' said Julie, a little indignantly.

'Hear, hear,' said Mandy. 'If I wasn't a bloody super model I'd never have become Chief of Cleveland Police.' She drained the pint. 'Right, I've got to hit the hay. I'm knackered and need to be up and at it tomorrow, despite being jet-lagged. See you later, kids.'

The next morning, Nick was making Julie's breakfast of steak, eggs and buttered spinach. She came into the kitchen in jeans and loose blue cashmere sweater. 'That smells beeftastic! What am I getting?'

'A medallion of beef, fried egg and buttered spinach. Any good?'

'Of course! I can't believe you do this for me every morning.'

'Why wouldn't I?'

'Because normal people have a bowl of cereal, or a slice of toast.'

'Well, that's no good. To do great work, you need a good breakfast. It's not like it takes very long. This idea of breakfast being sugared cereal is so 20th century. We need to get over it. Our grandparents knew better.'

He wrapped the steak in foil and set it to rest, then cracked two eggs into a frying pan. When everything was ready he unwrapped the steak and put it onto a hot plate with the eggs. 'Here you go, it's not fancy, but it'll taste good.'

She had her eyes closed as she chewed. 'This is delicious meat. Where is it from?'

'An organic, grass-fed place in Lancashire called Gazegill. I ordered a box of their meats, remember?'

'Oh, yeah. God, it's totally lush.'

She ate the whole thing in double-quick time.

Oh, luv, while I think on it, can you pick me up some Bio-Oil moisturiser from the wholefood shop down the road? I used the last of it last night.'

'Aye, no worries. We can't go unmoisturised. Mind, I wish somewhere else local sold it other than that place. It's all organic jumpers and hemp seed porridge.'

'I know what you mean. But they all mean well in Gaia, even if the whole vegan thing is a bit holier-than-thou. That place is a mecca for anyone selling New Age, alternative therapies.'

'I don't understand why all that so often goes with being a vegan. Can't you be vegan and not believe in having your pet dog's chakras massaged, or think you can cure cancer by...I dunno...sticking a daffodil up your arse whilst humming?'

She laughed. 'It does seem to pull in a large community of New Agers and environmentalist activists.'

'And a lot of the LGBT community seems to revolve around there, too. Can't see the link between sexuality and the soya bean myself. I think I'm too much of a nihilist for all of that.'

'Yeah, I know what you mean. But then, I'm all for being green and not being overly materialistic. Money can't buy you love and I think the people who go to that place are fellow believers in that regard.'

'That could be one of your manifesto points, when you stand for Parliament. You can be the anti-materialistic candidate.'

'Well, it'd be nice to hear someone say something like that. This endless pursuit of acquiring ever more stuff doesn't seem to make us any happier, beyond a certain point.'

'Well, money may not be able to buy you love, but it can buy me a second-hand car.'

She put a finger in the air. 'Ah, talking of which. Sid up at the

Hardwick garage says he's got a couple of Mercs. We'll go up there after work and take a look. He'll give me a good deal on one of them, because he knows I'll get all the parts from him for servicing.'

'What variety of Merc?'

'Dunno yet. And the word you want is *model*, not *variety*.'

She finished her food, gave him a quick tight hug, nuzzled his neck, and did her usual little squeeze of his crotch while licking the inside of his ear, then left for work.

He tried not to take such little daily intimacies for granted, knowing that at least one reason she performed them was to give his spirits a little lift, whether they needed lifting or not. They added a little charge to his psychic battery, and that gave him more positive power to draw on when his mood was low. It was all part of his psychological support system along with his judicious use of Phenibut to stablise his dopamine levels. It wasn't perfect, far from it, but it got him through and getting through was as much as you could reasonably hope to do when you had the depression gene in your DNA.

As he walked down Norton High Street to the Gaia shop, hands in the pockets of his leather jacket, he reflected that at least he wasn't so upset that he was hitting himself in the bollocks, like poor Paul Richardson had. That act of self-loathing kept returning to his mind. Not much shocked him any more, but that really had. The boy must have been in a terrible state of mind to do that.

Nick stopped walking, filled with a burst of emotion, the thought of the upset boy, briefly too much to take. He sat down on a wooden bench to compose himself.

Why hadn't an adult intervened in his life? It had to have been obvious that he was coming apart at the seams. He couldn't have hidden it from everyone, or could he? He certainly couldn't hide it from Josh. Why hadn't McGregor done anything? That was negligence. The more he thought about the teacher, although he seemed genuine when confronted, so much to do with these deaths revolved around him.

Although Paul's cause of death had still to be established, suicide had to be the most likely. He was so keen to die two days beforehand, that can't have just evaporated almost overnight. And he was furious with him when he'd saved his life. Absolutely furious. It was all a heavy, sad weight to carry.

Nick closed his eyes, said a silent prayer for Paul and went on his way.

Pushing open the door to the wholefood shop, a mobile over the door tinkled. The whole place had that universal smell that all wholefood shops have - a mixture of herbs, wood and patchouli. He picked up the Bio-Oil from a shelf of toiletries. There was only one person on the till, and a queue of four waiting to be served. The elfin girl in a green t-shirt and draw-string ecru non-sexist pants was talking to a pink-faced young lad with blonde dreadlocks. Of course she was. He smiled to himself. In such circumstances, Nick was torn between being impatient to be served quickly and efficiently, and feeling like such a non-corporate, community operation like this should be celebrated. Everyone is in such a rush these days, but here they would take time to talk to you, if you wanted to talk. Run as a non-profit co-operative, it really was Hippy Central.

Deciding to exhale slowly and not worry that it would take 15 minutes to pay for this single item, he rested his weight on one hip and turned to read a large noticeboard which was cluttered with cards and posters offering a myriad of alternative therapies and services, everything from 'White Light Healing' to 'Phrenology Therapy' and 'Organic Colonic Irrigation'. Another notice offered to put you in touch with your Spirit Guide.

Although it was all very earnest, it was hard to take it all that seriously, and he grinned to himself again as he noticed there were three people selling handmade dreamcatchers. Were they all genuine about these things, or was it just a bit of fun? How much fun could colonic irrigation be, organic or not? And what do you do with dreams when you've caught them? We live in strange times. People need something to hang onto, something to believe in. It was understandable enough.

'Excuse me,' said a clipped, crisp Teesside voice, pronouncing excuse as "ex-kuooze". He turned to see a lean woman in her 30s, smooth, straight brown hair tied back, dressed in a black tracksuit top and black sporty Lycra leggings. She was holding a piece of paper.

Nick stepped to one side. 'Sorry. I'll get out of your way,' he said. 'Thank you,' she said with a quick smile, as she pinned the sheet of A4 paper to the board. It was a poster for something called Save The Earth Day and called on 'Nature Warriors to rise up and fight back'. The location of this fight back was a gathering on Saturday in Stewarts Park, Middlesbrough. It was typical of so many of the notices on the big board, which seemed to take themselves and their worldview very seriously. Fair enough, the state of the environment was a serious issue, to say the least, but sometimes a bit of humour helps make your cause more acceptable to the masses. After all, everyone and everything dies in the end. Sometimes it seemed as though humans were destined to be a very short-lived lifeform in the history of the earth. A kind of mycelium that messed things up for a bit, but was too intent on killing itself, one way or another, and would be all gone soon enough to leave the earth and indeed, Gaia, in peace.

The sporty woman had a quick word with the girl behind the counter. 'See you on Saturday, Alice,' said the girl and gave her a wave, as she left.

Yeah, if you had to wait 15 minutes to get served somewhere, this was as interesting a place as anywhere. Of the dozen people in there, you wouldn't really see most of them in any other walk of life, but they had been pulled into the Gaia shop's orbit. Here they could find like minds and make new friends. Some of them looked incredibly perky, fresh faced and almost radioactively healthy. Others were thin, rather drawn and sickly, with greyish complexions. If they were all vegan or vegetarian, it was clear, standing in that queue, that it suited some of them very well indeed, and others it was making very unwell. Still, he admired them for trying to find a route through life that was positive and didn't hurt anything, or anyone. Life needs idealists, no matter how unorthodox or unachieveable their hopes and dreams are.

Eventually, he paid the girl for the Bio-Oil and walked back home. It was a pain in the arse not having a car. You got so used to being able to go anywhere, at any time, with minimal effort. As it was, he'd have to cycle the three or so miles to their allotment to get some veg, in a stiff breeze and with the threat of rain in the air now.

Their allotment was a place to get some release from the daily pressures of life. Growing your own food was one of those win-win deals. You felt better for both the doing and the eating.

Unlocking the gates, he wandered down to their patch. This was the time of year when you had to start to turn over the soil and prepare for the spring. A lot of the plots looked pristine and were planted in early broad beans and cabbage. Nick looked at their two beds of soil. The last of the winter kale was still green, but the remnants of the brussels sprouts were battered now, so he pulled them up and tossed them onto their compost heap. They'd laid one whole bed down to green manure and planted rye to fix nitrogen in the soil. It looked lush and thick.

Nick picked enough kale for their evening meal and went into their shed to make himself some tea. They kept a camping stove and mugs in there. Easily the best thing about having an allotment was sitting and looking at your allotment with a mug of tea in hand. So that's what he did whilst drawing out a plan of what they were going to grow and where. Julie worked hard on the plots in terms of digging, but it was his choice as to what to grow, largely because he was the family chef. He didn't go in for anything exotic. A small herb bed, rows of carrots, beetroot, shallots, garlic and courgettes, along with some rocket and mixed salad leaves would give them most of the vegetables they'd need, for most of the year.

After finishing his tea, he tidied up their small but snug improvised shed, made largely from old wooden doors and bits of hardboard, swept the floor with a stiff brush, gathered the kale in a carrier bag and got on his bike. He was just tucking his jeans into his socks so as to protect them from the bike chain, when a woman ran past at speed. He immediately recognised her as the woman who had put the poster up in Gaia. Wow, she could really shift. If she was a vegan, she was one person it really suited. She could certainly run, that was for sure, as she was fairly speeding down Oxbridge Avenue and crossed over the road, heading off up Hartburn Avenue.

'How come this is only three grand, Sid?' said Nick. 'It looks mint.' He kicked at the tyres of the silver Mercedes e320 Elegance two-door. To his eyes, it looked like a big version of a sports car.

Sid pulled on a roll-up, cupped behind his hand. 'It's nine years old and has done 135,000 miles. You'll need to look after her, Jules.'

Julie ran the flat of her right hand over the silver roof. 'She's gorgeous. Sleek, lovely black leather seats, with a walnut dash. It's a total bargain. I'll read up on what knackers on them first. Tyres look like they've got about 10,000 miles on them. They'll cost a bit to replace.' She flipped the bonnet and propped it up, peering inside while pulling on a pair of blue neoprene gloves to protect her hands. Nick stood and watched in awe as she pulled on various cables and inspected bits of metal. It was all voodoo to him.

'The fuel injectors are filthy, Sid.'

'Aye, lass. I know. You can flush them easy enough. Brake pads have got some mileage in 'em. Electrics need some work.'

'You're telling me. What bloody cowboy has had a go at these?' she pointed to a spaghetti of wires.

'You know what blokes are like, Jules. They always reckon they can sort their cars out, but they can't and end up botching it.'

She started laughing. 'Whoever had this last has managed to hook up his hazards to his brake lights. Well done, son.' She began fixing the problem, laughing as she did so, as though contemptuous of the wiring she was making right.

Nick looked on, a prickle of excitement flashing up and down his spine. Her knowledge of cars was exotic and mysterious to him. Exotic and sexy, especially when wearing her outsized navy overalls with nowt underneath, as she currently was.

'The fella I bought it off was a total doyle, like,' said Sid.

'There's a surprise, eh,' said Julie, emerging from the engine compartment with a grin.

'Mercs run forever. You'll get 100,000 miles out of this yet, mebees more,' said Sid.

'You're right. There's only one problem, mister,' said Julie, hooking an arm around the old man's arm, a man she'd known for all her life.

'What's that, luv?'

'We've got no money, Sid.' She kissed the old lad on the cheek. 'You can have his old Beamer for parts and scrap.'

'Nick's old motor? That's alright, that is. Make a good £500 car for someone to run for a year.'

'Aye, but the starter motor is shagged and that's just for starters,' said Julie.

The old man took a last suck on his roll-up and cast it to the ground.

'Look, luv. How much can you pay me a month for this motor?'

'An embarrassingly low amount,' said Nick.

'Just say how much, kidda.' He ran his leathery, motor oil-stained hand through his thick white hair.

Julie wrinkled her nose and gave him a squinting, defensive look. 'A hundred quid, Sid? Sorry, we're so skint!'

'That's alright luv, a hundred? OK, pay me a hundred a month for 24 months, I'll have the old BMW and that's us squared off. By the time you've paid for it, you'll need another from us.'

'Are you sure, Sid?' said Nick.

'Aye. No problem.' He stamped on the remains of the cigarette.

'You are a fabulous man,' said Julie, hugging the small, thin bloke. She handed him the BMW's keys.

'I am, like. I've always sorted you for motors, Jules. Remember I got you your first car back in the early 80s. A Datsun Cherry in orange, wasn't it?'

She bent at the knees a little. 'Aw, I loved the orange Cherry. That rust bucket went on forever. Datsun Cleveland sponsored the Boro at the time. I was so proud of that car.'

'Just promise me you'll get all your parts through me. That's how I make my money.'

'Of course, Sid. Where would I be without you?'

He held up the keys to the Merc. 'Give us another kiss and it's yours.'

She hugged him and kissed him on the cheek.

'You're a lucky lad to be married to this one, Nick,' he said, giving

135

her the keys.

'Don't think I don't know that, Sid.'

'She was the best-looking grease monkey I ever had in this place. You know I used to get lads coming down just to see this one.' He nodded at Julie, his arm around her shoulder. 'Pretending like they wanted to buy a car, but they really just wanted to chat her up.'

'That is true,' laughed Julie. 'Well, I was dressed so sexy in oily overalls and a manky old baseball cap. I learned everything I know about cars here. And it was very progressive of you to take a 17-year-old girl on, back in the sexist days of 1981.'

'I don't know what progressive means, luv.'

'It means sort of open-minded,' said Nick.

Sid made a face. 'It's all bollocks, that. You came to me and asked if you could work for me over the summer holidays. I didn't care if you were a girl, I needed someone to do all the dirty jobs. And you know what she did, Nick? She stayed late every day, and would strip down engines and, looking at the Haynes manual, like, put them back together again. By the end of the summer she was my best mechanic.'

'Rubbish. I wasn't. Rob Draper was. But I did learn a lot. And I did it all over again the next summer. It was great. I loved it, even though I had to put up with a lot of sexist shite from some of your lads.'

'Aye, well, it's not called Hardwick for nowt, luv. A lot of them lads had a hard wick for you.'

They all laughed. This was the great thing about being part of a community. Everyone could help everyone else. Why wasn't all life lived like this, instead of being so corporate and fractured? As Nick drove the smooth, silent Mercedes away, he let out a sigh.

'I really like Sid.'

'He's a lovely old sod, isn't he?'

'Yeah. And I love this car. It's so smooth. It feels super posh. There's so much power under my right foot. We've got a great deal with this, Jules. I just hope it doesn't cost too much to run.'

'It will eat fuel but then it's not like you'll be doing 100,000 miles a year in it. I'll give her a full service. I love these cars. It feels like you're in a big sports car, but it's got seats in the back. It won't be as fast as the Porsche, but it won't be far off and it'll cruise at 100 like a hot knife through butter.'

'It seems virtually new to me.'

'Nah, it's really worn out.'

'Not as worn out as the old BMW was.'

He turned onto Norton High Street. As they approached their house, someone was knocking on their door.

'Who's that?' said Julie, as they slowed to a halt.

'Shit, it's Josh. What does he want at 7.30 in the evening?'

He pulled into a parking space and got out of the car.

'Hey Josh!' he called out to the boy who was looking very agitated, as he knocked on the door with his knuckles.

'Nick!'

'What's wrong, Josh?' Nick put his arm around the boy's shoulder.

He was visibly panting, his eyes darting from side to side, in something of a panic.

'It's...it's Emily LeBron...she's dead! And I've done something very wrong.'

Emily LeBron. #5.

CHAPTER 11

Julie unlocked the front door, put a calming hand on the small of the lad's back. 'Sssh, just settle down and come in,' she said, in a slightly cooing tone.

'You don't understand. I found her,' he said, his voice breaking into a squeak at the end of the sentence.

'Come into the kitchen and tell us all about it. I'll put the kettle on,' said Nick, trying to keep a cap on his emotions at hearing another girl had been killed.

Julie patted one of their kitchen stools. 'Now, sit down and tell me all about it, Josh.'

The boy rubbed at his hair, leaving it as a bird's nest and launched into one of his word expulsions.

'I was walking home from college and you know the cycle track is just before the bridge over the old railway track I was walking past that and there was what I thought was some clothes over by the hedge, right beside the track and I don't know why I thought it was important but I just thought oh I'll go and see what that is and I walked towards them and as I got near I could see it wasn't clothes it was Emily and she was lying on her back with her arms by her side and she had on the clothes I'd seen her wearing earlier in class and that was a blue hoodie and a pair of black trousers and I ran as soon as I saw it was her and kneeled down beside her and shouted her name and she couldn't answer because she was dead and I just knew somehow she was dead but I had to touch her to make sure and I touched on her neck and she felt weird and warm but she wasn't breathing and then I'm sorry but I went a bit mad...'

'Oh, my god, what have you done, Josh?' said Nick. 'You didn't do anything to her, did you?'

'Yes. I'm sorry. I shouldn't have but I did. I couldn't help it. Or or or or or...erm...I don't know why I did it. It felt like the right thing to do.'

Julie licked her dry lips and took the boy's hand. 'Tell me what you did, Josh.'

The boy looked frightened and was still panting, his mouth slack. Tears welled up in eyes. Nick had never seen him cry. He didn't do that sort of emotion, not normally.

'I just thought it was the right thing to do. I'm really sorry. The police will think I killed her. It looks like I did.'

'Josh, look at me,' said Nick, speaking slowly and precisely. 'What. Did. You. Do?'

'I kissed her. On the lips.'

Tears spilled down his cheeks in heavy droplets.

'Oh, Josh, why did you do that?' said Nick.

'I don't know. I was alone with a girl and that never happens to me.'

Julie's face was set in a frown. 'Josh, be honest with me, did you do anything else? Did you touch her anywhere else?'

The boy's silence made Nick's guts sink to his boots. He'd obviously done something. His blood turned to ice.

'She was dead, she couldn't know anything.'

'You've done something wrong, though, haven't you?' said Nick, shaking a little.

The boy nodded up and down.

'Tell me.'

'I touched her breasts. I squeezed them and passed my hand over them. They were big, I couldn't not do it. I've never felt any before.'

'Oh, christ, Josh,' said Nick, putting his head in his hands.

'I know. I can see how it looks to anyone looking at me.'

'Did anyone see you?' said Julie.

'Yes.'

Nick closed his eyes again. 'Who saw you?'

'I don't know their name. I turned and saw a woman dressed in black looking at me from the road. I know I've done wrong. I know.'

'After you touched her, what did you do?' said Nick.

'I ran out of the field, down The Avenue and went home and thought about it for a while but I knew I'd done something bad and came here. Please help me. Please.'

'OK, OK, settle down. You have been a bad lad. There's no way you should have done what you did. Right? Do you understand?' said Nick.

'Yes Nick. I just wanted to have a feel...'

'Shut up. I don't want to hear it. I'm going to have to tell the police about this. I'm sorry, but I will have to,' said Nick. 'Do they know she's there?'

'I don't know.'

'So you didn't report it?' said Julie.

'No.'

Nick picked up the car keys. 'I'm going to see if she's still there. You, lad, are going to stay here with Julie.'

The Merc purred all the way down to Bishopton Road West. Clearly, the body had been found and the police informed because there were police cars everywhere.

He pulled onto the pavement and walked down to where an officer was standing in front of the entrance to the track that led to the cycle path.

'I'm sorry sir, this is a crime scene; you can't enter,' said the young copper.

'I know. Is Mandy Beale here?'

'Aye, she bloody is,' came Mandy's distinctive broad Yorkshire voice, as she strode up to him. 'What brings you 'ere?'

'I've got to tell you something. Emily LeBron was found by Josh. Let me explain.'

He took her to one side and explained everything, but excluding, for now, his touching of the body. She stood hands on hips, breathing heavily through her nose and listening intently. When he'd done, she asked him, 'Did he kill her, do you reckon? Is he our killer? You've got to admit it, all these killings can be connected to him.'

Nick shook his head. 'No. He's innocent.'

'Is he? He's messed up in the head, that's what he is.'

'He has Asperger's, Mandy. That is *not* being messed up in the head. That's just being different.'

'Look, Sunshine, I'm not bloody bothered what you want to call it, the lad's not right in the 'ead...'

'...I totally and utterly reject that. You're wrong.'

140

'Am I? I've got a dead young lassie over there. He found her. Or he says he found her. He also says he was seen by a woman. Then he comes to you knowing he's been seen at the scene of a murder and he starts to spin it for you.'

Nick tried to keep control of his rising anger. 'Look, he isn't capable of being that conniving. I've known him since he was 10 and in all that time he's not once been able to lie to me, let alone concoct a story and stick to it. He doesn't have that capacity. His condition doesn't allow it, even if he wanted to.'

'Ah, but 'e's a growin' lad. He's changing. Who's to say he can't do exactly that now? Look, I know what you're sayin' to me, but I wouldn't be doin' my job right if I didn't suspect him of being a serial killer, would I? I'm going to have to pull him in and question him and I'm going to have to do it now. Is he at your house?'

Nick nodded.

'Right, I'm going to get DI Bowes and 'ave a word wi' him now.'

'Bowes? Christ. OK, can I sit in with him?'

'No, you can't. You're not his father. You've no legal right to be there. His mother will have to do.'

'Good luck getting hold of her. She'll be out drinking with some bloke. She's always out.'

She let out a sigh and looked around as SOCO arrived. 'Alright then, if she's not available, you can sit with him but you cannot, under any circumstances, say anything to him and guide his answers. You can be there as a calming presence for him and for no other reason at all. Say anything prejudicial and I'll charge you with perverting the course of justice, right?'

This wasn't the fun Mandy Beale they saw socially, this was the serious copper. And she was a ruthless, unsympathetic woman.

'Right. I'll text Julie to let her know we're on our way.' He quickly tapped a message out. 'The thing is Mandy, there's something else you should know before you speak to him. He actually kissed the dead girl on the lips, and he touched her breasts.'

She looked at him in horror. 'He did what?! Bloody hell, Nick, and you're telling me he's alright in the head!'

'He didn't mean any harm. In his brain it was OK for the moment.

In his logic, he knew she wouldn't be offended because she was dead. And he wanted to know what they felt like as he's not had a relationship with a girl and it's a source of great frustration to him. Then he realised he shouldn't have done that and came and told me and Julie.'

'You're hardly selling his innocence to me, Nick.' She turned to one of her officers. 'Suzie, get DI Bowes. I'll see you at your house, Nick. Give me his mother's phone number.'

He dialled it up on his phone and she entered it into her own device. Then drove home in the new car, his stomach doing somersaults of worry. What the hell was going on? He couldn't even think straight. Surely Josh would have an alibi. But then he spent so much of his time on his own, he probably didn't. Even so, Nick was 100 per cent certain that he wasn't capable of murdering anyone, but then...you think you know someone, but do you really?

He got back a few minutes ahead of Mandy and Bowes. Julie was sitting with Josh in the living room, drinking tea. The boy seemed to have calmed down.

'Mandy will be here in a minute. She's bringing Vic Bowes with her.' Julie made a disgusted face. 'Are you OK to talk to the police, Josh?'

'Yes. I have nothing to hide. I will be honest.' He did his big exaggerated nod.

Nick gestured for Julie to follow him into the kitchen.

He whispered in her ear. 'I'm worried they're likely to go hard on him. Mandy's under massive pressure. She's very suspicious and thinks she has to consider that he's spinning us a story because he was spotted with the body.'

She shook her head. 'Did you tell her he's not capable of that sort of deception?'

'Yeah, but she's not sympathetic. She doesn't know him like we do. And you know Bowes. The man is a lunk head.'

'Where's his mother?'

'Mandy was going to call her but y'know what she's like these days...' he made a drinking gesture. 'She'll likely be out on the drink or the worse for wear.'

Their bell rang and Nick went to let Mandy and Bowes in, along with PC Suzie Smith.

'Right, where is he?' said Bowes, striding in, all but ignoring Nick.

'In the living room.'

'Just don't let him go hard on him, Mandy. Josh gets very upset if he's bombarded with questions and feels under pressure. He can get confused and angry,' said Julie. Mandy looked at her but said nothing. She was in professional hard mode and also couldn't be seen to side with them against her DI.

Nick followed them into the room.

'Now then, Josh. I'm Mandy Beale. I'm Chief of Cleveland Police, this is Detective Inspector Bowes and PC Suzie Smith. As you know, we've come to ask you some questions about Emily LeBron and the other girls that have died. Is that OK?'

'Yes,' said Josh, and nodded.

'Good lad. We just want to find out the truth, that's all.'

'Let's all sit down,' said Nick, knowing that a room full of people towering over Josh would freak him out. Thankfully everyone did as he said.

Josh leaned forward, his hands clasped together between his knees, eyes flicking between the adults in the room.

'Josh, did you kill Emily LeBron?' said Bowes, ploughing in hard from the get-go, staring into the boy's eyes.

He shook his head. 'No, of course not.'

'Are you sure?' asked Mandy.

'Yes. Thank you.'

'Are you sure? Because I think you might have done,' said Bowes. 'Even if you don't remember doing it, that doesn't't mean you didn't.'

'If I don't remember doing it, I can't confess to it, can I?' said Josh, getting a bit smart-arse about it, but still calm. Nick looked at Bowes. Josh's reply had tweaked his temper and put colour into his cheek. Mandy was also looking at her DI, as though keeping an eye on him.

'Don't try to be clever, lad. Cheeking the police will get you into trouble.'

'Why is being clever a bad thing? And why is telling you the truth being cheeky?' said Josh, with a frown.

'You know fine well,' said Bowes, eyebrows raised.

'And now why are you asserting what I know when you can't possibly know what I do or don't know? This is poor logic, Inspector Bowes,' said Josh, still calm, taking everything literally as he so often did.

'Move on, Vic,' said Mandy, realising this was getting nowhere.

'Were you with anyone this afternoon?' asked Bowes.

'I was in 6th form and then walked home on my own. That was when I found Emily.'

'Where were you on Sunday morning?' asked Mandy.

'In my room.'

'Can anyone else confirm that?' asked Bowes.

'No. I was on my own.'

'What about your mother?' Bowes again.

'She hadn't come home from wherever she was.'

PC Smith made notes as he talked.

'What about on Monday between 4pm and 4.30pm?' said Mandy.

'I was in my room. I get in from 6th form at 3.55pm usually. And no, no-one can confirm that. Mother didn't get in till after 9pm.'

'Emma West was murdered at about 8.30am on Tuesday. Where were you at the time?' said Bowes.

'I leave the house for college at 8.30. Mother had left for work at 8.00am. So I was in the house or just leaving the house. And no, that's not an alibi either. I can see from your point of view that the probability of me being guilty is relatively high.'

Bowes turned to his boss with eyebrows raised.

'Do you spend a lot of time on your own?' asked Bowes, turning back to Josh.

'Yes, I have Asperger's. I like to be quiet and to have things calm and predictable, if possible. So yes, I do. I always have done.'

'So apart from when you're in school, you have no one to vouch for where you are when any of the murders happened?' said Bowes.

'You could look at the activity on my IP address and you would find I am using the internet from my home, which is a sort of alibi, is it not?'

'Josh, internet activity does not prove where you were,' said

Mandy.

'Well, who else could it be using the internet at my house?'

'You might have set up some software to make it look like you were online when you were not in the house at all,' said Mandy.

Josh sat back and folded his arms defensively. 'That's a very good idea.'

Bowes asked him more questions about Paul, about Paul's parents and then about the dead girls.

'So you didn't like Connie, Emma and Emily because they'd been nasty to Paul?'

Josh nodded. 'They were cruel to him.'

'How?'

'They insulted him by saying he was fat and had a small penis.'

Josh didn't seem to be feeling embarrassed to say this to Mandy and Bowes.

'That's very interesting, Josh. Now tell me about the photos you took. What did you take them for?' said Mandy

'I've told Nick all about this.'

'Well, just tell me again.'

Josh let out a big sigh. He was getting tired and feeling hassled and stressed, Nick could see it, even if Mandy and Bowes couldn't.

'I know it's weird to you NTs, right? But it's how my head is. I like to study things and order them. I wanted to really look at all the females I am involved with at school because you can't stare in real life. Doesn't that make sense to you?'

'Not really. Normal lads don't behave like that. So why did you number the photos?' said Bowes, edging to the front of his seat.

'In order of attractiveness.'

'Don't you think it's odd that your 3, 4 and 5 have died in that order?' said Bowes. 'Because I do.'

'Oh, you're really not thinking straight about this,' said Josh, now snapping at him, getting agitated.

'I beg your pardon,' said Bowes.

Nick leaned forward. 'I think Josh would appreciate a break, Mandy. He's getting stressed.'

'I've got killer on the loose. We're all stressed,' Bowes said. 'So shut it, Mr Guymer. I'll handle this any way I deem appropriate. I know you fancy yourself as a...'

'...alright Vic, alright,' said Mandy, putting a hand up to him.

'I'm fine, Nick,' said Josh, standing up. 'As the logic of this situation seems to escape you, Inspector Bowes, let me explain. My #1 and #2 were my two female teachers. If I was working through those photos, killing people, those two teachers would be dead, wouldn't they? And they're not. Those two photos were not taken from my locker. Also I didn't have photos of Paul or his parents, numbered or otherwise, so how do you explain that?!' He stuck his jaw out, defiantly. 'You've got to think harder, Bowes, or you'll never work this out.'

'I really think that's enough questions, Mandy,' said Nick, seeing what was coming.

'I'll be the judge of that,' Bowes said, turning back to the boy. 'And I'll thank you to address me as Detective Inspector Bowes, lad. Don't try and be clever with me, son. I've seen it all before.'

'Your fear of cleverness is exactly your problem. You must meet a lot of stupid people in your line of work but I am not one of them. You're not very good at this, are you?' Josh raised his voice a little in saying that.

'You're in big trouble as it is. Your mother will be back home soon and I'll be telling her about your cheeky attitude.'

'Settle down please, Josh,' said Mandy. 'We just need to get to the bottom of these killings. Now, answer my questions, please. Why did you touch Emily on the breasts and kiss her?'

'I wanted to know what it was like. She was dead and would never know. That makes sense to me and you can't say that's not true. It may be unconventional but I'm unconventional. I did not harm her.'

Bowes spoke forcefully. 'Did you kill her, Josh? You did, didn't you? You poisoned her. Paul was brilliant at chemistry, his teachers have told us that. He taught you how to do it.'

Bloody hell. The look that came over Josh's face told Nick everything. The lad was upset and panicking. He paced around the room.

'You don't know anything, Bowes, you're stupid. That's just a moronic thing to say! Stating shit you've made up is not a substitute for finding out the truth. You're only trying to make me confess to it because you're so shit that you can't prove anything! It is lazy policing. You know it and I know it!'

Bowes stood up. 'Well, just tell me then. You know you want to. Then I can stop asking you questions. Because the questions will keep on coming until you do.'

Bowes had been doing this on purpose. This was his technique - nag and agitate, in order to provoke a confession. But Josh wasn't a regular perp.

'Ok, son, I know you've done something wrong, but you can make it right by telling me everything.'

'No!' he screamed it so loud and piercingly that PC Suzie Smith visibly leapt in her seat.

Julie came into the room. 'Is everything alright?'

But Josh had totally snapped and was raging now, his face pink and contorted, flecks of spit flying out his mouth as he yelled.

'This fat shit says I'm a murderer. You fat ugly shit! Fuck off! You thick shit! You fucking fucker fuck off!!' His voice got higher and more strained with the emotion, his face contorted and wild. He was gone, he was out of it and going utterly ballistic. It could get worse yet.

'Don't speak to me like that, young man. I'm the police,' said Bowes, hands on hips. But that just made things worse.

Josh screamed again and began marching around the room in a stroppy childish way. 'Oh you're the police are you? Well I don't care. I wouldn't want your brain for a million pounds. You're fucking stupid, that's what you are.' He made lunge at Bowes as though to hit him, letting out a yell as he did so. Bowes backed off, putting his hand to his face thinking he was going to get nutted, but Nick stepped in between them and pushed Josh away.

'Settle down, Josh,' he said, firmly.

Julie strode forward and embraced the boy in a bear hug, trying to hold him still to calm him down. 'Sssh, sssh, there there...don't worry, Josh...sssh, it's all going to be alright.'

But Josh wasn't having it. He wrestled free of her and ran at

Bowes, pushing him back, making him fall onto the sofa, then running at Mandy fists flying, his fury expressed only by growls and hisses, slaver running down his chin. But Mandy, at over 6 feet 2 and with a long reach, grabbed him by the wrists in a tight grip and held him at arm's length.

'Alright, young man. Calm yourself down. Julie is going to look after you. We're leaving the room now. That's all for today. Thank you for your help.'

Nick led Mandy, Suzie and Bowes out of the room to the kitchen, and spun on his heel as they came in, jabbing a finger at them.

'That, Bowes, was exactly the opposite of how you should have conducted it! I told you, didn't I? I told you what he's like and you just ignored what I said, like I had no perception, and you got it wrong big time. You can't treat him like you can some Teesside scumbag. His Asperger's isn't an act, it's not something he's ever, ever, ever going to shake off. He won't grow out of it, you've totally, totally misunderstood what makes him who he is. Treating him like that was very, very close to actionable abuse for a boy with his condition. You tried to bully him. And I will report you if you do it again. You have to behave properly. I don't care if this is a murder investigation, you treat people right and you didn't treat him right. And by the way, I'd remind you that he's innocent until proven guilty. You can't bully your way to a conviction, you need evidence and the lad's right, you've not got any.'

Bowes ignored him. 'He was going to cough to it, boss. We only need a good go at him one more time.'

It was very awkward. Bowles was simply a mean, old-fashioned copper, but they got on well with Mandy socially. Yet Nick had always harboured the idea that there was something about his character that Mandy really didn't like, and that sometimes, the feeling was mutual. She was hard-faced. The job had made her that way, and he understood that, but even so. From the moment she'd given him a chance to beat the crap out of the rapist Sean O'Connor, a chance he'd passed up on, he'd felt he'd gone down in her estimation.

'That's just bullshit and you must know it is,' said Nick, in disbelief.

Bowes stared at him, fierce and defiant.

'I'd remind you that some twat is killing girls. I don't have time to be nice to people whether they're daft in the head or not.'

Nick groaned and rubbed his eyes. 'He's not daft in the head. You can't steam into him. He won't have it, Bowes.'

'Hey. I'm the law. He'll have it if I want him to have it.' Bowes was sweating heavily, his pink jowelly, bovine head large and heavy on his neck. Christ, he was being defensive and stupid.

Nick tried to keep calm. 'Again, that's totally wrong. He can't take it and you know as well as I do that anything you got out of him under such duress would be laughed out of court. You'll also look terrible if revealed as a bully who picked on an innocent Asperger's boy without any evidence. He isn't a murderer. He couldn't do it and keep quiet about it, for one thing. Think about it. He was the one that came and told us what he'd done to Emily's body. He couldn't keep that bottled up. He knew it was wrong.'

Mandy leaned against the bench, arms folded across her chest.

'Nick, I've got to find this killer. I think it could be him. I say "could", not "is", but you've got to see this from our position,' she said.

Bowes turned to his superior. 'If I get him to cough, boss, it saves us all a lot of trouble. Loonies kill people and he looks like a proper loony to me, the way he goes on. When he's in a temper, he could do anything. I've just seen that with my own eyes. Exactly the sort of whacko what would do this. He obviously gets taken with notions. There are always friends and family what think he ain't done it, when the fucking sod 'as done it. Let me remind you of several things.' He counted them off on the fingers of his right hand. 'One. The first girl killed was the one who insulted Paul Richardson. If, as we currently think, Paul killed himself, Josh might see it as her and her now-dead friend's fault. Two. He took all those photos and numbered them. Three. The girls have died in the order he numbered them. Four. He was seen with the body of Emily LeBron and he was, let's not beat about the bush, abusing her corpse. Five. He's no alibis.' He turned to Nick, 'And you want to tell me that I shouldn't have him as my number-one suspect? You're bloody daft. You're blinkered by your relationship with him. You might understand his Asperger's better than I do, but you're too close to see what's really going on.'

Nick shook his head, staring at the floor. 'No I'm not. You're wrong. I understand him, you don't. You're treating him like he's a crazy person. He's not. He's just differently constructed. Your lines of logic don't apply to him. I understand that you have to talk to him about Paul and the girls, though you've not a hope in hell of personally doing that now, you've fucked that up royally, but you need to be looking elsewhere for the culprit.'

Bowles sneered. 'With all due respect, I'll run this investigation the way I think best and I'm getting sodding tired of being told by you, Guymer, how to do my job.'

Nick looked at him, feeling almost beyond angry but knowing now, after his last two encounters with the copper, that this was how he worked. He tried to wind you up, to get rise out of you, or to get you to transgress so he could arrest you. He wasn't rising to the bait.

'Trying to get a confession out a boy with Asperger's by bullying him is a waste of time. You know fine well that even if he confessed to the murders, it'd be inadmissible evidence obtained under duress and I would personally testify to that. This was supposed to be an informal chat, you treated it like he was a scummer in one of your interview rooms. Stop being defensive and get real, Bowes. Mandy, you don't even know how all these people died yet, do you?'

'Don't I? Oh.'

'What? So you do?'

'We have a better idea.'

'Well, how did they die?'

'That's classified.'

'Come on, Mandy. However it happened, Josh couldn't carry those girls on his own to where they were found.'

'Maybe he has an accomplice.'

'Were they poisoned?'

'Yes.' She turned to the DI and PC. 'Come on Vic, Suzie. We need to talk to the LeBrons.' She turned back to Nick, as they left. 'I know

150

you mean well, and this is stressful for all of us, but remember, I've been doing this job for decades and if I had a pound for every friend or family member who says their mate or son hasn't done it, when they bloody 'ave, I'd be very rich. People do terrible things, Nick. I'm sorry Josh got so upset, but I'd be lying if I said this was over for him yet. I simply can't rule him out just because you tell me he's innocent. Like I say, people do monstrous things all the time.'

'You think I don't know that? Remember who you're talking to, Mandy. I've got very good cause to know that. Jules and I have both been shot and she was nearly gang-raped, remember?'

She paused and looked to one side of him, before turning back. 'Yeah, sorry, of course.'

They left. Nick went to the fridge and took out a bottle of tonic, poured it into a glass, threw in some ice and a big slosh of vodka. He drank half of it, stood, closed his eyes and took a deep breath. This was heavy shit. Not least because, for all his solid defence of Josh, there was a small poppy seed of doubt in the vast ocean of his belief in the lad. Bowes was a crude, lumbering copper, but he'd been on the job for 45 years. He wasn't totally stupid. Nor was he corrupt. He had no interest in nicking the wrong person. So, even if he was an arsehole, his sure belief in Josh's guilt couldn't just be dismissed out of hand.

Julie was sitting with Josh, the TV on a sports channel showing basketball, when he walked back in.

'They've gone. Are you alright, kidda?' said Nick with half a smile.

'Yes, thank you. My mother will be here soon to take me home. I'm sorry, Nick. I went...' he made his lips vibrate and wafted his hand at his head.

'I'd told them not to...well...it's done now.'

'You believe me, don't you?' said Josh.

'We both believe you, don't we, Jules?'

'Yeah, we do.'

'How can you prove you didn't do something? There is no proof of things you haven't done,' Josh said, applying his rigid logic, as usual.

Nick sat down next to him and put his right arm around Josh's shoulders. 'Don't worry about this. The police are panicking because of how many people have been killed. They'll have other suspects too and eventually they'll get hard evidence against someone.'

Josh nodded. 'I just want to go home to my room and not come out until it's all over. When I'm in my room with Stanley, I understand everything, it's safe and life isn't such hard work. I just stay there, walk Stan twice a day, and that's it. It's nice. Being out in the world is exhausting and I'm shit at it.'

Nick swallowed down his own emotions. 'Yeah, I totally understand that. I feel like that sometimes, too. Maybe that's what you should do. Take a few days off school to get over this upset. You can stay in touch with the other kids by your phone or laptop, if you want.'

'I might do that.'

'Before your mam gets here, Josh, is there anyone at the school who you think could be responsible for these deaths? Any teacher, or kid, or worker at the school who has been behaving oddly?' said Julie, taking his hand. 'Someone who might have taken those photos out of your locker, for example?'

'It could have been literally anyone, but they had to have had a key. I've still got my key, so it must've been unlocked by the master key taken from the office.'

'That's interesting. What's your gut instinct as to who it is?' said Nick.

'I don't have those. I don't know what they are.' Josh looked at him with his big, eyelash framed eyes, with a vacant sort of expression.

'Aw, bless you,' said Nick and hugged the lad tight to him, and kissed the top of his head. 'You're a good boy. You really are.'

'I hope so, Nick. I want to be. Sometimes, it feels like I'm an alien who looks like a human, but very much is not. You NTs have so many things in your life, like gut instinct, that I just don't understand. It's like if a German asked you to describe a feltzsengeinheimer.'

'What's that?' asked Julie.

'A word I just made up.'

They both laughed and that made Josh laugh, which was nice to see.

'C'mon kids, group hug,' said Julie as they stood up.

The three of them wrapped their arms around each other, and, in the manner of a football team, began bouncing up and down for a full minute, laughing as they did so.

'That was brilliant!!' yelled Josh, as they separated. 'God, I wish you were my parents.'

CHAPTER 12

'I could've cried my eyes out, when he said that,' said Nick, as they got into their pyjamas, later that evening.

'Me, too. I feel so protective towards him.'

'I'm going to say it. I wish we *were* his parents. His mother is AWOL. When she picked him up, she was obviously tired and a bit pissed. She's had enough of him, or is unable to deal with him. I don't want to be overly judgemental, who knows what stresses and strains she's gone through with him, but I wish we could look after him...I worry so much about him. His mother is clearly sick of having to deal with him.'

'When I was calming him down, after you'd left the room, it felt like he was a baby who needed to be comforted. But once he'd come back to himself, he was like a 35-year-old university professor. Intelligent and sophisticated. It's like he lives several lives simultaneously.'

'Jules, he can't have killed those girls, can he? Don't default to what you want to be the truth, but to the reality.'

She pulled the quilt up to her shoulders. 'No. I *can* see why Mandy might think he has, but when you know him...'

'...I know. It's impossible to imagine. I really gave it to Bowes and her hard, you know. I really had a pop and said I'd report them if she or Bowes treated Josh like that again.'

Julie snorted. 'Who would you report it to, like?'

'Obviously, I hadn't any idea, it just sounded right. I think there'll be a rift between us and her now, you know.'

'Well, give it time. These things often heal over. Everyone is stressed out.'

'Yeah, but she's still not forgiven me for not beating Sean O'Connor up when she invited me to.'

'Mandy's hard as nails, but you know she means well. She's just trying to do her job efficiently, but she allowed Bowes to go over the top on Josh and wasn't sympathetic enough to his state of mind.

It's not in her interests to do that, really.'

'I'd told them not to do that and Bowes just ignored me like I knew nothing. That was what really made me mad.'

He turned out the light and lay on his back, looking into the darkness.

'The person responsible for these deaths has to have something to do with the 6th form.'

'Yeah, it's clearly not random murder. Why don't you give the lass from the office a call...'

'...Janey James?'

'Yeah, she's the secretary, so the whole place revolves around that office. She's the biggest cog in the admin wheel and she'll know of any conflicts, anyone who is behaving oddly, or maybe a teacher who left recently and has some sort of grudge against the place.'

'Yeah, good idea, I'll call her tomorrow, she gave me her number. She lives on Aiskew Grove, near to where I grew up.'

'I'm sure the police will have interviewed her as well, of course.'

'What's so scary is that the killer or killers are walking around, probably doing a job, and no-one thinks they're insane, but they must be to have killed these girls and maybe Paul and his parents, too. I want crazy people to look like Charles Manson.'

'Yeah, crazy people often look entirely normal. The sooner they're caught, the sooner the pressure will be off Josh.'

The following morning, he made the call.

'Hello, Janey, it's Nick Guymer.'

'Eee, hello, Nick. To what do I owe this call?'

'It's a bit awkward. Can I meet up with you on your lunch break?'

'Err, well, I've got the day off, as it happens and Friday as well. I'm taking a long weekend break. Going to the Lakes to do some walking with a friend.'

'Oh, that's nice. Me and Jules love walking. We don't get to do it enough.'

'But we're not going until after lunch. So why don't you come over now, if you like?'

'That's great. I'll be right with you.'

It was nice to get into the new car, not least because it had been valeted and was spotlessly clean, and not loaded with rubbish. He'd soon change that. He drove down Bishopton Road West, past where Josh had found Emily near the cycle path, which was now taped off. It looked as though the forensic team had set up a tent over where the girl had been. It was protected by several officers. Turning down Fairfield Road, he took a right up Upsall Grove, which ran across the top of Palm Grove, where he'd grown up. This was tidy, respectable, suburban Stockton. All modest, neat houses, with modest neat gardens, built in the late 50s to mid 60s. Acres and acres of housing stretching out to the west of Teesside. It was the sort of place he couldn't wait to move away from, aged 18. It had all seemed so stifling and dull that leaving it behind felt as much a duty as anything else. But now he felt differently and could see it had a welcome, calm, quietness to it.

Aiskew ran off Upsall on the right. He drove past the turning, and slowed down as he passed the snaking strip of green nature which threaded its way across the west of Stockton, ending up in Hartburn. This was Greens Beck, where Connie McQueen had been found and was where Nick and Jeff and others had spent a lot of summer holidays in the 70s. It was just a bit of park land, scrub and hedgerow, either side of the stream of water. Nothing dramatic, but it had been protected from being built on, and as such, was a nice little bit of nature in the suburban landscape.

Nick took a left up Auckland Way and parked the Merc on the side of the road, walking back around to Greens Beck and the small wooden stile that marked the path through the strip of woodland. Walking briskly, he took the path and had a look around. You only had to get a few yards down it to feel like you were in the countryside. It was remarkable really and had been why, as kids, it felt like you were on a bit of an adventure when messing around in the beck. It also allowed you to traverse the west of Stockton without walking along a road, except for a brief few yards.

He could see where the body had been found on Monday, because the police yellow-and-black tape formed a barrier around the area, though there was no police presence. It was only 50 yards from

Aiskew Grove, and to the right were the backs of the Auckland Way houses. But there was no way anyone could see someone putting a body here. If you parked right by the entrance, once you were onto the path you were invisible to anyone else, apart from other walkers, of course. It offered great protection for a murder, or to place someone who had been murdered.

Back in the car, he took out his phone, loaded Google Maps and zoomed out of the Greens Beck area. Something leaped out at him, right away. All three girls had been found beside this off-road track and cycle path that wove through Stockton. This one in Greens Beck was where Connie had been. Emma West had been beside a track that led up to the college, and Emily LeBron beside the old railway line, running north out of Stockton.

He placed a red flag where each had been found. That made it clear. They were all in places which connected up via off-road paths, largely not overlooked by houses. Around town, you could be picked up on CCTV cameras, but on these tracks there weren't any and while the tracks were well used, they were never very busy and there was plenty of opportunity to kill someone without anyone seeing you, especially if you had someone to keep lookout for passing dog walkers or cyclists.

The locations had to be significant. Putting the phone away, he drove to Janey's house and pulled up outside. It was a bungalow, one of many in the area. For some reason, that was surprising. Bungalows were for retired people in their late 60s, not 52-year old single women.

'Hello, Nick,' she said, answering the door to his knock. She gave him a big, pink-cheeked beam and he followed her inside, noting that, dressed in a loose blue linen sweater and trousers, she looked much more at ease than she had at the school. Her hair was also loose, rather than tied up. She had an attractive, generous vibe to her, and unusually, he automatically felt relaxed in her company. Normally going into someone's house was a source of massive inhibition and awkwardness for him, but not this time.

'Shall I put the kettle on?' she said.

'Well, it's too early for a vodka, I suppose,' said Nick.

157

She flicked a strand of brown hair off her pink cheek. 'Ha ha, yes, well...there are times when...' she laughed again. 'Do you like a drink, then?'

'I do. Too much.'

She gave him a small smile and then turned her mouth down. 'Me, too. It's in our blood, I think, as Northeasterners. I drink every day. Can't wait to get in from work and have a G & T, especially with all the stress at the moment. It's really upsetting.'

That was something of an early, quick confession.

'If you have anything like a social life, not drinking can be very difficult. Me and Jules drink a lot as well...well, not every day, but not far off.'

'I worry about it. But I like it, y'know? I don't get really drunk, but...I don't know...it's an issue for me.' She took two mugs out of a cupboard.

'I actually had a longish period of being teetotal a few years ago.'

'Well done, you.' She filled a kettle. 'Tea or coffee?'

'Tea please. Green if you've got it.'

'I do. I like green, too.' Another nice smile. 'So why did you stop drinking?'

'Well, I suffered, and still do, from depressive episodes and drink seemed to provoke them. Sometimes, anyway.'

'Aw, poor you. Depression is an absolute curse.' She busied herself with cups. 'I'm glad you felt you could tell me, though. Men bottle it up more than women, I think.' She seemed an instinctively sympathetic person.

'Well, my therapist...'

'...you're in therapy? Snap. Ha ha.'

She folded her arms across what his mother would have called 'an ample bosom' as the kettle boiled.

'Do you find it helps?' asked Nick.

'Yeah. I've been going for a few years now. When you live on your own, things can go round and round in your head. Therapy allows me to get them out.'

Nick looked out the kitchen window to a small well-kept back garden, with clumps of daffodils in two corners in front of a fence.

'I can totally see that. I don't really like Marc, my therapist. He sort of annoys me. But I find talking to him useful. When you pay someone to listen to you, you can say anything you want to them without it having any implications in the rest of your life; whereas, if you spill your guts to a friend or partner, once it's said, it can't be unsaid and you've both got to live with it forever.'

She nodded sympathetically. 'That's just how I feel. I suffered with depression myself, after my marriage broke up, that's when I started going.'

'I'm sorry to hear that. How long were you together?'

'Twenty years, if you can believe that.'

'Was it a case of, the kids leave home and there's no point in staying together, so...'

'...very much so. A classic situation.'

'Did you see it coming?'

She raised her brown eyebrows, as though still surprised. 'Oh, no. He came in from work one Friday, said he was miserable and I was the cause of the misery and he was leaving. The kids were at university. The next day he was gone. Within a week his lawyer had started divorce proceedings. And I don't mind telling you, Nick, I fell apart for a while.'

'I think that's to be expected, Janey. Literally overnight, your life was turned upside down. That's a hell of a kick in the teeth.'

'Totally. I was in my early 40s and the life I thought I was going to have, was ripped apart.'

'Life can be tough. God knows, I know that.'

She smiled. 'Yeah. It's not all sweetness and light, sadly, as the last few days have all too well proven.'

The kettle clicked off and she poured water into two mugs and then added a green tea bag, which Nick was glad to see, as it was the correct way to do it so that the hot water didn't scald the tea.

'The daft thing is, after a few months, I could see that he was right.'

'Your husband? Why do you say that?'

'Well, he *was* miserable. We'd stopped having fun. We'd stopped laughing. We'd stopped doing stuff together. I'll be honest with you,

Nick, we'd stopped, y'know, everything.' She made a hand gesture from her head to the floor, as if to indicate they had stopped even touching each other. 'We lied to ourselves for a long time about it. The kids filled in the hole, but when they left...there was just nothing. He was right. We'd run our course and now, I'm glad we did go our separate ways.'

She passed him the mug.

'Thanks. That's very sad though, Janey. That you should spend so many years with someone, have two kids with him, and then for it to all fall apart.'

She gestured for them to move into the front room. Nick sat on one end of the dark yellow velvet sofa, she on the other.

'It is and it isn't. I spent months feeling terrible about myself, but now, I see that it was the right thing for both of us. We never fell out, not really. We still see each other to talk about the kids and everything is fine. I know I've had much more fun and been happier than if we'd stayed together. It had just run its course.'

Nick folded his arms across his chest and nodded. 'Yeah, sometimes the bad stuff ends up being good stuff. Me and Jules went through...well...we split up...mostly due to me. I was an undiagnosed depressive. Jules got sick of me and my cold behaviour and left. Rightly so. But slowly, slowly we got back together. Took it careful for a long while. I understood myself more, I could see things from her point of view more, she understood depression more, and since then we've loved our life together and we've never been happier.'

She smiled. 'Aw, that's lovely and romantic. I'm happy for you.'

'So, you live here on your own? There's no Mr Janey James in your life?'

'Nope. I'm young, free and single. Well, not young, obviously, ha ha. When you've had one long relationship, I've found it makes the thought of getting involved with someone again rather...' she let out a sigh '...oh, I don't know...intimidating, I suppose is the word. You end up fearing the break-up before you've even started going out, if that makes any sense.'

He nodded with a smile. 'That makes total sense. I was thinking earlier that that was exactly why I never asked you out all those years ago, even though we had always got on well and we enjoyed our disco grope...'

She yelped out a high-pitched titter. '...disco grope, indeed. Ha ha. How romantic. Sorry. I interrupted you.'

'No, all I was saying is that back then, when I really fancied a girl, I was always thinking about the pain of the break-up, before I even started going out with them, and that was why I was inhibited in asking girls out. I avoided future upset, by not even getting involved.'

'Eee, Nick, that's bloody mad, that is, lad.' She shook her head, pitifully.

'I know. It was born out of insecurity, due to my home life falling apart with mam going bonkers and dad being emotionally closed down. Thankfully, I got over that when I became a student at Newcastle Poly. Everything changed, almost overnight.'

'Oh yeah? Why was that?'

'Primarily because, for some reason, I had quite a few women absolutely throwing themselves at me from day one, largely just for guilt-free sex. It was brilliant and it boosted my confidence, taught me to enjoy the moment and not think about the future so much.'

She laughed again. 'Well, I would certainly have been one of those girls, if I'd gone to college with you. I was quite the party girl before I got married.' She raised her eyebrows and gave him a knowing, somewhat saucy look.

'And for what it's worth, Janey, I certainly would not have resisted if you had done. Not for a moment.'

'Well, now, isn't that a funny thought? The things we might have got up to, eh.'

There was a pause as both of them briefly thought about what that meant. Nick stared at her black Crocs. She was wearing pale blue socks and had narrow ankles.

'You know, it's funny,' she said, raising the mug to her pink lips.
'What is?'

'Meeting you after so long. It still feels like I know you, but I obviously don't, or not as an adult. OK, we sat together in English

161

class for two years but that was a long time ago. But even so, I feel like we're old friends and I could tell you anything. I don't think I've ever felt like that before. It's very odd.'

He reflected for a moment. 'We used to make each other laugh a lot in English, do you remember? You used to draw rude cartoons of Hutch, the teacher.'

She laughed, leaning forward and really bellowing. 'Oh, God, I forgot all about that. Do you remember the "Hutch sucks cocks" one, that we got the knack for?'

'Remember it? It got pinned on the noticeboard and we got hauled over the coals by the deputy Head, once she saw it.'

She laughed loudly again, rubbing her eye. 'Oh, dear. And you totally took the piss and apologised to her for it not being especially anatomically accurate or something.'

'No, what I actually said was, in my typically smart-arse way, that it was clearly not a naturalistic depiction and was obviously a cartoon and you could tell this by the gargantuan size of the penis. As such, it was intended as a satire on the permissive society with Hutch being the authoritarian figure corrupted by contemporary culture...or something like that, anyway. I've always been good at making up bullshit theories on the spot.'

'Oh, my god, you were a smart arse, weren't you? But I'd drawn it, so you took the blame for me. Cartoon, indeed! Ha. Well I'd never seen a real-life penis so I had little to go on except biology textbook drawings and graffiti on bus stops!'

She smiled, laughed a little more and sniffed. 'Oh, dear. Happy days. We had a lot of silly things like that happen to us. What year was that?'

'Fourth year, I think. When you think about it, I suppose we spent a lot of time together over two years.'

'It seemed to go on forever. And our disco grope, as you so romantically call it, was the Christmas disco.'

'Yeah, I finally plucked up the courage to ask you to dance, after a mere 18 months of sitting next to you.' He laughed. 'Not my finest moment. And even after that I wasn't sure if I should or could ask you out.'

'Oh, well, maybe I should've given you the come on more obviously, but I was young and quite innocent, "Hutch sucks cocks" cartoons aside, not that I really knew what "sucks cocks" even meant. I think I thought it was slutty for a girl to ask out a boy. That was what we were brought up to think back then.'

'There were some strange notions about life in the 1970s.'

She put her mug down clapped her hands together. 'Oh, I remember now! You were obsessed with that girl, the blonde girl, what was she called...err...Shawn...Shawn Yeadon. You were mad about her.'

'Well recalled. I was mad about Shawn.'

'Yes, I remember being jealous of her. She seemed quite a worldly-wise girl and was pretty, which was the absolute opposite of me. Did you ever end up going out with her?'

'Not really. I did the same thing with her as I did with you. I won't go on about it. Anyway, you had a series of highly unsuitable boyfriends, didn't you?'

'I had three, I think. And unsuitable is the word. Yes. As I recall they were a little too frisky for my liking. Hands all over me. I wasn't prepared for that until a bit later. It's funny how naïve we were compared to kids today. They're so sexualised, so early.'

'So how come you didn't object to our disco grope?'

She gave him a mock, withering look. 'Because you were a nice shy boy, and the idea of you touching me wasn't threatening at all. Those three boyfriends were just thoughtless idiots, you were different.'

He knew this was the moment. He had to ask.

'Janey, I'm going to ask you something about that night, that I've long wondered about. It's a bit rude though, is that OK?.'

Her eyes widened. 'Oooh, I like a bit of rude. I don't get much these days. Go on.'

'Well, I'm sure you don't remember this as clearly as I do...'

'...you might be surprised about that.'

'I...err...' he laughed, a little awkwardly '...I had my hands on your bum, slid my right hand between your legs...' he felt his cheeks heat up. 'Bloody hell, this is way more embarrassing than I thought it

163

might be...' he rubbed at his temples.

'Ha ha, you've blushed.'

'Well, so have you.'

'That's because I remember it so well and I was the one getting felt up!'

'Oh, I'm not sure I can say this now...it's too...'

'Go on...I think I know what you're going to say, anyway.'

'Well it was just that it was like your gusset was so hard and unyielding. It felt like it was welded with a steel bolt. It felt like a chastity belt.' He couldn't help but laugh loudly. 'And ever since I wondered what you were wearing. You don't have to tell me. I just had to ask. Sorry.'

She put her head in her hands and sobbed with laughter.

'I'm sorry, Janey. I'm a bit sick in the head, really. What a thing to remember. I'll get going. Sorry, I didn't mean to embarrass you.'

'No, you bloody won't. Sit down.' Her eyes were streaming with tears of laughter. She pulled a tissue from up her sleeve and wiped her eyes and sniffed her runny nose.

'Oh, my god. That's so funny.' She sniffed again. 'I can explain! Well...err...I was wearing my mother's 1960s panty corselette which was partly made out of rubber, if you can believe that. It was a vicious garment and it hurt quite a lot, actually, but it did hold all your fat in, and I was a chubby girl, wasn't I?'

'Were you?'

'Yes. I've always struggled a bit with my weight.'

'Well, you're not struggling now.'

'What, you mean I've let myself go?!'

'No, just that you're not fat.'

'Well, I was back then. I didn't want to look fat so mother gave me this weird garment. It was like a bullet-proof vest only with underwear attached. You hooked it together between your legs. There probably was metal involved somewhere. Because Lycra didn't exist, the fabric was interwoven with some sort of vulcanised rubber and that's why it was so solid. But if it's any comfort, I was wearing it for you.'

'For me?'

'Yes, for you. I wanted to look good for you, didn't I?'

'Oh, Janey...you didn't need to do that. I liked how you were in class.'

'Well, I'd assumed you didn't, or you'd have asked me out, so I tried to be skinny for you, like Shawn Yeadon was.'

He put his hands over his eyes. 'Oh, god, I had no idea you were so keen on me. I was so dumb, so insensitive. Sorry. '

She just laughed. 'Oh, it doesn't matter. It was just teenage silliness.'

'Weight is such a modern obsession. Jules was telling me about thigh gaps the other day and how girls all want one.'

'Is Julie skinny?'

'Not skinny, no. Her weight has gone up and down from a 10 to a 14. When she had her miscarriages, she found it hard to put weight back on for a while.'

'Oh, poor lass. How many has she had?'

'Two. The second at 18 weeks.'

'Oh, no.' She put her hand over her mouth. 'I'm so sorry for you both.'

'Yeah. She was our little girl, Joni. I saw her, tiny, perfectly formed little body. Poor little mite just couldn't make it.'

'Aw, that's heartbreaking. You poor things.'

'Yeah...' he cleared his throat, feeling tears coming, despite his resistance. 'Sorry, Janey. Sometimes, it just catches me by surprise. It's still raw, really.'

'That's OK. Sod it, let's have a drink,' she said, getting up. 'I feel upset for you. I've got some cans of gin and tonic in the fridge, is that alright?'

He was keen. 'Yeah, just one should keep me under the limit. Thanks Janey.'

As she disappeared to the kitchen, he stood up, ran his hands through his hair and tried to get himself together. This was heady stuff. Now his emotions were running high.

'Bollocks to glasses,' she said as she returned, giving him a can. 'Cheers. Here's to what we were and what we're going to be.'

The gin and tonic tasted wonderful, too wonderful. It was all he could do to not suck it all down in one.

'Feel better now?' she said.

'Yeah, thanks.'

'When we were kids, I think we thought life was straightforward and uncomplicated, when it's anything but,' she said.

'Yeah. I miss being innocent,' he said.

She took a sip. 'What a funny thing to say.'

'The world is far worse than we knew when we were smooching to Barry White and I was feeling you up, all those years ago, Janey.'

'Hmm, yes, as recent days have showed us. These murders. Oh, my god.' She groaned and sat down.

'Yeah, and that's why I called you in the first place. I think the person who is doing these killings simply has to be something to do with the 6th form, right? Is there anyone that you could even speculate might be responsible? Anyone who is odd, or has said something strange. I know I'm grasping at straws but I want to find out who's doing this, not least because Josh is being put under pressure by the police. He's their number-one suspect.'

She looked at him wide eyes. 'Josh?! That's ridiculous. Josh wouldn't hurt a fly.'

He explained about his connections to the murders.

'Ah, so those were his photos. Right. Well, that's all well and good, but the fact remains, Josh is a lovely boy. I know he's got his issues, but when he comes into the office, he's always polite and well mannered, and from what I know about it, he deals with his condition very well. He's never been violent.'

'Given they've all been poisoned, whoever has done it would need some knowledge of chemistry in order to know what to administer and in what quantities. It is probably fast acting and doesn't leave any obvious residue.'

'Well, George Tyers is the 6th-form chemistry teacher. He's vile. He wears sandals all year round with awful socks. He's gross.' She pushed away from herself, as though trying to wipe Tyers aside.

'OK, but is he a serial killer?'

'Well, that's just very hard to imagine, but then, what does one of those look like? He could have made the poison, I suppose,' she said.

'I do feel like someone is trying to make Josh look guilty.' He explained about the numbering of the photos. 'Let's just pretend I'm right, who would have the opportunity to do that to him?' he asked her.

'Well, there's Mike McGregor...'

'...yeah, what's your view of him? You said before that he looks at girls for too long.'

She looked askance and held her hands up briefly. 'I'm sorry, but he's the sort of man I really dislike.'

'Why's that?'

She raised her top lip in an Elvis-like sneer. 'He pays lip service to being modern and liberal, but he's not. Aside from looking at the girls, I've heard him talk to some of his friends at various college-related social functions. He's an old-school sexist pig. Sorry, but that's my view.'

Nick told her about how he'd referred to Heather Leary as a 'stunner'.

'Oh, yes, that's absolutely typical of him,' she said. 'But he's popular with the governors and other important people. He's very clubby, if you know what I mean, and that's how he got to be deputy Head, relatively young. My view is, like a small minority of male teachers, he's overly interested in the girls. They're 16 to 18, some look a lot older and are quite mature, others are still silly teenagers. And some of them *are* stunners, but regardless, you've got to leave all that at home and be professional. The language he used to you, to my mind, is wholly inappropriate and if he'd said it in my presence, at college, I would have reported it to the Head. That's how strongly I feel about it.'

'That's pretty much what Jules said, too. I judge people by the words they use. And he failed my "good guy" test, right there and then. Do you know anything else about him?'

She took a long drink. 'Not much, no. He lives in Hartburn on his own.'

'So he's not married and doesn't have a partner?'

'No, which tells you something, possibly. I don't know. Maybe that's harsh...no, what am I saying? He's a sexist creepy shite, that's

167

not harsh at all.'

'OK, so who else teaches Josh?'

She looked past him, thinking. 'Err, Henry Kilbane, physics. He's a lovely older fella in his mid 60s. Karen Trimble, maths. She's a bit boring but nice enough, about our age. Outside of his classes, Alice Coates trains the basketball teams, one of which Josh plays in. She's new this academic year. One of those sporty, fresh and bouncy type of women. But very nice, too. Always cheery and can't do enough to help you. Super fit. Not an ounce of fat on her, lucky cow. Henry also runs the Robotics club, which I know Josh goes to, along with Heather. They do stuff with drones; building them and flying them. The kids in that club make me laugh. They're all *so* nerdy. I say that affectionately.'

'What about other non-teaching workers?'

She looked out of the window and finished her can, letting out a small belch of fizz. 'Brenda Coker is the other secretary, she's there right now. She's a nice lady in her 60s. Not the serial killer type, I'm thinking, not even in an Agatha Christie murder mystery. There's any number of maintenance staff, dining staff, counsellors, cleaners; all sorts, really. On top of that are visitors, parent governors, not to mention the occasional OFSTED visit. It's a really busy place. Much more diverse and interesting than when you and me were students. My office is a whirl of activity from 8am till after 5pm. There are so many facilities and options for the kids nowadays.'

Nick finished his can, too. 'So how easy is it for a stranger to just walk into the place unannounced?'

'Easy. Basically, anyone could walk in, go to an office or classroom, and if it was unlocked, go in and steal anything. Staff are supposed to lock their rooms at all times, when they're not in. But I'm sure some forget. But there is CCTV on the main entrance, so they would be caught on those. You could go through all the film, identifying every person and then try matching visitors to the sign-in book, but it'd be a huge task to do that and hard to know exactly who was who. I agree with you, I think it's someone who is already at the college, or who has good reason to be there regularly. It must be. But what is their motive?'

Nick finished his tea and leaned forward. 'Yeah, it's clearly specific to McGregor's form class.'

'Is it, though? Paul Richardson's parents were obviously not part of that class.' She got up. 'Another drinkee?'

'I'd love one but I'd best not. I'm driving.'

'You don't mind if I do, do you?'

'Knock yourself out. It's your long weekend.'

'Yeah, I love a long weekend. My pal Hilary is driving us to the Lakes this afternoon, so I don't need to worry about that.'

He looked at his watch as she went to the kitchen. It was just 11.30am. It was good going starting your second drink before noon. In a way, he felt a bit jealous of her. There's nothing like early drinking, while the rest of the world is going about its business. It's also the sign of someone with a drink problem of some flavour. Probably a G & T flavour.

She returned with a large glass, full of ice and a slice of lime. Clearly, she'd put two cans into it. Fair play. You do what you've got to do to get through life. He wasn't about to be even one per cent judgemental, but he found himself hoping she was OK, while rather suspecting that she really wasn't.

She sat down heavily, just along from him on the sofa. 'You know what? I'm beginning to think somehow and for some reason, Paul and his parents were killed by someone else. Their deaths are part of a different crime, or a different agenda.'

Nick watched as she took a big drink, thinking about what she'd said.

She crossed her right leg over her left and bounced it up and down, as though in contemplation, staring at a large impressionist painting on the wall opposite, hung above the gas fire, of a rural fields and hills scene. 'Perhaps whoever killed the girls just copied how the parents and Paul were killed?'

Immediately as she said that, Nick could almost physically feel the cogs in his brain drop into place, unlocking a problem.

'Shit. That's such a great idea, Janey. That makes a lot of sense.' He leaned forward as his thoughts coalesced. 'His parents were one murderer; the girls, another. And, think about it, who wanted to kill

169

Paul more than anyone else?'

'I don't know,' She shook her head, making a long strand of hair spill across her face. She pushed it behind her ear.

'He did. Paul did. He wanted to kill himself. I stopped him. But, as Josh said to me, the urge would not have gone away. When I found his parents dead, my first thought was that Paul had killed them. Only the subsequent deaths took me away from that idea. We began looking for an outsider, but it's not an outsider, it's Paul. Paul poisoned his parents, then poisoned himself. And that's the end of that. He took whatever it was, lay down on the gym roof, bless him, and let death happen.'

'When I think of what must have been going through that poor boy's head, it just makes me shudder. But you know what that means? That means someone else knew how he'd done it, and copied it for the girls.'

Nick pulled on his bottom lip in contemplation.

'Maybe, or maybe he found out how to do it, he was great at chemistry, and then he showed the person that went on to kill the girls how to do it. Yes!' He slapped his leg. 'That's what's happened, y'know. And, in that way, he got his revenge from the grave on the girls that had humiliated him. The poisoning was done in such a way that it would not be easily detected. Something has been used which the body can metabolise into elements that already exist in the body, so you can't spot the drug itself.'

She looked at him with wide eyes. 'Paul was doing chemistry, physics and biology. He came to us from Ian Ramsey as a straight grade-A student. He was very, very bright, at least before he started having his problems. Maybe he knew what to take. Maybe it's his "recipe", if you know what I mean.'

'Yeah, maybe. But why did that matter? Why did being hard to detect how he'd kill himself matter? He was standing in front of a train 48 hours earlier. He wasn't bothered about such niceties then. It doesn't make sense that he'd suddenly think, "Oh I know, I'll kill mother and father and myself and make it hard to detect why".'

'I disagree. If it's not possible to tell what chemicals have been used, you make it more difficult for it to be worked out where they

170

came from. So if he didn't want to get who supplied them into trouble, that's why he'd make it hard to know what it was.'

He nodded and gave her an admiring look. 'You're really very clever, you. Mind, I always used to copy your homework.'

She beamed at him, a drink flush to her cheek now.

Nick sat and thought about it for some time. 'This George Tyers, your sandal-wearing chemistry teacher. Could he have taught Paul how to kill someone without it being obvious? Or could he have been giving him some chemicals that bent his brain?'

'Well, he is vile, I don't like his fashion sense, but murder...I just don't see him doing that. In fact, I would suspect McGregor over him. It's his form, after all. He'd see Josh putting the photos in his locker. You found them in his office. And we both think he's a creep with a dodgy attitude to girls.'

'He also studied chemistry at University.'

'Did he?! Well, surely he's a better bet.'

'Yes, I agree. The hard thing about this is, it's hard to imagine any human doing these crimes. The person doing them is, in all probability, going home to the friends and family and just behaving like nothing is wrong.'

'That is weird. The thought that someone I see every day is killing children, is too awful to contemplate.'

'Well, someone is doing it. And the next photo, #6, is Jenny Wells, who is Julie's step-niece.'

'The Australian girl? Is she really?'

'Yeah, Julie's dad moved down under and started a new life. Jenny and Jade are his grandkids. They look quite like Jules, only with those mad painted and shaped eyebrows kids have.'

'Julie must be good-looking then, because if we're talking about girls who are stunners, she and her sister could definitely be filed under that category, though both are quite different girls.'

Nick took out his wallet. 'This is me and our Jules when we were on holiday in California.' He showed her a picture of them, arms draped around each other's shoulders, taken on Santa Monica beach as the sun was low, sinking into the liquid mercury blue Pacific, both tanned after three weeks of sun, Julie in a black bikini and

Aviators, blonde hair spilling over her shoulders, and him with a chestnut brown tan, bare-chested in black shorts. It was easily the best picture of them together they'd ever taken. Usually, one or both of them looked odd, with eyes half-closed or a bright sun highlighting their wrinkles. This was an accidental work of art. He'd put the camera on a timer and set it on a low wall. They were both a little drunk, relaxed and unselfconscious and it was a really hot evening. Even he knew they looked great in it, even though it was, in a way, not real.

'Bloody hell, Nick, she looks like a movie star. You both do. Oh, my god, I feel so jealous. And look at you: all muscles.' She sighed. 'You look like a really lovely couple.'

'We got lucky with the lighting on this. It made us look better than in real life. And I must say that Jules had just let off a vicious, sulphurous fart, due to eating a massive burrito of refried beans, which is why she's laughing. Reality is always less glamorous than photos.'

She sighed again, still looking at the photo. 'You say that but I wouldn't mind some of that glamour. God. That looks so brilliant. You both look fantastic. I can't believe you're the skinny shy lad I sat next to for two years. You both look like rock stars.'

Nick took the picture off her, feeling awkward, and put his wallet away, feeling he'd just been guilty of one of the 21st century's worst crimes - the 'look at me and my wife's great life' crime. He'd not meant to. Or had he? He was proud of being married to Jules. But even so, he knew it had played badly and he'd misjudged the situation and had actually been quite selfish.

'Janey, is the college doing anything to protect the kids? It is still open, isn't it?'

She nodded. 'There are a team of officers patrolling the school. But, to be honest, the kids have been killed out of school, probably on their way to, or from the place. Parents and friends of friends are collecting kids at the end of the day, but there's only so much you can do to protect them.'

'It must be a frightening and horrible time for everyone. Almost unbelievably so.'

'I think some will stay away now and you can't blame them.'

'Well, I suggested to Josh he have a few days out of it and just to stay in his room.'

'That seems a shame, but may be sensible.'

'He just needs to settle his mind down. He likes spending time on his own with Stanley, his dog.'

Janey sighed and finished her drink in three gulps.

'Look, I've got to go, Janey. It's been lovely to see you. Thanks for the drink.'

She looked at him with a smile already informed by the gin. 'Aw, it's been great to spend time with you.'

'We've both changed a lot, I think, but something of who we were, as teenagers, is still here and now.'

'Yeah, I'm not sure we change that much.'

He walked out of the living room to the front door, and opened it, letting cold air in. Without giving him a chance to resist, she pulled him in for a tight hug.

'Oooh, it's been lovely having you here. Come and see me again,' she said, on tiptoes, pressing herself into him, as they embraced and this time he instinctively and irresistibly pressed himself into her. And immediately felt he shouldn't have.

CHAPTER 13

'I love this motor more and more,' said Julie, as Nick drove the Mercedes south down the A19, out of Teesside and into North Yorkshire on Friday afternoon.

'It is very smooth and quiet,' he said.

'I wonder what dad's farmhouse is like?'

'He said it's run down. So we should feel right at home.'

'Well, it's not like we dressed up.'

'When I was at Janey James's bungalow yesterday...'

'...Oh yeah, what was she like? We didn't get chance to talk much about it last night, I was so tired after work. Odd to live in a bungalow at her age.'

'Yeah, I thought that, but she lives on her own, so has no need for a lot of space. Kids are in their 20s and have left home. She seems to live a nice, quiet life there.'

'No fella?'

'No. She was divorced 10 years ago. Mind, she was on the G & T before noon.'

Julie turned to him and gave him a raised eyebrows look. 'Mind, I'm all for early drinking when you're on holiday...'

'...which she was. She was having a long weekend in the Lakes. Even so...it looked a bit like...I dunno...'

She traced her centre parting with an index fingernail. 'Is she an alkie?'

'Put it this way, it wouldn't surprise me. But she was a nice girl at school and didn't seem to have changed much. I really liked her and she had some good ideas about the deaths.'

'I don't remember her from school.'

'She remembered you, mostly via your brothers.'

'That's typical, I'm afraid.'

He coughed and drummed his hands on the wheel nervously. 'Jules, I don't know if I did right, but I showed her that picture of us on Santa Monica beach, just to show her what you looked like.'

'Oh, yeah, I like that one. The light is low, so you can't see the stretch marks on my thighs.'

'So that was an OK thing to do?'

She frowned. 'Yeah, why wouldn't it be?'

'Well, I thought she looked a bit upset...no, that's overstating it. Wistful perhaps. And then I wondered if maybe I was rubbing her nose in our "happy couple" status a bit.'

Julie blew her nose on a tissue and looked out the window at the rolling fields, green with spring wheat.

'She probably fancies you and was hoping our relationship was on the rocks, so she could steam in and enjoy the pleasures of your substantial flesh.'

'Huh. I think you're probably right, given the way she hugged me close before I left.'

She sighed. 'Well, can't blame her for copping a feel, like that. We've all done it, at one time or another.'

'Don't you mind?'

She sniffed. 'I like that you've told me. But nah, I'm not possessive like that, am I? There's no point. I feel a bit sorry for her, actually. It doesn't sound like she's a predatory woman. She's probably lonely.' She grinned at him. 'If she does it again, don't reject her, it'll only make her feel bad about herself. I know you're not going to do anything with her.'

'I did feel it was a bit of an imposition, but obviously not an unpleasant one. And I felt I shouldn't or couldn't push her away.'

She shrugged it off as though it was of no consequence. 'Think of it as a social service, luv. Everyone needs a hug sometimes.'

Nick shrugged. 'But if it was man pressing himself into a woman, you'd not say that. You'd say it was abusive to do so uninvited.'

She nodded. 'I would, you're right, but that's because of the nature of the power balance between men and women, and also because women can't rape men, by the definition of the law. That's why a woman hugging a man tightly, pressing herself into him, is not as threatening to the man as a man doing it to a woman is. And that's before we even think about the likely imbalance in physicality.'

'Yeah, I get that. It did make me feel a bit uncomfortable, though, and it wasn't something I had a choice in. She was on me before I could leave.'

She snorted. 'Frankly, if being made to feel "a bit uncomfortable" by a man was the worst thing to happen to women in this world, I'd be out of a job. I'd trade the rape, abuse, torture and murder, for a quick hug of uncomfortableness.'

And in that moment, as so often happened when they spoke, he realised he was guilty of not seeing the bigger picture and of making a false equivalence between the male and female experience.

She went on. 'It sounds to me like she's a nice woman who is a bit starved of affection. Middle-aged women become weirdly invisible in our society. Whereas men get old and are thought craggy and experienced, women are just regarded as undesirable, wrinkled old bags, who've outlived their usefulness as mothers and are only good to be put out to pasture. It can be a cold, hard world for women of all ages, and it only gets colder as you get into middle age on your own. I've got you to desire me and make me feel good, but she won't have that, even if she's got friends. Friends can't seduce you, make love to you, be turned on by you, or make you feel physically desirable. And we all need to feel like that, no matter what age. That'll be the root of an overly intimate hug, in my opinion.'

He shook his head and glanced over at her. 'Sometimes you really amaze me how insightful and broadminded you are, Jules. A lot of women would be going round there and getting in her face.'

'Yeah, but there's no point in that. And to be fair, she's single, she can try it on with anyone she wants, married or not.'

They travelled west on the narrow country road for a couple of miles. 'It's up Banks Road, isn't it?' said Nick.

'Yeah, just up here on the right.'

He braked hard and turned up a single-track road which climbed steadily for a mile.

'This is amazing, Jules. So beautiful. Look, you can see all the way west towards Hawes in the Pennines.'

She gasped at the lovely open rural vista. 'God, I really miss living in the countryside. I'd love to live round here, but it's too far from work, really.'

'Maybe we should move from Norton and look for somewhere south of Yarm again. Somewhere we could get a long lease on maybe. Get properly settled in the country.'

'Yeah, maybe we should. As long as it isn't overrun with mice like the last place we had. Here we are,' she said, pointing at a dirt track. 'It's up there.'

He swung the Merc off the road for 400 yards, arriving in front of an old farmhouse, which had been pebble-dashed at some point about 50 years ago, but was now crumbling away. An old Ford Ranger was parked up alongside a muddy Jeep. The property was surrounded by dry stone walls, parts of which had fallen down into heaps of stones. In the field beyond, sheep grazed quietly. A long, well-worn footpath ran past the front of the house and into the distance, following the contours of the land, steadily heading downhill into a sprawling valley.

The old farmhouse had damp patches in the walls and the window frames looked rotten. The smell of coal smoke, a lovely familiar smell from childhood, swirled around in a gusty northwesterly.

'My god, run down is the word for this,' said Nick, getting out and looking around the junk-strewn yard.

'Yeah, but look at that, what a view,' said Julie pointing at the panoramic patchwork of brown and green fields, stretching right up into the hills of North Yorkshire, 30 or so miles away. A sheep made a baa-ing noise and it seemed to echo for miles across the wild open landscape.

A cold afternoon breeze blew, as they walked to the back door. Robbie opened it as they got there.

'Hey you two, you made it. Hello, Jules.'

'Hi, dad,' she said, with a smile.

'Helluva location, this, Robbie,' said Nick, shaking his hand.

'It is. Now, come in, I'm afraid the whole place is in a mess.' He called out. 'Sheryl. Carly. Girls. Nick and Julie are here!'

The two women came through to the kitchen, followed by Jade and Jenny.

After the greetings were over with, they all sat down around a large rectangular scrubbed pine kitchen table. Two big pots of tea were made.

'Are you taking time off school?' said Nick.

'Listen, mate, we're not going back to that place until they catch the bloody drongo that's killing people,' said Jenny, in a typically confrontational sort of Australian manner. She was dressed in a black roll-neck jumper, low-slung baggy blue jeans, ripped at the knee and turned up at the ankle, trainers and a Melbourne Victory FC baseball cap.

'Are a lot of girls staying off?' asked Julie.

'I think all of them are,' said Jade. 'They should close the bloody place down, if you ask me.'

'We thought it was for the best if we all came over here,' said Carly. 'Strength in numbers and all that.'

'And we're like a million miles from anywhere, here,' said Jenny. 'I can't even get reception on my phone.'

'You've got an internet connection, Jade. It's hardly living in the Third World,' chided her mother. 'It's not forever. Just until they catch this killer. I want you to be safe, and here is safe.'

'Have you any idea who it might be?' asked Nick. 'Any idea at all? It must be someone to do with the school.'

'Jen's got an idea, haven't you?' said Jade.

'What's that, Jen?' asked her mother. 'You've not told us.'

Jenny put her long fingers together. 'Listen, it might be a bit wacko. But why kill teenage girls and not boys? Why? Because he's after girls, isn't he? Girls in our class. OK, Paul died too, and his parents, but that's a separate thing, it must be. Paul was screwy in the head. He topped himself, I think, maybe his parents too. I don't think that's anything to do with Connie, Emma and Emily being murdered. We've got a girl killer. And that's the significant thing.'

'They're just crazy, Jen, you can't apply logic to crazy,' said Robbie.

Jenny was so self-assured and forceful that her disparaging look at her granddad's words was enough to destroy his argument.

'Okay, there's a lot of different flavours of crazy, but when you kill a teenage girl, what are you uniquely doing, over and above killing a boy?'

Her father shrugged but Nick just stared at her. Then it came to him strongly. 'You're stopping her having any kids. Is that what you mean, Jen? That's the unique thing about girls. They can have children.'

Jenny nodded. 'Exactly. When he kills girls or women, he's stopping reproduction.'

'But that makes no sense, honey,' said Carly. 'If you kill boys, you stop them reproducing as well.'

But Jenny had that all worked out. She shook her head. 'No. No you don't. Well, yes you do, but only in one sense, because they're dead, but overall you don't. If it had been boys killed and not girls, the girls would still have a load of kids, just not with those boys. You get me? I mean, god knows, there's plenty of sperm to go around, yeurgh puke, but if you kill girls, you significantly reduce how many kids are born. If those three girls each had a typical two kids, that's six off the total, right there. And I think whoever is doing it, is doing it to girls specifically for that reason.'

'That sounds too weird,' said Carly, looking puzzled, but it made perfect sense to Nick.

'But killing girls *is* weird,' said Julie. 'I think there could be something in what you say. In my work at Teesside Women, I see women who are involved with men that have very extreme psychological issues with women's fertility. They see menstruation as dirty. They seek to control the woman's fertility, sometimes keeping her permanently pregnant. I mean, there's a whole strand of abuse specifically related to fertility. That's a mentality that's out there.'

'Jesus Christ, Julie. What sort of sicko world do we live in?' said Robbie. 'How do you cope with all of that sort of thing?'

'That's not the half of it, dad. And I cope because I have to help people.'

'I think you're a bloody hero, girl,' Robbie said.

Nick drank some tea. 'I was talking with Janey James, the college secretary, and she is less than enamoured with Mr McGregor. What's your view of him, Jenny? He's your form teacher, so you see him every school day.'

She gave him a withering look and rolled her top lip upwards, revealing her even white teeth.

'What does that mean, Jen?' asked her mother. 'Has he said something? Has he done something?' Her voice was raised in concern.

'Nah nah nah...he's just a creep. So many men are creeps, he's just another one,' she said.

'And how does that manifest itself?' asked Julie.

'He looks at you for too long. Y'know what I mean, Jules? He looks at your arse. His eyes are always going downwards to your crotch, or to your chest. Just a quick glance. He touches you on your back or arm, if he can find an excuse to touch you, he will. Stands too close, like he wants to breathe your air. All standard creep shit.'

She was only 16, but she seemed so much older and wiser.

'Is that right?' said her mother. 'Is he like that with you, too, Jade?'

'I don't see him often, not like Jen does. The times I have, he is a bit of a perv, mum.'

Julie nodded, leaning on her elbows on the table. 'And that makes you feel really uncomfortable, Jen?'

She screwed her face up. 'Yeah, kind of. But I'm used to it, so no more than just being around boys and men generally. They all do it. Their eyes are always on you, looking at your tits and arse. They're all obsessed with sex. You can't walk down the street without them looking you up and down. I mean just fuck off mate, eh!' She shuddered.

'Hey, no swearing,' chided her mother.

Nick glanced at Julie, knowing this was something she'd often talked about and had dealt with from an early age.

'Oh, god, I know.' Julie shook her head. 'We all put up with it. It's an oppressive thing that only women endure. And you know they think it's a compliment that they're lusting after you. It's not. Keep it to yourself, you prick!'

Jenny laughed loudly and hi-fived Julie. 'Yeah, sister!'

'I just can't believe it's happening,' said Carly. 'Those poor families of the kids that have died. Your heart breaks for them. How have all these kids been killed?'

'They were poisoned,' said Nick. 'But in a way which was hard to detect. They were also either killed on, or taken to, public footpaths that run from the west and to the north of Stockton.'

'Really? Which paths?' asked Jade.

Nick explained about Greens Beck and the old railway line, now footpaths and cycle paths.

'Do you know those paths?' asked Nick.

Jade nodded vigorously. 'Yeah, we run on them in cross-country, don't we, Jen? There are a lot of off-road routes through Stockton. You can easily stay off the roads, go across the school fields and along tracks. When you're on them, it feels like you're in the countryside.'

'Yeah, they do feel like that,' said Nick. 'Do you do cross-country in games classes?'

'No. It's a cross-country club. There are 15 of us. We do competitive cross-country for County Durham. We're top of the league, mate. We're bloody great.'

'Oh, that's brilliant. So, do you train for that?'

'Yeah, Miss Coates sets the routes and she drives us in the school minibus to the county events. We do runs every other Sunday. She does basketball training on the other Sunday.'

'OK, what's she like? Do you like her?' asked Nick.

'Yeah. She really drives us on. Hard but fair. That sorta thing. She's the reason we're top of the league, I think. Before her, I heard that the 6th form were nowhere, but since she came in September, that's all changed,' said Jenny. 'I think she's ace. She's a total machine.'

'Those paths are well used, though, aren't they?' said Julie. 'It's not like they're deserted all the time? You couldn't just carry a body down there without being seen.'

'They're actually quite quiet, except when school is kicking out,' said Jade.

'But you've never seen anything unusual or suspicious?' asked Nick. 'No-one hanging around?'

'No. Nothing,' she said.

'Jenny, you know Josh, don't you?' asked Nick.

'Josh? In my form class? I don't *know* him. I don't think I've even spoken to him. He's got Asperger's like Heather Leary. They're kinda...' she hunched into herself '...I know it sounds harsh, but they're hard to get on with. They're outsiders. I mean, I am as well, but in a different way. They're too weird for me, though all the kids say that Josh is alright. He's super brainy. But I've kinda ignored him.'

Nick wondered if that was why Josh had put her in the middle of his numbering system.

'I've seen him around,' said Jade. 'He's nice-looking but Jen's right. Kids like them are hard work. That probably makes me seem like a really bad person.'

Jenny interjected. 'That Heather girl, man, is like some sort of professor. She's 16 going on 60. She's not just a clever kid, it's like she's...like she's from another planet. When I've tried to talk to her, it's like she can barely even see me, I'm so far below her...it's weird shit, man. If you told me she was an alien I'd, like, totally believe you.'

'How do you know him?' asked Robbie to Nick.

'Oh, it's a bit complicated. He lives next door to where I grew up. My dad was good to him, and I met him when I was sorting out my dad's estate nearly seven years ago. He took on my dad's dog. He went through a phase of sleeping in our allotment shed. We...well...we just like the lad. His parents are divorced and don't look after him very well, in my opinion. But he's a lovely lad, he really is. And you're right, Jen, he's super clever. At the moment he's obsessed with probability and statistics, but he used to be obsessed with owls, would you believe? That's just how he's made.'

'Josh is our friend,' said Julie. 'We look out for him as much as we can. His home life isn't very supportive. We...well...Nick, tries to help him get through life. It's a struggle for him sometimes. He doesn't have the ability to see how what he says or does might affect others. He's a lovely lad but doesn't really have much emotional empathy. He has to remember how to behave in any social situation and he spends a lot of time on his own. The problem is some photos he took.'

She explained about the photos and the numbering, to astonished looks from the two girls, after which everyone went quiet. Jen looked around the table. 'Well, I'm going to say it if you're not. That sounds like a kid that could kill girls. He sounds weirdly obsessed. What number was I?'

'Well, that's why I raised it. You were number 6.'

Jen put her head in her hands. 'You mean, I'm next? Bloody hell!'

'It's OK, honey, no harm will come to you here,' said her mother, taking her daughter's hand.

'The police know all about it, too. They'll probably come out and see you,' said Julie.

'Josh didn't do it,' said Nick, knowing it would sound overly defensive.

'Whatever,' said Jenny with an insolent shrug. 'But he was Paul's pal. Paul was a straight-A chemistry student. Maybe he taught Josh which poisons do what to the human body, killed himself and left Josh with the info to do likewise. It's one big sicko plot.'

'Well, I think the first half of that is right. But Josh *is* innocent,' said Nick.

Robbie ran his hands through his thick head of silvery-white hair. 'I'm sure the police are aware of all this. I just hope they catch whoever it is soon.'

Sheryl leaned on her elbows, cupping her mug in both hands. 'Well, whatever you say, I think this boy with Asperger's sounds very suspicious, y'know? Taking photos like that is weird.'

'He's not guilty. He can't keep secrets. He has no ability to deceive.'

Jade shrugged and made a face. 'OK, but maybe...maybe he's developed one. Those kids don't stay the same forever. They grow and they change.'

Nick didn't want to think that might be even one per cent true.

Robbie turned to Nick. 'Look mate, while you're here, can you give me a hand carrying some bags of cement and other building stuff? I can't do it on my own and, as nice as it is to have a house full of women, it's no good when you want a bit of muscle.'

'Sure. Let's do it.'

They went out of the kitchen, walked across what once upon a time had been a large farmyard, and into an open barn where a lot of building materials were stored, along with tools and equipment. 'I'm gravelling the front path round to the driveway so we need to shovel it from these big dumpy bags into wheelbarrows and take it around there. Shouldn't take us long.' He handed Nick a shovel and they began filling two large, deep wheelbarrows.

'So you must be stressed out beyond belief, Robbie, with these murders.'

'You can say that again, mate.'

'How are the girls coping? They seem like tough kids.'

'Jade, being a year older, seems to be strong, but Jenny has had some sleepless nights and now she's number six, that's not likely to get better.'

Nick threw another shovel of gravel into the barrow. 'Well it's her form class that is being murdered. It's bound to be upsetting for her.'

'Yeah, and she's going through a difficult period, anyway.'

'In what way?'

'She's just coming to terms with being gay, mate. Don't say anything. She thinks we don't know or realise. But it's pretty obvious.'

Nick took a break, stood for a moment and thought about how she was. 'Oh, right. Now you've said, it does seem obvious. Not that it had occurred to me previously. Then again, I'm not great at reading people. She seems like a lovely kid to me, both of them do. Intelligent and confident.'

'They are. Jen puts a lot of front on, but she's quite sensitive under all that bluster.'

They lifted the barrows up and took them across the yard to the front of the house, tipping them into a heap on the remains of an old gravel path, now overgrown with grass, then trudged back.

It took four trips to shift all the gravel.

'Bloody hard work, that, Robbie,' said Nick, wiping his brow. 'You're a good shape for a bloke of your age, though.'

'Yeah, maybe. I'll bloody feel it this evening, though.'

'Listen, Jules works with kids and young people, just as part of her work. Why don't you ask her to have a chat with Jenny about the whole gay thing?'

'I did think of that, but decided against it. Jen will be fine. She doesn't need mollycoddling. She's not that sort of kid. She's really just a moody 16-year-old.'

Nick wondered how true that was. Your sexuality is such a big thing at that age, and if you're feeling like you're not with the programme that everyone else is with, it had to be difficult.

They went back into the kitchen. Carly was cooking on a large stove, the smell of frying onions, garlic and ginger filled the air. Julie walked in. 'That smells good,' she said, as Carly added curry powder to the large, wide pan.

'Chicken curry is always a favourite here,' said Carly.

'I've just been watching Jen doing breakdancing. She's amazing at it. You've never seen anything like it. She's so limber,' said Julie.

'She's bloody good, isn't she?' said Cheryl, turning from the stove. 'She did local competitions back in Oz. Don't know if it's such a big thing here.'

'Breakdancing? What? Like all the spinning on your head business?' said Nick.

'Yeah, but it's so much more than that. It's like a combo of gymnastics and dancing. Go and have look, she's in the big front room,' said Julie.

He wandered through and was surprised to hear Kraftwerk's *Tour de France* album playing. He had a fondness for German electronic music since hearing their album *Autobahn* in 1974. A large blue foam mat was laid out on the living room floor and Jen was gyrating and doing forward rolls, leaping up onto one foot, twisting around, dropping to her knees and all the while to the rhythm of the music. It was a real performance art. She finished the routine doing a rotating one handed spin and a mid-air rotating volley, like a footballer leaping to connect with a crossed ball.

'Wow, that was incredible,' he said, clapping as she turned the music off. With a broad smile she did a bow. 'I didn't know this was your thing, Jen. That was sodding brilliant.' He found himself laughing from of the joy of witnessing it.

She gasped for air. 'Yeah. I've always loved it. Been doing it for years now.' She panted, getting her breath, her cheeks flushed pink with the exertion. 'Just trying to keep my chops in shape. I need to find a competition somewhere.'

'Honestly, that was brilliant. Have you ever thought about doing musical theatre?'

'No, mate. What do you mean?'

'I mean plays that have music and dancing in, like *West Side Story* only updated, modern stuff. Me and Jules saw something a year ago up in Newcastle, it was set in New York in the early 80s about a love affair between two girls in different gangs. It was great and had street dancing scenes, in that kind of style, as part of the narrative. It was really good.'

She cocked her head to one side. 'That's sounds bloody great. You know what mate, I've never thought of doing anything like that, but it's not bad idea at all.'

'I'd never have thought you'd dance to Kraftwerk.'

She grinned at him with her dark blue eyes. 'Oh, I love the old school. Lots of 80s vibes. Grandmaster Flash, Run DMC and Afrika Bambaataa.' She pulled on her baseball cap and hitched up her baggy, low-slung jeans. 'You're a rock guy though, aren't you? Not your thing, all of this.'

'I like all sorts of stuff, including 70s disco. Jules tells me I'm not a bad dancer once I've had a few drinks.'

'I love old disco. Melba Moore, Dan Hartman, KC and the Sunshine Band, that kind of thing.'

'Oh, yeah, those are the records that were played at our school discos. You know big Jeff, who was at the restaurant with us? He runs a string of record shops, if you're interested in vinyl, he always has loads of that sort of stuff in stock and he'd all but give it away to you because it doesn't sell. He also gets in old 80s 12-inch remixes in his auction room boxes and no-one wants them. So if you fancy getting into vinyl, you could do so for almost zero money.'

She gave him her big-jawed wide smile of pearly whites. 'That sounds cool. There's kids at college who collect records. I know

Heather Leary does. She's a big Bowie and Metallica fan.' She stood hands on her hips and nodded. 'Mother's got some old vinyl. I might see if we can get a turntable. Yeah, that sounds cool.'

'I'll ask Jeff to look out for one for you - people come into the shops all the time offering them for sale.'

She smiled. 'Cheers, Nick. You're alright, you are, for an old dude.' She danced forward and flicked a light punch at his belly.

'Hey, I'm not that old! Alright, OK, I am. At least compared to you. But it doesn't seem long since I was 16.'

'I'm just kiddin' you. How old are you, anyway?'

'50-bloody-2. I still can't believe it. Time goes so quickly.'

She raised her sculpted eyebrows. 'You really don't look that old, Nick. Not a day over 49, anyway.'

She cackled a cracked guttural laugh.

'Thank you very much, madam. I know you're taking the piss but I'll take 49! That's how bad it is.'

'Ah, age is all bullshit, mate. Even I know that with only 16 notches on my belt.'

'It's easy to say that when you're a limber 16-year-old, less so when you're walking along and there's a big clang and you turn to find something large and important has fallen off you.'

She laughed again and blinked slowly at him, letting her eyes close for a second, before opening them again. 'I guess so.'

Her default attitude was quite brash and in-your-face, but chatting to her now, it was quite obvious that underneath, she was a soft, sensitive young woman.

'So how are you coping with the stress of this weird situation at 6th form?'

She rubbed her forehead. 'It's better being out here than being in Stockton. It feels safer, so I'm unwinding a bit. I've been, like, mega-stressed out. And now I'm worried about this number six business. But then, I do feel safe here.'

'Did you know the three girls who've been killed?'

She flopped in an armchair and he did likewise, opposite her and beside the window.

'Yeah, I did. They weren't mates but I talked to all of them regularly.'

Nick cleared his throat. 'Josh tells me they were horrible to Paul. Did you know about that?'

'Oh, yeah. They were...' she wiped sweat from her forehead '...well, to be brutally honest, they were three bitches.'

'Really?'

'What happened to them was terrible. But I'm not pretending they were angels, because they weren't. They were dirty bitches.'

Nick frowned. 'They were...sexually active?'

'In Oz we'd call 'em fuck buckets. Everyone knew it. They worked as a threesome. I heard all sorts of rumours about them. I mean...you know...bad stuff.'

'This might be important. Tell me everything. Don't worry about the language you use.'

She pulled her long, strong legs up under her.

'Well, the thing is, Nick, I heard that they were having sex with an older man, as a threesome, and doing it for money.'

'Really? Was that just salacious rumours?'

'I think it was true.' She looked him in the eyes. 'Some kids, you just know they're bad kids...do you know what I mean? They almost stink of it. I couldn't tell you why, but those three were very tight and they talked in a way no other girls in the form did.'

'So when they took the piss out of Paul for being overweight and having a small penis, that was typical of them?'

'Totally. Everyone in the gym that day - and I was there - everyone felt sorry for Paul, even though Paul was annoying and strange. But the girls didn't care. They thought it was funny to humiliate him. It was like they felt superior and had this worldly knowledge that we humble teenage virgins couldn't understand. Oooh, his cock is small, I mean, so fucking what? Y'know? Who cares? They totally misjudged their audience. Paul was bloody mortified, Nick. A few of us went over to him to say not to take any notice, but he was gone, mate. He couldn't be comforted. I felt so sorry for him. He was vulnerable and they knew that and they gave it to him with both barrels.'

She stopped, but still muttered words under her breath, as though reliving it.

'Do you think Paul had sex with them, Jen?'

She stroked her strong chin. 'Oh yeah, definitely. And they probably made him pay them. Like I say, they worked as a team.'

Nick thought about it for a moment. The idea that he was getting his revenge on them from beyond the grave was now never more believable.

'That's really interesting. I'm sure they'll catch the man responsible soon, Jen. And if they don't, I bloody will. I'm not having whoever it is stitch Josh up for this.'

'Well, even though he looks a bit suspicious, I hope it's nothing to do with Josh. Like I said, he's an outsider, like me. So I understand a bit about how he might feel. Outsiders get made scapegoats for all sorts of things. Being different is hard at our age.'

He didn't reply immediately. 'Why do you feel you're an outsider?'

She stood up, walked to the window and looked out towards the hills in the far distance, her back to him.

'Oh, I don't know,' she said, a little wistfully.

'Don't you? I think you probably do, Jen.'

'You think you do?'

'I'm an old bugger, so I think I might have an idea.'

She turned around and looked at him with her blue eyes. 'You know, don't you?'

He smiled and held his hands wide and open, to encourage her to talk.

'If I tell you something, can you tell everyone else? I just can't have the conversation. I know this is a bit weird 'cos I don't really know you...' she stopped, thought about it briefly '...but that seems to make it easier, and you seem like a nice guy. Is that alright? I have to get this out of me, it's eating me up.'

'If that's what you want, yeah, of course. I'm cool with whatever you want to tell me.'

She smiled. 'Yeah, you are a cool guy, I think. And you already know, don't you?' She rested her weight on one hip.

'I think so. But you should say the words. It'll be empowering.'

She cleared her throat and stood facing him directly as though addressing a court. 'I'm gay. I'm a lesbian. I have no interest in the male of the species, sexually. I never have and I never will. The thought of it actually repulses me. And I feel the exact opposite for girls. And at times, Nick, it's bloody hellish, mate. I mean, I'm an Aussie. Aussies aren't gay. We're all alpha whatever. So it's kinda weird. Like, Jade has boyfriends and she has, y'know, a physical thing with them. She tells me about it. Even though to me it is barfo gross.' She put her finger in her mouth, as though to make herself sick. 'But I can't have that, or I don't have it and I don't know how to go about sorting it all out. It's making me really pissed off. I want to have a girlfriend, there are girls I like...but how do you know if they're gay? I'm scared and intimidated by the thought of asking a girl out, and I just don't want the attention that I know it's going to bring if I come out. I just want it to be normal, not weird and it will be thought weird. Even if people are supportive, that in itself is not normal. Do you get me?'

He nodded and smiled. 'Totally. Your sexuality is as normal and natural as mine. It shouldn't be a big deal to express it. If it's any comfort, whilst acknowledging your struggle, it's nothing compared to the fight you'd have had when I went to 6th form in 77-79. Back then, no-one was gay.'

'You mean, no-one admitted to it?'

'I mean, if you weren't gay yourself, it wasn't on your radar at all. I actually knew two lads who, with subsequent reflection, were obviously gay, I mean, really obviously, but it literally never occurred to me. Not even when I was sharing a bed with one of them, after a party somewhere. I thought we were just crashing out.'

She laughed. 'You had sex with him?'

'No. To be honest, if I'd realised what was going on, I'd probably have had a go, just for the experience, even though my heart wouldn't have been in it. But I passed out drunk before that could happen. I have this lingering memory of the lad talking dirty to me, but I'd had eight pints of real ale and was soon comatose.'

She roared with a deep, woody laugh. 'Well, I've not even been that close with a girl.'

He thought for a moment. 'You know what, Jen? I think this will surprise you, but your family already know you're gay.'

She pulled a face. 'What?! How could they know that? Has Jade told them?'

'They just do. I think it's been obvious to them for a while.

She winced and briefly covered her face with her hands. 'Oh, god. I hate this. I just don't want to talk about it to them.'

'That's fine. That's what I'll tell them. But you should join a support group, or something more social. Then you'll get to meet other young women. Now it's out in the open, you can do that, can't you? It's no big deal.'

She blinked slowly again. 'I guess so, yeah. I'm a bit scared of coming out, though. Kids might be weird about it and take the piss.'

'Only the wankers and arseholes. And they're weird about everything and everyone. Besides, everyone's gay these days, man. I'm probably gay. So's Jules and your granddad too...he probably goes out to discos in arseless leather chaps.'

She let out long laugh at that and began to take up her exercise mat.

'Jenny, at the risk of being a boring old fart to someone as young as yourself, the thing I've learned in life, albeit very late on, is that accepting who you are, for good or bad, is the easiest path to take. Don't fight with yourself. Don't regret being yourself.'

She stacked the mats in a corner. 'How did you learn that?'

'Oh, I suffer from depression, not all the time, often in short episodes of intense darkness and I've been close to ending it all a couple of times, but since I've totally embraced that as a part of who I am, it's made dealing with it easier. It's still horrible when it smothers me, but I understand it and myself better and so I can deal with it. And the good thing is that I've realised that people - not many people, admittedly - but friends down the years, they liked that which made me who I am. Even the dark stuff. Julie often says that she can now see that the emotional, funny, understanding, non-macho side of me, is also part of the moody, depressed, upset man, who feels there's no reason to live. I didn't get one without the other. So all I'm saying is, being who you feel yourself to be right now is 100 per cent the right thing to do, and everything that everyone likes about you is because of who you are, and that includes your sexuality.'

She cracked her knuckles and laughed a little, then stood up. 'Bloody hell, Nick. That was a helluva speech, mate.'

He held his hand up. 'Sorry, I didn't mean to go on...'

He turned to go, but she grabbed him by the arm and made him turn around.

'Thanks, Nick.' She pressed a wet kiss on his cheek.

He smiled. 'That's OK, we outsiders have to stick together.'

CHAPTER 14

'So what's your prediction for today?' said Nick as he, Jeff and Julie got on the X67 bus from Stockton High Street to Middlesbrough, sitting opposite each other at the back.

'I've got a feeling in my water that we're going to lose by the odd goal,' said Julie, dressed in jeans, battered black leather biker jacket, Boro scarf and hat.

'I'm a great believer in your sweet, delicious, if suspiciously vodka-flavoured water,' said Jeff. 'It's got mystic properties.' He smoothed out his long, greying beard and wafted it at her, giving her a mad look.

'This is true. You've got the best water when it comes to predicting Boro's results. We've played 37 league games this season, how many have you called right?' asked Nick.

Julie pulled her woolly hat down over her ears and shivered a little.

'This has been a very good year for my water; one of the best ever, I think. I've got 9 scores exactly correct, and 29 results right.'

'Only eight results wrong is amazing! We should gamble on your water and make a load of money,' said Jeff, dressed against the cold in a big green army great coat, complete with large brass buttons.

'The only season I tried doing that, my water dried up and I had the worst season ever. Betting jinxes my psychic skills.'

'Well, win, draw or lose, this is a bit of a treat for me to go the football,' said Jeff. 'Seems ages since I've been.'

'You've not been missing a lot of quality,' said Julie. 'But then, I could have said that for 75 per cent of my 40 years of going to the match.'

'Call me old fashioned, but I prefer the Boro being mildly rubbish. It feels like all is right in the universe,' said Jeff.

'This is true. I like one cracking season where we win a lot, but anything more feels as massively self-indulgent as eating three breakfasts,' said Nick. 'I've still not got over 2006's UEFA cup run, yet.'

They got off at the bus station and walked down to Doctor Brown's on Corporation Road, one of Nick and Julie's regular pre-match pubs.

'Town seems much busier than usual,' said Nick looking around at the crowds of people milling around.

Jeff raised his right index finger. 'A brief perusal of these people would tell you that this not the normal Saturday afternoon Middlesbrough shoppers, nor your typical Boro fans. I smell hippy in the air, mixed with dreadlocked anarcho, assorted bunny strokers and tree huggers.'

'How do you know that, Jeff?' asked Julie, chuckling, hands jammed into her jacket pockets as a cold wind blew in from the northeast.

He made a wide-armed gesture. 'Easy. Every other punter has got hemp trousers on, and hand-knitted jumpers made out of lentils are everywhere. I actually think it's a demo, of some sort.' He pointed to some women who had a hand-painted banner saying 'Save The Earth'.

Julie nodded. 'Oh, yeah, I heard about this. Someone at work was talking about it. Save The Earth is a green organisation. They're probably organising it here for maximum exposure, with the match being on.'

'Not sure the Boro fans will have too much empathy for a man with blonde dreadlocks and non-sexist, vegan trousers and a "Meat Is Murder" badge,' said Jeff, with a snorting laugh, as they passed one such dude. 'Then again, most trousers are vegan, I suppose.'

'Not if they're cheesy,' said Julie.

The three of them pushed through the gathering crowd and went into the pub. Inside, it was a lot less busy. Match days were quieter than they had been when Middlesbrough were in the Premier League, with crowds of 10-15,000 instead of 25-35,000.

Nick bought them each a double vodka and tonic and they leaned against a wall by one of the windows. Outside, the protesters milled around in ever-greater numbers.

'Here's to your water being wrong,' Nick said, clinking hers, then Jeff's glass.

'Cheers. I'm going for 1-0 to Birmingham City,' she said.

'Right, I'm putting a tenner on that,' said Jeff, tapping at his phone.

'You'll jinx it, Jeff, I'm telling you,' she said.

'Yeah, but think about it. If I jinx it, it means the Boro don't lose, if I don't, it means I win. Either way, everyone's a winner, baby, that's the truth, as those great philosophers, Hot Chocolate, once so eloquently expressed it.'

'Their first single was on Apple, you know,' said Nick to Julie.

'Oh. How. Interesting.' She made a mock yawning gesture.

'Aye, it was a reggae version of "Give Peace a Chance", added Jeff, as he finished placing his bet. 'Unsurprisingly, it flopped and they were dumped immediately. More interesting still, drummer Tony Connor joined them after being in the highly collectible prog rock band, Audience.'

'Really? Now, I didn't know that,' said Nick, with glee.

Julie laughed. 'You two are a right pair. You're genuinely impressed by that, aren't you?' She slapped at Nick's arm.

'Well, yeah. It's a top obscure fact that the big man has unearthed there.'

She just shook her head and grinned.

They took a drink. Jeff looked out of the window. 'This is going to be a decent-sized demo when it kicks off. So what's it all about, again, Jules?'

'Not sure. I'll look it up.' She did a search on her phone. 'Ah, right. Save The Earth are, like I thought, an environmental pressure group.' She scanned through their website. 'The usual stuff, pro-recycling, organic, vegetarian, anti-car and anti-pollution.'

'It's so hard to know the value of a load of people going on a demo. Will it really have any effect on any of those issues?' said Jeff. 'Half the time, demos are just people trying to make themselves feel morally superior, I reckon. All these "Not In My Name" signs they've got, they get right on my wick. Whatever it is, no-one said it *was* in your name. Even if you're on the other side, it's still not in *your* name. It's all very self-focused, that. All very look-at-me.'

'Maybe, but the right to protest is crucial in any democracy, isn't it? And wanting to get together with like-minded people is natural enough,' said Julie.

Jeff cast her a cynical look. 'Is that the future politician speaking? Me and him went on a CND demo in 1980 in Newcastle just because we were trying to cop off with two lasses.'

Nick grinned at the memory. 'Oh, aye, that is true. Rhona and...'

'...Dagmar. Lovely big-breasted German lass. Nipples like saucers.'

'In fairness, I believed in the cause,' said Nick. 'And in the nipples like saucers.'

'The cause being getting into said ladies' pants,' said Jeff, stroking his beard and moving his bushy eyebrows up and down. 'Followed by the swift deployment of our nuclear weapons.'

They cheered, laughed and clinked glasses. Julie went back to her phone.

'A lot of this group's ideas are reasonable enough, though I'll be damned if I start eating soya.'

'I was thinking something along those lines when I was in Gaia getting the Bio-Oil. In fact, now I think about it, while I was queuing, a woman came in and put up a poster for this event. That place is full of this sort of eco-warrior types. They all mean well, and whether you think they're hopeless idealists or the cutting edge of a new age, at least they're not just accepting the status quo.'

'You just fancy hippy girls,' said Jeff, dismissively.

'She wasn't a hippy and I didn't fancy her. She was more sporty, actually. A Lycra job.'

Julie continued reading the website. 'Not sure this lot are hippies. Not a lot of love and peace on their message board. It's pretty confrontational and apocalyptic. They're also calling for a public policy of population control in order to conserve the earth's resources.'

'Ah, that old classic,' said Jeff. ' "To all the ladies giving birth, it's the murder of the planet earth". Who's that?'

'Easy. It Bites, from the *Eat Me In St Louis* album,' said Julie, without looking up from her phone.

The two lads looked at each other in shock.

'I knew that'd surprise youse two. Egremont's finest, were It Bites.

Francis Dunnery. Blonde guitar player and singer. Sexual desire tends to fix musical info into my memory. I saw them in London. He was a really brilliant guitarist and had gorgeous, innocent but troubled eyes; sexy and vulnerable. But he wore really, really horrible jeans. I remember thinking, those would have to come off. Oh, yes. Never got near him, sadly.' She grinned to herself at the recollection.

'Despite unpleasant trousers, it was also on a Greenpeace compilation album. Always thought it was a bit of a harsh sentiment,' said Nick.

'Yeah, people don't like to be told how many kids they can or can't have...' said Jeff '...especially by Cumbrian rock bands.'

She looked up. 'And how would you enforce it? By infanticide or forced sterilisation? Also, because of the post-war baby boom, we need an expanding population so that the young people can pay for all the old people.'

'Yeah, but they're right about an ever-expanding population being a drain on the earth's resources,' said Nick.

'Surely, you solve that by expansion of renewables, reducing consumption and ending dependence on oil, not by forcing people to only have one kid,' she said. 'And by increasing wealth of developing countries. Most people have less kids when they get better off.'

Nick stared out of the window. Most of the protestors were under the age of 35, with a smattering of colourfully dressed hippy pensioners, too.

'It seems odd to me that the police have allowed this to happen here on match day,' he said.

'I don't think it's official. They put out a message on their Facebook page and on Twitter about an hour or two ago. They're starting here, walking the full length of Corporation Road, then going down Linthorpe Road to end in Albert Park where they're promising there'll be speakers, refreshments and, god help us, falafels.'

Jeff have a comedy yelp. 'Lord save us from the falafel. Like eating a ball of garlic-flavoured sawdust. Any event at which falafels are for sale, forfeits my support. I need a big face-full of fried meat if I'm going to support your cause. And talking of food, do you know you two really stink of garlic?'

'Oh, god, do we?' said Julie, licking the back of her hand and sniffing it as it dried. 'Oh dear, that is a bit eyeball frying.'

'We were at Robbie and Sheryl's gaff yesterday. She cooked up a big pan of curried chicken, there must have been half a pound of garlic in it,' said Nick. 'Was bloody good, though.'

'Oh, aye, you said you were going over there. So you had a nice afternoon?'

'The girls are staying there until the murderer is caught,' said Nick. 'We had a good time, didn't we, Jules?'

She nodded and jerked a thumb at him. 'And he managed to help Jenny to come out as a red-hot lezbo and via him, tell the rest of the family, even though they all knew anyway.'

Jeff raised his bushy eyebrows. 'Ah, red-hot lezbos are a speciality subject of mine.'

Julie put her fingers in her ears. 'La la la...don't want to hear.'

Jeff laughed and flicked at his hair. 'I'm not surprised her family already knew. I mean, it *was* obvious, wasn't it? Or am I just incredibly perceptive, like some sort of omniscient hairy sexual god?'

'I have to say, I didn't spot it at Big Meat, did you, Jules?'

She shrugged. 'I didn't pay it any thought. I am not as lesbian fixated as you boys.'

Jeff put his hands in the air in acclaim. 'Ah, y'see, it's just me. I have special powers of sexual understanding. I didn't say anything because I thought it wasn't in doubt. That being said, I have no idea why or how I knew that. It's not like she was smoking a pipe and reading Virginia Woolf.'

'I also may have persuaded her to get into vinyl records. She's a brilliant hip-hop dancer...'

'...honest, Jeff, you've got to see her. She's incredible. More like gymnastics, really. She was spinning on her head, then rolled onto her shoulder, leapt to her feet, and broke out into this stretchy dance thing, did a tight forward roll. It's like she's made of rubber. And all on the beat to Kraftwerk. Can you believe that?' said Julie.

Jeff put his thumbs up. 'She sounds like a proper star. I wonder why she didn't mention it at Big Meat? If she had, I could have told her I've got literally five boxes of 12-inch mixes of early 80s jazz funk, electronica, early rap and other stuff that no-one will ever buy. She can have the lot for free.'

'I did tell her that. Can you look out for a turntable for her as well?'

'Oh, I've got one in the back she can have. Tony D'Ianno brought it in, along with his big woofers. They'll be great for her. Hey, I'm glad you're getting on as a sort of family unit. I liked them all.'

'I must say, I enjoyed being there and I almost never enjoy that sort of thing in someone's house,' said Nick.

'They do make getting on with them easy,' added Julie. 'They're just very take-us-as-you-find-us. And the girls are so sharp, clever and funny.'

'This is all good news, I just hope this murderous bastard is caught so the girls can stop worrying, and that Josh can rest easy as well. Between you and me, Mandy is totally shitting bricks, she's in a terrible mood the whole time. If she doesn't catch the perp soon, the top brass will come down on her like a ton of lead.'

'But she is the top brass,' said Nick. 'She's the boss.'

'There's always brass that's more top than you,' said Jeff.

'Well, I hope she's gone off the idea of Josh being guilty of these heinous sodding murders,' said Nick.

Jeff made an uncomfortable gesture. 'I wouldn't be so sure about that, man,' said Jeff, a little too quietly. 'There's a lot of circumstantial evidence against the lad.' He held up his hands. 'I'm just sayin', I'm not passing judgement. Don't look at us like that. It's not my fault. You know what Mand is like. The more protests of innocence there are, the more she thinks her suspect mighta done it.'

Nick wanted to protest, but there was no point.

'C'mon let's have another round. There's nothing we can do about Josh right now. And I have a feeling we'll need to be a bit pissed to witness the Boro's performance today,' said Julie, going back to the bar.

Nick turned and looked out the window again. There was some chanting now, and quite a lot of shouting.

'They're getting a bit wound up. I bet the Old Bill has arrived to break it up,' said Jeff.

Although for most of its length, Corporation Road was a wide main road, the far end, where Doctor Brown's was located, was narrow and one way.

More chanting broke out.

'More people: no earth. More pollution: no earth. More cars: no earth. More oil: no earth!!' Each statement was followed by a double clap. They were all facing down the road, and began to move off as one. It was a powerful noise.

'You know, what? I don't like the look of this,' said Nick, feeling concerned.

'Me neither. Bad vibes, ahoy, if you ask me,' said Jeff.

When you grew up in the 1970s, fights were a common part of life. From seeing violence kicking off at school, to seeing it start on the terraces or in pubs, you developed a sixth sense about trouble from an early age. It was a metaphysical thing, hard to express or pin down, but a very tangible sense, nonetheless. It was something to do with the mood of people who want a fight, something to do with the noise they make and the shapes they create with their bodies.

And suddenly: It was on.

Julie had just returned from the bar holding three glasses and put them down on a table, when the crowd began to yell and gesture at something out of their sight. Sirens went off. Car alarms, too. Then there was a crash of shattering glass, probably one of the big plate-glass windows of a nearby bar and grill.

'Christ, it's all kicked off,' said Julie. 'I don't like this, it looks bad.'

Some blokes left the pub to have a look at what was going on, the prospect of watching violence, a perennial entertainment for some.

There was a big surge of people up the road and a lot of angry yelling. More glass broke somewhere. Then, just as quickly, a sea of people ran back down the road, spilling over the pavement and down Beech Street, which was a short lane, and also across the pavement onto Marton Road.

The men who had left the pub to look at what was happening, came running back in.

'Chaos out there, like!' one yelled. 'Coppers everywhere. Riot squad! Looks like someone threw a firebomb.'

And he was right. A sweeping wave of police, the front row of which was in riot gear and shields, advanced down the road, dispersing the crowd. It was a hell of a show of strength. Surely a totally over-the-top reaction to a bunch of green activists.

The police ran past the pub, made sure everyone was scattered, turned around and headed back up Corporation Road.

'Bloody hell, that was a bit bloody heavy duty,' said Nick. 'It's not like they're a bunch of terrorists.'

But it wasn't over.

Beech Street was opposite the pub. Nick pointed at a transit van pulling up. 'Look at this. They're up to something.'

Half a dozen people got out dressed in balaclavas and army fatigues, all of them carrying something in each hand. All six initially sprinted at speed towards the pub. Five peeled away up Corporation Road, one didn't, but ran towards the pub. Black balaclava, army fatigues. Nick pointed his camera and took a photo just as the figure reached the window.

'Fucking hell...get down!' yelled Nick, as two bottles were thrown through the window. Instantly, the smell of petrol hit his nostrils.

The petrol bombs exploded as they crashed through the glass. He hit the deck first, Julie was down quickly too, but one of the bottles hit Jeff on the back of the head, and in the blink of an eye he was engulfed in yellow, orange and blue flames.

'Jeff!' yelled Nick as it exploded.

Julie screamed. 'He's on fire!'

The big man was engulfed in the strangely beautiful flame. What the fuck do you do when someone is on fire?

But Jeff was quick. The bottle had hit him on the head, the pain of which had sent him sprawling to ground, but, immediately realising the situation, he ripped the big army coat off and as he did so cast aside most of the flames. But his head was still burning.

'Your hair's on fire, man!' yelled Nick, grabbing a pint of lager off the table and, without hesitation, pouring it over Jeff's head, extinguishing the flames, as bar staff and other drinkers did the same to extinguish the burning petrol, like a half-pissed fire brigade.

Jeff got to his feet, roaring like very, very, angry bear, lager dripping from his drenched hair.

'You absolute fucking bastards!!' he yelled and ran for the door to administer retribution, followed by Nick, Julie and at least half the pub.

But outside it was some shade of carnage. Glass everywhere. Broken windows. Police. People running. A waste bin had been set alight, sending black smoke and orange flames into the sky.

'It was him!' yelled Jeff, pointing at a figure running away at speed, with a black balaclava, already zooming past the police, who had now pulled back, probably waiting for more numbers. The demo itself was dispersing into disparate groups, fear in some people's eyes. The petrol bombers were clearly not part of the demo. They had hijacked it, coming at it from two sides, in two gangs.

'Get that bastard!' yelled Jeff, running faster than Nick had ever seen him run. Even so, he was being outpaced by the man in the army clothes who was very light on his feet, sprinting away down Corporation Road at speed. Nick accelerated past him. 'Go, Nick! Get that fucker!' Jeff yelled, having to slow down.

Nick pounded the road as fast as he could, but didn't make any ground up because the man was so quick, taking a sharp right down a one-way road, right in front of an oncoming car. It looked certain that it would knock him down, but in one leap he was on the bonnet and then running over the roof of the car and leaping off the other side. It was cat-like and almost beyond agile.

Nick had to let the car come out of the road before he could take off after the escapee, giving them at least five or six seconds to get further ahead. The fleeing man had turned into a pedestrian area, sprinted up a walkway and then just bloody well stopped in his tracks. What the fuck was going on? What was he doing?

Standing hands on hips, he had to be getting his breath. Nick used the last of his energy to sprint up to him, but he didn't move, not even as Nick closed on him. Instead, he just looked right at him. Nick was 15 yards away. 10 yards away. 5 yards away. Almost within reach now. Grab the fucker. Take him down. Why the hell had he stopped and let himself get caught? Watch out. He might have knife or a gun. A hundred thoughts ran through his brain as he approached.

Nick lunged with the intention of rugby tackling him to the ground, his lungs burning with cold air. But as he made his move, like a gymnastic on the parallel bars the man sprung onto the railings, up and out of his grasp, did a handstand on the metal rail, and whooped as he dropped backwards over the side, to the concrete ramp below, landing on his feet, squatting down and doing a forward roll to take the pressure off the 12-foot drop, then leaping up and sprinting away at speed, all in one seamless move. He was down the ramp, through a car park and gone.

Fucking hell. That was intentional, almost a tease. Come and get me; whoops, no chance! You can't catch me. Nick took out his phone from his back pocket, aimed it at the fleeing figure and took a photo, as he watched him sprint away, leap onto a five-foot-high wall, somersault over it and, arms raised, drop behind it.

It was like it was a performance. An art form.

As he got his breath back, he just stared at where the man had been, with his hands gripping the railings, body upside down, legs pointing to the sky. Replaying the escape scene in his mind, a jolt of electricity twanged his heart. He'd seen something every bit as agile and gymnastic as this yesterday.

Jenny.

So many of the same moves he'd done were the same as those that Jenny had done in the room at the farmhouse, especially that tumbling forward roll. That firebomber was certainly some sort of athlete.

As he walked away, Nick knew that his subconscious was getting to work on this and that at some point, hopefully not too far in the future, it would spit out a whole lot of truth.

He walked back to Corporation Road in search of Julie and Jeff, still trying to get his breath back, his lungs still burning. They were waiting for him, sitting on a low wall.

'What happened? Are you alright?' said Julie, running up to him.

'He got away. He was amazingly agile. I think he's one of those freerunners.'

'What? What's that?'

'They're lunatics that run across roof tops. It's like acrobatics, gymnastics and running all rolled into one,' said Jeff, coming up behind Julie.

'What's happened down there?' said Nick, nodding back down towards the pub where now a large number of police in fluorescent jackets had sealed the area off.

'The demo has totally dispersed. More police arrived. We didn't even see anyone getting arrested,' said Julie. 'We talked to one of the hippy demo people and he said there were four bombers who came from this direction. They broke the shop windows, ensuring the police went into riot mode. Then the six we saw arrived. This fella reckoned they set out to cause mayhem to disrupt the demo.'

'Aye, he said there's an extremist element in Save The Earth. Thinks they're responsible. Bloody nutters.'

'I knew the petrol bombers were not part of the demo, they hijacked it,' said Nick. 'Did any get arrested?'

'Nope, they were all too quick, like the one you went after,' said Julie.

'Can we get a cab home, please,' said Jeff. 'I stink of petrol and lager and burnt hair, which normally I wouldn't mind if it was at the end of a big piss up, or after fixing a car on Bonfire Night, but not on a Saturday afternoon in the Boro. We've missed kick-off, anyway.'

'Aye, let's get home. I'm totally knackered,' said Nick.

'I'm not surprised. You ran like the wind,' said Jeff. 'Fastest I've seen you go since you played on the wing in the Ian Ramsey rugby team in 1976.'

'Still wasn't quick enough. He was fast as a pro athlete. Did you see him run up and over the car?'

'Yeah, that was amazing. You need serious power and speed to do that.'

'It was like he was gymnast. He did a handstand on the railings and then dropped backwards fully 12 feet, landed, did a forward roll and sprinted away, all in one move. It was amazing.'

'Freerunners are pretty fearless. I've watched some amazing footage on YouTube,' said Jeff as they walked down to the taxi rank. 'But what the hell were they doing with petrol bombs? What was the point in all of that destruction?'

'Fuck knows,' said Julie, bitterly. 'There's some sodding weird people around, right now.'

'Can you come round ours later? Bring Argie,' said Nick.

'Tricky. Come to mine...'

'...yeah, but I'd rather not run into Mandy,' said Nick. 'Sorry, but you know how it is.'

Jeff, ever practical, shrugged. 'I get you. But she won't be there. She's working half a night shift, and she goes home after those.'

'OK, cool. Yours it is.'

CHAPTER 15

Nick got out of a hot shower.

'Are you decent?' said Julie, coming into the bathroom.

'For you, never.'

'That was the correct reply.'

She sat down on an old wooden chair and put her hands behind her head, looking him up and down, as he dripped water onto the bath mat.

'Are you alright, luv?'

He nodded, grabbing a towel off the radiator. 'Yeah, I'm fine. Why?'

'Good. Give us a look at you.'

'What do you mean?'

'I mean give us a look at you.'

'Why?'

'Never mind why.'

He unwrapped himself from the towel and stood in front of her.

'Is something wrong, or are you just perving?'

'I worry about you.'

'Why?'

'You look a bit thin. There's almost no fat on you.'

She leaned forward and nipped at the skin on his hips and ran her fingers down his abs.

'Do you feel OK?'

'Yeah, like I said, I'm fine.'

But her knitted eyebrows suggested she didn't agree. He looked down at himself.

'Isn't this what I'm normally like?' he said.

She shook her head. 'You're down to a really low body fat percentage, luv. I'm worried about why you've lost weight. I think it's all the stress over Josh. You've been tossing and turning in bed, and not in a good way.'

He rubbed at his wet hair. 'Yeah, well, until they catch this killer,

I don't see the worry abating, really.'

He went and looked at himself in the full-length mirror in the bedroom. 'Christ, Jules, I didn't realise I'd lost that much weight. I've not looked at myself for a while; preening in front of a mirror isn't one of my lifestyle choices. But I can see what you mean.'

She kissed his neck and slapped his bare backside.

'Don't go wasting away on me. I like you meaty.'

'I wasn't lithe enough to catch that petrol bomber.'

'I'm not sure anyone would be. He was incredible. The way he ran over that car was amazing. So light on his feet.'

He began drying himself. 'Yeah, he was a gymnast, alright. I was just thinking how, in some ways, he was like Jenny. She did similar sorts of forward rolls in the middle of her hip-hop dancing.'

'Just what was to be gained by the destruction of the pub and the shops? OK, it made the demo into a big news story, but it won't have done Save The Earth's reputation any good, nor added credibility to their cause.'

He pulled on a sporty grey V-necked t-shirt, socks, underwear and a pair of old jeans, thinking about what she'd said.

'Well, maybe that's why they did it. To make Save The Earth look bad. Have they made any statement about it?'

'I don't know. I'll look it up downstairs.'

'You know what these pressure groups are like, they're often a moderate group, but with a radical faction within them who want to take it over,' said Nick.

'That's what one of the demo blokes said to me and Jeff. They can tend to get quite territorial.'

'Well, no-one is a winner, if you ask me. It was just a bloody stupid thing to do,' said Nick, as they went downstairs to the kitchen.

'Right, let me fix you a drink, luv. What's your poison?' asked Julie.

'Have we got any red wine?'

'Aye, we've got a bottle of Cab Sauv from Kwik Save. The best wine £2.97 can buy.'

'Sounds about my level in the vino market. Give us a big glug of that. It'll give me some extra carbs, from which I might gain a bit of weight.'

'Good thinking. There's frozen spicy potato wedges in the freezer if you fancy some when we get back later.'

'I know. I made them. Trouble is, when you're used to a low-carb life, eating carbs is quite hard work. They make you feel bloated and heavy really quickly. Or they do for me, anyway.'

She unscrewed the cap on the wine. 'We'll just have a livener before the cab arrives. You just need to stop fretting about Josh. It's making your motor run too fast.'

'These jeans are loose now.' He pulled the waistband out.

She stopped and took a look. 'Oh yeah, you've lost about an inch off your waist. Still, at least it'll make it easier for me to get my hand down there. Which is the important thing.' She got a glass from the cupboard, and pointed at him. 'I love an in-trouser feel-up. Reminds me of being a teenager.'

That made Nick laugh. 'Well, you don't need to sell that to me. As you well know, I still believe dry-humping is the finest sex anyone can have.'

'Hey, big man!' said Nick, as Jeff opened his front door.

They did a double high-five and went into his large kitchen.

'I stand before you singed but undefeated,' said Jeff, arms out wide. 'Whisky, gin, vodka or wine?'

'Aye, that'll do: all in the one glass,' said Julie.

They laughed.

'How's your hair?' she asked, as he fixed a drink.

'About half an inch shorter in places. If you'd not been so quick to pour beer on my head, it'd have been a lot worse. Have you seen the local news reports?'

'No, what have they said?' asked Nick.

'Doc Brown's wasn't badly damaged apart from broken windows. Same goes for the other bar and the shops.'

'Any arrests?'

'No.'

'But, do you think the bombers underestimated the police presence?' said Nick.

'Yeah, I do. As an aside to that, Cleveland Police went in heavy with some riot squad because they had intelligence that there was going to be trouble. They arrived early and started breaking up the demo to try and stop anything kicking off, but as it turned out, the trouble hadn't even arrived. As I said to Mandy, the demo crowd were all crusty and hippy types and were obviously shocked by the bombers. The bombers were interlopers. If I ever get my hands on that bloke who threw that bomb, I'll batter the sod. I shit myself. I've never been on fire before, apart from once when I was so stoned, I lit my beard instead of a joint. Tried to smoke it, too.'

'In honour, you should dig out "Burning for You", by Blue Oyster Cult,' said Nick.

'Good call. Or to half-quote Jimi, you can stand next to my fire.'

Argie wandered in with a colouring book.

'Hello Arg,' said Nick, ruffling the lad's long fair hair. He grinned up at him.

'Rainbows are great,' the boy said, pointing to a multi-coloured arc he'd drawn with wax crayons. 'Every colour is in a rainbow. There's nothing that isn't! And you can't see one in the dark.'

He seemed very pleased with this fact.

'You're growing into a little philosopher you, Argie,' said his dad. 'What else have you drawn?' He turned over the page to find a head-like shape coloured in with patches of orange and yellow and red. 'What's this?' asked Jeff, pointing at the image.

Argie took the book off him and with his little index finger pointed at the head. 'The red is thinking hard, the orange is being fed up and the yellow is feeling nice.' He said it like it was obvious.

'That's just brilliant, Arg,' said Nick.

'You're dead good at art, you are,' said Julie.

'Aye, I don't know where he's got that from, I can't even paint a door,' said Jeff. 'Owee son, it's time for your beddy-byes. Say night-night to Julie and Nick.'

He lifted Argie up and carried him upstairs, laughing and giggling as Jeff made silly noises at him.

'He's growing up so quickly. He'll be at school next year. I think he's really bright, y'know,' said Julie. 'What he said there was almost profound. And what a thing to think up - assigning colours to your brain.'

'Yeah, more importantly he seems a happy, self-contained little boy. I hope life doesn't wash that out of him.'

Soon Jeff returned. 'It's amazing. He gets into bed, puts his head on the pillow and it's like someone has flipped a switch. He drops off almost immediately. A year ago it was the exact opposite. Funny things, kids.'

'Will you get his hair cut when he goes to school?' asked Nick. 'It's quite long already.'

'I will if he wants it cut. I won't if he doesn't. I like him with long hair, it gives him a shaggy dog look. He'll probably grow up to hate rock music, tie-dye, long hair and everything else I love, so I'm not letting go of my little freaky-looking boy just yet.'

'Does he have any friends yet?'

'He plays with other kids at nursery, but they don't seem to do friends at this age. I think that's a thing that develops in a year or two. From what they tell me, he's well-behaved and polite and quiet. I like that. That's what I'm trying to instil into him: have some manners and don't be a twat. So important. Working in the shop has taught me that over the years. Just say your please and thank yous, it makes so much difference to the quality of your own life, let alone anyone else's.'

'Well, that's what my mam always told me, "be a nice lad, and have good manners", and she was right,' said Nick, adding, 'It doesn't sound much, but it's a great lesson to learn.'

'Yeah, I'm no fan of the 21st-century progressive parenting. Children should be seen but not heard. When we were kids and were out with the parents, we didn't dare say anything. You just sat there and kept schtum. He can have all the creative expression he wants, but there's no way he should be annoying other people while he's doing it. I'll never be one of those parents who lets their kids run around a cafe or restaurant and gets on everyone's wick.'

'I think you're doing a fine job with him. We were just saying how bright he is,' said Julie.

Jeff nodded. 'I know every parent thinks their kid is going to be a super brain, but the boy has got something. You can see that with his drawings and colourings.'

'The way he related colours to thoughts was amazing,' said Nick. 'In some ways, it's always seemed to me that young kids are smarter than adults. Their wisdom is ignored in the adult world, but it's still wisdom. Didn't Hair Bear used to say that babies are born knowing everything and as you grow up you forget it all?'

'Well, you do if you're stoned out of your box all the time, like HB was. But Arg is growing into himself now, that's for sure. I was thinking yesterday how devastating it must be for those girls' parents to have their kid taken from them at 16. To think that they'll have gone through all the stuff I'm going through with Arg, seen them grow and develop and then...it's beyond appalling.'

'Has Mandy said if they've got any leads?' asked Nick.

'I'll be honest with you, she thinks Josh is likely to be the killer. And that twat Bowes is pushing at her, telling her to arrest him quick, before he kills anyone else. They've got no-one else who even vaguely seems connected to the deaths. Not yet, anyway.'

'But he isn't,' said Nick.

Jeff raised his index finger. 'I know, I'm just telling you why. Right? Don't shoot the messenger. You might as well know why.' He counted the points off on his fingers. 'One. He was friends with Paul. Paul knew all about poisons from his chemistry A-level. He had textbooks in his house about it too and there's some dropper bottles in the shed. They don't know what it is yet. She thinks he made some poison for Josh, to use to get revenge on the girls. Two. Josh spends a lot of time on his own, so doesn't have an alibi for any of the murders. Three. He took those photos of girls and numbered them in the order they're being killed. Starting at 3 with #1 and #2 being in honour of Paul and parents. Four. He's obsessed with girls sexually. Last, all were killed on or near to the old railway track around the same time of day, just after school. And he walks that way home and by his own admission was seen next to the last body.'

He took a drink and looked from Julie to Nick. 'I'll tell you this, if there's no murders in the next few days and Josh is at home and is only going out to walk the dog, Mandy is set to come down hard and arrest him.'

'But that's all circumstantial evidence,' said Nick, feeling a little desperate. 'And pays no regard to what he's like as a boy. It'd mean he was lying to us and Josh doesn't lie. He couldn't maintain a lie. He came to us and confessed what he'd done to Emily. He didn't have to do that. In fact, he wouldn't have done that if he was trying to cover what he'd done.'

'Aye, I get you, like, but Mand just sees that as an elaborate double-bluff and all part of his scheme, because he knew he'd been seen, so he tried to explain it away before it was reported, even though it's not been reported, or not yet, anyway.'

'But Jeff, you know what he's like. He could *not* do this. Why would he?' said Nick. 'He's not crazy, or no more crazy than any other teenager.'

'To be fair, I don't know him like you do. I chat to him in the shop, but that's not knowing someone. You've taken him under your wing, you know him better than any of us, but Mandy would say that just makes you more blind to his crimes.'

'But her case is all circumstantial and supposition,' said Julie. 'There's no hard proof of his involvement in the murders at all. Not one shred of hard evidence.'

'True and that's why he's not been arrested. She doesn't want to be busting an innocent Aspie kid, it'll be bad PR for the force if he's not guilty. But she's just waiting on an opportunity to get a warrant to search his room and his laptop.'

'I'm sure Josh and his mother would volunteer for that to happen just to clear his name, even without a warrant,' said Nick. 'Or he would if I have a quiet word with him. It'd all have to go through me. And we'd both have to be there. Or I can just get his laptop and hand it in. Anything to make this be over.'

Jeff nodded. 'OK, I'll let her know. But I reckon she or Bowes'll just think that's a chance for him to delete anything incriminating.'

'Well, that makes absolutely no sense at all,' snapped Julie, annoyed. 'Because he'd have done that already if he really is that Machiavellian. If he's clever enough to do these murders, he's clever enough to remove all trace of anything incriminating on his computer, isn't he? He's exceptionally computer literate. So what they're saying there is total garbage and I'll tell Mandy so, if needs be.'

Jeff held his hands up. 'OK. Like I say, I'm trying to help, Jules. Don't shoot me, I'm only the big hairy man.'

'What poison has been used?' asked Nick. 'If it's so lethal, where is it now? Where is Josh keeping it? How has it been administered? When could he have administered it? As far as I know, none of the girls disappeared for any length of time. They were just found after school. That suggests it was done quickly sometime after school finished. Unless he's got access to powerful chemical weapons, I don't see how that's possible.'

'Has the specific poison been identified, Jeff?' asked Julie.

'She's not said anything about that, but they think all of the bodies were in the same state and thus were all killed the same way with the same gear.'

'I've read up on this. Some poisons quickly metabolize in the body and don't leave any trace, except for elements you'd naturally find in blood, so you never really know what's done for them,' said Nick.

'It's sodding terrible, the whole thing, from top to bottom. The idea that another girl has to die to prove Josh's innocence, is sick. I can't bear it,' said Julie, rubbing at her forehead. 'And #6 is Jenny. I can't handle the idea that she might die. I...I...I just can't.'

'They are aware of that.'

Julie put her face into her hands.

'Well, no-one has died since Tuesday,' said Jeff. 'Let's hope it stays that way. Let's change the subject. The whole thing is doing my head in and it's making me and Mandy butt heads because I basically agree with you, and I bloody hate us rowing.'

'Sorry to hear that, man,' said Nick.

Jeff waved away his sympathy. 'It's just life. Hey, better news: I won 75 quid, Jules. Your water came through again. It was 1-0 to Birmingham. Bang on the money.'

'I know, it's bloody good water. I felt that one quite strong.'

'It's like a predictive form of cystitis,' said Jeff.

'Exactly like that.'

'Sounds like a shite game, winning goal in the last 10 minutes. It's all a bit desperate. I can't see Mogga getting out of this. If he wasn't a club legend, he'd have been got shot of by now,' said Nick. Julie nodded.

'Gibbo, unlike most chairmen, is loyal to his managers, which is good, but you know what it'll mean. At some point, probably in October, things will have got so bad he'll have to sack Mogga, when really, he should have done it by now. We need a big new change, if you ask me. Maybe get a foreign manager in for the first time. We're treading water and need something new to reinvigorate the club,' said Julie.

'Is this you talking or your water? Because if it's the latter, I'm piling on a big bet.'

'Oh, it's my water. Deffo.'

'Right. I'm blobbing a hundred on that. New foreign Boro manager in October.'

Jeff got up and fixed them more drinks.

'I love it in here. Your kitchen is better than your living room,' said Nick, leaning on the large pine table.

'I know. I spend all my time in here, unless I'm playing records, then I have to go into the music room. I should hook the turntable up to speakers in here, really. Just never seems to be time.'

'How many records have you got in your collection now, then?' asked Julie. 'I know you men like to measure absolutely everything.' She held her hands apart by about a foot.

'God, I have no idea. When I shifted it all up here from Harrogate, the removals people reckoned there were about 12,000 albums, 5,000 CDs and 3,000 singles. How accurate that is, I have no idea. I've got to stop snaffling the best stuff from the shop. This week we got a dead hippy collection in and in there was Caravan, Gentle Giant and Hawkwind's debut records, all first pressings. I mean, "come to daddy", y'know? Can't resist that. Then someone brought in a huge collection of 60s 7-inch singles, in amongst which were some Yardbirds EPs. I mean, I can't resist that sort of thing either, so they went home with me. I should sell the CDs, really. I never play them. Would probably bring 20k into the shop 'cos a lot of them are rare or are box sets, but I just can't face not having sterile little boxes of plastic in my house.'

'I keep saying that. I only need CDs of music not available on vinyl, so I could easily lose 2,000, but I just can't face it. It gives me the Fear.'

'Aye, well, that's because of the great 1989 album collection sale. I told you at the time, you'd regret it.'

Julie laughed. 'You tell this story like it's a relationship break-up when all you did is sell your records.'

'It was profound, man. I should never have done it,' said Nick, shaking his head.

'How much are his records worth now?' she asked Jeff.

'Nick's? Probably 30 or 40 grand.'

'Oh, so it's not worth me killing him to inherit?'

'No. He's worth far more to you to keep as a sex slave. Basically, records are not worth much in the grand scheme of things, even rare ones. We get excited over a record valued at the same price as 12 cans of premium beer or a joint of beef. It's mad really; it's its own little world, which is why we like it, I suppose.'

'Everyone needs a hobby,' said Julie.

'What's yours then, Jules? You don't have one, do you?' asked Jeff.

'Yes I do.' She said, nodding.

'What is it?'

She paused briefly.

'Masturbation.'

She said it in such a dry, flat way that it caught Nick and Jeff off guard, taking a couple of seconds to sink in, before they broke into laughter.

'Surely that's a lifestyle choice, not technically a hobby,' said Nick.

'Aye, you can't collect a wank,' said Jeff. 'And there's a sentence I never thought I'd ever utter.'

Nick's phone vibrated with a text message. It was from Janey James.

'*Can you give me a quick call when you have a spare moment?*'
He turned the phone to Julie.

'Oooh, she'll want you to go round there and service her.'

'Who is this splendidly wanton woman?' asked Jeff.

'Janey James.'

'Ah, yes, a well-upholstered girl, even aged 16.' He did a juggling gesture in front of his chest.

'And still is,' said Nick. 'Though they must be somewhat lower now when unfettered.'

Jeff turned to Julie.

'She was well into him for about two years, on and off. They sat together in English. I used to tell him, but he wouldn't have it. I used to think that he couldn't believe getting a nice, well-breasted girlfriend would be that easy, so he moped around after Shawn Yeadon instead, even though he couldn't even pluck up the courage to ask her out, and despite the fact that he only had to say "let's go out" to Janey and she'd have been all over him like white on rice.'

'Oh, I've heard all about his many failed school romances. He didn't like going out with girls because he couldn't bear the idea of breaking up with them. Mad.'

'Hello! Can anyone hear me?' Nick waved. 'I am still here. I can hear you talking about me.'

'So Janey is a single woman, eh? If me and Mandy fall apart, I wouldn't mind sniffing around her. She was always a nice girl, but I had the feeling she was the sort who might, after a couple of drinks, unfasten her hair, strip naked and give a chap a thorough good seeing to with all available orifices. The quiet girls are always the ones most likely to be swinging naked from the chandeliers at the end of the night.'

'Ha ha...hey, I wasn't a quiet girl and I like a bit of naked chandelier swinging as much as the next horny chick,' said Julie with mock indignation.

'Janey lives in a bungalow, you can't have a chandelier in a bungalow,' said Nick.

Julie laughed. 'No, she'll be straddling the standard lamp, luv. Whatever happened to standard lamps? And why were they standard? And which standard were they judged against?'

'Well, while you two work out that conundrum, I'll give Janey a call.'

He went into the front room.

She answered right away. 'Hello, Nick. Thanks for calling me back so quickly.'

'No worries. How're the Lakes?'

'Oh, we didn't go in the end. It was too cold, they reckoned it was below freezing on the fells, and we both just fancied sitting in and having a few drinks. So we stayed at home.'

The clink of ice was clearly discernable, as she took a drink. Bless her. Most Northern Britons admire someone who can really bloody drink.

'That makes sense. It was cold this afternoon. We had an eventful day in Middlesbrough.'

'Oh, yeah, you were going to the football. Did you see any of the trouble?'

'We were caught up in the middle of it. I chased down one of the petrol bombers, but he got away.'

'Really?!'

'It was horrible, Janey. We were in the pub they firebombed. Jeff caught on fire, but we put him out with the help of lager.'

'Oh, my god, is he alright?'

'Yeah, he's fine. Me and Jules are at his house, right now.'

'Are you? Oh, right.' She sounded a little disappointed.

'So why did you want me to call you?'

The ice clinked again, once, twice. 'I've had an idea...about the murders of the girls.'

'Oh, yeah? What's that?'

'Well, as they were all killed after coming to or leaving 6th form for the day, I looked at the timetables for each of them to see if they had anything in common.'

'And did they?'

Another clink of glass as she took another drink of what Nick assumed was gin and tonic.

'No. Nothing at all. They were all in different classes, all had different teachers, all in different parts of the college.'

'Oh. Right. Well, I'm sure the police will...'

She interrupted him. '...but the one thing, the single one thing they all had in common was...'

Even more ice action. Nick waited patiently. If she needed to drink, he could wait.

'...are you still there, Nick?'

'Yeah, I'm here, Janey.'

'Sorry, the line went quiet.'

'So what was the one thing they had in common?'

'They all had a class, or a club, with Alice Coates, the sports and fitness teacher. Sometimes as part of their extra-curricular activities, others as part of their courses.'

'Really? That is interesting. Jade and Jenny Wells mentioned her. She runs the cross-country team and takes them to competitions.'

'As I told you before, she's very nice. Very competitive, apparently, but then that's the nature of sport, isn't it?'

'Does she have an assistant, or is there another sports teacher that she works with?'

'Yes, that was what I was going say.' She swallowed more drink. 'Geoff Powell is the other sports teacher. He takes the boys for rugby and football, primarily. He's the senior teacher and has a supervisory role to look at the health and fitness of all the kids. He talks to them about diet and exercise. So even if he doesn't teach them, he knows them all.'

'Right. So even if the girls didn't have a class with him, he'd know them?'

'Yes, he has an office next to hers in the same block. If she was taking the girls' basketball club, say, Geoff will still be in and around the place the whole time. He would know every one of those girls who were killed, and more importantly, would have been around when the girls were doing their team training or clubs.'

'What's this Geoff Powell like?'

'Typical sports master. You remember what the male sports masters were like when we were at Ian Ramsey together.'

'Macho bullies and lecherous pervs?'

She made a small laugh. 'Well, yeah. Exactly. And we all thought the females were lesbians who spied on us in the showers.'

'So Powell is lecherous?'

He heard her put the glass down on a table.

'Not like in the 70s when they'd actually take girls out. He's lecherous in a similar way that Mike McGregor is, if you get me. The occasional inappropriate comment, he looks at the girls for just a little too long, will contrive to find a reason to turn and look at their backsides when they pass him in the corridor. That sort of thing. He probably thinks no-one notices, but I notice and I'm sure other women do too.'

'Isn't that how male teachers behave, more generally?'

'No. As I said to you before, you've got to leave all of that behind, and most do, especially the younger teachers who have grown up with this stuff being rule number one in their training. Powell is in his early 40s like McGregor; they still feel entitled to get their jollies looking at pretty 16, 17 and 18 year olds. Just because they don't take it any further, the way they used to in the 70s, they think it makes them innocent. But I don't like it.'

'OK, but how do you go from perving at the girls to being a mass murderer?'

'That, I'm afraid, isn't a question I can answer.'

Nick thought for a moment. 'Can you contrive a reason for me to come into the college, so I can get to talk to Powell and to Alice Coates? I also want to see if I can get from the college grounds to the old railway path without going on Bishopton Road West. Obviously, that'll look a bit weird if I'm just roaming around college grounds, but if I'm with you, it'd look more innocent. That could be the route the killer took, either to kill the girls, or to take them, already dead.'

'Oh, god, just those words make me go cold. Yes, I can come up with some excuse for you to come in on Monday.'

'Does anyone there know Josh is the number-one suspect?'

'No. The police haven't told us anything. So I'm pretty sure that's not generally known. If you'd not told me, I'd not know. One person or maybe more will know, though.'

'Who?'

'Whoever is setting up Josh to look guilty.'

'Ah, yeah. Good point. OK, well, I'll leave that with you, Janey.

If you can come up with a reason for me to speak to them, and then maybe we could take a walk across the grounds.'

'Ok, Nick. Come in at 2pm.'

CHAPTER 16

On Monday, Nick parked the Merc in the Stockton Sixth Form College car park, hitched up his now loose-fitting jeans, wrapped a yellow-and-green silk scarf around his neck and zipped up his leather jacket against a stiff northeasterly. March seemed to be the coldest month these days.

'Hello, Janey.' He stood in the doorway to the college office. She looked up from her computer and smiled.

'Eee, hello, you.'

'It's bitter out today, like.'

'Eee, I know. It's Baltic. I like your scarf. Makes you look like a Swedish student who is youth hostelling across Europe.'

He laughed. 'I do like a silk scarf. You've got a very smart suit on. Really suits you.' She was wearing a charcoal pinstripe.

'Thank you. It's Nicole Farhi.'

He almost said that she had been Julie's favourite designer, when she had been more interested in clothes than she was these days, but stopped himself.

'Should I sign in?' he said, pointing to the visitor book.

'No. Best if there's no hard evidence of you being here, I think. The whole place is very quiet. All the kids are staying away this week. The Head sent out an email to all parents yesterday telling them to stay away.'

'Yeah I had a word with Josh yesterday and he told me. He's happier being in his room, anyway.'

'It's probably for the best. Some teachers are in for half days, doing preparation, marking and other admin.' She handed him a pin-on 'visitor' badge. 'Now, this is your story. You're interviewing George about kids' health and the obesity epidemic, and Alice about the success of the cross-country team. OK? You're a freelance and your articles will be in the *Stockton and Darlington Times*. No-one reads that so when they don't appear, no-one will even notice. I'll say you only want a few minutes of their time.'

'Brilliant. You're good at subterfuge, Janey.'

She gave him a conspiratorial grin. 'You have to be in this place, on a day-to-day basis, just to keep it all running. I saw Alice come in earlier. She's such a hard worker. She's often here even when she doesn't have to be. Come on, I'll take you to the sports block.'

She locked her office. 'Do you remember your way around? she asked.

'I remember where the gym was, but nothing looks familiar. It's all changed so much. Jeff was saying he bets they don't have a smoking room these days!'

She laughed. 'No, I mean, can you imagine? Times really have changed so much since our day.' Her shoes made a click-clack sound as they walked, echoing around the quiet corridors.

'It's spooky without all the kids here,' said Nick.

'I know. I can't wait for things to get back to normal.' They turned down another corridor. 'Alice first?'

'Fine.'

She stopped at a blue door, tapped lightly with a knuckle and opened it. 'Hello, Alice. I've got Nick Guymer here for you. He's a journalist and wants to have a very quick chat about the success of the cross-country side. I said it'd be OK.' That was clever. Effectively, she'd given her no choice but to see him.

'Really. Oh...err...OK, send him in,' said the teacher, as though he was a pupil.

Janey turned back to him. 'Geoff's office is next door. I'll let him know you're here.'

Alice Coates got up as he walked into the small, overly warm office. Wearing black Lycra sportswear and white trainers, she was the epitome of 'sports teacher'. Perhaps in her late 20s at most, at five feet six or so, she was lean but powerful looking with broad shoulders, strong thighs and bulging calves. That had to be all the cross-country running. She made a polite smile but seemed surprised to see him. Probably didn't get many visitors at the moment.

'Come in, Mr Guymer.' She seemed hesitant. Suspicious, almost.

'Call me Nick. Only the police call me Mr Guymer.'

She made a short polite laugh and sat down. 'OK, Nick. What would you like to know?' She sat perfectly still, hands together on her lap. Her eyes flicked over his shoulder to the door, as though she was expecting someone to come in.

'Is it OK if I record this?' he said, holding up his phone. 'My shorthand isn't what it was 20 years ago.'

'I'd rather you didn't. Just take notes.'

She spoke in a terse, but unspecific English voice. Fortunately, he'd brought a notebook with him, but her defensiveness was notable.

'OK, so this is your first year here, I understand.'

'Yes.'

'Did you come from another school?'

'Yes. Well sort of.'

'And where was that?'

For a moment she paused, as though this was something she didn't want to disclose. She just stared at him. Her small glossy pink tongue emerged to lick her lips. Five or six seconds passed before she replied.

'I was a fitness instructor in the army.'

'Wow, that sounds tough.'

'Challenging, certainly.'

'Was that locally?'

'Catterick.'

'So why make the change to teaching?'

'I wanted to be involved in education.'

'So when you came here, you turned the cross-country team into this all-conquering juggernaut? Is that a passion of yours?'

She looked away from him and down at her trainers. There was a tap at the door. She visibly jumped in her seat and stared with wide eyes at the door. 'Yes?'

A bearded man put his head around the door. 'Sorry to disturb, Alice. Ah, Nick Guymer?'

Nick nodded.

'Geoff Powell. I'm next door when you've done. I've just got to nip out for five minutes, let yourself in if I'm not back.'

'Thanks, mate.'

'Sorry to interrupt, Alice.' He held up an apologetic hand.

She just nodded.

'So you've had a lot of success with the cross-country team?'

'Very much so.'

'How did you turn things around?'

'Oh...err...strict training sessions. Measuring results. Improving fitness and stamina.'

'So is it all quite scientific?'

'Very much so. The body is a machine. When you know how yours is set up, you can fuel it to perform far more efficiently.'

'That must take a lot of dedication on the kids' part and on yours.'

She looked back in his eyes. She looked hard and a little soulless. Maybe you had to be in this game.

'Dedication and discipline. Yes. A valuable lesson for them all to learn. The weakest members have simply been weeded out to make the group stronger.'

'So would you say you're quite ruthless?'

She frowned. 'In what way?'

'In a "my way or the highway" sort of way. They either get with your programme or get out.'

She didn't hesitate. 'That's correct. Elite sport has no time for the inadequate or the weak.'

'But you lost poor Emily LeBron. She was one of your runners, wasn't she?'

'She was.' She nodded but didn't look sure.

'What a terrible business these murders are.'

She blinked and nodded again. 'She wasn't...any more questions?'

'She wasn't what?'

'Nothing. I was just going to say, she wasn't the fastest runner, so her loss won't diminish the group's performance.'

That was a weird thing to say, the sort of thing Josh might say - totally lacking in empathy and without any comprehension of how it might be construed. Maybe she was some flavour of Aspie, too.

'So do you run competitively yourself?'

'No.'

'So what are your passions in life, Alice?'

'Passions? What's that got to do with anything?'

'Well, it seems that you're very dedicated to helping the kids get fit and be...'

She interrupted him. 'It's not about just being fit. It's about winning. About learning to win and learning how to be the best. I like winning. I like being in control. These children are growing up in an era where to be second is to be nowhere. They should be prepared for harsh realities.'

Nick wondered what Julie would make of her. She was cold, but then, if it had been a bloke, you'd think nothing of it. Men tend to be emotionally repressed and admired for it, we unfairly hold women to a different standard.

'Have you always liked cross-country?'

She allowed herself a thin, quick smile. 'Orienteering was my passion. Still is.'

'Oh, I remember trying that when I was a pupil here in the late 70s. I was hopeless at it because I can't read maps and don't know my left from my right, half the time.'

'With all due respect, there's no excuse for that. If you won't learn, that shows weakness of character.' She made no expression as she spoke. Again, it seemed unintentionally rude.

Nick looked her in the eyes. 'If you don't mind me saying, that's a strange thing for a teacher to say. We're all different, we all have different qualities. I'm no good with maps, but I'm good with words. We can't all be good at everything.'

But she clearly wasn't impressed. 'Is that all, Mr Guymer? I must be getting on.'

'Yes, thanks, Alice.'

He stood up. She stood up. They looked each other in the eyes one last time, shook hands and he left.

Wow, she really was an ice queen. Jade and Janey had both said she was nice, though. Maybe he'd somehow rubbed her up the wrong way and rather typically not noticed.

He tapped on the next door down.

'Come in.'

Geoff Powell was a kind of throwback to the sort of games master he'd had as a kid. Very much the alpha male, he wore a beard, but not in a fashionable style, and had closely cropped hair. Sitting in a swivel chair, he didn't even bother to stand up, merely leaning forward, hand extended, legs spread wide apart, as though to own the space. He spoke with a broad North Yorkshire accent.

'Now then, Nick. Janey said you wanted to do a piece about how we're working with kids to stop 'em being so fat and get 'em fitter.'

'Yeah, I just had a word with Alice about the cross-country success she's having.'

'Oh, aye.' He picked up a Biro and tapped its nib on his desk. 'What did you reckon to her, then?' he said, not looking at him.

'Very determined. Focused. Reserved.'

'She's a weird one. Sometimes hot, sometimes cold. I call her the Arctic Roll. Sort of hot but sort of cold. Sometimes it's like she's got no blood in her veins. But if you ask any of the kids, they all like her, which is weird, really.'

'Why is it weird? Janey said she was very nice.'

'Yeah, I know. She likes her. She says she's funny. When I work with her, sometimes she's cheerful, sometimes she's stoney. Maybe she doesn't like blokes, if you know what I mean.'

Nick had to make a quick assessment. While he couldn't always read people very well, it seemed very likely that Powell, given his attitude, his body language, and taking what Janey had told him into account was, what is still sometimes called a 'man's man'; in other words, he was an unreconstructed male chauvinist. He gambled that if he played up to that, he'd probably get more out of him.

'Yeah, could be a pipe smoker. Grip like a vice, I reckon, that one.'

Bullseye.

It had the desired effect, immediately. Powell wasn't stupid. He would know fine well what he could and couldn't say in polite society, and especially in the PC school environment. But Nick, having identified himself as one of his kind, could see the teacher visibly relax.

He grinned, revealing an even set of large white teeth.

'You're not kidding. Might need some WD40 and a spanner, to get in there,' he laughed and stretched out his legs and put his hands behind his head.

Nick knew exactly how to play this. 'Aye, no chance of losing your watch down there, eh.'

That made Powell laugh heartily and grip his wrist. 'Ha ha, no. Unlike my ex-wife. Where's me watch gone, luv?!' He rocked on his chair in laughter. 'I'll just get me mag light and I'll go and have a look for it. Ha ha ha. No, I think it'd be like a sparrow's arsehole, wouldn't it?'

It was weird talking like this. It made Nick feel uneasy.

'So do you not get on with her?'

Geoff shrugged. 'She's young and new. Sometimes she's full of ideas and really upbeat, other times it's like she doesn't give a shit. The job can do that to you, though. Anyway, what can I do for you, Nick? Do you want a coffee, by the way?'

It was a chance for a bit more alpha male behaviour. 'No, I'm fine. I could use a vodka, to be honest. The stress of coming down here is getting to me.'

'You mean them murders? Fucking disgraceful, if you pardon my French. I mean, what the hell are the police doing? There was loads of them around here for a couple of days, but where are they now? They're bloody useless. How can someone kill three girls just like that? In broad daylight! And leave them in a public place? How can they do that? It beggars belief. The police are shit, if you ask me. Half of them that came here were fucking thickos. You despair.' He seemed genuinely angry.

'Did you know the three murdered girls? Did you teach them?'

'I only take the lads, Ice Cube Tits in there takes the girls, but I do nutrition and exercise lectures for all the kids, so they were in for those. All three were what we used to call good-time girls. All proper shaggers from what I overheard. They didn't deserve what 'appened to them. I mean, it sickens me to my bloody guts.'

He spoke with real and convincing passion.

'So who the hell is doing it, do you reckon?'

He pulled open the bottom drawer of his desk and took out a half bottle of whisky and two glasses. 'Fancy one? There's sod all to do here, really.'

'Aye, go on,' said Nick, partly to keep him onside, partly because he really did feel like a drink.

'No ice, I'm afraid,' said Powell, pouring two good belts of Glenmorangie.

'No bother, man.'

'Right, well, cheers, Nick. Good to meet you.' He clinked his glass against Nick's.

It was a smooth, flowery, delicious hit of powerful booze.

'That's a nice drop, Geoff.'

'Aye. Don't tell anyone you had it here. Bit of a no-no.'

Nick made a mouth-zipping gesture.

'What I don't understand is why the girls that were killed were all in the same form. Janey said they were all in Mr McGregor's.'

Powell shook his head. 'I have no idea.'

'So what's McGregor like, then?'

'He's a prick,' said Powell, taking a drink and wincing at the powerful whisky. As he said *prick* spit flew out his mouth, because he said it with such force.

'Yeah?'

'Yeah. He's a perv, isn't he? Fucking disgraceful. Blokes like him should be banned from teaching kids.'

'Is he? What does that mean exactly?'

'Oh, every school or college I've ever worked at has one.'

'What does he do, like?'

'Oh, he doesn't *do* anything. He's too much of a ponce for that. He's the sort to get a crush on one of his girls. It's pathetic.' He warmed to his theme. 'Look, look, any red-blooded man would sneak a look at some of the lasses here. They come in all tits and arses. Tight leggings and jeans. Sports gear. I mean, come on. They tell you to leave all of the sex stuff outside, but that's going against nature. You can't. You know as well as I do that we all do it, even if we don't admit it. We're programmed to look at a nice pair of tits or whatever, even if she's 16.'

Nick couldn't allow himself to agree with something he so profoundly disagreed with, not even in these circumstances, so took a swerve on it. 'I can see what you mean.'

Powell raised his finger. 'But...OK, you cop an eyeful when maybe no-one's looking, but that's it. Nothing else. Anything else would be 100 per cent wrong. Only a sicko twat would take it further. But McGregor is a toucher, isn't he?'

'A toucher? You mean he touches girls sexually?'

'No no. He's all about a hand on the small of the back, a hand on a bare forearm, on a thigh, or around the waist. That's all so wrong, in my book. In my opinion, he's a weirdo, and by the way, I can imagine him killing a lass.' He jabbed a finger at Nick, as he took a hit of whisky.

'What? Really?' Nick leaned forward. 'Are you serious?' he said, remembering Jenny had said something similar.

'Oh, yeah. He's a coward, is McGregor. A wimp. The *Gazette* said last night that the lasses were poisoned. That's just his style. He couldn't commit an act of violence, but he could do something snide like poisoning.'

'Have you told the police that?'

He gave Nick a big sneer. 'Have I fuck as like.'

'OK, but why not?'

Geoff cracked his knuckles. 'Look Nick, I could give the coppers a list of all the shite people who work here, but it's just *my* view of them. I've no proof against anyone, have I? And I have no idea why McGregor might want to kill anyone, unless he's just bloody cuckoo, but I don't think he is. Also he's deputy Head, so if I tell them he's a perv, later when this is all over, if he turns out to be not guilty, that'll come back to bite me.'

Nick took a drink and thought for minute.

'What do you think of Janey in the office?'

Geoff poured himself another single malt. Nick turned it down.

'Janey? She's the star of this place, she keeps the whole place functioning, but sadly, the bloody bosses have no idea that's the case.'

'I used to go to school with her. Came here with her, actually. She does seem really good at her job.'

'She is. And she's got great tits, let's not forget those wonderful

229

puppies. She's a divorcée and is probably gagging for it.'

Divorcée? Who said that word in the 21st century? Geoff was really so old school.

'Why was it those three girls killed, do you think?'

'No idea. Like I say, I think it's McGregor. He's probably killing the ones who wouldn't let him feel them up. Disgusting.' He paused again and drained his glass. 'Those lasses had a reputation. It could be a sex thing with him. It really could.'

Nick nodded. 'Hey, do you know Josh?'

'Josh? Oh, yeah, he's a spaz kid, isn't he? Do you know him?'

'He's Asperger's, not a spaz, Geoff. Get your abusive terminology right. Yeah, I do. I'm a good friend of his. I look out for him. His parents divorced and took their hands of his wheel. He's very bright, but struggles with fitting in and doing the right thing, sometimes. But he's a lovely lad. OK?'

Powell held up his hands in apology.

'Sorry, Nick. I wasn't taking the piss. Sorry, I should watch my language. Yeah, I know the lad. Good at basketball. He never gives me any grief. And he's a very fit lad and pretty strong. A good runner. He's not one I need to get to lose weight.'

'Yeah, he's in good shape. So he doesn't give you any grief?'

'No. He gets the piss taken out of him, sometimes, because he's not your normal boy. I like him. He's a nice lad, you can tell that. Mad about girls, but they all are at his age.'

'Yeah, I know. But that's good to hear you like him. So let's talk about fitness, Geoff. You run this diet and exercise class.'

'I devised it. It's a programme. They've let me run it across the whole two years. There's so many bloaters these days, we need to stop them pushing crisps into their face and drinking pop all the time. There's literature available for parents on how to feed their children.'

'It amazes me that this even needs doing.'

'Yeah, well, loads of parents are bloody idiots. It's not said enough, in my opinion. Idiot parents are the problem and all the liberal hand-wringers want to excuse them for just being shit. You've got the bloody internet, do some learning, you dumb get. That's what they should be told. But they won't, they just let them eat sweets and processed food. It's child abuse. It is. It's child abuse.' He sat back after jabbing his finger in the air. 'Sorry, I get passionate about this. Kids are kids. They don't know sod all, but their parents who feed them crud are absolute twats in my view and that's why I started the nutrition and exercise class, to try and beat some good information into the kid's brains and bypass the fat, idiotic parents.'

His language was, to say the least, uncompromising, and ironically would have made a great article.

'What sort of info do you give them, George?'

He ran his hand over his closely cropped hair.

'I keep it simple. No point in going into too much biology. I tell them to largely ignore what they've been told about so-called healthy eating by the NHS. That's full of shit. They've got the so-called Eat Well plate which is basically a carb bomb and exactly why everyone is a fat sod these days. It tells them to base their diet on carbs. That's wrong. We know that now. So I tell them to lay off sugar and fruit juice, don't worry about fat, eat more butter and protein. Only have more carbs if you're really physically active.'

Nick laughed. 'I totally agree. I've been low carb for a few years now. I was pretty fat and it sorted me out really well.'

'Oh, yeah, it'll do that for most people. And you look in brilliant shape, Nick. You must do weights as well.'

'Yeah. Just at home with free weights. I've put on loads of muscle just doing that. It's taken years, though.'

'In rugby training we low carb between games, high carb directly after a game to put glycogen back into the muscles. But we've bred a generation of fat kids by telling them not to eat fat. It's bloody perverse!'

Nick found himself warming to George. He seemed to really care about the kids. Yes, he was un-PC, loud and crude, but he had their welfare at heart and by contrast, when he'd met him, he doubted Mike McGregor did.

'I think it reprograms your body. I struggle to put weight on now. Because of all the worry over Josh, I've lost some weight and I'm probably well under 10 per cent fat now and I think that's too low when you're not an athlete. It leaves you open to infections.'

'Why are you so worried about Josh? He's not ill, is he?'

Shit. The fact he was prime suspect wasn't common knowledge. Should he tell him? He took a chance. A big chance.

'George...' he cleared his throat '...don't tell anyone this, but Josh is pretty much the primo suspect for the murders.'

The colour drained from the sports teacher's face. His bottom jaw dropped open.

'You are fucking shitting me!' His voice was raised again. 'How do you know?'

'I can't tell you that. But it is true. They can't prove it yet, but they're trying to and don't have any other suspect at all.'

Powell stood up and went to his window looking out on playing fields. He was shaking his head, as though he'd taken a blow in a boxing match. Nick heard him blow out air and then suck in a deep breath through his nose, before turning around.

'No, no, no, I'm not 'avin that. That's bloody rubbish. Is that the police's best effort? Fuck off!' He made a dismissive gesture with his arm, as though knocking the idea away with an invisible tennis racket. 'How? Why?'

'It's all circumstantial. He...he took photos of the girls in his class, on the quiet, while they were doing sports. He numbered them on the back according to how much he fancied them and they've subsequently been killed in that order.'

'Bloody hell fire. Are the photos dirty?'

'No, not at all. He just likes to look and...' he made a masturbating gesture.

'...yeah yeah, I get you. That's normal teenage boy stuff. We have to virtually stop some of them having one off the wrist in the showers. So is someone framing him? Did they get hold of the photos?'

'I saw them in McGregor's office. But they'd been taken from Josh's locker.'

'McGregor again. See? He's a wrong 'un.' Powell jabbed a finger, then shook his head and sat back down heavily.

'Have you seen anyone behaving weirdly? Any suspicions at all?'

asked Nick.

'Literally none.' He knocked down the last of his whisky. 'But what does a child murderer look like?'

'I just need a break. One bit of evidence to disprove Josh's guilt, one bit of evidence to at least suggest it could be someone else. But whoever has done this has gone about it with a ruthless efficiency. The girls' bodies, and the Richardsons', had been almost respectfully laid out, arms by their sides. They haven't just collapsed.'

Geoff scratched his dark brown beard. ' "Respectfully"? That's a weird word to use about a murderer. You don't respectfully murder someone.'

But as he said that, a lock dropped in Nick's mind. Not the only lock to the door that had the murderer behind, but an important one nonetheless. He made a conscious choice not to tell Geoff Powell anything more.

'Well, thanks for your help, Geoff. I'll write this piece up to highlight the good work you're doing. It seems important.'

They stood up. 'Cheers, Nick. I'll look out for it. The Stocky and Darlo *Times*, is it?"

'Err...yeah...hopefully.'

'OK, well good luck.'

Janey was sitting at her computer when Nick walked back into the office. She looked up with a smile.

'There you are. How did it go?'

He thrust his hands in his pockets and thought for a moment.

'Alice was pretty frosty. Didn't say much. She's seems quite tough-minded.'

Janey frowned. 'Really? Are you sure?'

'What do you mean?'

'Well, that doesn't sound like her. She's always cheerful with me. She's dedicated to her work, but...'

'...hang on, that *was* Alice Coates, though, wasn't it? I mean, you saw her.'

'Well, yes, it was. Of course. How could it be anyone else?'

Nick sat down and put his fingers together in a pyramid. 'Geoff

Powell said she was frosty with him sometimes. Calls her the Arctic Roll because sometimes she's warm and sometimes cold.'

She flicked the switch on the kettle. 'Well, he would. He's a sexist boorish dickhead. Any woman who isn't tarted up with her tits out, probably seems frosty to him. He probably thinks I'm a lesbian.'

'Hmm. He's certainly an alpha male. Sits with his legs apart.'

'I hate that. Probably got nothing to show off in that department, anyway. Usually the way of it.'

Nick smiled but was deep in thought. Something wasn't right somewhere. Coates was a bit of a cold fish with him, but Janey and the girls thought otherwise. It had to be for a reason. Maybe she just didn't respond well to men. If so, fair enough. He couldn't blame her for that, given the way the world was.

'Thanks for helping me, Janey. I really appreciate it. Now, I've got to go across the fields and see if it's possible to get from the back of the college to the old rail track footpath where the bodies have been found.'

'I'll come with you, so it doesn't look odd. I can make out I'm showing you around the grounds as a visitor, if anyone asks.' She looked around herself. 'Oh, bugger it, I'll lock up, let's get going.'

She threw on a woollen overcoat and they went out the main door. As they were doing so, Alice Coates came up behind them and Janey held it open for her.

'See you, Alice!' she called out cheerfully, but Alice just ran off in the direction of Bishopton Road West, seemingly totally ignoring her.

Janey stopped and watched her go. 'That's odd. She's normally chirpy.'

'Well, she wasn't chirpy when I met her. She gave me the creeps a bit, to be honest. There was something cold and distant about her.'

'Funny. I suppose she does have rather chilly moods occasionally. Maybe it's just her time of the month. Right, let's go around the back of the gym. Oooh, that sounds a bit naughty. All sorts of things always went on behind the back of the gym at Ian Ramsey, remember?'

It was the sort of remark that Julie would routinely make; in fact, in some ways, they were very similar women.

She considered. 'Actually, we can't get to the back of the gym from here. We'll have to go out the fire doors. Let's just go this way first.'

She led him past the Stockton Town F.C. building, towards St Bede's school next door, taking a path out onto a large expanse of grass. To their right was a running track, the rest of it was marked out as four or five football pitches.

'Stop a minute, Janey,' he said.

She pushed a strand of hair off her forehead, as a cold wind whipped across the open space.

'What is it?'

He pointed in the distance. 'See beyond the undergrowth and bushes? That's a bank of scrub land which leads down to the old railway line and paths where, at one location or another, the three bodies were found. Now, one thing is clear, there's no way anyone could get away with carrying a body, even if it was in a bag or whatever, across this open space without anyone noticing. And you certainly couldn't do it three times.'

She dug her hands in her coat pockets and looked 360 degrees around her. 'You're right. If it was done at the college there's no way they're coming over here, it's just too exposed. Let's go back into the college and out the back fire doors.'

They retraced their steps, went inside and through to the actual gymnasium. Nick pushed at the metal bar and opened the door outwards and stood outside. Janey pushed it shut and stood alongside him.

She pointed into the middle distance. 'That's a housing estate and look, there are informal footpaths running down this bank and around the end of the housing estate. The fields are up that bank. This is a lot more protected if you were trying to get a body out.'

They walked down a slope onto a path through some landscaped trees and bushes and emerged on to Ashmead View and a new, smart, red-brick housing estate.

'There's no way they could have come through here with a body without being seen,' said Nick. 'Let's go around the other side.' They went back to the footpath and took left around the last house.

'This is it! This is how they've either done it or have gone unnoticed,' said Nick. 'This is perfect.'

He pointed at a long straight strip of scrub land. Walkers had made a path in the grass. It was set down from the football pitches above, but also hidden from the back of the houses by a fence. Walking down it they were soon beyond the pitches, into more landscaped scrub, then took a right and within two minutes were at the old railway track.

'From here you can get to where the bodies were found without ever having to go on a road, and you're protected from sight by greenery on either side of the cutting made for the railway,' he said.

'And it's quiet, too,' added Janey, looking around. 'So we know it is possible. What we don't know is if that really is how it was done. I still think carrying a body of a teenage girl is a real effort to go to. Would you really get away with not being seen three times?'

'Maybe they were seen, but nothing looked amiss.'

'How can nothing look amiss when you've got a body in a bag or rolled up in something?'

'Maybe they looked like landscape gardeners and had the body in a green big bag in a wheelbarrow, so people thought it was just some compost.'

She scrunched her face up. 'Nah, it still beggars belief. Witnesses would come forward. But what it does show is that you could get from the college to the cycle path without going on the road. I think that's important. Come on. If we walk up here we'll come to Bishopton Road West, which is my way home.'

'Oh, are you walking? I assumed you'd be in a car.'

'I used to. My new regime is to walk, just to get exercise. I'm sat on my fat arse all day as it is.'

'It's not a fat arse, Janey.'

'It's fatter than Julie's, judging by that photo you showed me.' She said it too quickly, as though it had been on her mind. He felt guilty again for showing her that photo.

'It's not a competition, man. They're two fine arses and believe me, I'm an expert in arse aesthetics.'

They walked slowly along the track. 'Are you now? Is that your special little thing?' she asked, smiling.

'I'll have to take the fifth on that.'

'I'll take that as a yes, then.'

They walked past the spot where Emily LeBron had been found. It was still sealed off with a white tent and guarded by an officer.

'Well, I've got to go back to the car park to pick up my Merc. Do you want to come with me and get a lift home?'

'No, you're OK. I'd better walk. It's not that far.' She turned to face him. 'It's nice spending time with you, even though it's in such terrible circumstances. It's good to have you in my life again, even if it's just briefly.'

As he reached the Mercedes, he stood for a moment, admiring it. It was so clean and silver and sleek. He was just about to get in when he noticed a figure coming out of the college; it was Alice Coates again. Now dressed in grey, she must have gone back for something, she now she had a small rucksack on her back. She messed with something on her wrist, a heart monitor maybe. And off she sprinted onto Bishopton Road West and went left. Nick got in the car and turned over the engine and pulled out left onto the road and kept her in sight. Bloody hell, she was fast, probably going at about 10mph, judging by how fast he closed on her going at 20mph.

But she wasn't on the road long, turning off down the same track he and Janey had just walked up. He slowed down and watched her disappear, heading south. Driving on, at the first opportunity he parked on the side of the road, took out his phone, found Google Maps and typed in Stockton-on-Tees. Getting in as close as possible, he traced the path she'd gone down. Fully paved, it came out on a bend in Darlington Road, just beyond his old teenage drinking haunt, the Stockton Arms, then continued as worn mud or sand path into open country, heading south to Preston Farm Industrial Estate, seemingly just petering out under the A66, though it could just have dwindled to a narrow pathway through fields, invisible to the Google Earth camera. It meant you could leave town and only have to cross one road.

Throwing the phone onto the passenger seat, he accelerated away to the junction with Fairfield Road, took a left and gunned the Merc down to Greens Lane and onto where it joined Darlington Road, with Julie's workplace on his right. Left again, he looked at his watch. He'd done it in three minutes, was he in time to see her emerge and where would she go? It was just under a mile and a half. She'd have to be doing an almost Olympic pace to have beaten him, but she had a head start while he'd looked it up on the phone.

He didn't have to wait long. A few seconds later, she came out, still doing a good pace, not even breaking stride to cross the road and disappear down the track on the other side. The fact she was obviously very familiar with the tracks where the girls were found - Jade had said they used them for cross-country training - made him feel suspicious of her, but surely that was ludicrous. She wasn't a murderer. It was surely some pervy bloke like McGregor who got his kicks by snuffing out teenage lives. It's always a pervy bloke who kills girls.

Still, the fact was, she could traverse Stockton at speed, being fit and so fast, and she could do so without ever being caught on a CCTV camera, because there weren't any on the tracks. It was an undeniably great way to get around town anonymously, which surely had to be why the girls' bodies were left there.

It was 4.20pm. He drove around to the Teesside Women Centre and parked next to Julie's mid-blue Porsche, got out and leaned on the boot until she knocked off at 4.30. Soon she emerged, pulling on her bike jacket, chatting to a short woman with shoulder-length, straight brown hair.

He gave her a wave.

'Hello, you. What are you doing here? Is everything alright?' said Julie as she approached.

'Fine, yeah. I was just in the area.'

She turned to the other woman. 'You've not met Nick, have you, Julie?'

'No. But I recognise him from the picture on your desk, Jules. Hello, Nick.' She smiled a wide smile showing even teeth.

'Hiya.'

'Julie is also a Julie,' said Julie. 'What's the collective noun for a gathering of Julies?'

'Err...that'd be an intimidation of Julies.'

The two women laughed.

'Right, I'm off. I'll see you tomorrow, Jules,' she said, waving a goodbye to them both. Julie turned to Nick.

'So how come you were sniffing around my parts?' She yukked a laugh.

'It's a long story, but I've got a couple of ideas about the murders. I want us to go and see Josh together.'

'What? Now?'

'Yeah. Not for long, then we'll go home and I'll cook us one of my special cheese, bacon, sausage and black pudding omelettes.'

'What do you want to talk to Josh about?'

'First, I just want to make sure he's OK and not going batshit crazy. Then I want to ask him about some of his teachers, especially McGregor the form master, Powell the games master and Alice Coates, who takes him for basketball. I'll explain it all later.'

They drove the short distance up Greens Lane, onto Fairfield Road, left on Lealholme Grove, right up Palm Grove. Even though he'd left home over 30 years ago, the route was burned into his DNA. Julie parked in front of Josh's house, Nick just behind. It was still some shade of spooky to see the house he'd grown up in, now housing a new family, creating a new, and hopefully happier history within its four walls.

Nick rang the doorbell and waited, unsure if Josh was in and if he was, would he bother to answer the door? No-one answered, so he left Julie at the front and walked down the pathway on the right of the house, to the garden at the back.

Josh's room light was on. The fact it shared a wall with his old bedroom still freaked him out.

'Josh! Josh!' Nothing.

He probably had headphones on, so he picked a small clog of mud from the border and lobbed it at the window. As soon as he did so, he saw the head of Stanley, the wire-haired terrier, appear, looking to see what had made the noise on the window. He wasn't a big dog, so he must be standing on a chair to even reach the window.

Nick waved at the dog, wondering if he would recognise him. The dog saw him waving but didn't bark. He wasn't the barking sort. A more placid dog, you'd never find. He tossed another lump of mud. Finally, that brought Josh to the window. Nick waved at him. 'Open the door, Josh!'

By the time he got to the front, Josh was already at the door.

'Hello, Julie! Hello, Nick! Have you come to see me?' he said, happily.

'Of course we have. Who else would we have come to see?' she said, giving him a peck on the cheek as they walked in.

Nick put his arm around Josh's shoulder. 'Are you feeling OK?'

'Yes. It's been great.'

'What has?' said Julie as they stood in the narrow hallway.

'Being in my room. No hassles. I love it. But I like that you're here. You look great, Julie. Your hair's great.'

'Thank you. You do seem perky.'

'This is when I offer you tea, isn't it?'

'Yes. Let's all have some green tea,' said Nick.

'I can make that happen,' said Josh, raising a finger and going into the kitchen and filling the kettle.

'Is your mother still at work?' asked Nick.

'Yes. She's working late and won't be back until after nine.'

Nick wondered if she really was working or if she wasn't just getting laid by one of her, apparently many, intimate male friends.

'Let's have these in my room,' said Josh as he poured the hot water onto tea bags. 'I don't like it down here.' It did seem cold, unloved and unlovely.

As they walked in, Stanley jumped down off the chair by the window and came up to Nick, his tail wagging.

'Now then, Stan. How are you, old boy?' He got down on his hunkers and gave the dog a proper tickle and stroke. There was an extra touch of grey to his blotchy fur these days. He had to be well into double figures now.

'How old is Stan now, Josh?'

'12. That's 84 in dog years. He's really old. He could die soon.'

'Don't say that Josh. He's got years yet,' said Julie, perching on the side of his single bed, noting as she did so the used tissues on the floor beside the bed and visibly shuddering.

'He could do. Terriers often get to 16, but he might not. You never know. Animals die all the time.' He was right of course, but it was a typically Asperger's, overly logical way to look at a much-loved pet.

'So, what have you been up to?' Nick sat down alongside Julie. Josh took his position at his workstation on his black cloth swivel chair. His laptop was on the desk.

'It's been great. I've been in touch with everyone on Skype. Everyone is shit scared of being killed, understandably. People like being alive. Honestly, I think I'd learn more just being in here. You waste so much time at school. Even just going there wastes time, I've got loads more done just getting out of bed and sitting here and working.'

'What have you been working on?' asked Nick.

The lad swivelled around in his chair and tapped at his keyboard.

'Statistical probability. It's absolutely fascinating.' Suddenly, he was the older Josh mode. Talking like a student in his 30s. He held the computer up to them. It displayed a spreadsheet of incomprehensible figures. 'It's amazing how, when you build probability into any cause and effect, you can almost always predict the outcome. No matter what it is. It is as though there are immutable laws of the universe and when you unlock those doors of perception, everything appears as it is: infinite.'

Nick laughed. 'I didn't know you'd been reading Aldous Huxley,' he said, recognising the quote.

'*The Doors of Perception* was on that reading list you gave me.'

'Oh yeah, I forgot. That was about two years ago.'

'I'm still working my way through it, but there's only so much time in any day for reading in between school work, dog walking and masturbation.' He put the laptop down on the desk. Nick and Julie looked at each other, amused. He was just stating things as they were, not even trying to be funny.

'Well, it all looks very complicated.'

The lad made a face at him. 'It's not that hard. If I can understand it, anyone can.'

'No, you're actually super clever, Josh,' said Julie.

The boy turned back to his laptop. 'And something great has happened,' he said.

'Oh, yeah, what's that?' said Nick.

'Me and Heather Leary have been talking about her drone business by Skype. You know what is weird? Talking to her on Skype is really easy, talking to her in real life is really difficult and embarrassing and I can't speak properly sometimes. Why is that?'

Julie grinned at him. 'It's probably because you're one step removed via the technology, so you don't feel so exposed or pressured.'

He sat upright, drummed hands on his lap and looked into the middle distance.

'Yes! That makes sense. I can't touch or smell her. It's less intimidating. You're so clever, Julie.'

She smiled broadly back at him.

'Is she setting up a drone business, then?' said Nick.

'Yes.' He reached across his desk and picked up a small object and handed it to Nick. 'What do you think this is?'

He looked at it closely. 'This looks like the sort of small pen you'd get at Argos. Smaller, if anything.'

'I know, but it's not. It is one of Heather's prototype drones. She built it. It's amazing. She lives on Bedale Grove, half a mile away. She flew it here and in through the open window. And no-one would ever know, because it's so small. You can barely see the propellers. She's calling it the Bee because it looks like a bumble bee.'

Nick looked at Julie in amazement and passed it to her. 'That's incredible.'

'How did she fly it here?' asked Julie.

'It's got a GPS and a lens built in. She stood in the fields at the back of her house with the controls, then used a camera feed to her phone in order to guide it in through the window.'

'Bloody hell. This is incredible. Don't such things already exist?' said Nick.

'They do but not to such a high spec, or quite that small. She's getting a patent on all the electronics. Her dad is sorting it all out.'

'The possibilities both invasive and positive, are endless,' said Julie, handing it back to the lad.

'She's amazing. And I actually think she might like me.'

'I'm sure she does. Why wouldn't she? You're a nice lad,' said Julie, with a smile. In response, Josh just pulled his cross-eyed face, then laughed.

'Josh, what do you think of Alice Coates - Miss Coates, your basketball club coach?' asked Nick.

'What do I think of her?'

'Yeah. Do you like her?'

'Yes. She's says nice things to you even when you've been shit.'

'So you find her warm?' said Nick

'I've never touched her. But she's probably warm.'

'I didn't mean that. I meant you find her sympathetic and friendly?'

'Oh. Yes. Warm. Sorry, I forgot. I like her. She's really good. She helps you get better without making you feel bad about yourself. Unlike some teachers.'

'And what about Mr McGregor? Do you like him?'

Josh just stared at him blankly. 'I have nothing to say about him.'

'Why not?'

'Because he's just there. He's...he's nothing. Just a teacher.'

'Is that how most kids feel about him?' asked Julie.

'No.'

Josh could drive you crazy. He would just answer a question and not elaborate unless you asked him to. It was all so much hard work, sometimes.

Nick leaned forward. 'Who doesn't feel like that?'

'Girls.'

'Girls? And why is that?'

'I don't know why. I'm not a girl.'

'What do girls say about him?' asked Julie, sensing the way the conversation was going.

Josh looked at her wide-eyed and held up two fingers, touching each finger to make a point. 'One. He stands too close to them. Two. He touches them on the arm, back or hand. They say it's creepy. I don't really know what that means exactly, but I know it's not a good thing.'

'Why haven't you told me this before? It could be very important,' said Nick.

'You didn't ask me this before.' In Josh's world of logic that was perfectly sensible.

'But he was OK with you?' said Nick.

'What does that mean?'

'He didn't do anything to annoy you?'

'Yes, he did.'

'What did he do?'

'He ignored me. He ignores the lads. He's only interested in the girls.'

Julie rolled her eyes at Nick.

'OK, what about Geoff Powell? Do you like him?' asked Nick.

'No. He's a fucking cunt,' said Josh, immediately and without pausing for thought. He could say extremely emotional things without emotion, and that was always a bit disconcerting.

'Sorry, I swore, but he's a fucking twat...sorry, I swore again, but he is a cunting, shitting fucker.' He began laughing, throwing his head back and laughing loudly, caught up in the rudeness of the words.

They let him settle down for a minute.

'I know you're being all serious and adult with me. But I'm still a kid who finds swearing funny. And I think I should be allowed to.'

'Yeah, but you do know that in saying that, it means you're not,' said Nick. 'You've got to have an older, outsider's perspective in order to say that.'

'Oh. Right. Fucking hell.'

'Yeah, OK Josh, that's enough now. Don't push your luck,' said Julie, pointing at him, in disapproval. 'A bit of swearing is OK but don't get crude, it doesn't suit you.'

Josh blushed and looked away, knowing he'd overstepped the mark.

They sat quietly for half a minute.

'Sorry, Julie. I get weird ideas in my head. Obsessions and I can't let them go and then I go over the top. It must be part of my...' he vibrated his hands on either side of his head '...my head thing.'

Nick leaned forward. 'Josh, if the police come and interview you, promise me you won't say that to them. They'll get the wrong idea. Do you understand? You don't have to lie to them, but just don't say you get obsessions and go over the top, right?'

The lad looked at him with his pretty almond-shaped eyes and then pointed. 'Ah, I see. Because that sounds like a mad loony who might who kill girls.'

'Exactly,' said Julie.

'Well, maybe I am,' said Josh.

'Don't say that, either,' said Nick.

'Have there been any murders since I've been on my own, in here? No. Maybe that's why.'

Again he was flat and emotionless and, for the first time, quite creepy.

'It's not something to joke about,' said Nick.

'It really isn't, Josh,' added Julie.

'I'm not joking.'

'But you haven't killed anyone, Josh,' said Nick, patiently.

'Well, you say that, but I ran the statistical probability calculations and it looks pretty certain that I did. Only an idiot wouldn't think so.' He turned back to his laptop, tapped at the keyboard and then passed it to Nick. It showed a graph with two curves intersecting at one point.

'I can't understand this, I'm rubbish at maths,' said Nick, passing it to Julie, who scrutinised it.

'Basically, what it's saying is that you tick all the boxes for most of the variables and unknowns. Is that right?' she said.

'Yes. That's right, Julie. That proves it's more likely to be me, than it is to be anyone else.'

'But surely you can prove anything with statistics,' said Nick.

'That is a cliché often said by people who don't know anything about mathematics. What you really mean is that statistics can be interpreted and presented with bias, but the actual numbers are immutable.' He was in full college professor mode now.

'OK, what I mean is, you've found a statistical way to prove your guilt, but you're not guilty, are you?'

'I trust numbers more than I trust humans, or myself. Numbers don't mess you around. They don't insult you or make you feel bad. Numbers don't make you cry and make your brain want to explode. Numbers don't make you so confused that you don't know how to behave.'

Nick tried not to show it, but he was horrified to hear him talk like this. And it was obvious what the police would make of it. Vic Bowes would just haul Josh off to the station if he said these words in front of him. It sounded like, for all the world, Josh wasn't in control of himself and didn't know what he had or hadn't done. It sounded like he was a crazy loner. And the killings had stopped, he was right.

For the second time, Nick had maybe 0.5 per cent of doubt in his mind of Josh's innocence.

'But there's statistics and there's actual real life, isn't there? Likelihood isn't the same as fact, Josh,' he said. 'You didn't kill anyone.'

'I know what you're saying. But I can't prove I didn't and, it sounds to me like at some point I've got to prove something which can't be proven. And in those circumstances, likelihood is the only thing the police have to go on. I've sat here and thought it all through at length. I know I freaked out when Mandy Beale and that detective inspector had a go at me, but I can now see her point of view. The data all points one way.'

Julie pushed a strand of hair behind her ear. 'But you do know you didn't kill the girls. You would remember doing it. Or at least you'd remember having the thoughts about wanting to do it, and, as far as I can tell, you don't. You'd have told us if you did. You told us what you did to Emily.'

'But that doesn't matter. It looks highly probable I did it, and unless I have hard evidence I didn't, which I don't, then I am likely to be thought guilty.'

He spoke calmly and rationally.

'OK, let's go at this from another angle,' said Nick, taking the laptop from Julie. 'What is the weakest chain in the link to prove you're guilty? What is the least likely event?'

Josh leaned over and pointed with a long, slim finger at a green dot on the screen. 'Access to the poisons that killed the girls. It's hard to get that sort of thing. But that is offset by my association with Paul Richardson who was brilliant at chemistry and could have sourced the relevant chemicals and given me the recipe, so to speak.'

Julie stood up and looked at the screen. 'But you know what, Josh? See your list on the left of the graph which itemises all the points to do with the murders, you've missed off something fundamental which skews all your other numbers.'

'Have I? What?'

'Motive. You haven't included motive. All you've done is broken down possibility, you've not assigned any value to motive. See? You've marked the business with the photos high, but there's nothing to evaluate why. Do you see what I mean? Your motive for those photos was so you could sit and look at girls and play with yourself, in the peace of your own room. That's why you took them, isn't it?'

'Yes.'

'So that was your motive and it's a convincing motive. All teenage boys and many men for that matter do that. It's quite normal behaviour. So you need to account for that. Normal motives reduce the probability of you being the killer. If your motive was because you hated the girls and they had all been horrible to you and you wanted to use the photos as a kind of voodoo doll, that would make the likelihood of you being the killer go up.'

He took the computer and stared at the screen, chin on his right hand, then looked up at her.

'You are fucking brilliant. Sorry. But you are. How have I missed that in my calculations?' He slapped himself on his forehead. 'This changes everything. It's like...oh, man...I'm going to have to re-do all of this...it's all wrong. All of it. I'll still be the most probable but the numbers will shift.'

'See, that's the thing about life, just when you think you've got it all sussed out, something comes along to contradict everything you thought you knew,' said Nick, standing up and patting Josh on the shoulder. 'Now look, promise me you won't show any of this to the police. You don't want to be putting ideas in their head. So don't store it locally, put it on your private cloud server. Because your laptop will be the first thing they want to go through. So don't have anything on this thing that you oughtn't, right? No pornography. No pictures of girls. Right?'

'I see what you're saying. But I don't have anything like that on here. A teenage boy would be an idiot to do that because your parents or a teacher could just open it up and see it. So you'd keep anything like that locked down on a private server that no-one else even knew existed.'

'Is that what you've done, Josh?' said Julie, eyebrows raised.

'To answer that would surely compromise both you and me.'

CHAPTER 17

'I don't mind telling you, he creeped me out on a couple of occasions,' said Julie, throwing ice into two glasses, and pouring them each a large vodka from a litre bottle of Smirnoff, adding fizzy water and lemon juice. 'Sometimes it's like talking to a college professor. Then he's a 16-year-old silly boy. It's like you're dealing with two different people.'

Nick took the glass and went into their living room, flopping down on the sofa and putting the TV on in search of football and finding a game.

'I've got a lead weight in my gut. I'm sure he's going to get arrested, y'know. I'm sure he is. And I don't think he's in any fit shape for the consequences of that.'

Julie sat in their leather armchair and took a big drink.

'Is there any chance at all that it *is* him who's done this? We might have got him all wrong. We think he can't lie. But maybe we're making a big mistake in thinking that. It would be easy to interpret our meeting with him as being all about him trying to find a way to admit his guilt. I'm not saying he *is* guilty...but for the first time, I could see that he might be.'

'Yeah, I'm sure he's not guilty, but not quite as sure as I once was. Maybe we need to build a case against him, instead of building a defence. We keep thinking the defence will prove his innocence but in fact, trying to make a watertight case for his guilt would serve us better.'

She sucked another big gulp down and nodded. 'How did it go at the college?'

'Oh, yeah. I've got a lot to tell you about that. There's a route out of there which can take you to the paths that traverse the town. No CCTV or anything.'

He told her about his meetings with Alice and Geoff.

'What puzzles me about her, is that my experience of her and Geoff too, was that she's cold and distant. But the four Js' - Josh,

Janey, Jenny and Jade - is the opposite. This wasn't a subtle difference. It's like she's totally different. Why do you think that is? Is she just distant with men?'

Julie hooked a thumb into her bra strap, readjusted it and took a drink.

'Well, think about it. That sounds like she's approachable to women, but defensive towards men. That's not that hard to grasp, is it? She feels uptight and stressed by men, but can be herself around women and children.'

While he thought about that, he got up, went to the music room and returned with half a dozen records, dropping the needle on Todd Rundgren's *A Wizard, a True Star*.

Julie closed her eyes. 'Oh god, I love this album. "Sometimes I don't know what to feel" is right on the money, at the moment.'

'Going back to Alice Coates, I hear what you say about her. But if that was the case, why was Josh so complimentary about her? He really liked her and found her very positive. At 16 he's not a child, really.'

She pulled on her bottom lip, contemplating the situation. 'Well, yeah, but he's still 16, maybe her issue is with the adult male. If so, I totally understand. You know what I'm like, I prickle with suspicion in any alpha male environment, or when talking to a bloke like that. Basically, I hate macho blokes. Macho blokes are where so much trouble starts for our society...and for the whole bloody world.'

'I knew that by the time I was 15. All the boys I liked didn't try to bully you, or make you feel bad. They just accepted who you were. They didn't have this weird agenda to define or prove your maleness. But I have to say something. Geoff Powell, right, he was boorish and sexist and I got him to open up by being likewise...'

She interrupted him.

'Really? How did you do that? That's amazing to me. I've never met a man who is less sexist than you. How can you assume that role so easily?'

He shrugged. 'It's hardwired into all of us. Or into my generation, anyway. It's so easy to drop into it. You don't even have to try hard.

Actually, as a writer, it interests me how we can flip these cultural switches and go from one mode to another.'

She folded her arms across her chest. 'I won't ask what you said to him. I'm sure I don't want to know.'

'No. Well, it wasn't too bad. Actually, it was almost the sort of thing me and Jeff say together, but we do it in a post-modern ironic way. So that makes it alright and you can't have a pop at us for it.'

'If you say so, darlin'. But I hear a lot of old-school sexism dressed up as post-modern irony.'

'But he said something which I think is really, really important, which I'd never thought of.'

'Out of the mouths of babes and sexists...'

'...exactly. We were talking about the killings and he said, "No-one kills anyone respectfully," and that struck me as profound.'

She narrowed her eyes. 'Isn't it just a statement of the obvious?'

'Think about it. We know Emily LeBron was laid out, arms by her side. Mandy told us the other two girls were likewise. This is the thing. If you're killing someone, it's usually out of hatred or anger, right? And when you do that, do you care how their bodies are when they're found? No, you don't. But all the girls' bodies - and Paul's parents, too - were found laid out nice and respectfully. The exception was Paul Richardson on the gym roof, he was in a sort of 's' shape, lying on his side. That was how he'd died. He wasn't laid out like the other kids. His death is different.'

She squinted at him. 'Yeah, I see that totally.'

Nick took a sip of vodka and thought about it some more.

'Well, I'm obviously guessing, but to me, it suggests the killer had respect for the girls, as though they had to be killed, for some weird reason, but even so, the killer acknowledged that they were good, decent people. So much so that they killed them in as quick and painless way as possible. No bruises. No hurt. No pain. Maybe he tried it...'

'...he or she,' interrupted Julie.

'...yeah, he or she, tried it out on Paul's parents first, and Paul somehow found out and administered himself the same poison. Remember there was up to 24 hours between his parents' death and his. Plenty of time to find out who murdered them, confront them, say, "I'll tell the police if you don't give me some of the poison. I want to kill myself". We know he really, really wanted to die. That's why he wasn't laid out. He died where he fell.'

'Right, so that means the deaths are part of an agenda. It's not personal, it's about something greater and over-arching. It's not to do with the girls as people.'

'Exactly. They're casualties in a war. However the killer imagines that.'

They sat and listened to the brilliant music, wrapped up in their own thoughts.

'The killer must have a cause, but what cause?' said Julie, glass to her mouth.

Nick closed his eyes and let his mind open and relax. Some minutes passed...more and more minutes.

Then in a flash of understanding more akin to an electric shock, he opened his eyes.

'Shit! I know what this is about, Jules!'

'Eh? What?' said Julie, who had been falling asleep.

He got to his feet and paced across the room.

'Jenny had it right. Remember what she said: killing girls stops reproduction. It's a ploy to stop growth of population. Nothing personal, but every girl you kill, you reduce the future population. It's a hardcore green environmentalist eco-warrior-type of person. It's a form of eco-terrorism. And whoever it is, is setting Josh up for it. That's why they started with Paul's parents. They knew he was depressed and suicidal and that they could make it look like he killed them and then himself, and who was his best mate? Josh.'

'Oh, my god. And Josh had taken those photos and numbered them. Put those things together and the fact he spends so much time on his own that he'd not have an alibi for the murders...'

'Exactly, and that means the killer knew Paul and knows Josh and had access to his locker to steal the photos.'

'It's McGregor, isn't it? It bloody is. It has to be. He fits that bill and the photos were on his desk,' said Julie, also standing up. 'He knows both boys well, he knew Paul's state of mind - Josh had reported to him Paul was behaving weirdly,' she said, taking a black hair clip from a table and fastening her hair up on the back of her head. 'He's even got a chemistry degree, so knows what to administer to poison people. It has to be him. It just must be.'

'Yeah, it is hard to see past him. Geoff Powell thought it was him, too. Said he was a creep and a toucher. I wonder if Mandy has had him interviewed? He must have been by now.'

'Why don't they arrest him, then? Surely, if we can see this, the police can. Blokes in their 30s kill more often than 16-year-old boys.'

'Yeah, but he wasn't seen feeling up a dead body, was he? There's more circumstantial evidence against Josh and none against him.' Nick paused. 'I guess for all we know, they might be going to arrest McGregor. We just don't have a clue and I don't really want to have to ask Mandy and she won't tell Jeff, because she knows he'll tell me.'

'The problem now, as ever, is how do we get hard evidence against him?'

He thought for a moment. 'I know how. We find out where he lives, break into his house and find the poison he used. He'll surely still have some because he won't have stopped the killing yet. He's just waiting until Josh is in school again.'

'Will he? Surely he'll expect a knock on the door by the police?' she said.

'Well, he won't have it on the hall table with a big black skull and crossbones over it saying "Poison". He'll have hidden it, but anyway, they'll have interviewed him at school, not at home. There'll be extreme ecological literature in his house.'

She took her laptop out of her work bag and typed in McGregor's name into a people search website. 'Common, but here we are. He lives on Phoenix Gardens. Michael McGregor, 39. All the others listed are too old or too young.'

Nick put the address into Google Earth. 'What number is it?'
She told him.
'Interesting. Guess where that is.'
'Err...near the college?'

'It's off Oxbridge Lane and is flush up against the cycle path. He's about a mile from the college. He just goes straight up the track to Bishopton Road West, or he turns off and takes the worn path up to the 6th form gym, the way me and Janey went. Looks like it's a small house and with just a Yale lock on that door. You could get in there, couldn't you, Jules?'

She looked over his shoulder. 'Easy that, aye. Trouble is, it's illegal.'

'Not as illegal as murder.'

'Well, if we're going to get in there, we'll need to wait until we know he's in school, and lord knows when that's going to happen.'

'If I'm right, there will be no more murders, at least not until Josh is at school. Then it'll start again.'

'But we can't let that happen. Not least because Jenny is next on the list!'

'She can't leave the farmhouse or be out of anyone's sight. There's no way she can be attacked if that's the case.'

'Oh, god almighty. We've got to stop this killer or help the police to stop them, or just do anything we can. It's so sodding scary.' She texted her father to tell him about their ideas and telling him to continue to keep Jenny safe and away from school until an arrest was made.

Tuesday morning dawned overcast and damp.

'Jules. Can I ask you a bit of a rude question?'

He spoke while serving pork sausages, sweet potato rosti and buttered spinach to her for breakfast.

'What?'

He poured coffee for them both.

'It's about Janey James.'

'What about her?'

'I think she wants to have it off with me.'

'I don't blame her. I should rent you out.' She laughed and grinned up at him.

He groaned. 'Jules man, I'm trying to...oh, forget it.' He sat down and sighed.

She stopped eating and put a hand on his arm.

'Sorry, luv. So was she flirting with you again, yesterday?'

'I think so, yeah. Nothing too dramatic, but she stands a bit too close and...I don't know what to do about it. She's a nice lass and possibly a bit lonely. How do I say, basically, you're lovely, but I can't have sex with you?'

She ate her food and cleaned her plate, washing it down with black coffee.

'Thank you for asking me this,' she said, more serious now.

'What? Why?'

'I'm just glad you can ask me. Dealing with being attracted to, or by someone, is an issue in married life. And we all need to know how to deal with it.'

'Does it happen to you?'

'Occasionally. I'll be honest with you, I quite like it when someone who seems nice flirts with me, as long as it's not offensive, obviously.'

'Do you?'

'Well, yeah. It's a natural human thing to enjoy admiration. Maybe especially once you get to middle age. I've been known to touch someone on the arm, as a sort of flirt. I mean, if it got more serious, obviously I'd draw the line, in no uncertain times. But just being a little affectionate with someone is fine. It's one of the colours in the rainbow of life. That's what I think, anyway. Being massively in love with you doesn't stop me being attracted to other people, and I'm sure it doesn't for you. But it's what you do about it, isn't it? I'm not a fan of open, promiscuous relationships. They're almost always emotionally destructive. The evidence is pretty watertight on that.'

'Yeah, I'm certainly not interested in that. But I do like her being attracted to me. I like that I think she wants to shag me and in a selfish way, that's why I don't want to be harsh with her, but I don't want to lead her on, either. That seems unfair to her.'

She folded her arms across her chest. 'Sexual attraction is one thing. Love is another. We're together because we love each other. It also happens that we're sexually attracted to each other. But it's the love that binds us together. I don't believe anyone stays with

255

anyone long-term just for sex. It's not enough.'

'That's so true. Love lives in the top-floor penthouse apartment in the skyscraper of life, lust works on the reception desk.'

She grinned. 'Beautifully expressed. Anybody would think you're a writer.' She got up. 'If Janey gets more forward - and she probably will - just tell her that you only have sex with me, but tell her she's lovely and if you weren't with me, you deffo would shag her senseless. Which is true, isn't it?'

'I guess so. Makes me feel like I'm being unfaithful to you even saying that, though.'

'Oh, man, don't be daft, it's just being realistic. If you handle it that way, you allow her to feel good about herself, and feel she hasn't really been rejected. And you should enjoy her attentions. You should feel good that she's attracted to you. Bookmark it in your psyche, so you can revisit it when you're depressed. OK? You've got to embrace the positives in life, especially when your brain is set up the way it is.'

He shook his head, feeling some degree of disbelief. 'That's so open-minded. If it was happening to you, I think I'd be very jealous.'

'Well, I would have been when younger, but I'm a world-weary, gnarly old bitch these days and I'm not in the slightest bit insecure about you and me, and I know life is complicated and messy for us all. It's also a backhanded compliment when someone fancies your fella. I'm only surprised you're not having to beat lasses off with a stick every day.'

'That's never going to happen. I'm too weird for that.'

'Weird and gorgeous.'

They hugged each other tightly and gave each other a little feel-up.

Once Julie was away to work, Nick got in the Merc and drove the couple of miles to Oxbridge Lane, parked on Waltham Avenue, the next street along from Phoenix Gardens, and walked back to look at McGregor's house. Oxbridge Lane was another route in his DNA, having walked it hundreds, if not thousands of times, to get from Palm Grove to the High Street, or in the summer, to get to Ropner Park. A fine mist of rain was falling now. He zipped up his black leather jacket and dug his hands into his jeans, as he turned down the small cul-de-sac, full of small red-brick houses and one-storey blocks of flats, all of which had been built in the last 25 or so years. It was quiet and modest, and in the summer would be quite leafy.

The road curved around to the left a short distance, then right, the cul-de-sac capped with the back of two blocks of houses. A path led around to the front and joined up with a path that led onto the cycle track which traversed Stockton. McGregor's house was the last one in a block of three. With no houses overlooking his front door, he could walk out onto the cycle track without being seen. In fact, if he wanted, he could get to and from the college without ever going near a road.

Nick walked onto the cycle path, which had a white line painted up the middle to try and enforce some order on users. There was a couple walking in the distance, and a cyclist coming towards him, but it was, by and large, quiet and tree lined. He went back to the house, walked up to the door and rang the bell, hearing it ding-dong.

There was no reply, and he could tell there was no-one in, so he went to the window and peered into the living room. Christ, what a mess. There were papers, books and magazines strewn all over the place. Three empty mugs were on a cheap-looking wood coffee table. It was an ordinary enough room. Everything looked like it had come out of flat packs, so it had a budget look about it, even though McGregor had to be on a decent wage as a deputy Head. Maybe he spent all his money on exotic poisons. He squinted at a bookshelf on the far wall but couldn't really make out any titles.

It was a quiet little corner of Stockton, this. Like Hartburn more widely, it was neat and tidy and ordinary, in a nice way. The sort of place that outsiders might think didn't exist on Teesside, given it was largely reported as an area of industrial wasteland and terminal decline.

He strolled around to the back of the houses. Each backyard was just a small square of concrete slabs, and had a four-foot wooden fence around. Wheelie bins stood in a row inside the gate. Pushing at it, he went in and peered in the bins. Empty.

He looked in the kitchen window. Unremarkable. No bottles of poison. He turned away, but as he did so, something in his peripheral vision moved. Turning back, he got a glimpse of a figure leaving the front door in a navy blue hoodie. It wasn't McGregor, though. Too tall and fair-haired.

Nick sprinted around to the front of the house, passing no-one as he did so. They had to have taken off down the cycle track. He looked south, there was no-one there at all, but to the north the figure in the navy blue hoodie was running at speed away from him. Nick put his head down, like a sprinter, and took off. After 30 yards he looked up and could see he'd gained on the figure. He put his head down again and forced his leg to go faster. Soon he wasn't far behind them, maybe only 40 feet away. Most of his brain power was being taken up by pushing his body hard and so he hadn't realised; hadn't realised who the figure running away from the house was. He should have spotted it immediately, but hadn't, largely because it was so unexpected, or because subconsciously, he just didn't want to. But as he approached them, he knew who this was. There was no denying it.

It was Josh.

'Josh! Josh! Stop!' he yelled, trying to catch his breath. The boy heard him and turned around, slowing down to a halt.

'Hello, Nick.' He was breathing heavily. He had a funny look in his eyes. Scared and intense. The sort of look he had when he was going to into one of his freak outs.

Nick reached him and put his hands on his hips, as he caught his breath. He looked at the boy, all sorts of horrible thoughts going through his brain, trying to think how to deal with him.

'Are you alright, Josh?'

'Yes.'

'Are you sure? You look upset.'

The lad didn't reply and just made an 'I dunno' short of shrug.

Nick licked his dry lips. 'Josh man, I just saw you come out of Mr McGregor's house.'

That shocked the boy. 'What? How could you have done that?'

'I was at the back. You must have been there when I rang the front door bell. You were upstairs, weren't you?'

'No. I wasn't there. Not me. No.' He shook his head firmly. But he couldn't lie to save his life.

'It's alright, I'm not upset with you. I just worry about you. You know that. I want to protect you.'

'Nick. You're not my fucking father, even if I am the son you never had. I don't need your fucking help!'

That really hurt like a knife into his soul. But now wasn't the time to indulge in personal emotions.

'Even so, why were you in there?'

'I fucking said I wasn't and I fucking wasn't!' He was shouting but his eyes betrayed the truth.

'Josh, I know you...'

'...no, you *think* you know me. You know the me you meet, you don't know the me you don't see. I'm not one person. Now, in this moment, I am not the Josh you like. So leave me alone.'

'Don't say that, Josh. Especially don't say it to a police officer.'

Josh had begun walking away, but stopped, turned around and walked up to Nick so he was right in his face and hissed at him in a fury. 'Fucking leave me alone or I'll fucking hurt you. Right?'

It was horrifying. His eyes were their normal blue but somehow a thousand shades darker. It was how he'd been that day with Mandy Beale. It did seem like he was different person when these furies took over him.

Not knowing what to say or do, he just stood and watched Josh break into a trot and run away from him, an icy shard of fear running the length of his spine. Somehow, even then, he knew what had happened and as he half-ran, half-walked back to the house, his mind was already in a maelstrom.

The front door was ajar. He pushed it open with his elbow so as to leave no fingerprints, and walked up the carpeted stairs. There were two bedrooms and a bathroom. One bedroom door was wide open. He walked in and saw what he expected to see: Michael McGregor, dressed in black trousers and a blue shirt, lying dead on the floor in a crumpled heap. Oh, fuck.

Take a photo. Take photos of everything. He'd regretted not doing so at Paul Richardson's house. Meticulously, he took photos all around the house, making sure he didn't touch any surface, then left, leaving the door ajar, knowing he should report the body, but unable to yet work out what the implications were. His mind was shattered into a million fragments of information and emotion. The body wasn't going anywhere. It could wait to be found.

This felt like a moment of crisis. And for the last 40 years, when he'd had a major crisis, he'd turned to Jeff for help. And that's what he did once again.

'Alright man,' said Jeff, answering his phone.

'Jeff, it's Nick,'

'I know it is. Phones tell you who's calling these days, remember, granddad.'

'Sorry, yeah. Some bad shit has happened and I need to go over it with you to sort things out. Are you in the shop?'

'Yeah. What sort of bad shit are we talking about? You've not killed someone, have you?'

'No, I haven't. But I think Josh might have.'

As soon as he got to the shop, Jeff took him next door to the Royal Oak.

'Two large single malts please, Jock,' said Jeff.

Nick waited until no-one was in earshot before saying anything, taking their usual table by the window. It was only 11.40am so the pub was quiet except for a few crumpled and defeated people, for whom it was never too early for a drink, bless them.

'Right, well, let's have it, then,' said Jeff, knocking his glass against Nick's.

Calmly, he explained the events at McGregor's house, then showed him photos of the body.

Jeff was good in a crisis, able to keep his head when all around him were losing it and that fact helped Nick's boiling emotions to calm down to a simmer. He looked up from the pictures of McGregor's body.

'This fella has been killed while standing up and has collapsed.' He cleared his throat and took a big swallow of whisky. 'You know what this puts me in mind of?' He tapped at the screen with his right

260

index fingernail.

'No. What?'

'Remember when we found Susan in her house in Malton? God rest her soul. She'd taken the poison, it had hit her as she was standing up and she just crumpled in on herself, remember? She was lying really unnaturally.'

Nick leaned forward and put a hand on the big man's bare forearm. Susan was his birth mother, after all.

'Yeah, yeah, you're right. It's just like that.'

'His body is at a really unnatural angle. It looks like he's dropped down and keeled to one side. His legs are weirdly tucked underneath himself. If you remember, with Susan, we worked out that the cyanide hit her so quickly, she was dead before she hit the floor. This looks exactly the same.'

Nick took the phone from him. 'You are totally right. Good thinking, man.'

Jeff raised his right index finger to a 45-degree angle. 'But why would Josh have done this? Yes he was at the scene of the crime, but let's just put that to one side for a moment. Why does he want to kill McGregor? He's not said anything against him before, has he?'

'No. He just said "he's there". But I'm beginning to wonder if I've made the mistake of thinking Josh was some sort of innocent who was unable of lying and conniving. The way he was with me today was scary.'

Jeff smoothed out his long beard. 'But you know he can freak out. And when any of us do that, we become like other people for a moment.'

'Yeah, I know...I dunno, this was different, Jeff. I've got to be honest, it's totally undermined my belief in his innocence. I mean, he told me and Jules he was the person most likely to be guilty.'

Jeff pulled a face. 'Yeah, but...he was talking about stats, wasn't he?'

'That's what we thought. But maybe we were naïve.'

He let the single malt burn his throat as he looked out at the High Street, another day just passing like it was normal and no-one had been murdered. The ability for the world to keep turning no matter how messed up your own life had become, was perpetual testimony to the insignificance of all of our individual travails in the scheme of existence.

'I don't know what to do, Jeff. Do I report the body? If I do that, that means I have to say I saw Josh. Then Mandy will have him arrested and god knows what'll happen after that.'

Jeff looked out of the window at the grey damp day in contemplation and said nothing for a while. The best thing about having lifelong friends is that when one or both of you is thinking, or weighing something up, there is no social necessity to say anything.

After a few minutes, Jeff took another sip of whisky. 'You're overthinking all of this. Your whole focus is on Josh not being guilty. If he's not guilty, he won't get sent down for it.'

'Oh, come on, man. Innocent people get sent down all the time.'

'True, but not an innocent Aspie kid like Josh. And don't forget, if he really is responsible for any of these murders, he needs dealing with, no matter what. I don't think he's guilty, but Mandy has done all along and, y'know, she's the professional. She's no beef, for or against the kid, it's not personal. There's just no-one else in the frame. Maybe it's best to leave the authorities to sort it out. If you start hiding it from the police, you'll end up with Mandy's knee on your throat. You know that.'

'But if I report today's events, they'll come for Josh. And he'll blame me.'

'But Nick, man. He *was* in there. Now, there are two basic options. One is, he went there and killed him. Two is that he was asked to go there and he found him and that's part of a plot framing him for the murders. Those are the only two possible scenarios. '

'Yeah. You're right. He lied to me. Lied in my face. I feel really upset by that...and by...by...by some other stuff he said.'

'He's a 16-year-old kid; Asperger's or not, he knows how to hurt the grown ups. We all did. When you're that age, you're not mature enough to understand the long-term implications of your words, but my god, the teenager is an evil shite when it comes to being nasty and hurting people's feelings. It's part of the gig. Don't take it to heart, man.'

But it wasn't that simple. He had so much tied up emotionally with Josh. They'd almost died together at the Flynn farm fire. Like it or not, he *was* like a surrogate son. And Nick saw so much of himself in the boy, so much so that he couldn't think objectively about him and what he had or hadn't done. Maybe this is what it was like to have a son.

He sank the remains of the single malt.

'I totally get how you're feeling, but the dead people, the dead girls, they're more important even than your feelings about Josh,' said Jeff. 'Next on the list is Jenny. Think about this. How would you feel if he killed her and you knew that you could have prevented it by telling the police what you know?'

That sent a shiver down his spine so cold and electric that it brought him to his senses.

'Yeah. You're right. '

'And, look, Mandy is old school, she's got size 15 hobnail boots and is as subtle as a flying mallet, but if she gets the merest whiff of his innocence, she'll let him go. She's straight up and down. She wants to nick villains. I know it doesn't seem like it, but she's altruistic about being a copper. She wants to make the world, or at least Teesside, a safer place. She's not one for nicking people just to get conviction rates up, not least because if she did that in this case, the real murderer is just going to slaughter some other kids. She needs to get the right perp. So she'll be fair and, let's face it, you've already given her and Bowes a proper bollocking over treating Josh right...'

'Is that what she said? "Proper bollocking"?'

'Yeah, man. She'll never tell you, but she listens and absorbs and considers. All of it is wrapped up in this hard shell but under that, she learns and understands.'

'Before I do this, I have to call Jules.'

'Of course you do. I'll get us a round in while you do that.'

He went outside and called her.

'Hello, gorgeous.'

'Jules. I need your advice.'

He explained the details of what had happened.

'What should I do?'

She didn't say anything for a while. He listened to her breathing while she thought about it. The Ingleby Barwick bus arrived at the stop opposite the pub, let two people off, and then pulled away.

'Do what Jeff says. You can't keep a cap on this. You'll get in trouble for perverting the course of justice. That's serious stuff. Call his mother or leave her a message and tell her about today and that you've got to report the body and thus Josh's involvement. She'll have to be there when they formally question him.'

'OK. They won't have a lawyer. Can you call Gaunty and make him aware of the situation?'

'Of course. Oh, god.' She let out a heavy sigh. 'This is awful. What's Josh done? I'm not sure I believe he's innocent any more and I can't bear the thought we've totally got him wrong. Is it possible he's developed some sort of personality disorder?'

'Well, he seemed to be aware that there was more than one Josh, so I'm not sure what flavour of crazy that is, but it doesn't seem right. I've *never* heard him talk like that before. He threatened me, Jules. But then, he could just have gone into a special, scared freak-out mode after seeing the dead body.'

'Keep me updated.'

Nick rang off and went back inside as Jeff sat down with two drinks.

'Jules agrees with you. I just hope Josh doesn't totally lose it again,' said Nick, as he called Vicky, Josh's mother. It went to voicemail. 'Hi, Vicky, it's Nick Guymer. I'm sorry to have to tell you this but I think Josh is in a bit of trouble. I just caught him leaving the house of his form teacher Mr McGregor and McGregor was dead, I'm afraid. He denied being there. But he was and he was very odd in his behaviour. I have to report the death and will have to tell the police about Josh being there. I'm sure they'll question, or perhaps even arrest him on the back of this, so expect a call from the police. Our lawyer Jon Gaunt will be aware of the situation, if you need him. He's a very good public defender. I know this is an awful situation. I'll see you soon.'

He looked up at Jeff. 'Bloody hell. This is a proper shitter, Jeff.'

'Yeah, but don't lose faith in the lad, yet. Nothing is proven. And he could still just be being framed rather expertly. Let me tell Mandy about McGregor and Josh. Probably best if you're not too in her or her officers' faces.' Taking a big drink, he stood up and went outside the make the call.

Nick's stomach burned hot with nervous worry, fearing the coming avalanche of events. To occupy his mind he looked through the photos he'd taken in McGregor's house. The first one was of the messy living room. Had it been ransacked, or was he just very untidy? The latter seemed more likely. Three mugs on the table. McGregor lived alone, who were the other two for? Was one Josh? Was that how the poison had been administered? Forensics would find that out.

Jeff returned and raised his bushy eyebrows and blew out air. 'The ball is rolling.' He took a drink and held up his hand, counting off points on his fingers. 'First they'll get to McGregor's and make that a crime scene, then get SOCO in, then go to see Josh. She wants to formally arrest him for evidential and procedural reasons, but she said that they'll use an officer who is a specialist in dealing with people who are a bit...y'know...unusual. So, that's something. Just sit back, let it all happen. He'll be fine. He'll be questioned at headquarters in Middlesbrough. You'll be able to visit him, if they hold him for long. They might not, though, they might decide he's deffo not guilty and let him go.'

'They won't. If I know him, he'll try and be clever and will put himself in the clarts doing so. Or, he'll just go apeshit and they'll have to section him or something.'

'Nah, that won't happen. Mandy's learned her lesson on that. She said as much to me. Like I said, she won't admit it to you, but you taught her a lesson there.'

Nick felt heavy with worry and his impotence in the situation. How could he prove Josh's innocence? Only by finding the real murderer. But what if that *was* Josh?

Jeff let him muse on his feelings for a bit. 'Oh, one other thing she told me. They've found what killed Paul Richardson and are now testing the other bodies for the same stuff.'

'Oh, yeah? What was it? Cyanide?'

Jeff shook his head and rolled the alcohol around his mouth. 'It was more obscure than that. She told me the Latin names for it but I'd never heard of it. But the interesting thing is this, right? You mix the two chemicals together. On their own, they're safe, but put them together and they're deadly.'

Nick leaned forward. 'How doesn't it kill the person whose mixed them?'

Jeff cocked an index finger. 'Ah, you only combine them on your target's skin.' He held out the flat of his hands. 'You have one cloth in each hand, each soaked with a different chemical. You put one on the person's skin, then the other on top of it. You'd have to be careful not to touch both yourself, so the killer probably wore surgeon's gloves.'

'Christ, that must be powerful stuff. How long does it take to work?'

'It's fast acting, in the same way cyanide is. But you wouldn't even necessarily know. They don't burn or itch on their own, but once they're mixed, your skin absorbs them and it knackers you within a minute or three. She said the lab reckon it doesn't actually technically kill you for an half an hour or more, but it renders you unconscious, not far off instantly.'

'So nobody really suffered?'

Jeff shook his head. 'If they did, it'd have been just like getting instantly very sleepy or woozy, apparently. It sounds to me like it was chosen for that reason. A quick painless death. Like you were saying - a respectful death. If there's a good way to go out, it seems like this was chosen to achieve that.' Jeff flicked at his long curtain of hair, smoothed out his beard. 'Actually, you know what? All these deaths started with the Richardson parents. Why were they killed? If Paul did it, why? Abuse, is my guess. He was getting it up the arse from an Uncle Ernie or his dad, even. He quite clearly lost his mind, applied his chemistry knowledge, somehow got the chemicals, killed them, then a few hours later, did himself in. But someone else knew what he was up to and saw Paul's work and thought, I'll do that to girls. I don't know how McGregor fits into that, but I'm sure that's the order of events.'

'Yeah, let's see...' he took out his phone '...they were called Terri and David.'

Nick looked through the Google results. 'Hard to know which ones are them...hold on...fucking hell.'

He dropped the phone in shock. It bounced on the table, skidded and dropped onto the floor.

'What is it?' said Jeff, bending down to pick up the phone, putting it on the table.

Nick struggled to organise his thoughts for a moment. He looked at his phone again.

'It says here, in the obituary in the *Northern Echo*, Terri and David Richardson "were committed environmentalists and regional organisers for Save The Earth".'

'What?!' Jeff grabbed the phone from him and read the obituary, then looked up at Nick. 'But...but...that means...'

'...I know. As Jenny said, killing girls reduces the population and the demands on the earth and Save The Earth believe in population control.'

The two of them, faces set in frowns, thought about it for a minute. They looked in each other's eyes.

'I can't work out how, but I have a feeling that demo in the Boro is now very significant,' said Jeff.

'You're right. What did we see? A demo full of hippies and assorted New Agers. We also saw firebombers hi-jacking the event. If that is a radical splinter group, is it possible that the Richardsons were "conservatives" and actually it's the radicals that have killed them because of that?' said Nick. 'And they disrupted a peaceful demo to make a point to the mainstream STE group that there will be trouble if they hold any more demos. It's a threat to try and overthrow the group.'

'There's no fury like the evangelical's fury. That's for sure. These sorts of people tend to hate those in the movement that they feel are not as ideologically pure as they are, more than anyone else. It's like with left-wing socialist types. They hate each other far more than they've ever hated the Tories.'

'Does Save The Earth have an office or a meeting place?' asked Nick.

Jeff looked at his phone. 'No, it seems to organise around its Facebook page, which is a closed group, so unless they've made a post public, I can't see it. The last of those is for the demo in Middlesbrough.'

Nick looked at it on his phone. 'I'll see if I can join it.' He clicked the relevant button. 'I wonder what criteria they apply to membership?'

It didn't take long to find out. A message was immediately sent to his Facebook inbox.

'Here we go. It's a list of questions.'

'Read them out, then. Let's see if we can pass their test.'

'One. "Are you concerned about the future of the Earth?" Well who's going to answer no to that? Two. "Are you prepared to be radically active in campaigning?" '

'Well if you failed on those first two you'd not have even bothered to apply to join the group,' said Jeff.

'Three is more interesting. "To be a member of STE you must submit your name, address, contact number and email address. All information will be kept confidential. If you are approved as a member you will be given a unique social media identity with which to contribute to the STE group page." '

'Clearly an attempt to be covert.'

Nick shrugged. 'Yeah, but not a very good one. Facebook posts still have an IP attached to them somewhere in the mix. You could still be traced. Also, if I fill this out, how can they verify that I'm who I'm purporting to be? I could easily fill in your name and address et cetera. There's nothing in this to match me to the info I give. Not even a request for photo ID, which would still be easy to fake, especially when you're just emailing it in.'

Jeff sneered at him, cynically. 'They're just playing at it, if you ask me. It's more like one of those left-wing student societies that existed at Newcastle Poly when we were there, remember? It was all combat trousers and up-against-the-wall rhetoric, but in reality, just another social group and a way to meet people of like minds. It was Citizen Smith, only without anyone as funny as Wolfie. This lot are not a hardcore eco-terrorist group, no matter how they might want to pretend they're some sort of underground green movement. The police have probably already infiltrated it, just to keep an eye on them. That is, if they think it is in the slightest bit dangerous. You could tell what they were like from the sort of people who gathered for that demo. It was more New Age than anything else. They'd not hurt a fly for fear of being subjected to instant karma.'

Nick's phone vibrated as a text arrived from Josh.

'The police are outside. I'm sorry. I've let you down. Apologise to Julie for me, please. It's been great knowing you.'

Nick slung the whisky down his throat. 'We need to get to Palm Grove, Jeff.'

They left the Royal Oak and jumped into Jeff's white van.

'What did the text say?' asked Jeff as he took off for Fairfield.

Nick passed his phone to him. 'It doesn't sound good.'

'Is that an admission of guilt?' said Jeff, glancing at it. 'I don't think it is, not necessarily.'

'I don't know what to think.'

'Frankly, I'd be amazed if it was. I just don't buy it,' said Jeff as he drove down Oxbridge Lane. 'Even if he's got it into his head that he's guilty, I still don't think he is.'

'Why not?'

They'd gone down past the cemetery, around Oxbridge roundabout and halfway towards Greens Lane before Jeff spoke again.

'It's just a gut feeling. I just can't imagine him doing what had to be done to kill those people. And I still don't think he's got a rock-solid motive.'

'You don't need a rock-solid motive if you've lost your mind,' said Nick, biting off a loose nail sliver on his little finger. 'Paul proved that.'

As they turned up Palm Grove, the scene before them was amazing. There were six police cars parked on the right-hand side of the road.

'Oh, fuck, they've gone totally over the top. Why do they need all this presence?' shouted Nick, as Jeff parked up further down the road.

'Don't do anything daft!' yelled Jeff, as Nick tore open the van door and ran towards Josh's house.

His heart was pounding in his chest up into his throat. This was wrong. Josh was a nice boy. He was *his* boy. Yes you can make misjudgements of character but you can't mistake a funny, clever boy for a mass killer.

'I'm sorry, sir. You can't go any further, there is an ongoing incident,' said a police officer, holding out a hand to stop him as he sprinted towards Josh's house. Nick felt like nutting the lunk-headed idiot in the face.

'Josh is my friend. I'm his school guardian. I know what's going on. I need to speak to him.' The fact that such a role as school guardian didn't exist, felt irrelevant.

He moved to walk around the officer, but was held by the arm. 'I'm sorry sir, you can't go any further.'

As that happened, the door to Josh's house opened and he came out, an officer on either side of him. Neighbours all stood on their doorsteps, watching the action unfold.

He seemed calm. His head bowed. Where the fuck was his mother?

'Josh! Josh!' called Nick. He was only 30 feet away. 'Don't worry. We'll sort it all out for you!'

Josh turned to look at him and gave him one of his unaffected smiles. 'Will you look after Stanley, Nick? He needs his walk. He's not had it today.'

'Of course. I'll come and see you later. Don't worry, lad, everything will be OK.'

The two women officers guided him into the back of a police car and then sat either side of him.

'You heard that? I've got to pick up his dog,' said Nick, to the copper in front of him.

'I'll just check,' he said and spoke into his phone, becoming distracted as he did so. Useless. Nick simply sprinted past him to the house, throwing a dummy to another officer with ease, and arriving at the front door, where Stanley stood, observing what was going on with his usual placid disposition.

Nick scooped him up into his arms and kissed him on the top of the head.

'This must be familiar for you, Stan. Remember when I picked you up from next door, all those years ago? Well, it's déjà vu all over again, fella.'

He snuggled into the dog's warm fur, then was aware of a figure standing in front of him. It was Vic Bowes and he was grinning at him in a sickly manner.

'You again, Nick Guymer. You do like a crime scene, don't you?'

The man smelt of stale sweat and weary desperation.

Nick put Stanley down and stared at the policeman in the face, eyes wide and unflinching.

'Why do you think you're even here, you prick? Why do you even want to speak to Josh Jones, eh?'

'Hey, language, Guymer. I'm a copper, remember? We've had info, haven't we?'

Nick jabbed him in the chest. Hard. 'I'm taking no lectures from you, you greasy dumpling.'

'Watch it, son. I can nick you anytime I want.'

'If you want to nick me, I'll give you a fucking good reason, because I'll fucking beat the snot out of you so hard that you'll wish you were dead and don't think I won't fucking do it because I'd fucking love to.' With every 'f', spittal sprayed out of his mouth into Bowes's face.

Nick was on the verge of tears, his eyes glazed with upset and in no mood for Bowes's bullshit, taking out his upset on the policeman.

In his blind passion, he hadn't noticed Jeff approaching.

'Now now, let's play nicely lads, shall we?' he said, as ever, pouring oil on troubled waters. His big arms and hands placed around each of their shoulders, beaming in his beatific sort of way

'Just so you know, Vic. I made the call about this. Me. Right? So, the reason you're here is because of me. I know you hate me because I'm better than you at this shit, and I don't blame you for that, because laying off blame for your own inadequacy is class 101 in the self-loathing textbook,' said Nick.

'You fancy yourself too much, Guymer. That kid is a killer. He's going to jail for the rest of his natural.'

Jeff, dropping into one of his madman roles with ease, leaned into the copper. Nose to nose. And made a manic, grinning face, all teeth, hair and beard and then let out a strange, high-pitched chirping noise, made with his lips, like he was a robin on acid. Then backed off, both hands raised in apology, as if it was nothing to do with him. Bowes, like many before him, just stared at Jeff, bewildered at his lunacy.

Nick scooped up Stanley again, closed the door and, alongside Jeff, left the scene.

As Jeff drove them away he turned to Nick. 'Where to now?'

'Middlesbrough cop shop. That's where they're taking him.' He texted Jon Gaunt to tell him to get down there. 'Gaunty will look after him.' He stroked Stanley, who had immediately settled down on the front seat beside him, putting his head on his paws, looking up at him with dark brown eyes. What a great dog. Nick stroked him constantly, to comfort his own shredded nerves.

'Where's his mam?'

'Still at work, I presume, she's not been in touch yet. I told her where Josh would be. I just hope he's coping. They just need to not bombard him with questions. He responds badly to noisy pressure. It seems to shut his brain down and you don't want someone with a lack of inhibition in the first place, kicking off. I mean, you didn't see him last time. He gave Mandy and Bowes both barrels, and then some.'

'Aye, she did mention it.' He snorted a laugh. 'All water off a duck's back to her, like.'

As Jeff crossed the Tees, heading to the A66 to take them into the north of Middlesbrough, he drummed on the wheel, deep in thought. 'If we just say for a moment that Josh is totally innocent, who else could be responsible? It has to be someone who goes to or works at the college, doesn't it? McGregor is dead...'

'...that doesn't rule him out. He could've been killed by someone else to stop him killing more girls.'

'Good point, Batman. Still think it's more likely that he wasn't guilty and the real murderer did for him before he found out, or to stop him finding out, or to shut him up,' said Jeff.

'Don't forget this might not be just a single murderer, there could be at least one other person involved in order to take the bodies to where they were found...'

Jeff shook his head. 'No, you're forgetting that we know the toxins and how they work. I favour the killing on the spot theory, because it's so quick. Bang, on go the chemicals, they collapse and that's it. Who else at that college is a potential suspect? The gym teachers?'

'Coates and Powell? I'm not ruling them out but then, I'm not ruling out any teacher.' Nick stroked Stanley in contemplation. The doggie had gone to sleep.

'There's one person we've not considered, y'know...' said Jeff '...not even for a moment and...well...maybe we should.'

'Who's that then?'

'You won't like it.'

'Won't I?'

'No.'

'I'll be the judge of that. Who?'

'Janey James.'

Jeff raised his bushy eyebrows at him, as though in shock. 'Think about it for a minute. You yourself said she's the hub of that place. Everything revolves around her. She's got access to information on everyone who works there, and on every kid, too. She's in a perfect position to set up whoever she likes for murder. She knows where everyone is, she knows where everyone lives. Everyone has to sign in at her office so she knows who goes where, and what they do when they get there. She can move around the whole building with impunity. Everyone knows Janey. If she was in a classroom, taking photos out of Josh's locker for example, she'd have access to the locker master key, and no-one would give her a second glance. She's part of the fixtures and fittings. Perfect cover.'

Nick instinctively revolted against the idea, not least because if he was honest he bloody well fancied Janey and didn't want her to turn out not to be the nice person he thought she was, let alone be a mass murderer. But he also knew enough to know that lust can blind even the most perceptive person and he wasn't even that.

'I get what you're saying. It's just that...having spent some time with her, she seems so nice.'

'I know and she's got those magnifico chestular assets, and no-one wants to see those behind bars. But, even so...it's worth thinking about. Was there anything she's said which might in any way be construed to be anti-population growth or anything very eco-warrior?'

Nick sat and thought for a moment. 'No, not really. Or nothing that struck me that way. She was concerned we might have got caught up in the Boro demo. That was all,'

Jeff nodded. 'Well, one thing is for certain, she wasn't one of those freerunners, not with tits that big, you'd topple over!'

But Nick had stopped listening. Something had stirred in his subconscious. He could almost feel it moving as it began coming to the surface, like it had been birthed deep in the sea bed of his mind, had been nursed and weaned and now, too big to live down there any longer, came swimming up to the surface, gasping for breath and needing to have its freedom.

Ideas and understandings are wholly and totally metaphysical, and yet when they appear in our thoughts fully formed, you wonder how you didn't see it this way before. How was this truth so obscure and masked for so long, but was now so clear? Why the hell didn't you realise this earlier? Why didn't you see what was literally in front of your face? Why didn't you let your mind connect two things you had seen, but had not, until now, connected?

Nick turned to Jeff and put his hand on his bare arm, just below where he'd rolled up the sleeve of his denim shirt. Stanley woke up, stretched and yawned. Nick tickled him on the tummy. The dog yawned again, and settled back down.

'This is no time to admit to being gay and propose marriage, though if have to, I'll say yes, just to get my hands on your record collection in the inevitable divorce,' said Jeff, indicating left to turn off the A66, heading toward the police station on Bridge Street West.

'No touching below the waist, though.'

'Jeff, man, I've just...I've just realised something.'

'Is it that I'm a red-hot sex god?'

But Nick was already skimming through the photos on his phone.

'We're almost at Mandy's Palace of Power, so gird your loins, not that I have any idea what loins are, or what girding might involve. I imagine you'd need one of those 24-hour panty corselets of our youth...not that I ever wore one, though, lord knows, I needed to.'

'Janey wore one at that Christmas disco,' said Nick, distractedly looking at his phone.

'Really. Ah! I see! And that explains the rigid gusset which has so long puzzled us?'

'Aye.'

Jeff turned into the police station car park and took the first parking space, coming to a halt with a judder as he stepped on the brake too hard. Nick held his phone out under Jeff's nose.

'What do you see in this photo?'

The big man took the device from him and held it up close to his eyes. 'You know what? I have no idea why phones are called smart. This is stupidly small. I don't see what it is. Oh, hang on...is it from Doc Brown's in the Boro?'

'Yes. Exactly. I took that about three seconds before that person, right in the middle of the photo, threw the petrol bomb that set you on fire.'

'Twat!' Jeff jabbed his finger at the phone, as though in retribution. 'I'm gonna get you!'

'And I've just realised who that is,' said Nick.

'What? How can you know that? They've got a balaclava on.'

He leaned over. 'See their trainers?'

Jeff squinted. 'Yeah, white with a purple flash. So what?'

'What else are they wearing?

'How many more questions do you want me to answer? Err...let's see...black sports top and some sort of sporty, Lycra leggings which are...err...black, purple and grey.'

'Anything else, strike you?'

Jeff groaned. 'I don't know. Stop trying to make yourself look clever and tell me what's on your mind.'

Nick took the phone from him and pointed at the figure. 'We referred to this person as "he" but this is actually a woman. I thought it was a man because her legs are so well developed and she doesn't really have pronounced hips. But this is a well-developed woman. And I know who it is and it's blowing my mind.'

Jeff took the phone off him. 'I can see what you mean, I think, at least now you've said. To be honest, I'm just saying that, it's not obvious at all to me.'

Nick flicked at the screen to reveal a second photo of the firebomber, just as they had let go of the bottle full of petrol and looked at the slightly blurred picture. Yeah, it was her. You could tell by the bright green eyes.

'See this?' He let the phone rest on Jeff's hand. 'It's Alice Coates.'

'What?!'

'True fact. I'm 100 per cent certain. Same shape of legs, exact same sportswear. Like a typical sexist idiot, I assumed that someone so athletic and fast was male. I'm embarrassed I went to such an easy default.'

'Woah, woah woah. Hold on, neddy. Wow. So when you met her, did she know it was you that had chased her? She must have done. Maybe that's why she was - what was it Powell said - Ice Cube Tits? She was super defensive and scared that you knew what she'd done."

'She only got one brief close-up look at me as I approached her, but I was moving fast.'

Jeff rubbed at an eye. 'Hang on, if you're right, what does this mean? Is she the killer? She can't be.'

'Why not?'

He looked at the photo again. 'I don't know. I'm just being bigoted, probably. It goes against everything we think about women. Men are war-mongering bastards, women give birth and nurture. A fast, fit, muscular woman like this just doesn't look like a killer in our cultural universe.'

Nick chewed his bottom lip. 'And I've just realised something else. I saw her putting the notice up in Gaia about the demo when I was buying the Bio-Oil. She knew the lass who was on the till. The lass even said, "See you, Alice." Christ, how come I didn't recognise her when I met her? She was encouraging people to go to a demo that she was planning to disrupt. But if the idea is to wreck the Save The Earth organisation, why would she try to get people to it?'

'You're overthinking it. She just wanted to make a big splash and scare more people, probably.'

A car pulled in beside them. 'Ah, it's Gaunty, look,' said Nick, giving him a wave.

They got out of the van and shook hands with Jon Gaunt. Born in Eaglescliffe, he was six foot, unshaven, had scruffy thick white hair, wore a denim shirt and jeans and had leathery tanned skin. In his mid 60s now, his roots were in the late 60s counterculture, such as it was in the northeast of England. Driven almost wholly by idealism and political commitment to help the poor and the oppressed, he worked for the Public Defender Service in Darlington, funded by Legal Aid.

'Now then, Gaunty. How are you?' said Nick.

'Fine. Hello, Jeff. How's that shop of yours?'

'All good, mate. You're looking well.' He pointed at his tan.

'Had a few days in Ibiza. Drug busts. Had to get some local kids out of jail. So what have we got here, Nick? Julie gave me only a few details.'

As they walked into the station, Nick went over all the main facts. Gaunty nodded, quickly and quietly absorbing them.

'They've arrested him? He's 16? Never been in trouble? If it's all circumstantial, I'll have him out of here as soon as. Sounds like an overreaction.'

His words calmed Nick's nerves a bit. He was such a good man to have on your side.

Nick pulled open the police station door and they strode into the reception area. All the staff knew the lawyer well.

'Hello, Gaunty,' said the sergeant on the desk, looking up from a computer screen. 'What brings you here?'

'Alright, Jim. Young boy, Josh Jones. Just arrested in Stockton.'

The copper stood up and looked at some sheets of paper on his desk. 'Oh, aye.' He picked up a phone and hit an internal extension number, spoke briefly to someone and then put it down again.

No sooner had he done so than a locked door was opened and Vic Bowes came out looking very pleased with himself. He clapped his hands together, looked at Nick, Jeff and then Jon Gaunt.

'You're too late, Mr Gaunt. He's already confessed to the whole bloody thing. Banged to rights.'

CHAPTER 18

'You've bullied it out of him. He's innocent. It'll never stand up in court!' raged Nick, his blood instantly running hot.

'This is your last and only warning, Mr Guymer. I'm tired of your insults and attitude. Shut it or I'll nick you for...'

But Gaunty intervened, speaking in a clear, firm, confident Teesside voice, 'No you won't, Bowes. Mr Guymer is perfectly within his rights to dispute your bald statement of the boy's guilt. You may find his language strong, but he's under a lot of stress and, so far, has not broken any laws, therefore you are not allowed to arrest him and if you do, I shall bring a harassment charge and we will win and you will lose and you will look very foolish. I suggest you do not want that to happen.'

Bowes just shrugged. 'He's always in my face, this one,' said Bowes to the sergeant, dismissively jerking a thumb at Nick.

'I will need to see young Josh. Is his mother here?' said Jon Gaunt.

Bowes nodded, knowing he had to do what the lawyer wanted. 'Wait here. I'll make the arrangements.' He left.

'Thanks, Gaunty,' said Nick, with a smile. 'That was a nice little speech.'

'Vic's an arsey sod. Always has been. Now, Josh's mother will be sitting in with him. You're going to have to wait here. You'll only get access to him as a visitor, if they hold him in the cells here and I'm hoping that will not be the outcome.'

'If the only evidence they have on Josh is his own confession, how good a case would that be?' asked Jeff.

'That would depend on so many different things. Without hard evidence it would be difficult to get a conviction and I'd be surprised if the CPS even let it proceed to court.' He lowered his voice. 'The unique thing here is the multiple murders. They're under huge pressure and that can do strange things to the police force.'

'You mean they might fit him up?' asked Nick.

'Not if they think he's innocent, but yes, if they think he's guilty but can't prove it sufficiently. That's just my personal view based on 45 years in the business.'

'If they charge him, rightly or wrongly, what would happen to him next?' asked Nick.

'I'd ask for him to be bailed but given the crime, that's likely to be turned down. Then he'd be kept on remand at the Young Offenders Institution whilst CPS looked at and decided if it should proceed to court. While there, he'd have a medical assessment. This would likely be down in Wetherby. The local place closed recently.'

'Bloody hell,' said Jeff. 'That's miles away. And he'd be with some really hard kids. He'd not survive that. He's a gentle, clever lad.'

'I hear what you say, but that is nonetheless what would happen. It'd be tough for him, there's no point in saying otherwise. There is little special accommodation made for someone with Asperger's. Prison is harder on them than on most.'

'Shit. I should never have told you to make that call, Jeff. This could be the death of the boy.'

'If you had withheld information about McGregor, you'd have got into some very hot water, trust me,' said Gaunt. 'You had no real choice.'

The locked door opened again and Vicky, Josh's mother came out. She'd clearly been crying. 'Thank you for coming, Mr Gaunt. Thanks for asking him, Nick.'

'How's Josh?' asked Nick.

She pushed at her mess of loosely permed hair. 'Remarkably calm.'

'You do know he is nothing to do with these murders, don't you?' said Nick.

'I'm bewildered by it all, Nick. I had no idea that he was even under suspicion.'

'Were you present when he confessed?' asked Gaunty.

She swallowed hard and nodded.

'Was he coerced in any way?'

'Not at all. We sat down. The officer - a nice woman - said something like, can you tell me what you know about the murders of your classmates and right away he said, "I am most likely to have killed them, I'm afraid. I'm sorry". And that was that.'

'Follow-up questions?' asked the lawyer, a frown setting into his heavily creased face.

'She said. "Are you sure?" He said he was sure. Then she asked if he was confessing to the murders of - and she read out the three girls' names.'

'What did he say to that?' asked Nick.

'He said that no-one was as likely as he was to have killed them. She asked again if he *did* kill them and Josh just looked at her, you know, with his blank expression and said he didn't know how it couldn't be him but he had no memory of killing them. There were more questions this time about Mr McGregor.'

'Did he confess to killing him?' asked Jon Gaunt.

'No. He said he'd got a text from McGregor and had gone to the house in response to it. I actually saw that on his phone. It's true. He did. He showed me and the officer the text. It just said he wanted to meet him at his house and there was an address. That's all. When he got there, the door was open. He went in and walked around the house and found McGregor's body. Then you rang the bell, he didn't know it was you and, at the first opportunity, he ran for it.'

'So he's categorically denying killing McGregor and all of the Richardsons?' said Gaunt.

She nodded and look around herself wildly. 'Yes, Mr Gaunt. I just can't believe any of this. I'm shocked to my bones. My Josh is a good boy. You know that, Nick. He can't have...he hasn't...'

Vic Bowes came out of the secure area of the station and stood hands on his hips, sweat stains under his arms, tie loosened. 'We're ready for you, Mr Gaunt.'

'Just a minute, I need a word, Jon.' Nick tugged on the lawyer's arm and took him to one side while Jeff put his arm around Vicky's shoulder.

'Me and Jules talked to Josh the other evening. He's working on statistical probability. He said to us he thought he was statistically the most likely to have done it and had worked it all out, Julie pointed out that he hadn't assigned motive to any of his stats and...well...he should re-do them. He may have done so and for some reason, it's made him feel he's even more guilty.' He ran both hands through his hair. 'Christ man, this is so complicated. There's a lot more to tell you.'

'OK. I understand. I note he didn't confess to the murders, as Bowes said he had. He didn't. He seems to have said he considers himself likely to have done it and that is *very* different. My aim right now is to prevent them charging him today. Buy ourselves some time.' He whacked Nick on the shoulder and gave him a stern smile, then turned to Vic Bowes. 'Right, I'm all yours.' And he walked through the door.

Just as he did, the door to the station opened and Julie walked in. She gave a little shiver.

'Eee, it's cold today. Hello, Vicky; hello, lads. How's things going with Josh?'

Nick stood up, took her by the arm and went outside, so that the sergeant couldn't hear.

'What's happened? she said, worry set into her face.

Nick explained, as she concentrated on his words.

'But...he surely hasn't actually confessed to murdering the girls. He's acknowledged being the most likely. Just as he did the other night.'

'Exactly. I just said that to Jon. I think that's what he is going to push in order to prevent them from charging him today.'

'Thank god for Gaunty. Vicky looked wrecked.'

'Sorry, I've no sympathy for her. Sure, you're upset about what your son may or may not have done, but how about being in his life more?'

Julie licked her lips and looked into the distance, thoughtfully. 'Yeah, well, let's worry about Josh first.'

Before they went back in, Nick told her about Alice Coates and the Middlesbrough petrol bombing, got out his phone and showed her the pictures.

'Are you sure, it's her?' she said.

'Yes. Positive. The eyes.'

'It explains why she was so agile and was able to get away from you. I mean, she's obviously a brilliant freerunner.'

'And is totally built for it. I thought, when I met her, what powerful legs she had.'

He took her cold hands in his.

'I've not had time to consider this properly, but is it possible Coates is the killer? Remember what Jenny said at your dad's house?'

'About the population control? I suppose it is, yeah. Why don't we try and get the police to search wherever she lives? If it's her, there'll be evidence of the poisons, surely.'

'Well, that'd be great, but on what precepts can they do that? They can't just say, "Oh, Nick Guymer thinks you were a firebomber, give us a look in your house", can they?'

'Shit, I suppose not, but they should know of our suspicions, so they can investigate.'

'No. We're going to have to do that.'

'What? How?' She looked at him incredulously.

'You and me are going to prove she's the lunatic behind all of this.'

She raised her eyebrows and blew out her cheeks. 'You reckon? OK. I'll take your word for it.'

They went back inside. Jeff was chatting to Vicky and she was laughing at something he'd said. Jeff could be very funny, but this was no time for laughter. It annoyed Nick and he realised he really disliked her. She was one of those rather childish people for whom life was all about themselves and anyone else, son included, seemed to be an optional extra.

There was nothing to do but sit and wait.

As they sat, Nick got on his phone and did a search for Alice+Coates+army+Catterick.

There was nothing.

When Jon Gaunt emerged, he had a half smile on his lips.

'How's Josh?' asked Nick, standing up, noting his mother wasn't quite so quickly concerned.

'He's doing well, all things considered. No freak outs, which is good. I'd almost say he's enjoying this.'

'What?' How?' said Nick, puzzled.

'Well, he's highly intelligent, and, as such, he's enjoying the new experience. But - and it's a big but - he has no concept of what will happen to him if he's charged.'

'Can we see him?' said Julie.

'I don't think that's a good idea. The more coming and going he has to put up with, the more stressful it might become. I'll tell him you're thinking of him and will see him tomorrow.' The lawyer looked around. 'Can we go out into the car park? I think it'd be for best.'

They adjourned outside under the cold, grey skies.

'OK, look. I've told them that Josh has not, in actual fact, confessed to anything, other than to a probability. He's been steadfast about that, too. He's not said, at any point, that he put chemicals on the skin of the girls and killed them. In fact, he's said he has no memory of doing that. He looks at this forensically. Everything he's said is 100 per cent accurate. Overly so, if you get me.'

'That's typical of him,' said Nick.

'However, they're going to hold him for 24 hours. But not charge him. They've said they're going to question him more tomorrow, part of the not-too-much-stress strategy. I'll be present.' The old lawyer scuffed at the gravel in the car park with his foot. 'I think they've nothing hard on him.'

'So why are they holding him without charging him?' asked Julie.

Jon Gaunt didn't reply immediately, as he cogitated on the situation, finally letting out a sigh.

'My view is they're leaving it for 24 hours to try and firm it all up. The problem here is this: They can charge him and send him on remand, during which time they can gather more evidence...or not, as the case may be. It's the easy option for them. We want to avoid that at all costs to preserve Josh's sanity. I've been to where he'd be held...' he shook his head '...it's a brutal place full of cruel, vicious villains, the mentally ill and the violent. Putting Josh in that environment would be...shall we say...destructive, for the lad."

'Oh, my god, it sounds like hell. So, basically we've got 24 hours to prove he's innocent?' said Nick. 'Or for all intents and purposes, he's dead.'

Gaunt nodded. 'If we can't plant serious doubt, they'll charge him and let the CPS sort it out. That's clearly their intent. They want to announce they've got the killer, Bowes especially. It's his last big case, isn't it? He wants to go out on a high. Of course, if another death happens while he's in here, the same sort of death at least, then that'll help his case. But obviously we want to avoid that.'

'We do because the next is Jenny Wells, who is my dad's granddaughter,' said Julie.

'Really? Good god.' He shook his head. 'This is a very difficult case.'

'So he'll be held in an actual prison cell?' said his mother, still clearly in some sort of shock.

'Yes. But he's fine. Don't worry. They've been careful not to trigger his negative reactions. They know if they do, it'll only invalidate any future court case. They're being careful to keep very calm and not clutter his brain with questions. To be honest with you, I've known a lot of Asperger's people over the years, and Josh is one that is obviously totally at ease on his own in a small room. In fact, the thing we'd hate - the deprivation of choice and freedom - actually plays to his strengths. He likes calmness and things not to change and when you're in a cell, not much changes.'

At last, they all went silent. Just 24 hours to prove his innocence. Jesus Christ, how the hell were they going to do that?

'OK Batman, how exactly are we going to catch this killer?' said Jeff, as he drove them back to Stockton, behind Julie, who was driving the Porsche.

'Back to our house. First, we do in-depth research into the 6th-form teachers Alice Coates, George Tyers and Geoff Powell. A real three-laptop job, right?'

'OK. Then what?

'First, we find out where Coates lives - I've got an idea where that might be - and then we break into her house and look for evidence of poisons. We know she's capable of extreme behaviour, throwing firebombs, and we suspect she's a green extremist. We have to think she's our best bet.'

'Shouldn't you tell the police about her being one of the firebombers?'

'No. I'm telling them nothing until we've got this stitched up tight. I'm not giving Vic Bowes anything. He can fuck right off. I'm going to rub his fucking nose in his own crapulence.'

'Fair enough. I'll keep schtum with Mand. So where does Coates live, do you reckon?'

'South of Stockton. Somewhere just out of town. The path I saw her running ends up by the Preston Farm industrial estate and the track petered out. You wouldn't run there and then turn around and run back, I don't reckon. So I think she lives down there somewhere, or near to the track. We'll find out exactly where by searching the electoral register.'

They ground to a near halt in slow traffic.

Jeff spoke. 'The trouble with this case is...'

'...case? It's a case?'

'It's a case. We've had a lot of cases, we just never call them cases, but cases they be.'

'OK, so what about *this* case?'

'Six people have died but for two different reasons. That's what I think. The girls were killed to stop them having kids, Paul killed himself and his parents,' said Jeff.

'I still find it hard to believe that anyone could think that killing a few Teesside girls is going to make any difference to the population of the earth. It's mad. It doesn't surrender to logical thought,' said Nick.

Jeff ran his fingers through his beard, waiting for traffic to move through roadworks. 'Yeah, but I suppose when you're totally committed to something, logic and proportion fall sloppy dead, to almost quote Jefferson Airplane. In other words, once you're convinced of a cause, you just think you're making your small contribution to that cause. In their loopy universe, you kill three girls, you stop six or seven kids being born. You've done your bit.'

Nick stroked Stanley, who was wide awake now and probably hungry and thirsty. 'Don't worry Stan, I've got some stew in the fridge with your name on it. You always liked my stew, didn't you?'

Jeff glanced over at the dog, sitting upright on Nick's lap. 'He's the only dog I've known who you literally expect to start talking at any moment. I'm sure he can, he's just choosing not to. Also, he really should be wearing glasses. I've always thought that he's got a professorial look to him.' He gave the dog's right ear a little tickle.

'Yeah, I hear what you say about having a cause. There's some more research to do. Have such schoolgirl deaths happened anywhere else in the country, or even worldwide? Maybe it's a movement?'

Jeff nodded. 'Yeah, yeah, yeah, this is all making much more sense. Once you build in the righteous belief a cause gives you, anything is possible. Even so, Save The Earth were anti-population growth. Why wasn't that enough for the bombers?'

'Probably because STE aren't a serious group. Like you said, they're a hippy and student gathering, wanking themselves off on the idea of rebellion, while mummy and daddy invest in property for their inheritance. OK, I'm probably being a bit OTT, but that's their basic vibe. The bombers are for real. They mean it, man, and they don't want a watery version of what they believe in getting all the attention.'

They stopped off at the shop to pick up Jeff's laptop, then went on to Norton. After feeding, watering and walking the dog, picking up his shit in a small bag, Nick returned home to find Julie and Jeff in the living room listening to Tangerine Dream's *Ricochet* album, a large vodka and tonic on the coffee table for him.

They set to work, saying very little as they went after information.

Nick looked into Alice Coates, putting her name into Google. It brought her up on the college website, on which she was pictured, staring back at the camera, hair pulled back, small features, unusually green eyes. Not smiling. Like himself, she wasn't very photogenic and seemed frozen in the camera's headlights.

She'd worked for the army at Catterick, so he entered her name+army+Catterick into the search engine again. Still no results. The only Alice Coates that came up at all were people who were clearly not her.

'I'm getting nothing for Alice Coates in the army.'

'Maybe she's lying and wasn't in the army,' said Jeff.

Nick made a face. 'Nah, it's too easily checked. If you're going to lie, you'd make it harder to disprove.'

'I've got her home address, I think,' said Julie. 'I've had to pay some money to People Finder, but I've got her...err...right...let me look this up...'

'I bet it's south of Hartburn somewhere,' said Nick.

She took a drink and entered the post code. 'Yeah, good call, Guymer...' she studied the map '...it's what was probably, once upon a time, a farmhouse out beyond Hartburn Village.'

'So she was probably running home when I saw her,' said Nick. 'And just like McGregor, she can go to and from her home without even going on a road.'

'She actually goes past McGregor's house,' said Jeff, looking at a map of the area on his laptop. 'He would have gone to work on the same route. Maybe they struck up a thing with each other.'

'I don't think so, Janey would've almost certainly have known about it, if they had,' said Nick.

Jeff stroked his beard. 'I'm looking at the college website and the chemistry teacher is this bloke, George Tyers...'

'...Janey mentioned him. Said he was vile and wore sandals with socks.'

'Oof, that is vile,' said Jeff. 'No call for that. Can you find his address on People Finder, Jules? He'll be about 60 or 61.'

She got to work.

'What are you thinking, Jeff?' asked Nick.

'Yer chemmy teacher has access to dangerous chemicals - brilliant, aren't I? And if Paul used them on himself and his parents, he has to have got them somewhere. I'm just wondering if Tyers lives near or alongside the cycle path and could therefore have left his house, done a bit of girl killing and gone home without anyone ever seeing him. And again, no CCTV to catch him doing anything.'

'Here we go,' said Julie. 'George Tyers, 62, he lives at 98 Castle Close, Stockton. Where's that? I've not heard of it.'

Jeff did a search. 'Bingo!' He made a klaxon noise and pulled an imaginary horn. 'It's off Bishopton Road West, just along from St

Bede's school, not far from 6th form at all, and there's a pathway at the end of the street, right by his house! And that leads onto the main cycle path heading north and south. So he could leave his house and take that route to school, just like Coates and McGregor. And they could all get to and from each other's houses, without going on a road. That's a very strange coincidence, don't you think?'

Nick bit his bottom lip. 'I know what you mean, but those tracks traverse several miles in total, and a lot of houses are right by them.'

An idea occurred to him. 'Maybe Alice Coates doesn't come up on my searches, apart from 6th form, because she's just changed her name.'

'Married, you mean?' said Julie, looking up from her laptop.

'I was thinking divorced. There's no sign of a man in her life. She's reverted to using her maiden name.'

'I'll see if I can find her in births, marriages and deaths,' she said. 'How old do you think she is?'

'Not over 30. I'd guess 28,' said Nick. 'Try to find her in North Yorkshire. If she worked at Catterick she'll either have lived there, or locally.'

Jeff cracked his knuckles and stared at a map on his screen. 'I'm looking at the centre of Middlesbrough, right? And I'm tracing the route Coates ran, with you in hot pursuit, and it's pretty obvious that if she kept leaping from roof to roof, only going to ground in little back streets and alleyways, she could get away some distance before she's picked up on any CCTV cameras in town.'

'Yeah. She planned it out. She'd probably have been parked somewhere out of the way and worked out a freerunner route to and from it,' said Nick.

Julie made a squeaking noise. 'Eeek, I think I've found her. Alice Teresa Coates married Colin Thurston at Scorton Methodist Chapel. 11th June 2011.'

'Where's that?' asked Nick.

'North Yorkshire, innit?' said Jeff, loading the map. 'Yup, it's north of Catterick. Nice little village set around a green. Must have been where she lived. You'd not get wed there otherwise. Might even be where she grew up.'

Julie was still typing, humming to herself as she did so. 'It's fizzin' amazing what you can find out about people, if they don't tick all the relevant boxes to lock down their information. Colin Thurston lives on The Green, in Scorton. He was on the electoral roll there as living with Alice Thurston in 2011, but *not* in 2012. She's gone. He's still there. So that's the story. They divorced last year. It can't have lasted much more than 12 months. And I bet she left the army, as well as getting divorced. A whole new start, like...just a minute...' She searched for Alice Thurston+Catterick+army. 'Yes! Get in! Got her. She was a physical instructor in the army. Must have got the job when she got married, then left on getting divorced, hence she didn't show up as Coates.'

Jeff bent down and stroked the dozing Stanley, who was lying flat out beside his armchair.

'Might be worth taking a trip down there and giving the ex a bit of a probing.'

'That'd be so weird, though,' said Nick. 'Stranger turns up at your door, knows you've been divorced and wants to know if the ex-wife is capable of murdering.'

Jeff raised his index finger. 'Ah, but anyone who divorced within a year is going to feel pretty bitter, or very relieved, or both, and so might be happy to blab about her.' Nick nodded.

'Shall we go down there tomorrow, Jules? You can chat him up a bit. You're good at manipulating men,' said Nick.

'You're not that challenging to manipulate. First pull up, then pull down. Repeat until desired result is achieved. Easy,' she said, distractedly curling a strand of hair around her finger, as she looked at the screen. 'We should pay a visit to Alice's house and Chemistry George's as well. If no-one is in, we might spring their locks and have a sniff around. We just need something to put doubt in the police's minds about Josh's guilt. Time's running out.'

'And sodding quick,' added Nick. 'Can you get off work tomorrow?'

She nodded. 'Just thinking about Paul Richardson. Why did he choose to kill himself on the roof of the gym? Why there? Is that significant? It must be significant.'

'It's an odd place, that's for sure,' said Jeff.

'Could just be random. He had to do it somewhere. You get a good view from up there.'

Jeff raised his finger. 'Ah, or alternatively, you can be seen from some distance, by someone. His death is then a trigger for something else.'

'What, though?' asked Nick. 'He died early Monday morning, Connie died late afternoon. I think you're right Jules, I think he was telling us something. I think he was associating it with death, just by being there.'

'And surely that means Coates or Geoff Powell,' said Julie. 'It's their facility.'

'But it's also where a lot of classes are held, where various school clubs meet and where kids play sport. It could be indicative of something to do with that,' said Jeff.

The three of them sat in silence looking at each other, the dog asleep now.

'This is hurting my lovely brain,' said Jeff, after five minutes. 'And I need my lovely brain so that I can recite the entire Frank Zappa discography in chronological order.'

CHAPTER 19

It was a bright and breezy morning. Nick parked the Mercedes beside a large circular patch of grass in centre of the village of Scorton, got out and took a look around. His stomach was churning with nervous worry for Josh.

'This is really nice,' said Julie, pulling on her leather bike jacket over a sweatshirt. 'It smells so clean and fresh.'

'It looks a bit like Norton Green, doesn't it?' he said, as they walked towards Colin Thurston's house.

'Yeah, except it's really peaceful and quiet. There's no traffic noise at all. Oh, god, it's so nice. I really miss living in the countryside. That house we had was infested with mice and run down, but it was in a lovely location. Let's find somewhere else like that.'

He put his arm around her shoulder and gave her a squeeze. 'OK, I'm up for that...here we are.' He pointed at a green door. The house looked old, maybe originally early 19th century. Made of small, hand-made red bricks with small and narrow windows, it was connected to houses on either side, both of which were very different in age and style, as indeed were all of the many houses around the green. It gave the village an eclectic, messy look, and was none the worse for that. North Yorkshire did a lot of villages like this. Hardly chocolate box, but nonetheless interesting and characterful.

Nick was about to rap on the door with the big brass knocker, when it suddenly opened and a man came out, almost crashing into him.

'Sorry, mate,' he said, pulling up short.

'No worries. Are you Colin Thurston, by any chance?' said Nick, trying not to let his tension show.

'Yeah. Who's asking?'

'I'm Nick Guymer, this is Julie Wells...' she smiled her best smile, head cocked to one side sympathetically. 'We're with Cleveland Police and are looking into the murders in Stockton. I'm sure you've heard about it.'

He closed his door behind him and turned a key in a mortice lock.

'Yeah, I heard about that on the local news. What's it to do with me?'

He was lean, with high cheekbones, grey eyes and full lips. In his early 30s, he wore a black fleece, black Lycra running leggings and training shoes. He was obviously about to go on a run.

'As you might know, three of the girls killed were taught by your wife, Alice, so we're just trying to get a picture of everyone involved at 6th form,' said Nick, thinking he was pushing his luck a bit by pretending to be a copper, but Colin Thurston bought it 100 per cent. Then again, why wouldn't you? No-one expects to be interviewed by people pretending to be the police.

'I didn't know that. Of course. How can I help?'

Julie took a pace forward. 'Tell us about Alice.'

As he talked, Nick looked him up and down. He was a good-looking man with sensitive eyes. 'Alice? You're probably asking the wrong man, I'm afraid.'

'Why's that?' asked Julie.

He looked into the distance. 'We...we had a whirlwind romance and marriage, but we fell apart just as quickly.'

Julie smiled. 'I'm sorry to hear that.'

'Oh, don't be sorry.' He raised his hands up in surrender. 'It was one of those things.'

'What sort of person is Alice?' asked Nick.

He frowned. 'Well, that's hard to say.' He shook his head. 'Err...she's very passionate and I liked that...at first. She's intense. She's incredibly fit and takes being strong and healthy seriously. We met at a charity running event.'

'Does she do freerunning?'

He frowned. 'Freerunning? No. She's into cross-country and orienteering.'

'Is she interested in politics?' asked Nick. 'We understand that she's interested in green and environmental issues,' said Nick.

He nodded and looked at his watch. 'Yeah, that's right. She's a vegan these days.'

'Would you say she's quite extreme in her views?' asked Julie.

He nodded right away. 'Oh, yeah. I mean, that's one of the reasons we broke up. She's obsessed with it. On every single level.' He blew out air. 'I just couldn't stand it any longer so we split up last year. I've tried to get in touch and patch things up, but she doesn't respond.'

'Why did she leave the army and go into teaching?'

'She wanted to work with children and help them to live good healthy lives and have a good attitude to life. She was very passionate about it, plus she didn't want to live around here after we'd split.'

'Did that go hand in hand with her increasing green outlook?' said Nick.

He nodded again.

'Was she concerned with overpopulation?' asked Nick.

'What?' The penny dropped with him. 'Do you...you don't think...you don't think she's...'

'...we don't think anything, Colin; we're exploring ideas, that's all,' said Julie.

'She wasn't specifically concerned about that, no. But she was always on about exhausting the earth's resources and wanting to start a green revolution. She joined some Facebook group called Save The Earth for a while, but fell out with someone there...I mean, I say fell out, I don't really know what happened. She just said they were all poseurs and err...what was her words again...err..."hippy wankers" and that wasn't her outlook at all.'

'So all this got too much for you?' said Julie.

He looked at the ground and winced. 'Yeah. I guess so. And...well...we shouldn't have got married at all. I knew really...'

'...knew you shouldn't get married?' asked Nick.

He winced again. 'I knew she...or rather, I didn't know, but I suspected, that she was actually gay, but in denial to herself about it. We just pretended for a while. But...well...it became obvious soon enough.' He looked at Nick. 'This is really embarrassing.'

'Don't worry about it. I get what you're saying. Does she have a partner or girlfriend now?'

He shrugged. 'I really have no idea. Like I say, I've heard nothing from her since the day she left, not even a single email. I've even sent letters to the forwarding address she gave me, but if she's getting them, she doesn't reply. Are you sure she's not in trouble?'

'Would you expect her to be?' asked Nick.

He rested his weight on one hip and scratched at his hair. 'I just don't know. I'm sorry. She means well. She really does. But it's hard to live with anyone who becomes evangelical about something. They get blinkered to any other point of view, y'know?'

Julie nodded. 'She taught the three girls who have been murdered. How do you think it'll have affected her?'

He didn't speak for a few seconds, pondering his response. 'It'll have upset her, but she's the sort of person who swallows emotion down and fears she'll look weak if she shows it.'

'Would you say she's a feminist?' asked Julie.

Thurston didn't hesitate. 'Absolutely. She didn't hate men, but she did feel they were all too often a malign influence on women and I agreed with her. It's pretty obvious when you see the way the world is.'

'So is she more comfortable in the company of women than men, would you say?' she asked.

He made a puzzled face. 'Why do Cleveland Police want to know that?'

'Like I said, we're just building a picture,' she said.

'I suppose she is. Yes. Now, I really have to get to going, if that's OK? I've got a cross-country race to run.'

Nick shook his hand. 'Thanks for your help.'

He walked away and got into an old Ford Ka and drove off.

'Well, he was so nice,' said Julie. 'A bit of a feminist with nice eyes - reminds me of another bloke I know.'

She grinned at him.

'I don't look as good in Lycra as he did.'

'I wouldn't let you out the bloody house in Lycra! C'mon let's get back home and pay Chemistry George a visit. We're running out of time. It's 9.15am. We need to get something to help Josh by no later than 5pm.'

Nick leaned on the roof of the car, as she pulled open the passenger door. 'You know what? I find it impossible to imagine Alice Coates killing anyone, let alone the girls she teaches. I just can't imagine it.'

She rested on the door and looked at him. 'You're just saying that because she's a woman. You've got to get over that preconditioning. You'd have no trouble thinking George Powell could do it, would you?'

'No. I wouldn't. And statistically, he's far more likely to be a killer than she is...'

'...but statistics only tell you what has happened, not what is happening. And from what Colin told us, she's not your average woman.'

'And we know from what he said, she must only relatively recently have begun freerunning. And we know how good she is at that already.'

She turned her face into the breeze, blowing back her hair. 'Well, that's only true if you're right about the firebomber. It might be someone who just looks like her. It sounds to me like she's what my mam would call "proper off on one".'

'Meaning she's crazy?'

'Not crazy, as such, meaning she's obsessed, blinkered or totally immersed. In Alice's case she's proper off on one about green issues and when you're off on one, who knows what you'd be prepared to do, or what crazy notions get into your head?'

Nick drove back to Stockton on the B roads.

'I think we pulled off pretending to be police, pretty well,' said Julie.

'Well technically, I said we were working *with* Cleveland Police, and that's true, in a way, isn't it?'

'I suppose so. Shall we try it again on Chemistry George?'

'No. If he's got anything to hide, that'll just make him clam up.'

'So why are we there?'

Nick turned off Bishopton Road West, turning up the leafy Castle Close.

'We'll think of something.'

'We'd better do quickly then, that bungalow at the end is 98.'

At the end of the road was a path leading down to the cycle track. Behind the bungalow was a garage-like building.

'That looks interesting,' said Nick, nodding towards it. 'I bet that's a workshop, or a garage converted into one. Look, it's had windows put into it on the roof. You wouldn't do that if you just kept your car in it.'

There was a front door and a side door. Side doors always seem less formal or confrontational, somehow, so he walked down to it and rang the bell. Julie went behind him and looked around the back yard. It was concreted over.

'Deffo a workshop,' she said, nodding and quietly adding, 'Just the sort of place you might keep dangerous chemicals.'

The door opened.

'Hello, Mr Tyers,' said Nick. How old did Janey say he was? 62? That meant he was teenager in the 60s, went to college in the 70s; so why did he look like 62-year old teachers looked like when he was at Ian Ramsey as a kid? He wore a beige cardigan with leather patches on the elbow, brown slacks, a blue open-neck shirt and open-toe sandals with brown socks. Urgh. Clearly the rock 'n' roll years had passed George Tyers by.

'I was expecting you this afternoon,' he said, in a gruff, coarse Stockton accent. He closed the door behind him. 'It's out the back here.'

Nick glanced at Julie, and made a gesture to suggest they play along with being whoever the teacher thought they were.

He led them out to the workshop and opened the door. Inside were two long wooden benches, shelves of jars and tins, tools hanging up.

'Quite a workshop you've got,' said Nick. 'What are all these jars and bottles?'

Julie picked a brown bottle up and inspected it. It had ridges on it.

'I work on experiments in here - for use in class. I'm a chemistry teacher. Can't do it in the house for insurance reasons. Ridiculous.'

'In case something goes boom?'

'Indeed. Not that it would, but insurance companies worry about such things.'

'Do you need a licence to have lots of chemicals in a workshop at home? Surely some are restricted,' said Julie. 'Or they might get stolen and used for nefarious purposes.' She looked around as she spoke. The place was packed with all sorts of bottles and jars. Some looked really old. It seemed likely he'd been filching this stuff from the college and other places he'd worked, for years.

'Oh, err, no. It's all...err...it's all fine. And safe.' He was suddenly a little edgy. Nick looked him in the eyes. He was nervous now.

Tyers pointed to a lawnmower. 'Here it is. It's not in great condition, but then you only paid £10 for it, didn't you?'

He must have sold it on eBay and someone was due to pick it up.

'I'm really interested in chemistry, actually. Always have been,' said Nick, always comfortable with making up a story on the spot. His CSE grade 5 was proof of his complete disinterest in chemistry and how rubbish he was at it. 'I wonder if you can explain something to me? I was reading how some Russian dissident was supposedly murdered by the KGB. And they did it by applying two different chemicals to his skin. On their own, the chemicals were not dangerous but when combined were highly toxic. Is that actually possible?'

This seemed to agitate Tyers even more and he shifted around on his feet. 'I don't know, do I? I mean...I don't work for the KGB.'

Nick forced a small laugh. 'No, but I just wondered if it was possible and which two chemicals they might have used.'

Tyer narrowed his eyes and looked at Julie, who stood hands in jeans pockets, quietly observing him, then he turned back to Nick. 'Well, I suppose it is. Yes, well yes, yes it is. That is the nature of chemistry. One thing added to another produces a third.'

He was more nervous now.

'So, would it be easy to get chemicals like that, or would it have to be a military thing?' asked Nick.

Tyers brushed dust off the bench with his hand, distractedly. 'Who knows? I'm but a humble chemistry teacher. Now if you'd like to take the mower...'

Nick pushed it one more time, choosing his words carefully. 'So you put a dab of each substance on the victim, they're absorbed by the skin, mix in the bloodstream and work their magic. Is that how you do it?'

Tyers stuttered a little and made his eyes flutter in a way that put Nick in mind of Ray Franks, his regional manager when he was a Littlewoods pools collector in the late 70s. 'Is that what? Err...I'm not a biologist...I don't know. Now, about the mower.'

'Oh, I'm afraid it's a bit too small for our garden,' said Julie, walking out of the workshop. 'Just keep the money, though. We've wasted enough of your time.' They marched away at pace with Tyers saying something about describing it accurately on the eBay listing.

Back in the car, Nick did a three-point turn and drove off. 'Well that was very informative. He was absolutely shitting himself,' he said.

'He went from grumpy old sod to nervous old man, just like that.' She clicked her fingers. 'And there were dozens, hundreds even, of bottles of god knows what in there. There was a bunsen burner, there was a centrifuge and what looked like a medical fridge. It was like a fully equipped laboratory, crossed with a garden shed. Have the police interviewed him, do you reckon?'

He nodded. 'Janey said they'd interviewed them all at 6th form in their offices. So they might not have been to his house and even if they did, if they just went to the front door, they might have missed the workshop tucked around the back.'

'That place had not been searched, that was for sure. There was thick dust on the shelves. When I picked up that bottle, there was a clear spot where it had stood. Nothing had been moved for a while. If they'd searched that place, there's no way anything would have been put back exactly where it had been.'

'Good point. And we can offer that to the police to put doubt in their minds over charging Josh. How can they send him down when they've not even searched that place?'

'And that bottle I picked up was old and it had poison of some sort in it. Or originally, anyway.'

'How do you know that?'

'That's what the ridges on brown bottles were there to indicate, back in the day. He could have reused it, of course.'

He drove down Greens Lane and parked up in Hartburn Village.

'Right, let's take a look at Alice Coates's place,' said Nick.

They walked up onto Darlington Lane, then right onto the cycle path, quickly heading south out of Stockton and into open country. Birds chirped their spring song, and a robin flew ahead of them, skipping from tree to tree. This was a little bit of rural Teesside that outsiders never hear about, let alone see.

'I've never been down here before,' said Julie. 'It's lovely. You forget how quickly it's possible to leave urban Stockton behind. Where does this lead?'

'Basically it peters out under the A66, beside the Preston Farm Industrial Estate and somewhere down there is the farmhouse that Alice Coates lives in.'

'Can she drive to it?'

'It's not on a road, but there must be a track to it, or how could anyone get furniture and stuff in?'

It was only a mile walk. The noise of the traffic on the A66 soon filled the air. As the concrete structure which held one of Teesside's main arteries in place came into view, Nick stopped and pointed at a building in the distance.

'There it is.'

They reached the end of the track.

'It's quite out of the way. Should we go and knock on the door?' said Julie.

'Deffo. Yeah. Let's play innocent.'

They walked down the rutted track to the old farmhouse, which you probably got access to from the industrial estate.

'No car here. Maybe no-one is in,' said Nick.

'She probably doesn't have a car. Wouldn't be green to have one unless it was one of those electric ones you can charge up, and there's not exactly anywhere to do that out here,' said Julie, as a blackbird flew over her head and across a grassy field to a hedgerow, clucking its song.

It was a large, sprawling place with several decrepit outbuildings. The house itself didn't look much better, with sections of what had once been pebble-dash having flaked off, revealing the brick underneath. The door and window frames were a 1950s green, but blistered and faded from years of weathering.

'I wonder why she lives here? She must be on a decent wage and could afford somewhere far nicer. She's really neat, smart and tidy, and this place looks the exact opposite of that,' said Nick as they reached the door and looked around. The A66 filled the air with white traffic noise, but aside from that, it was peaceful and still and really quite isolated.

'Weird that there's a retail park and industrial estate up and over there,' said Julie, pointing east. 'You'd never know from here. It's very private.'

'And there's no-one home by the looks of it,' said Nick, after knocking on the door and waiting. 'But, yeah, it's hard to believe we're just a couple of miles from Stockton Sixth Form College. Let's have a look around.'

They wandered to the back of the house and peered in a kitchen window. Two white mugs sat on the drainer. It all looked very basic and quite bare, frugal to the point of dereliction.

'This doesn't look like a home,' said Julie, looking in a window at what would once have been the back parlour but which had since been knocked through to make one big living room. 'It just doesn't have the lived-in look. There's thick dust on the window sills inside.'

Nick joined her. 'But there's a sofa an armchair and a coffee table, albeit really old 70s-style ones.'

'Hmm, but no TV.'

'You don't need a TV these days, just a computer.'

'She won't have broadband out here, though. No way.'

'Maybe she doesn't like TV. I mean, we only watch football and *Masterchef* on ours, don't we?' said Nick.

'True enough. I prefer the radio to TV, or listening to music. Life is too short to waste it watching telly. Even so, given she started at 6th form in early September, and must have been here now for at least six months to show up on the electoral roll, it still doesn't look lived in. There are almost no possessions. No magazines or newspapers. No ornaments and no pictures on the walls and the whole place is in quite a decrepit state.'

'Maybe she's moved out,' he said, hands in pockets, looking at a gang of sparrows dust-bathing in some dry, fine mud across the yard.

'Yeah, maybe. Something is weird about it, though.'

'Like what?'

'Don't know. I just feel it in my water. Something's not right about this. I don't think she's ever lived here. This is a bolt hole, possibly. Somewhere to hide.'

An air horn from a truck on the dual carriageway in the distance briefly filled the air.

Nick stared at her. 'Listen, I've just had a thought. Could it be that she is registered on the electoral roll as living here, but is really living somewhere else? And she's done it deliberately so she's not traceable. Do you get me?'

She clapped. 'Brilliant. The authorities think she's here, but actually she lives somewhere else and just runs down here to pick up the mail. This is so knackered she must be renting it on the cheap, so can afford it.' She pulled at her chin in contemplation.

'She's not doing that for any other reason other than deception,' said Nick. 'And why would she want to do that? Come on, let's go back to the car.'

'Could be that she's hiding from an abusive man, or woman,' said Julie as they walked.

'Colin Thurston?'

'Maybe. He seemed nice. But then...or maybe it's someone she's since met. We have service users at TW that have to go to great trouble to make sure their ex-partner doesn't know where they're living. Setting up what is effectively a false address is as good a way as any of avoiding your address being looked up on the internet.'

They got back to the Mercedes.

'Christ, we're not getting far in definitively proving Josh innocent, are we?' He looked at his watch as he started the car. 'How the hell are we going to do that, Jules? How?!' He slapped the wheel in frustration. 'Basically, we can't prove where Josh was when the murders happened. We have absolutely no evidence of any wrong doing by anyone else. All we have is a shifty chemistry teacher, and a fucked-up eco-woman who likes freerunning and firebombs, who had a boy kill himself on the roof of her gym. It all adds up to the square root of sod all. Meanwhile, the clock is ticking for Josh. It's already 10.30. Bloody hell.'

'Settle down. We're not beaten yet. This business about Alice's address is another chink in the police's armour. They have to check it all out, surely. Now, where does Geoff Powell live, do you know?'

'One of those new terraced houses on Darlington Lane, which, by the way, isn't far from the north end of the cycle track.'

'Let's go and see him then. Will he be in?'

'Seems likely, as school hasn't opened for business again yet. But what can we say to him? How is he going to help us get proof of Josh's innocence?'

'Just get driving,' she said impatiently.

He did as he was told.

'You said you thought he was genuine and that he was angry that Josh was the main suspect, didn't you?'

'Yup, 100 per cent. He refused to believe it.'

'OK, well that means he'll help us if he can, now that Josh is in custody.'

'OK, but in doing what, Jules? If he had evidence that Alice or anyone else had killed people, he'd have said. He's not holding that back. He's as in the dark as we are.'

'Alright, alright,' she snapped. 'It's the only idea I've got, he just might be able to spark off a thought, the way you say I did when you asked me what would happen next in *Kidda*. I had no idea what you were writing, but just hearing another voice seemed to help you.'

'Yeah, that is true. OK.' He took a left onto Darlington Road and then a right onto Yarm Back Lane which skirts the western edge of Stockton, eventually intersecting Darlington Back Lane. He turned right and soon arrived at a block of new red-brick terraced houses.Geoff Powell's was at the end. Nick parked outside and even as they were getting out, the teacher looked at his front window and saw them. He raised his dark eyebrows in acknowledgement.

'I warn you now, he's a bit of a lech,' said Nick as they waited by the door.

'Of course he is, he's a man.' She hitched up her old jeans and stuffed her hands into her leather jacket pockets.

The door opened. 'Now then, Nick,' he said, nodding. 'To what do I owe this visit?'

'Can we come in, Geoff, something's happened and I need your help.'

'Aye, no bother. And who's this?' he said, looking Julie up and down.

'*This* is Julie Wells,' said Julie, jaw set against him already, hating being addressed as "this".

'Jules is my missus,' added Nick by way of clarity.

'Nice to meet you, luv.'

The house smelt of new carpets and paint. He showed them into the front room. It was straight from IKEA. The walls painted beige, the carpets were a soft grey.

'New house, Geoff?' asked Nick.

'Yeah, just moved in a month or two ago. We used to live in Thornaby. After the divorce, she stayed there and I came here. I like it. I can go for a run out into open country easily enough. So what are these developments?'

He gestured for them to sit down on a new beige two-seat sofa.

'Josh has been arrested.'

'Powell raised his eyebrows. 'For the murders?'

'Yeah. They're holding him for questioning, they're going to charge him in about six hours, unless we can unearth some hard evidence that he couldn't have done it.'

Powell seemed very concerned. 'Shit. But you still think he didn't do it?'

Nick nodded and explained about Josh and his statements of probability. 'Look Geoff, if they charge him, they'll send him to a rough young offender's place in Wetherby to await trial and I don't think he'd survive that in his condition. The cops have always thought he was the one. So have you any suspicions at all about who else it might be, or just any idea whatsoever?'

'It doesn't matter how crazy or extreme,' added Julie. 'We're desperate.'

'I thought it was McGregor. I told you as much in my office. But now he's snuffed it. Are they sure it *wasn't* him and someone else has done for him?'

'I'm afraid Josh was seen leaving McGregor's house, after he'd been murdered. By me, as it happens. So while what you say is a possibility, it still doesn't prove it wasn't Josh.'

'Bloody hell. That lad isn't a killer. Anyone who's known him for a while could tell you that. He's not even a fighting sort of lad. I'll happily vouch for him, if that helps.'

'It'd help, but only in court. He won't survive in that young offender's place. It'll drive him out of his mind,' said Nick. 'We have to get evidence to stop that happening. If we could prove Josh was somewhere else when at least one killing happened, that would be enough for now.'

'Please rack your brains, Geoff,' said Julie, leaning forward, hands between her knees.

The bearded gym teacher sat back and stared out of the window, but said nothing for a full minute. Then, out of nowhere, he jumped as though hit with jolt of electricity.

'Yes!' He gripped a fist and punched the air. 'Heather Leary! Yes, get in! She'll be able to prove where he was when the murders happened.'

'Heather? How?' asked Julie.

'The drones, luv. She flies those drones out the back of the college two nights a week as part of the club that Henry Kilbane runs. That class was active when Emma West was killed. Henry told me. Maybe it was when the other murders happened as well; she flies them all the time, anyway.'

'So what? How does that help Josh?' said Nick.

'She builds them with a camera in, doesn't she? Josh himself told me that because he was saying that she could film the rugby matches from above the pitch. Come on, let's go round to her house and see if she's got drone footage, who knows what it might have filmed?'

For the first time in recent days, Nick felt the tight knot of worry in his gut loosen a little. This was a potential lifeline.

'She lives on Bedale Grove, but I don't know the number. Janey will,' said Geoff.

Nick called her immediately. She said it was 110. They went straight there. It was just over a mile, straight down Rimswell Road, then Fairfield Road, turning off down Upsall Grove all the way to Aiskew, where Janey was, then along Kipling and onto Bedale Grove, a street of semi-detached houses that were very similar in size and style to Palm Grove where he'd grown up, each with a small garden at the rear, backing onto a large open field, ideal for flying a drone.

Nick rang the doorbell. A middle-aged woman came to the door. She had shoulder-length ginger hair that Heather had obviously inherited.

Julie stepped forward. 'Mrs Leary?'

'Yes. Oh, hello, Mr Powell. What are you doing here? Is 6th form reopening?'

'It's not about that. Is Heather at home?'

'She's out on the field with her dad, droning.'

'Can we get out there from your back garden?' said Nick.

'Well, yes. What's this about?'

'It's complicated and is about the murders, but she's not in any trouble,' said Julie. 'Can you show us through to the back field?'

She did so, chattering away as she did, but Nick couldn't focus on her words. All he could think of was Josh sitting in that cell in Middlesbrough. Hopefully he hadn't kicked off and gone ballistic.

In the middle of the field were two figures. Heather, dressed in a baseball cap, black hoodie and jeans, was holding a box with an aerial on.

Geoff Powell took the lead, running up to her and her dad. 'Heather!'

She looked up. 'Hello, Mr Powell. You're not usually here.' She looked blankly at him then back down at her box, which Nick could now see had a Kindle-sized screen built into it.

'What's up?' said her dad, a balding, fair-haired man in his early 40s, in a lightweight blue anorak.

You could see Powell was a natural leader by the easy way he took charge, and began to explain the situation. Nick was a little bit in awe of him. He had an innate self-confidence which was totally alien to Nick.

'All the test flight footage is on my cloud,' said Heather. 'I haven't looked at most of it. There are so many hours. We're just testing flight, control and clarity of image. But it is all dated.'

As she spoke, Nick could see how like Josh she was. She shared his blank expression and intense focus and slightly unworldly quality.

'I'm sorry to have to tell you this, Heather, but Josh has been formally arrested for the murders. He's not being charged till later today. If we can prove it's not him, we can stop him ending up in jail.'

Like her schoolmate, she didn't engage her emotions very much. 'That's an odd thing to hear. Josh wouldn't hurt anyone. He's a gentle boy. And he makes me laugh.'

Her dad seemed a bit more sceptical.

'Well they must have their reasons, luv. Can we just bring the Bee home? Then we'll check the server,' said her father.

The Bee was duly returned to base. It was slightly smaller than an AA battery. She guided it back from somewhere in the distance to where they stood, so accurately that her father looked up and plucked it from the air.

'We saw this at Josh's. It just looks like a fat bee at a distance. The way you've made the propellers almost invisible when it's in the air is very clever,' said Nick. Her father grinned at him.

'It's the smallest drone in the world, as far as we know. Making everything as small as possible is the ongoing challenge.'

They went back to the house, Geoff talking to Heather's dad as they walked. Nick went to Heather.

'How is Josh?' she asked. 'Do you know?'

'He's in Middlesbrough police station, at the moment, in a cell. I'm worried about him.'

'Josh is great. He's so obviously not a murderer.'

'Yes, but you know he's been working on probability, and he's statistically proved he is most likely guilty.'

She rolled her eyes. 'Oh, that is *so* Josh. I wish he'd said, I would have disabused him of such a ridiculous notion. He gets fixated on ideas. We - I mean Aspies - we all do. He just needed to see it from a different angle. I could have helped him if he'd asked me.'

'I think he was too shy to do that, Heather.' He briefly explained about the photos, being careful not to say what Josh had been doing in his bedroom with them. 'He didn't want you to know he'd taken a photo of you to look at in private.'

She looked at him with a puzzled expression. 'I don't mind if he does. I'd have given him a photo if he'd wanted. I've taken one of him. Will you tell him that?'

'Of course.'

'Thank you, Mr Guymer.'

She spoke with the voice of an older person, in the same way Josh sometimes did. What fantastic outsiders they both were.

Inside the house, they went upstairs to a spare box room which was mostly taken up with two huge computer screens.

'Which dates do you want me to search for?' said Heather, sitting down, in charge of this Starship Enterprise.

Nick wrote them down on a scrap of paper.

'Have the police not asked you about this?' asked Nick.

'No, we've heard nothing from them,' said Heather's dad. 'Then again, they probably don't know what we do.'

They sat as Heather Leary skimmed through huge lists of files. Connie had been killed in the morning so, as she didn't drone in mornings, there was no film. But Emma and Emily had both been killed on the way home from school.

'This is the footage from that first day's drone class,' she said, clicking her mouse.

They all leaned forward.

The footage was mostly blurred as the device took off.

'Where is this located?' asked Julie.

'Skywards from the field behind 6th form,' said Heather.

They watched as the ground got further away and the picture opened out. Below was St Bede's School and Bishopton Road West.

'Wow, this a great-quality picture,' said Nick. 'And it goes faster than I thought.'

'There are many improvements still to be made,' said Heather, as the drone followed the road and then came back around in a sweeping arc, eventually coming to rest at Heather's own red-training-shoed feet.

'Well, there was nowt suspicious on that. Only people walking along the path. Is there any more footage, luv?' said George Powell.

She clicked on another file. 'This one takes a different route south. I was testing the maximum transmission distance and sent it down to Hartburn Village and back.'

It was fascinating to watch it take off and travel the mile or more over tree tops, filming as it went.

'Slow the playback down a bit,' said Mr Leary. 'Everyone is a bit of a blur.'

She did so.

'That's the Stockton Arms', said Julie, pointing to the corner building as the drone flew over it then banked around to retrace its flight path.

'Slow down...' said Nick, leaning into the screen. 'You're right over the cycle path there, look you can see the white line down the centre. 'Stop!' She paused it. 'And that's McGregor's house there, look...the path runs right by it.'

'There's no-one in sight, though,' said Julie.

Heather ran the film on. A cyclist passed through the frame, heading south. The drone changed direction again, aiming back towards Stockton Sixth Form College.

And then they saw it.

It only lasted four seconds.

But what an horrific four seconds it was.

All five in the room gasped as they saw it.

Heather turned around and looked at them with wide eyes. 'I didn't expect to see that. That is very surprising.'

'Play it back, Heather,' said her father, his forehead etched in a deep frown.

The drone had turned so it faced in the direction of the college, just at the point the track from 6th form, that Nick and Janey had taken, joined the paved cycle path. And there, at that point, held in the frame it had passed over the heads of two people. One a blonde-haired girl, the other, quite clearly, Alice Coates, dressed in all-black sportswear like a killer insect. And she had her hands either side of the girl's face. That girl was Emma West.

'She's got gloves on, like surgeon's gloves' said George. 'Is she...?'

'Yeah. She's administering the poison, you caught her murdering Emma West,' said Nick, his adrenalin racing, appalled at the sight, but simultaneously relieved that it proved Josh innocent.

He took out his phone. 'Jeff? We've got it! We've conclusive proof that Josh didn't kill Emma West. Will you tell Mandy?'

'Get in! One nil. That's bloody good news. Are you 100 per cent certain?'

'Yeah, it's film of one of the murders. We'll get copies made and bring them to Mandy.'

'So who is the killer?'

'Alice Coates.'

Jeff let out a cry. 'Bloody hell! I thought it'd be a bloke. Right, I'll get the big girl onto it. Where are you?'

He explained.

After ringing off, he turned back to the others, who had been talking amongst themselves.

'I've got the file for the afternoon Emily was murdered. Shall I run it?' asked Heather.

'Yes, please,' said Nick.

They watched as it took off. 'Is this going higher than last time?' said Nick

'Four times as high,' said Heather studying her notes. 'I was testing how well it performed in wind at greater heights. It's quite stable.'

'It's a panoramic view. You can see for miles,' said Julie. 'That's amazing. Stockton looks great from the air.'

'Can you freeze it?' said Nick. 'That's right above Bishopton Road West. There is where it goes over the cycle path and to the left is where Emily LeBron was found.' He pointed at the screen. 'And there's no-one down there at all is there?'

'No, it's clear,' said Julie.

'I'll speed the film onto when it's returning to base,' said Heather, skidding it along by nearly 12-minutes. Now facing into a setting sun, it passed over the same area. She paused it again. It had again captured, albeit in just two or three frames, the murder.

'You bitch,' said Geoff Powell, just under his breath, as the frozen image showed the same black sportswear-clad figure, this time bending over a body lying flat by the track, exactly where Emily had been found. As the video rolled forward, it took the drone towards the college. It had to pass over the building to get to where Heather was flying it from. As it made that manoeuvre, it clearly caught Josh walking out of the college. His distinctive mop of scruffy fair hair and long stride was easily identifiable.

Nick had to swallow his emotions down. Bless him. He was utterly, totally, innocent.

'That was an odd experience,' said Heather. 'A satisfying outcome, however. Are you going to get Josh out of the police station, now?'

'Yes. Thanks, Heather. We'll take him back to our place. I don't know what we'd have done without you. Can you make copies of those videos onto two DVDs, please? We'll need to show them to the police.'

'Of course,' she said. They stood by while she quickly burned the DVDs.

'Would it be possible for me to see him this evening? To come to your house, Mr Guymer?'

Nick glanced at Julie. She was smiling. 'Yeah, that'd be no problem.'

CHAPTER 20

At just after 5pm, he parked at Middlesbrough central police station and strode into the reception area with a lightness in his heart for the first time in what felt like forever. Josh was sitting there, waiting for him. He looked up and broke into a huge smile.

'Hello, Nick.'

'Now then, tiger. Are you good to go?'

He nodded and stood up. 'Bye, Sergeant Jones,' he said to the man behind the desk. Nick handed one of the DVDs containing the videos to the sergeant, who was clearly expecting it, keeping the other for himself.

'See you, Josh. Hope you enjoyed your stay,' said the sergeant.

'It was OK. I don't think the coffee had even been in the same room as actual coffee. The food was terrible. Possibly illegal! You should arrest your chef!"

The policeman laughed. 'Well, at least you didn't have to pay for it.' He leaned over the desk and held out his hand to shake Josh's. The lad just looked at the large paw.

'Shake his hand,' Nick said, leaning into him.

'Oh, sorry. I wondered what you were doing, Sergeant.'

They shook hands briefly even though Josh had no idea why, and went back to the car.

As they got outside, Nick put his arms around the lad and hugged him tightly. He absolutely stank of sweat. Josh just stood there motionless, not reciprocating the embrace.

'You've no idea how good it is to get you out of that place,' said Nick, patting him on the back. 'Have you been OK?'

'Fine. Everyone was very nice to me. It was a bit boring, but I can cope with being alone in a small space quite easily.'

'Yeah, Gaunty said that. You absolutely stink, though.'

'I do. I'm sorry. Even I can smell it, which research has proven isn't a good sign.'

'Well, you can have a shower at ours.'

'Am I going to yours? I thought I was going home.'

'Your mother's work commitments means she won't be home until late, as usual. So she's agreed you can stay with us for a few days, just while the police put the case to bed. Best if you're not left on your own too much, I think. You can sleep on our sofa and do all your homework in the music room. Is that OK?'

He raised his arms in the air, letting another waft of bitter sweat out. 'Yessss! Brilliant. I love staying at yours.'

'Julie's gone over to your house to pick up some clothes for you.'

'How's she getting in?'

'Using the spare key under the plant pot at the back. And I've got more good news for you. Heather Leary is going to come round to our place to see you this evening.'

'What? Really? How? Why?' His eyes were wide.

'She said she likes you. She wants to make sure you're alright and to have a chat.'

'Fucking hell. Is it a date?'

'Sort of. It's a just a social thing. Don't build it up too much.'

'Do you think she'll fucking kiss me?'

'She might...' Nick put his index finger over Josh's lips '...if you stop swearing. But don't go getting any funny ideas about doing anything else. Right? You know what I'm talking about.'

Josh nodded but was clearly excited. 'She saved me from going to jail. Thank god for the Bee.'

'It's an incredible device.'

'So have the police arrested Miss Coates?'

'I've not heard anything, but if they can find her, they will have, yeah.'

Josh paused. 'Nick? Why did she want to kill the girls? I don't understand. Is she just bonkers?'

'Yeah, you'd have to be to do that, obviously. I think she's on a mission.'

'What does that mean?'

'She's got a cause - environmentalism - and it's taken over her rational mind, somehow.'

'I don't understand. She's always good to kids. It doesn't make sense that she'd kill them. There's no logic to that.'

'Well, humans are not always logical creatures. I suspect in her mind, she thinks she's done the girls a favour.'

Josh sat quietly for a while. 'That is mad. She can't think that. And what about Paul's parents? Why did they have to die?'

'We've yet to work that out. But our best guess is that Paul killed them because he was getting abused or something, and then before committing suicide, he showed Miss Coates how to do it, knowing she might kill the three girls who had humiliated him. Then when Miss Coates found your photos and realised you'd numbered those three girls consecutively, she found a way to frame you.'

Josh vibrated his lips and made a high-pitched noise. 'That's really very mad and she's not that mad. She isn't, Nick. I know you're going to say that I don't get people properly, but my dysfunction isn't in understanding, it's in feeling what you NTs feel. I'm better at logic and reason and based on that, I think she didn't do it. It must be someone else on the footage who just looks like her.'

'I know it's shocking, Josh, but people can do shocking things that are out of character.'

But the lad wasn't having it. 'No. Sorry. That doesn't make sense. Whatever anyone does must be in character: by definition what they do, is who they are. So what you actually mean, Nick, is that people can do things that shock you because you don't fully understand their character, but you thought you did.'

Nick smiled at him. 'Yeah, I suppose that's right, professor.'

Josh smiled broadly at him, a smile that made Nick's heart float into his throat. He reached out and patted the lad on his leg.

'So what do you fancy for your tea? You can have whatever you want, or at least as long as I've got the ingredients.'

'Can I have your special meatloaf, jacket potato, peas and gravy? I'm starving.'

'Yeah, I can rustle that up for you. It doesn't take too long.'

'Yay! Foooooood!'

'Hello, Julie, I'm out of jail!' said Josh, holding his arms out wide as they walked into the house.

314

She gave him a hug and kissed him on the cheek.

'I'm very pleased for you, but you totally stink, lad. Go and get a shower. There's your sports bag with clean clothes in the bathroom.'

The boy saluted her and ran upstairs, making a happy humming noise.

'Right, he wants meatloaf, I'll crack on with that.' Nick went into the kitchen and took some beef mince out of the fridge and began preparing it.

'There hasn't been news of Alice Coates's arrest yet,' said Julie, sitting down on a kitchen stool. 'And I'm sure there would be because Cleveland Police would love to announce an arrest.'

'Maybe she's gone to ground. Or she's just at home and, as we don't know where that is, it'll take a while to unearth her. Which reminds me, I must call Janey and tell her what's happened.'

He added a little bit of rice crumb, herbs, salt and pepper and onion powder to the mince, shaped it into a loaf tin and put it in the oven. 'Can you do Josh a jacket spud as well, while I make that call?'

Sitting in the music room, in his big padded leather armchair, he called Janey.

'Hello, you,' said Janey, a smile in her voice.

'Hiya. How are you?'

'Well I've had the second gin of the evening, so I'm feeling quite nice.'

'Good. Have you heard about Alice Coates?'

'Heard what?'

Nick gave her as brief an account of the events of the afternoon as he could. She kept making little yelps of disbelief.

'So I imagine the police are looking for her now. I just thought you should know.'

'That was thoughtful of you, Nick. So she doesn't really live at the address she gave us?'

'No. It doesn't seem like it. It's virtually derelict.'

'Could she be staying with family?'

'She doesn't have any, according to Colin Thurston, her ex-husband, who me and Jules met.'

'Eee, I didn't even know she'd been married. She never said.'

'He was very nice, but they didn't last long. He said he thought she might be gay. He wasn't being horrible. It seems they both realised it was a big mistake quite quickly.'

'Oh, yeah. I assumed she was gay.'

'Did you? It didn't occur to me.'

'Oh, yeah, she smelt of it.'

'What does it smell like?'

She laughed. 'Not literally smells. I meant...'

'...I know what you meant, Janey. Anyway, I'm cooking Josh dinner so I'd better go. I just wanted to update you.'

'Is he OK?'

'He seems fine. They seem to have been decent with him, thank god.'

'That's good. God, I'm relieved. Well, it sounds like the whole nightmare is just about over. Or it will be when they arrest her. It'll be nice to get the college back open.'

'Yeah, it does. Thank god. Thanks for all your help.'

'That's alright, I'm happy to help. It's been such a terrible business.'

He rang off.

Wandering back to the kitchen, Josh came trotting downstairs rubbing his wet hair with a towel, now in a clean pair of navy jogging pants, t-shirt and hoodie.

'All fresh and clean?'

'Yes. That's the whole point of washing, surely? Who says "no, I'm more dirty now" after having a shower?'

Nick laughed. He wasn't even making a joke.

'Ah, here he is. The man of the moment,' said Julie, with a smile. Josh looked around himself to see who else had come in the room. 'I was talking about you, daft lad,' said Julie, tapping him on the belly with the back of her hand.

The lad smiled. 'I like being here. You're kind to me. That doesn't happen at home.'

He said it without emotion, more as a dispassionate observer, really. And that made it all the more heartbreaking to hear.

'What time is Heather coming?' he asked.

'About 8-ish,' said Julie.

'Great. This is brilliant. Why can't life always be this great?'

'The bad times make you appreciate the good times more,' said Nick.

Josh sat down on a stool and thought about that. 'Yes. I understand that. Waking up in jail this morning makes being here now feel nicer.'

Julie stood in front of him, hands on hips. 'You seem very cool about having to spend 24 hours locked up. Wasn't it horrible?'

Josh stared at her crotch for a little too long, then looked away, remembering not to do that.

'It was alright. If you're an NT you'd hate it. But it was quiet. There was only one other person being held and he was asleep and snoring because he was massively drunk. And the police officers kept looking in on me, and someone brought me a Kindle with loads of books on, so I could read. I wouldn't want to spend a month there, but for a day, it was fine. I also did a bit of homework.'

Nick took the litre bottle of vodka and poured himself and Julie each a triple. 'How did you do homework?'

'I asked for some paper and a pen and did some probability equations.'

'Eee, lad. You must be the only person who's ever done that in the Boro nick,' said Julie, shaking her head.

'Mr Gaunt came and checked on me twice. I like Mr Gaunt. He looked me in the eye, put his hand on my shoulder and asked if I was OK and I felt like he really wanted to know.'

'He's been a good friend of my family over the years. He's got a good heart and soul,' said Julie.

'I don't know what that means really. It's too metaphysical for me, Julie.' He pulled a face at her, stretching his mouth wide with his fingers. In return, she made a cross-eyed duck face. That made him throw his head back and laugh.

Nick finished making their dinner and served it up.

'I'm starving and this looks lush,' said Josh.

He ate at such a speed, it was a wonder he tasted any of it.

'Don't just shovel it in, Josh,' he said.

'Sorry. It's fucking delicious. Your food is amazing.'

'And *please* watch your language,' said Nick, whilst feeling happy that the boy liked it so much.

'Can I ask you both, something?' Josh said, scooping up a forkful of peas.

'You know you can,' said Nick.

'When Heather arrives, what do I actually do? I mean, literally.'

'She's just coming over to have a chat. You don't have to *do* anything. You can both go in the living room, sit down on the sofa and just talk about what's happened,' said Julie. 'I'll give you both a small glass of white wine, if you like, if she likes wine.'

'Oh, great. Right. Err...it's just that this has never happened to me before. I just want to do everything right.'

'You'll be fine, Josh. Take a tip from me. Don't overthink things. I was a classic overthinker. Don't be like me,' said Nick.

'Why wouldn't I be like you? You're great and your wife is fantastic, so being like you should mean I'll get a fantastic wife,' said Josh, in his flat, logical way.

Nick got up and ruffled the lad's hair. 'I just mean, don't worry about doing the right or wrong thing. Just be who you are.'

'Easier said than done. I don't know who I am.'

'Well that's the human condition. Maybe none of us do,' said Nick. 'All you've got to do is sit and talk and be nice.'

'Right. Yes. Good.' Josh nodded.

Right on 8.00pm the bell rang. Nick went to the door. Heather was there, wearing a green sloppy sweater, leggings and trainers, her ginger hair tied into a ponytail. Her dad was in the car. Nick waved at him, gave him a thumbs up and then let her in.

'Hello, Heather. Nice to see you,' said Nick, suddenly feeling as gawky as a teenager.

'Hello, Mr Guymer. Is Josh back?'

'He is indeed.'

'Is he OK?'

'He's fine.'

He led her into the living room where Josh was.

'Hello, Heather!' the lad said, his voice squeaking a bit, perhaps with nerves.

They stood looking at each other in the middle of the room, neither of them knowing what to say or do in such a social situation.

'Why don't you both sit down?' said Nick realising they needed a little guidance.

They did as he said, just as Julie came in with two glasses of fizzy white wine and the bottle under her arm.

'Do you like fizzy wine, Heather?'

'Yes, Julie. Thank you.'

She put the glasses down on the table. 'Right...err...don't neck it too quickly. Do you want some music on?'

'Yes please,' said Josh. 'Music helps fill awkward gaps in conversation. Nick, you told me that,'

It was weird. That was an embarrassing thing to say, but neither kid was embarrassed, because both of them lacked social skills, both lacked emotional empathy, and both had never been in this situation before. In a way, it was a blessing.

'What sort of music do you like, Heather?' asked Nick, although he already knew.

'I only like Bowie and metal, nothing else, at the moment,' she said, firmly, sitting down and taking her glass.

'You like Metallica, don't you?' he said, feeling Bowie might be too sexy for them.

'Yes.'

'Great, I'll pull some albums out of my collection for you.'

He went next door and took the first six Metallica records off the shelves, returned to the living room and put them on the table.

'OK, kids, if you need anything, we'll be in the kitchen,' said Julie, backing out of the room, leaving the door ajar.

In the kitchen, Nick stood looking at her, resting against the kitchen table.

'I felt so out of my depth there,' he said.

'I know. Me, too. It's an odd situation. From what I've read, some Aspies struggle with the idea of falling in love in the way we might understand it, but then...what *does* it mean?'

'Being with Josh makes me question everything I take for granted.

I mean, I love you. I love you so much. But what does that mean? How can I explain my love for you? What words do I use for that? I tell you I love you, all the time. And I'm being honest, as far as I can be. But if I had to describe what I mean by those words, I'd struggle.'

She took a drink. 'If you try to break down an emotional connection it just sounds weird. I love you because of...I have no idea. You know me, understand me and respect me. You make me laugh, you intellectually stimulate me and I love our sex life. All of those things are wrapped up into the word "love" but even then, the thing we have with each other is still something metaphysically beyond any of those words.'

'Sometimes I think we sell love as this big thing, when it's not really. It's just getting on and being nice with each other. It's companionship mixed with sex,' said Nick.

'Yeah, well, if you were impotent, I'd still love you.'

He put his arm around her waist. 'There's no chance of that. Quite the opposite, in fact.'

'Hmm, so I see.' She bumped her groin into his, grinning. 'What with all this worry, we've not had a good session for what seems like ages.'

'But how do we go about it with Josh being here? When we've had a break we usually go at it hammer and tongs. I don't want him hearing us.'

'We'll have to do it when he's out or at school. I'll nip home on my lunch break and give you a good seeing to.'

'This is what it must be like to have kids. Having to find a quiet moment for a shag.'

'Some people aren't noisy when they're having it off, though. So they'd be alright. It's just that we're groaners and screamers.'

'True. Y'know, we've only just met Heather but I sense she's a similar level or degree of Asperger's as Josh. They seem quite like each other.'

'I wonder whether, if you don't really have emotional empathy and are not really sure how to behave in every social situation, but you know the person you're with is the same, it makes things much easier.'

'I'm going to have peep in at them. I left the door cracked,' she said, getting up and treading gently out of the kitchen. She returned quickly, a big smile on her face.

'What's going on?' asked Nick.

She spoke in a whisper. 'They're snogging on the sofa! They haven't even put a record on.'

Nick was shocked. 'Really? That was quick work, they've not been in there long. Bloody hell. Josh hasn't kissed a girl before, I hope he works out what to do.'

'Well, he's getting some practice in now. Looked like he was doing fine. They were all over each other, hands up top and down below. It's quite sweet, really.'

'Well I think this has been brewing for a while from what McGregor told me in his office. They'd been told off for "inappropriate touching" at college. Maybe together they're really uninhibited because neither will be shy or embarrassed with another Aspie.'

'Actually, you're not wrong. I read about that being the case. What do we do if they just start having it off? Pour a bucket of water over them?'

They both laughed.

'The first time I had a girl round to my house, we ended up dry humping on the front room carpet.'

'I think I did as well. I couldn't wait to have a go at it, in fact.'

'So if Josh and Heather follow our fine example, do we just not say or do anything?'

She shrugged. 'God, I don't know what to do. Probably best not to let it go too far. They've plenty of time.'

'Yeah. We should exert some discipline on them. If they get on well for a while, they can take it further. We don't want to be drippy, liberal parents, do we?'

'We're not actually their parents, man,' she said, as he walked out the kitchen and pushed open the living room door.

Thankfully, they were now sitting at either end of the sofa. Josh had opened his laptop and was showing her a spreadsheet. They'd put on the black *Metallica* album at low volume.

'Do you need anything?' he asked, noting they'd barely touched their wine. 'Snacks or anything?'

'No, thank you,' said Josh, his face flushed pink.

'I don't eat after 6pm,' said Heather.

'Really? Why's that?' asked Josh.

'I like to have 12 hours in every day when I don't eat,' she said.

'Why?' Josh asked.

'So I don't get fat.'

'You're not fat.'

'It works then, doesn't it,' she said, perfectly logically, and smiled at him.

'OK, cool, well, let me know if you need anything.'

Nick and Julie stayed out of the way and left them as they passed the rest of the evening looking at Josh's probability equations. At 10.30pm, her father rang the bell and collected her.

'Was everything OK?' he whispered in Nick's ear.

He nodded. 'Fine. They seemed to get on very well.'

'No funny business?' It was a curiously old-fashioned euphemism.

'They had a bit of a snogging session, but nothing to worry about.'

Mr Leary blew out air. 'Good. Kids are stressful, aren't they?'

'It's hard to know what to do for the best, yeah.'

Once she'd gone, Nick turned to Josh in the living room. 'Did you enjoy your evening?'

'Can I tell you something very private?' Josh said, quietly in his ear.

'Of course you can.'

'We kissed each other. It was brilliant.' He said it in an excited whisper.

'Well, it is a nice thing to do.'

'She just asked me and then when it started I remembered what you said, that there was no right and wrong and that made me relax and get into it.'

Nick smiled and patted him on the shoulder. 'I'm happy for you. But don't be in a rush to take it further, yet.'

'Right, Nick. Thank you. Now I must go and have a wa...err...have a wee.'

He ran upstairs, Nick returned to the kitchen.

'What are you grinning at?' said Julie.

'Nothing. Just remembering what it was like to be 16 and having your first intimate encounter with a girl and how exciting it is.'

She blew out her cheeks. 'I'm exhausted by everything that's happened today. I'm off to bed.'

'I'll just tidy up down here and get Josh settled on the sofa.'

He pulled out a duvet and pillows from the airing cupboard. Josh returned from the bathroom.

'You'll be OK on here, won't you?' he said, as Josh changed into his pyjamas, got under the quilt and lay down.

'Yes. Thank you. What a day it's been. I'm so tired.'

'Well, you take it easy and get a good night's sleep. I'll put this glass of water down here, beside the sofa. Try not to knock it over.'

As he placed the glass on the carpet. Josh reached out his hand and touched Nick's. 'Thank you for looking after me. One day, somehow, I'll pay you back.'

Nick squeezed the lad's hand and felt tears glaze his eyes. 'There's no need for that.' But even as he said it, Josh had closed his eyes and dropped off to sleep.

Turning out the lights, he took at last look at his phone. There was a text from Jeff.

'Police arrested Alice Coates at 6.30pm. It seems as though she's got cast-iron alibis for when the murders happened. They're holding her overnight while they're all checked out. Somehow, she's not the killer.'

CHAPTER 21

Josh was still asleep when Julie went to work at 8.30am, so Nick gave him until 9 before taking him some green tea, then setting about making them a breakfast of sausages, black pudding, tomatoes, scrambled eggs and rocket.

'That smells great,' said Josh, unable to resist the smell of hot fat. He sat down at the table and yawned, ruffling his hair into a raggle taggle mop. 'I slept very well. I like your sofa.'

Nick put a plate in front of him and served up the food.

'Wow. Look at all this food!' he grinned at Nick. 'I'm starving again. For future reference, I always am.'

'Well, tuck in then. I've got some news for you.'

Josh began to demolish the plate at a speed that could probably win him an eating competition. 'What news is that?'

'The police caught Miss Coates and arrested her. But, I'm afraid, she can't have done the killings. She has a rock-solid alibi for each one and can prove she was elsewhere when the murders happened.'

'I'm glad about that. I like her. She's a nice teacher. And it was improbable that she was guilty. I was much more likely to be guilty than she was.'

'So, apart from you, who is statistically likely to be the woman in those Bee videos?'

Josh didn't reply. He just kept shovelling food into his face until it was all gone. 'Delicious. Thank you, Nick.' He patted his tummy. 'To answer your question, there are two ways to look at it. The first is to assume it is someone who we know of, a teacher or worker at the college. Of those, the most statistically probable is Mr Powell.'

'But we know it's a woman. A woman who looks very like Alice Coates. Possibly someone who has made herself up to look like Miss Coates.'

'The second option is to accept it is someone we don't know and thus can't assign probability to. We might also consider that the footage from Heather's drone does not show what you think it shows.

What you think was film of a murder and the aftermath of a murder, was nothing of the sort and thus not only is it not Miss Coates, there is no actual film of the murder. All in all. I favour the second as being most probable because the variables allow for many different outcomes. None of which is of any use to you in finding the killer. Can I see the footage?'

'Err...yeah, I don't see why not. I copied it onto a DVD.' He set it up for Josh and ran it, secretly hoping he would notice something they hadn't. Then he made them both more tea.

Josh watched it in silence. He was capable of sitting perfectly still. So much so that occasionally Nick found himself looking for signs of him still breathing, so motionless was he.

'So what do you reckon?'

'I'll need to put this into my probability spreadsheet before I offer you an opinion worthy of the name.'

He went and got his own laptop and began tapping at his keyboard for half an hour. Nick let him get on with it while he did his morning emails.

'Hmm. Well, statistically, it is very probably Miss Coates and it is very likely she killed the girls,' he said.

'But we know she can't have been there at this time.'

'Nevertheless, it is the most probable outcome given the facts we know; however, if there are other facts that we don't know, then all would be different. For example, if someone was pretending to be her.'

His obsession with probability was frustrating the hell out of Nick.

'Hmm, well, we're no further forward, then.'

'Data don't lie. But you're right. We're not. I shall put it on my back burner and let it cook.'

Nick finished a sausage. 'Look, do you fancy a trip out into the countryside? I really should go and tell Jade and Jenny about what's happened. I mean, Jenny is still the next on the list, so I know she's been stressed out by the whole thing.'

'Why not just call them?' asked Josh, with a frown.

'Because it's complicated, and important news is best given in person, if you can.'

Josh shook his head. 'You NTs have some weird rituals. But yes, I'd like to go for a ride. Thank you.'

Nick called Robbie to let him know they were on their way.

'Is it good news, Nick?' he asked.

'It's really complicated. A lot has happened. There haven't been any more deaths.'

'We've heard nothing about anything. The police haven't been in touch or even had a news conference.'

'Like I say, it is complicated. I'll explain it all when we arrive.'

'OK, thanks, Nick. Is Jules coming?'

'No, she's at work, but we've got Josh staying with us, so he's coming along for the ride, if that's OK.'

'Yeah, fine.'

He gave Jeff a quick call.

'Yo! Crazy dude.'

'Jeff, have they released Alice Coates yet?'

'Nope. Mandy is incredulous that it's not her. But two alibis have checked out and are 100 per cent concrete. They're working on the third now. But, as I said this morning, if two have proven true why wouldn't the third? She'll probably end up letting her go this evening.'

'OK, thanks, man. I'm just with Josh and we're going to update Robbie and family.'

'Righto. I thought this was the end of it, but it's looking like it isn't.'

Nick drove them south out of Stockton, but got stuck in traffic on the Tees Flyover. As they crawled along, he talked to Josh.

'So what do you think now about your evening with Heather?'

'It was enjoyable. I texted her this morning to thank her for visiting me.'

'Good lad. That's nice of you. Shows you've got good manners.' Nick nodded with approval and patted him on the leg.

'I know. I remembered what you said about that. There's something I don't understand, though Nick.'

'What's that?'

'Why does she want to touch and kiss me?'

'Oh, don't go down that road, Josh. Just accept it. don't question it. There's no point. She likes you. That's how you feel about her, isn't it?'

He didn't seem able to respond to that.

'You know I don't do the "feel" question, Nick. That's one of your NT things.'

'Well, you say that, and I know what you mean, but you do know what "feel" means, I know you do. Remember what you said when you first told me about her.'

'I do remember, but you need to ask me something less vague than "how do I feel".'

'OK, what did you like about last night?'

'That's more like it. I liked sitting next to her and talking about spreadsheets and drones. I liked kissing her and feeling her breasts and I liked her putting her hand down my pants and...'

'...OK, OK, Josh, I don't need to hear the grisly details, thank you very much.'

For a moment, Josh had a panic. 'I've not done anything wrong, have I? That was all OK, wasn't it? She initiated it all and I was happy to let her.'

'No, that's fine. For what it's worth I've always followed the same path and let women initiate sexual encounters. It always seemed the safer option as I was never too sure if I was correctly reading the signals they were giving off and didn't want to misjudge the situation.'

'Well, if I follow in your footsteps I won't be going far wrong.'

'I'll say this, though, it was very forward of her to do that.'

'It's weird being the object of a girl's desire or affection. I sort of don't believe it. It doesn't seem likely, even though I like it.'

'I know what you mean. I was just the same. I think it's a healthy attitude to strike. You don't want to go around thinking you're God's gift to women. Only arrogant idiots think like that. And I think a lot of women think it's a nice trait. Did she text you back?'

'Yes. She said she'd had a good time and would I like to meet in Ropner Park on Saturday afternoon and get some ice cream? I said yes. Does that means we're going out with each other now?'

'Definitely. That's a date, Josh.'

He gripped his hand into a fist. 'Yes! Get in.'

'Remember, no feeling each other up in public like you did on the sofa, though.'

Josh saluted. 'Keep your privates for private. That's what you told me and I will.'

'Good lad.'

'Thanks for helping me. Everything would be much more awkward for me without your tips. I'd probably have ended up running around the park naked with a hard on!' he laughed.

Nick smiled.

Eventually the traffic eased and they moved south on the A19.

'When you had your first date with Julie, did you end up kissing?'

Nick laughed. 'Yeah, and the rest.'

'Full sex?'

'I refer you to my previous answer. Julie was very forward, like Heather.'

'Maybe we like the same sort of women.'

'Yeah, maybe we do. I've never gone for demure, timid, girly-girly women.'

'Why not?'

'I don't know, really. It's how I'm made. I just like passionate, strong, intelligent women. Always have.'

'Why would anyone want a girlfriend who was passionless, weak and stupid?' said Josh, as ever, getting to the root of the matter.

'Men who want to control and manipulate women.'

'Why would they want to do that?'

Nick groaned. 'That, my shaggy-haired young friend, is too big a question to answer on a short trip like this. I'll ask Julie to explain it to you one day. That's her specialist subject.'

'Julie is brilliant. She should be a leader of something. Be mayor or an MP or something. She's so good at finding the right words to make an argument.'

'She's thought about it before now. Maybe she will. Our local MP just died, so there's a vacancy.'

They were in open country now.

Nick turned up the single-track road that led up to the farmhouse.

'Are you OK with Jenny and Jade? You can stay in the car if you want.'

'I don't know Jade. Jenny is OK. I don't think I've ever talked to her. She keeps herself to herself at 6th form.'

'She feels she's a bit of an outsider.'

'I suppose she is. Yeah. Not like me. She's not a loony toon. But she's not a mainstream girl. I don't know why, though.'

He considered mentioning her sexuality, but now didn't seem the right place or time, as he turned down the rutted mud track to the farm.

'I like it out here,' said Nick, pointing to the panoramic view west to the Yorkshire Dales.

'Why are big open spaces good, or thought attractive?'

Nick laughed. 'Only you would ask a question like that, Josh. It's an aesthetic a lot of people enjoy.'

'I know that. But I don't really understand it. I think I prefer small spaces. They feel more controllable. It seems wild out here. Like anything could happen.'

Nick pulled up at the house. A small red hatchback was parked at the side.

'Come on then, Josh.'

They got out and went around to the back door. Nick knocked and Robbie answered almost immediately.

'Hey guys, come in,' he said, pushing at his white hair. 'The wind has got up this morning. Ah, you must be Josh. Hi mate, I'm Robbie,' he held out his hand.

'Hello,' said Josh, shook hands and nodded.

'So what's been going on, Nick?' said Robbie, as Sheryl and Carly came in.

'Hey, you two,' said Nick, introducing Josh to them. Sheryl put the kettle on, smiling nicely at Josh. 'Well, it's complicated. I'll try and keep it simple. Some video footage taken from a hi-tech drone flown by a friend of Josh's, captured footage of two of the murders...'

329

'...wow. That's amazing,' said Robbie. 'Have the police arrested someone?'

'They did yesterday.'

The two women let out sighs. 'Oh, that's great to hear,' said Sheryl. 'What a bloody relief.'

'I'm afraid it's not that straightforward,' said Nick. 'The person arrested was Alice Coates, the 6th form gym teacher. I saw the film and it was definitely her on it, but she's got alibis for when the murders happened, so I think they'll release her later.'

As he was speaking, he knew something was up. They were all looking at each other oddly.

'I'm sorry, mate. That makes no sense,' said Robbie.

'Why not?'

'Miss Coates came here about 20 minutes ago. She's taken Jenny and Jade out on a cross-country run, so they can keep their fitness levels high. She's not a killer. And she's not in jail.'

Nick's mind spun in neutral, trying to grasp what was being said.

'What? That's not possible. She's in Stockton Police station,' he said, with a rising panic.

'She's not. She texted Jenny this morning and asked if she fancied a run to keep their fitness levels up. Jade wanted to go too, so they headed off no more than five minutes ago.'

'Are you sure it was actually Miss Coates?' asked Josh.

'Well, we don't know her, but the girls do,' said Sheryl.

'But the killer looked like Miss Coates. Miss Coates is in custody. Therefore the killer may be the woman who came here,' said Josh, without emotion.

It all crashed into Nick's brain. Jenny was #6, Jade was collateral damage. She was here to murder them.

'Where were they going?' said Nick, his heart beating fast.

'They were taking the track along the ridge, heading south, you get the best views,' said Robbie.

'Right, call this number.' said Nick writing down Mandy's mobile. 'Tell them who you are and where you are. Tell them I'm going after them.'

'Are you serious? Is it the killer?' asked Robbie.

'Yeah, and she's come for the girls. Josh, you can stay in the car or come with me. Are you up for it?'

'Fuck yeah,' said Josh, fearlessly.

They headed out of the farmhouse at pace. A clear path headed south, right along the contour of the land.

'They've got five minutes on us,' shouted Nick as they set off.

'They're fast, but we can make that up,' said Josh, settling into his stride. The boy was as fit as a fiddle, Geoff Powell had said as much. Nick knew he himself had good short sprints, but how he was over long distances was untested.

The land was open and clear.

'What do we do when we catch them up?' yelled Josh, running alongside Nick, with ease.

'Be careful! She kills by applying two chemicals to the skin. One has no effect. We have to be aware of that.'

'But how do we stop her?'

'I'll beat the crap out of her. She needs immobilizing. I can do that with one good hit. I just hope she's not killed them both yet. She'll want to do it in an isolated place.'

'Killing two people is harder than one, because the other can stop you,' said Josh, in between big breaths.

The wind howled in their ears as they pounded along the field track. All of a sudden it rounded a bend, opened up and plunged down into a shallow valley. In the near distance were three figures. One was in all black, the other two in red and royal blue training gear.

Thank god, the girls were still alive.

'There they are!' yelled Josh, and he accelerated past Nick, in his excitement.

'Take care, Josh!' yelled Nick as the lad moved away from him. There was no controlling him in this situation. Jesus, he could run, he left Nick behind by a yard every five seconds. Nick heaved for breath. His lungs were burning now. He was fit and strong but he was 52; Josh was 16 and in another league of fitness.

They closed in quickly. Even as he pounded along, panic was overcoming Nick. Whoever this woman was, she was a killer. But she had to apply two cloths of chemicals. That's what the video had shown. And she had to put on gloves to administer those. Now he thought about it, she would have to stop for a rest to do that. She'd have to pull on the surgeon's gloves, take out the poison and then administer it. That meant, while they were running, they were safe. When they stopped, that's when the trouble started.

Josh continued to move away from him. Shit.

The three women began to slow down.

He could see them come to a halt at the bottom of the valley, then disappear around a small line of trees.

'Josh!' he yelled. The boy looked over his shoulder. 'Wait for me! Wait!'

The lad put his thumb up and began to slow. Nick blew out a gob of congealed foamy spit, as he caught up.

'They've stopped. She's about to try and kill the girls.'

'How do we stop that?' yelled Josh, his face bright pink from the exertion.

'Keep calm! Let me handle this. Make sure she doesn't touch you. But if you get a chance to kick her hard, do it.'

In unison they ran down a slope to the line of trees. As they got to the bend in the path, they slowed to a trot, just as the two girls came into view.

Nick took charge, though exhausted.

The two girls turned to look at them as they arrived around the bend. They both waved at them, as they approached.

Significantly, the woman had disappeared. Nick assumed she'd gone behind some trees to pull on the gloves of death.

Gasping for breath Nick rasped, 'Get out of here! Both of you! Get back home! That woman is the killer. She's taken you here to kill you! Get away! Go back to the house. Now!'

The girls, stood looking at him like he was crazy, hands on hips, getting their breath back.

'What are you talking about? Why are you here, Josh?' said Jenny.

'It's Miss Coates, you're talking about. She's our teacher,' said Jade, licking her lips.

'It's not her. Even if it appears to be,' said Nick. 'We've got to go

332

now.'

'The real Alice Coates is in the police station. This is another one,' said Josh. 'We've got film of her killing Emma and Emily.'

The girls looked at them, understandably incredulous.

But it was too late.

The woman came running from behind a tree, blue latex gloves on her hands, and what looked like a small flannel in each hand, each soaked in the deadly poison.

'Get out!!' he yelled. 'Get away! All of you!'

The girls turned around and screamed as the woman, dressed all in black Lycra, lunged at both of them simultaneously, catching each of them on the cheek with one of the flannels. Bloody hell. That'd not kill them, though.

'Go!!' he yelled at a hysterical pitch which finally cut through their fog of confusion. And the two girls and Josh took off at speed, not on the track but down through open grassland, heading back towards the farm.

The woman was a clone of Alice Coates. It was definitely the woman he'd met in her office at 6th form.

'Who the fuck *are* you?' he yelled, intent on holding her up for long enough to allow the kids to get away, but keeping at least 10 feet away from her. But she wasn't for talking. Instead she turned, picking up a small rucksack. As she did so, Nick ran at her, lunged in with a Souness-style sliding tack, his body fully extended swiping at her legs in a scything motion. But she saw him coming just in time, jumped over his legs like a gazelle and took off in pursuit of the three youngsters.

Nick got to his feet. Oh christ, his legs were hurting, full of lactic acid from the run, already.

Now, he just couldn't keep up. She was Olympic fast. Worse yet, she was faster than the kids, and was gaining on them, still holding the cloths in each hand.

His legs felt heavy and his lungs burned as he went after her, the physical effort making bile rise into his throat, followed by vomit. He turned his head to one side and tried to throw up whilst running but simply had to stop to wretch out his breakfast; then, panicking that she was about to catch the three kids up, he took off again, wiping his mouth on his sleeve.

Now several hundred yards in front of him, running across open fields towards a gate and a dry stone wall, he could see the kids turning around and looking at their pursuer, getting near to them now. Oh, fuck. They were stopping at the wall, they must be knackered, and Coates was bearing down on them. Fear in his throat, he kept going, and saw the three of them split in three different directions. Left. Right. Straight on. That was a great idea. Smart kids. She'd have to pursue one of them. Which one?

Jenny.

#6.

Nick was getting a second wind, and feeling pleased that Josh and Jade were now putting distance between themselves and the killer. Josh was on his phone as he ran, hopefully calling the police.

But Jenny wasn't putting any distance between herself and the woman. She was 16, fit and strong, but no match for an adult athlete in her late 20s or early 30s. Neither was Nick, and he just couldn't make up any ground. He needed her to stop, but she wasn't going to do that until she'd caught and murdered Jenny. She was relentless.

It was an agonizing torture to see it play out in the distance as he pounded on. All it would take was one application of the other poison on the cloth to kill her.

But Jenny was brave and not for going down easily. She wasn't as fast as Coates, but she was exceptionally lithe and limber. Seeing the woman getting within a few strides, she threw her weight forward, did a roll, ending on a half-handstand, spun around 180 degrees and hit the woman full in the face with her right foot. It was like a footballer volleying a player in the head. Bam! A perfect strike, perfectly timed. It was a hip-hop move retooled as some sort of kung fu!

Nick yelled formless noises of encouragement to her. And it was a sodding good hit to the face because it had broken the woman's nose in an instant and sent her reeling sideways, stumbling and falling onto her backside as she did so.

These few seconds gave Jenny a chance to put some distance

between her and her attacker, and a chance for Nick to gain ground.

The Aussie girl took off again, and sprung up on a wide, dry stone wall. This gave her the advantage of height over Coates, but meant she couldn't run that fast because the wall was uneven and crumbling in places. Her attacker wasn't down long. In one leap, with blood running from her nose, nimbly she joined her on the wall, still in pursuit. This woman was insane. Why did she need to kill Jenny so desperately? She was also a freerunner and far more capable of running on a wall than Jenny was.

Her having been knocked down for a few seconds had allowed Nick to gain valuable yards and she couldn't run as fast across the top of the dry stone wall as he could across the flat field. He was now only 15 yards behind and gaining all the time.

Jen looked over her shoulder, and as she did, so, slipped on a loose crumbling stone, lost her balance and fell into the field onto her knees. She tried to scramble back to her feet but was now clearly absolutely exhausted, legs just not working properly, wading through metaphorical sand. Nick ran alongside the wall, finding some speed still left in his legs. Coates leapt down 10 or 12 feet in front of him and ran towards Jenny with the white cloths gripped in her hands.

It's often said that in moments of high stress, adrenaline can make your body do super-human things. And Nick really needed his body to do something super-human in this moment.

This was it.

Life or death for Jenny.

She could run no more and, heaving for breath, turned to face her attacker. Her fists, raised she lashed out, connected with the advancing woman's jaw but she had no power to her punch. She lashed out with her feet, kicking her on the shins, screaming now, screaming into the north Yorkshire air, the scream of someone who knew they were about to die.

What a kid, she was a fighter.

But it was such a simple task to put a piece of cloth into someone's face. It took no time to do and Nick was just yards short of being able to stop her doing it and his legs couldn't take him any faster.

He was four strides short.

Jenny screamed again as the poison was rubbed into her face, unable to fend the powerful woman off.

Nick pulled his right arm back and as he reached the woman, he smashed the hardest right cross he'd ever thrown in his life into her already bloody face. It was powerful enough to floor a heavyweight boxer and she reeled backwards, staggering, and quickly now only semi-conscious. Nick planted his left foot forward and swung a right again, connecting with huge power, knocking her up into the air and flat onto her back. As he hit her, a loud crack told him he'd shattered her cheekbone. Better still, he'd knocked her out. She lay in a heap of Lycra, mud and blood, a haematoma already swelling on her face.

Spinning around he looked at Jenny. She was lying on her back, where she'd fallen after being poisoned. Her eyes closed, mouth open, her chest rising and falling from the exertion. Could he touch her or would he get poisoned?

'Jenny! Jenny, I'm sorry, luv. I couldn't get here quick enough. How are you feeling?' He put his hand on her Lycra top.

She opened one eye and looked up at him. 'You throw a bloody good right-hander, mate,' she said, in her broad Aussie twang.

'How do you feel?'

'Fucked.'

'Oh, shit. I was hoping the poison might have evaporated or something.'

She propped herself up on her elbows. 'She got me in the face, mate. I knocked my bloody pan out. Couldn't keep going.'

'You did great. What a volley you got her with. Right in the mush. Brilliant.'

She kept panting. 'I was pleased with it. A bit of Aussie karate!'

'You look bright eyed.'

'Watch out! Behind you!' screamed Jenny.

Nick spun around to see the bloodied woman getting to her feet, clearly disorientated. Without hesitation he stood up, crashed another right hander into her face and sent her sprawling to the mud again. She lay motionless on her front, still gripping the two cloths.

Maybe he'd killed her.

Turning back to Jenny, he saw she was now sitting up. She spat to one side.

'I must be friggin' immortal, mate, 'cos I'm not feeling a lot like dying.'

She had mud stuck in her platinum blonde hair, which she picked out with her fingertips.

In his mind's eye. Nick replayed the moment when she'd first wiped the poison on her and her sister. It was with her right hand. And she'd used the right again in the field.

'Fucking hell. I think she wiped the same poison on you twice. That's what's saved you, kidda. She got mixed up who she'd given which poison to.'

She gave a disbelieving snort. 'Guess this was my lucky day, huh. But I don't understand why the bitch wanted to kill me.'

'It's not her. She's in Stockton police station.'

'Well that's her twin then, she's exactly the same. It makes no sense to me. How did she know me, if she's not my teacher? She did know me. She knew my best times. She mentioned them as we set off. And she damn well looks identical to my teacher. I reckon it's her, mate and the woman the cops have got, that's someone else pretending to be Alice Coates. All of which is pretty fucked up.'

Sirens blew on the wind coming from Northallerton.

'That'll be the police.' He pulled her to her feet. 'Let's get back up to the track.'

'What about her?' said Jenny, pointing to the prone body.

Nick turned and looked at her, lying still, the blood on her face drying from red to a dark brown. She was motionless.

Then he saw it.

The tear on the back of the right glove, and on the fingertip of the left. One torn on the wall, the other ripped when she tried to defend herself against Jenny's punches. Traces of the chemicals must have mixed in her bloodstream after soaking into the skin of each hand which, while not killing her as quickly as she'd killed her victims, was just as lethal nonetheless.

She was dead. Poisoned.

'I think we better just leave her to the professionals. She's died the way she killed.'

'Strewth! That shit is powerful. I can't believe she's dead, just like that...' her voice trailed off in the wind.

'Come on, let's get away from here.'

CHAPTER 22

Mandy Beale walked into the Wells's farmhouse and pulled off a pair of latex gloves. Everyone was sat around the table, the smell of Earl Grey tea mixed with a large pan of beef stew bubbling away on the stove. She looked around at everyone.

'Ah, you've made it, Jules.'

'Just got here. What the hell has happened...?'

'... I'm tempted to quote my predecessor and say it's a bad business. Have you given a statement to PC Smith, Jenny, Jade, Josh?' She looked at the three teenagers sitting together at the end of the table, the girls now changed out of sports clothing back into sweatshirts and jeans.

'Yes,' said Josh, on their behalf, making a big dramatic nod.

'You too, Nick?'

'Yeah.'

'Good.'

'Who is the dead woman, Mand?' asked Julie. 'How are there two Alice Coateses? There's no record of her having a twin, is there?'

'That, my blonde lovely, is a good question. I'm bloody glad we were so snowed under with paperwork that we hadn't got around to letting her go.'

'Well, she's not guilty of anything, is she? It was the woman out there who we saw on the drone footage,' said Nick.

'I'm not jumping to any conclusions about anything. One thing I do know is we have two identical-looking women, one alive, one dead. They obviously have to be twins. And yet you're right, there is no record of her having a twin.'

'And the woman in Stockton has confirmed she hasn't got a twin?' asked Nick.

Mandy nodded, her lips pinched together.

'How did she react when you told her?' asked Nick.

'We haven't actually told her. We've just asked her if she does.'

'Well, maybe she didn't know. Maybe they were both adopted at birth and the documents lost,' said Julie. 'I've heard of incidences of that at work, where people have no idea if they even have any family because they were given away or adopted at birth, especially if it happened abroad, and they moved here as babies.'

Mandy made a noise, put her right index finger on her nose and pointed with her left, a gesture she must have subconsciously copied from Jeff. 'The Alice Coates that is still alive was indeed adopted, not that she tried to hide that. In fact, as witnesses go, she's been very open and good natured.'

'That's what the Alice Coates I knew as a teacher was like,' said Jenny. 'She liked us kids.'

'It didn't seem in any way weird that she'd come to give you a private running class?' asked Mandy.

'She went out of her way to train us all. She'd train us on Sundays in her own time,' said Jade. 'So that's what it seemed like.' She turned to her sister. 'Thing is, Jen, she was a *bit* weird with us. I'm only saying this in hindsight. But she was more...' she paused to try and think of the right word '...kind of frosty. I mean, not as smiley and chatty as usual.'

'That's what she was like when I met her in the office,' said Nick.

'Maybe. But I didn't think anything of it,' said Jenny.

'It's all bloody crazy shit, if you ask me,' said Robbie Wells. 'That bitch must have been out of her mind.'

'She's out of her mind now, for sure. She's very dead and you did a good job of breaking her face, Nick. My question is this: were the twins aware of each other? Were they working together? Or is it a case of good twin, bad twin?'

'Did she ever mention family, girls?' asked Sheryl. They both shook their heads.

'You can't let the Alice Coates you've got in Stockton, go, Mand. She could be dangerous,' said Julie. 'You don't know.'

'I'm going to have to charge her this evening if I want to do that,' she said, sitting down at the big table.

'You can hold her for up to 96 hours if you think she's committed a serious crime,' said Julie, drawing on her experience as PA to a lawyer.

340

'Thank you, Julie. I do know that. But the fact remains, she's got a cast-iron alibi for the time frame of every murder, including Paul's and his parents. There's no way I can present that as a reason to keep her in custody.'

Nick sat chewing on his bottom lip in contemplation, his legs stiff and painful after so much running.

'What I need is evidence of conspiracy.'

'What does that mean?' asked Jenny.

Josh looked at her. 'It means the police need incontrovertible evidence that they knew each other - a film of them together, for example. Then, given she's denied knowing she had a twin, she could be arrested for conspiracy to murder, as a bare minimum,' he said.

Mandy gave him a little clap. 'There's a job on the Force for you with brains like that, Josh.'

He smiled. 'Oh, I'm far too clever for that.' He wasn't even trying to be sarcastic, but everyone laughed, anyway. Not that Josh had any real understanding as to why it was funny.

Nick was smiling at Josh's comment when a memory dropped into his brain, the way a coin drops into a slot machine.

'Oh, my god. I think I saw...' he put his hands to his temples and rubbed them to bring up the memory '...I think I saw them, not at the same time, though. I talked to her and Geoff Powell at the college and then me and Janey James went out to have a look at the paths to the cycle tracks. As we were doing that, Alice came out, Janey waved cheerfully at her and she blanked her. Janey thought that was out of character. But then, about half an hour later, when I returned to pick up the car, I saw Alice coming out of the college again. I just assumed she had returned to pick something up. But I bet it was the other twin, the nice one. In which case, I definitely met the woman who just died. She seemed identical to the woman in Alice's office.'

'How did you find her, Mandy?' asked Julie.

'I did a local TV and radio statement asking her to come to Stockton station. She did.'

'Why does she say she's not living at her given address?'

'She says her ex-husband had been hassling her, so she rented an empty old place south of Hartburn to put him off the scent, but in actual fact she lives in Thornaby. And even as I'm saying that, I know it sounds very dodgy. But then, she's very affable, and not in any way a murderous toe-rag.'

'We met her ex-husband. He seemed nice, but you never can tell,' said Julie. 'He did say he'd tried to get in touch with her. Maybe he was understating it.'

'Where does he live?' asked Mandy, eyebrows aloft.

'Scorton,' said Julie. 'He thought Alice was actually gay, but wouldn't admit it to herself.'

'Pffft, welcome to the club,' said Jenny, almost as an aside. Jade nudged her and winked.

Mandy drummed on the table. 'The fact remains, I still have zero reasons not to release her. We can think this and that, but without a shred of proof I can't charge her. And I think there's a good chance she is innocent of any crime.'

Josh cleared his throat. 'I suggest you go back to the footage from the Bee and analyse it properly over the last six months. Heather has hours of footage. She may have captured something.'

'We will, but that will take a lot of hours of work,' said Mandy. 'And I've got about three before I have to charge or release.'

'Obviously, you'll have searched where she's living in Thornaby,' said Julie.

'Yup, nothing obviously incriminating. She's either totally innocent or she and her twin have meticulously planned this.'

Josh just stared at her, his eyes wide. Nick glanced up at him, knowing that was his look when he was working something out.

'Have you asked her about Save The Earth?' asked Nick.

'Yup. She's a member, but isn't one of the radical ones. She says she was helping to advertise the demo but didn't go, and didn't throw a petrol bomb, and was convincingly amazed that someone might think she would have done such a thing. It must have been the dead woman that you saw throw the petrol bomb. They're physically very similar. And she was obviously a great runner.'

Nick took out his phone and found the photo he'd taken. The

screen was too small to really make out any detail.

'Has anyone got a laptop?'

Jade fetched hers and gave it to him. He loaded the photo onto the screen so everyone could see the dramatic image from Doctor Brown's.

'I thought it was Alice Coates because of the distinctive green eyes, and her legs are similar, the big calves and powerful thighs. She's also got the exact same Lycra running gear she was wearing when I met her in her office.'

'I wish I'd seen this earlier,' said Jenny, looking over his shoulder.

'Why's that, Jen?' asked her mother.

She pointed at the screen.

'That isn't Alice Coates, or rather, the woman that trained us, whatever her name really is.'

'Why are you so sure?' asked Mandy.

'This woman is much more muscular and well-developed. Her thighs and legs are thicker.'

'Are you sure?' said Mandy.

'Positive. I've paid her legs a lot of attention, mate,' she said, and raised her sculpted eyebrows at Mandy, very knowingly for a 16-year-old.

'So is it Dead Woman?' asked Julie.

Jenny shook her head. 'Nope. That woman wasn't a solid unit like this bitch. She looks like a rugby player, mate. Look at the quads on her.' She pointed to the bulge on the front of her thighs. 'Her calf muscles are huge. See that there...' she pointed at the extravagant curve on the back of her lower leg '...trust me, that is a major gastrocnemius muscle. You don't get one of those without serious gym work.'

Josh stared at her as she spoke.

'OK, so what you're telling me is Nick got this wrong in who he thought it was,' said Mandy.

'Kind of,' she said, hesitantly.

'Why the doubt?' asked Julie.

'Because it does look like Miss Coates's eyes. She has very distinctive eyes.'

Nick cleared his throat, took a drink of tea and said, 'But if it's not Dead Woman and it's not Alice in Chains, that means it's someone else. Someone else who looks like the other two.'

They all sat in silence for a few seconds, then Josh spoke in his quick, flat, matter-of-fact way. And having worked out whatever his brain had been cogitating on, as was his way he let it all spill out of his mouth without taking a breath.

'I think you'll find that there are three of them they're not twins they're triplets Alice Coates doesn't know the other two that's why she seems so innocent but the other two conspired to do the killings used her as cover knowing she'd have an alibi if they got seen and tried to set me up as guilty to keep you off the scent in effect the evil two are invisible they went into college when they knew Alice wasn't there and pretended to be her in order to get access to information about the girls and that explains why some met a frosty woman and some a friendly one, but the one that isn't dead is the petrol bomber and freerunner you saw Nick and she's the one you've got to find because rather than risk being caught and sent to jail she'll kill herself.'

'Bloody hell, Josh. How do you know all that?' asked Nick.

'I don't know, it just seems obvious now. It explains everything. And as there are very few triplets born every year, the probability that they were the only triplets adopted seems high and should be traceable for that reason.'

Mandy was writing in her small black police notebook as he spoke, then looked up at Josh.

'If she was going to kill herself where would she do it?'

'My guess is the roof of the gym,' said Julie. 'The whole thing rotates around there. It's the epicentre.'

'I really don't like nicking serial killers, and would far rather they topped themselves and do us all a favour, but the law obliges me,' she said, dialling a number and instructing officers to go to Stockton Sixth Form College, then hung on the phone. 'They're putting me through to Charlesworth, the coroner...' she made a surprised face at them. 'Hello, David. Yes it is a bad business.' She paused to listen. 'Gettaway. Are you sure? All three of them? Bloody hell. Yes, I will.

Thank you.'

She rang off and looked around the table.

'He's just had a load of tests back and the murdered girls were all in the early stages of pregnancy and the father was Paul Richardson.'

'Oh, shit. This changes everything,' said Nick. 'It's about abuse and revenge, not anything to do with population control.'

'The boy was being abused?' said Mandy.

'Yes. Hence his change to being hyper-sexualised.'

'That is gross,' said Jenny.

'Did any of the three girls mention anything to do with sex to you?' asked Mandy.

'I wasn't friends with them. I'm an outsider. I don't mix with that type of kid but the general view of them was that they were dirty. Isn't that right, Jade?'

Her sister nodded. 'They were promiscuous.'

'I'm an outsider, too. They never talked to me either, but he was going out with Connie for a couple of months,' said Josh. 'But he didn't tell me he'd had sex with them but his language changed and he said lots of rude things.'

'And by what the coroner tells me it seems likely that this happened around the same time. Maybe even on the same day.'

Julie rubbed her face. 'Oh, no. Then they fell out, they started slagging him off, that triggered some sort of simmering psychosis, and he killed his parents, then himself. What a horrible state of affairs.'

'Strewth, mate, this is one major exercise in sicko behaviour,' said Robbie, shaking his head. 'Even if it happened like Jules says, where do the murderous triplets come into the equation? What was their motive?'

'That, my friend, is a job for the boys and girls in blue,' said Mandy, standing up. 'And we will find a connection, though if triplet two really has killed herself, we may never discover their true motives.'

'I can't believe all of this,' said Jenny, hands behind her head. 'What the hell sort of weirdo pervert place have you moved us to,

345

mum?'

CHAPTER 23

The following evening, Nick and Julie joined Jeff and Guru in the Royal Oak.

'Four single malts please, Jock,' said Jeff, handing over a £20 note. They took their usual table by the window.

'Well here's to being stardust and golden,' said Guru, raising his glass.

'What a bloody day it's been,' said Julie. 'I feel so sorry for Alice Coates. What on earth must it be like to find out you've got two twins you didn't know about, one or both of them are murderers, and both have now killed themselves. That's just totally overwhelming.'

'Well at least she's alive and free to go home. What was impressive was that young Josh called it 100 per cent right in the end,' said Jeff. 'He went from being prime suspect to being prime detective.'

'When I saw him coming out of McGregor's house, I have to say, my faith in him was severely tested. He was so weird with me, but that was just him and his condition, when under severe stress. He does go into this other mental space, so it actually is like dealing with a different person.'

'Why did they kill McGregor, though?' asked Julie, sipping at the glass of Glenmorangie.

Jeff raised his index finger. 'Ah, I have news from le grande Mandy. They searched his house and took away an old-school written diary in which he documents his lust for teenage girls, but also an entry which mentions briefly seeing Alice Coates with "her sister" on his way home, the day before he was killed. So it seems likely he saw the two evil triplets together and that was what sealed his fate. They couldn't risk anyone knowing they existed. Mandy reckons they spent almost all their time apart, but the forensics are dissecting their phones and getting loads of info from them. They've pieced together a hell of a lot already.'

'I find their motives for murder elusive,' said Guru, tugging on a thick silver loop earring.

'Me, too,' added Julie. 'It's weird beyond belief. It has to be related to the girls' pregnancies, surely.'

'I had coffee and a sarnie with Mandy for tea and she's filled me in on what they've found out so far,' said Jeff. 'And, no, it's nothing to do with any of that. In fact, it's not really to do with anything.'

'Do they have families?' asked Nick.

Jeff shook his head. 'Nope. They were born as triplets in Singapore. Father was in the navy, and had an affair with the wife of an important diplomat. It was politically impossible for them to keep three bastard children, so they were, as far as they can tell so far, given to some adoption agency which farmed them out to other expats. Two, Liz and Bonnie, were kept together; one, Alice, was shipped back to England and brought up in Yorkshire, unaware of the existence of the other two. The people who adopted her were also in the dark. They're still alive and were shocked to have Mandy's mob turn up on their doorstep to tell her.'

'So were the twins brought up in Singapore?' asked Guru.

'Yeah, apparently. But it seems somehow, last year they found out they had a sister, by which time they had already drunk deep from the well of lunacy and had probably already begun their killing spree.'

'And what did they do for money? Did they work?' asked Julie.

Jeff tugged on his beard. 'Here's the amazing thing, if there weren't enough amazing things already. Their adopted parents died a few years ago. They were mega rich and left them a multi-million quid fortune. So they were independently wealthy.'

Nick got up to buy another round. 'So when did they come to Teesside and hatch their weirdo plans?'

'Last autumn. Mandy reckons somehow they got hold of birth records in Singapore, found they had a third "twin" and began to work out how they could use her as a patsy for their crimes.'

He raised his index finger. 'She's also had Interpol on, there's early evidence that they could be responsible for similar deaths in the Far East, Australia and Indonesia. Exactly the same MO. Bodies laid out, neatly. This was just the latest instalment.'

'Has she found a reason for how they arranged the bodies?' asked Nick.

'Liz has some sort of OCD. There's evidence of it in her flat. Everything just so. She just couldn't leave the bodies without tidying them up. Arms by their side, legs together.'

'But McGregor was sprawled on one side,' said Nick.

'The other twin, Bonnie, must have killed him on her own, then,' said Guru.

'Big points to the man with the shiny head,' said Jeff. 'That's exactly what they think.'

Nick went to the toilet. He'd just unzipped when his phone vibrated. He looked at it. Janey.

'Hello, Janey.'

'Hello. How are you?'

'I'm fine.'

'What are you doing?'

He looked down and laughed a little. 'I'm actually in the Royal Oak, in the little boy's room.'

'Oh, dear. I was just calling to get the inside info on what happened yesterday. I only heard what they said on the local news. Are you OK, are the girls and everyone OK?'

'Everyone's fine. It's all over. College can reopen. Look, I'll come round yours for a drink soon and we'll have a chat about it all. Is that alright?'

'Yeah, great. I'm so glad. Glad about everything. It's been so stressful.'

'It has and I'm still finding out things. It's a large, complex, difficult story to explain.'

She paused. He heard her take a drink as the ice clinked in her glass.

'Are you still in the toilet?'

'I am. I can't go now.'

'Why not?' She laughed a little.

He looked down at himself. 'It's hard.'

She laughed again. 'I'm sure it is. I'll see you soon.'

She rang off and he returned downstairs.

As he sat down, Julie said, 'They've found Paul had a secret cloud server and it's full of evidence that, as we thought from the very start, he was being sexually abused by his father and his father's brother. He seems to think his mother knew about it as well but wouldn't face up to it. Probably intended to tell me about it at some point at TW.'

'Oh, the poor boy. Oh, god. I hope they fucking nail the uncle,' said Nick.

'Oh, don't worry about that,' said Jeff. 'His online journal also documents how he stole the chemicals from George Tyers's workshop. As a top student, Tyers had taken him back there for additional work a couple of times.'

'That was why he was so shifty when we were there,' said Julie. 'He knew some chemicals had gone missing and he knew what they could do. So Paul used them to kill his parents?'

Jeff nodded. 'Yup. We'll never know for sure, but I think the two evil triplets were with him and that's why they were neatly laid out. Maybe the OCD one killed them? There's no way to know. In the approximately 24 hours between him doing that and killing himself, he seems to have been intent on getting revenge on Connie and her friends. A theory they're working on is that he was going to personally kill them, but something stopped him. Maybe he just couldn't face confronting them. But our two evil triplets had already arrived on the scene with the idea of using their sister Alice as cover for their latest murderous spree, knowing if they were spotted, everyone would think it was her. Liz had impersonated her at college; she was the one you met, Nick. Bonnie kept tabs on where Alice was, so Liz could have a free run of school. It was all a big elaborate game to them, they loved to scheme and plot it all out.'

'That must be why Janey reported Alice often being in school when she didn't have to be. That was Liz snooping around.'

'Exactly. And she nearly got caught out by your visit. But it's funny how they were all athletic and into running, despite growing up half a world away. That's triplets for you. In the course of being at the college, she saw McGregor's file on Paul's behaviour. It was obvious he was vulnerable. George Tyers has said this morning that he'd confessed to who he thought was Alice Coates, that some of his chemicals had gone missing, and that he suspected Paul had taken them on a recent visit. With access to the office, Liz knew where he lived, caught up with him somewhere, offered him a deal. Kill your parents, then give me the chemicals, and I'll enact your revenge for you. They'd used contact poisons in Singapore, Interpol think, but they're much harder to get over here. Paul is by now in a terribly distressed state and agrees, and he then goes and kills himself. After that it was just a matter of using Josh's photos to muddy the waters further and ensure they weren't caught.'

'But how did she even know of the photos?' asked Guru.

'Good point. This is where McGregor's diaries come in,' said Jeff, but Nick interrupted him.

'Oh, I get it. He was a perv. He would get the passkey for the lockers and go through them looking for girls' intimate stuff, gym clothes, underwear, anything like that; in doing so, he opened Josh's and found the photos.'

'The dirty bastard,' said Julie, contemptuously. 'Creepy shit.'

'That was actually their mistake,' said Nick. 'And they knew it. They accidentally got tied into only being able to kill when Josh was in and around school. What had looked like a great opportunity to frame someone for their murders, ended up tying their hands. They'd killed three in two days. God knows how many others they'd have killed, had Josh not gone into solitary confinement and then been arrested. I'm sure they planned to kill all nine girls in the photos, that had been the "game" and then they'd have moved on, but they boxed themselves in. Maybe they thought Josh would be out and about for another day or two. But by having Liz on the inside, it meant they knew where all the kids lived and which route they'd take to and from school. They killed McGregor, then used his phone to text Josh, hoping he'd be arrested and the whole case put to bed. Then they could move on to pastures new. I suspect one of them was nearby when I turned up, perhaps to photograph Josh at the scene of the crime, then send it to the police, or something '

'Why did McGregor have to die?' asked Julie.

'Because he saw the two evil triplets together. And Liz hated him.

351

Thought he was a slimeball. There's texts about that on her phone. So Bonnie went there and did the business,' said Jeff. 'And they mixed that with trying to frame Josh further. Which nearly worked.'

'So has Mandy got any evidence of their commitment to an eco-terrorist group?' asked Julie.

Jeff shook his head. 'Nope. Nothing. And nothing specifically against girls, either. We were looking for reasons which didn't exist. No reasons have been found.'

'What were they doing at the STE demo then?' said Nick.

'They were ghosts in the machine,' said Guru, cryptically. 'Everywhere and nowhere, baby.'

The three of them looked at him. 'Nah, sorry G, I have no idea what you mean,' laughed Jeff.

Guru thought for a moment. 'No, I have no idea what I mean either. Apologies to all sentient lifeforms looking for wisdom.'

They all cheered and clinked glasses.

'All that happened, I think, was they rode on the back of a small group of extremists, who wanted to basically smear STE and put them out of business for not being radical enough. The fact Paul's parents were in the STE was just coincidence. So somehow they heard about what was going to happen and just joined in,' said Jeff. 'This was just another game for them. It was all one big game being played out.'

'Actually, they were really anarchists, weren't they?' said Julie. 'They're complete outsiders who want to create anarchy, be it with bombs or murder. There's no green philosophy, no eco-terrorism, they're not wedded to anything other than to fuck things up and enjoy exercising the power of life or death. That's what they get off on. They're addicted to the mayhem.'

'And when the power was gone, after Liz was dead, Bonnie couldn't face life without that power and it was time to die,' said Nick.

'So the third triplet's body was on the roof of the gym, just as Josh said it would be,' said Jeff.

Nick nodded. 'It's a sicko tale of woe.' He blew out air. 'I'm so glad it's all over and life can get back to something approaching normal.'

'Is Josh still staying at yours, then?' asked Jeff.

'Yup. I spoke to his mother this morning and she's said that she's happy for him to stay with us full time, if he's happy to, and he is,' said Nick.

Jeff raised his eyebrows. 'Really? She wants to farm him out? That's a bit weird.'

'Well, the reason she's been working so late is due to a promotion she got. But she has to go to Manchester. She can't commute there every day from Palm Grove, but doesn't want to take Josh out of school with his A levels due next year. And change stresses him out. And I think she fancies being free of the responsibility of looking after him, so she can get down to serious shagging and drinking. So anyway, she asked us to step in. It was quite a shock.'

'Ah, so you're doing a bit of the old "in loco parentis". Always thought that sounds like an album by Van Der Graaf Generator,' said Jeff. 'Quick Guru, give me a catalogue number for a VDGG album.' He snapped his fingers.

'*Pawn Hearts*. Charisma CAS 1051. *Godbluff*. CAS 1109.'

They gave him a little clap.

'You could've just made those up, in fairness,' said Julie. 'But I know you haven't. Yeah, well, we like having Josh with us, and it seems to be good for him. The poor luv hasn't had a loving home to go home to for a while and he needs help and guidance at this time in his life, especially from a male role model. Plus we get lovely doggie Stanley into the bargain.'

'It's a very selfless act of you both,' said Guru, putting his fingertips together and nodding in a half prayer. 'The teenage boy is a challenging organism. A case of "I'm in the middle without any plans, I'm a boy and I'm a man". And then he's got Asperger's on top of that.'

'Well, it'll only be until September next year, when he goes to University,' said Nick, who was quietly thrilled to be responsible for the lad.

'Aye, but even so, having a 16-year-old around the house is a big change for you two. There'll be no wandering around the house naked,' said Jeff. 'And no noisy shagging.'

'We'll cope, won't we?' said Julie, smiling at Nick and squeezing his hand.

'And it'll be useful having a genius around the place,' said Nick.

'And the lad is happy with the situation?' asked Jeff.

'Yeah, he loves it at ours. It means he can keep sneaking looks at my below-the-waist parts!' laughed Julie. 'Teenage boys, eh, they don't change.'

'Well, in fairness, I do that too, Jules, and I'm 52,' said Nick. She slapped at him, playfully.

'How's he coping after events at Robbie's?' asked Jeff. 'I mean, being chased halfway across Yorkshire by a lunatic poisoner is a bit traumatic for most. Same goes for Jenny and Jade.'

Julie answered. 'The girls are tough Aussie kids. I mean they really are. Proper full of "fuck you and all who sail in you", so that and their loving family will get them through. And you know Josh, he's able to disengage his emotions from any situation, as long as he's not being hassled. So he's accepted it and already moved on. It helps that he's distracted by having his first girlfriend, Heather.'

Guru lit up. 'They got together? Ah, that's excellent news. I hope they find the meaning of the verb to love. I sensed they were kindred spirits.'

'Only you would quote Todd Rundgren,' said Julie. 'That's why you're lovely.' She patted him on the back of his tanned hand, grinning at him.

'We all need just one victory, and we're on our way.' The tanned, smooth, bald, leathery-skinned man smiled and raised his glass to her.

'I wish we could ask them why they've done what they've done,' said Nick. 'It was so clever and conniving, and yet...to what end? It seems utterly senseless.'

'Does it have to make sense?' said Jeff. 'Two people get loopy ideas and go sick in the head. You can never make sense of that. The story of the human on earth is dominated by the "what the fuck have they done that for?" narrative. We're idiot headbanger chimps and there's no understanding us.'

'Understanding people is like trying to look through milk,' said

Guru.

'I don't recognise that lyric,' said Jeff.

'It's not a song, Jeff. Just an observation.'

Julie drummed on the table and tapped her glass with a fingernail. 'Anyway, now all this horrible nonsense has been put to bed, I've got something to announce to you all.'

'What's that?' said Nick, shocked. 'You're not pregnant, are you?'

She looked at him incredulously. 'And how exactly could that be possible? I'm a reproduction Atacama Desert.'

'I dunno. You hear about miracles like that,' said Nick. 'An egg gets stuck up a tube and only releases itself after a few years.'

'I don't have any eggs up any tubes, thank you.'

'Have you won the Lottery?' said Jeff. 'If so, I have a first pressing of John Martyn's debut album on pink Island; it's yours for £300.'

She shook her head.

'Sadly, no. That would be tricky as I don't do the Lottery.'

'Ah, you must have a new job?' asked Guru.

'Not quite, but sort of.'

She looked at them all with bright, excited eyes.

'I've made up my mind. You all persuaded me. You are looking at the Independent candidate for Teesside North and Central in the upcoming parliamentary by-election.'

'Amazing!' exclaimed Jeff. 'You know you're going to win. The whole of Hardwick and Norton will turn out to vote for you. Your brothers and Jackie will frog march everyone to the voting booth under threat of violence.'

'Well, it's not going to be easy, but I have an outside chance. I just feel that I might as well. I've thought about it for 25 years.'

'I'd love to see you in Parliament,' said Nick. 'Asking questions at PMQs. Sticking it to the stuck-up wankers.'

'Let's not get ahead of ourselves,' she said.

'And it's plenty of coin. What is it - 70 grand and another 70 to run an office? That's sweet gravy,' said Jeff.

'It'd be more money than we've ever had,' said Julie. 'That's for sure.'

'What side are your politics on, left or right?' asked Guru.

'I'm neither left or right. Like most people, I'm a mix of all sides and none. And what does left and right even mean any more? It's an outdated notion. I'm just going to stand on a platform, tell people what I think would help our lives be better, but without any old-fashioned political tag. People are sick of political parties. I know I am. If people like what I say, I might do OK. If they don't, I'll crash and burn. It's going to be a hell of a battle to win the seat. But, in my favour, it's a three-way marginal, so the vote will be split. Hopefully, I can go through the middle. I probably only have to take 25 per cent of the vote to win.'

As they sat and talked about it for the rest of the evening, somewhere in his subconscious mind, Nick began to worry that this was the start of a big new battle - a big new and very dirty battle - but now wasn't the time for new concerns, so he swallowed them down, raised his glass and proposed a toast.

'Here's to the Right Honourable Julie Wells, MP.'

THE END

Books in the Nick Guymer Series

Published by HEAD PUBLISHING

1. Teesside Steal (2013)
2. Queen of the Tees (2013)
3. Teesside Missed (2013)
4. DJ Tees (2014)
5. Teesside Blues (2014)
6. Tyne Tees (2014)
7. High Tees (2015)
8. Teesside Meat (2015)
9. Teesside Shadows (2015)
10. King Tees (2016)
11. Teesside Dreams (2016)
12. Blood on the Tees (2016)
13. Teesside Outsiders (2017)

A Nick Guymer Comic Short Novel
Published by HEAD PUBLISHING

Knickers Always Go Down Well (2016)

Kindle/Paperback

http://www.johnnicholsonwriter.co.uk

About John Nicholson

John is a well-known football writer whose work is read by tens of thousands of people every week. He's a columnist for Football365.com and has worked for the Daily Record, The Mirror, The New European, Sky and many other publications.

Books in the Artie Taylor Series
Published by HEAD PUBLISHING

1. The Girl Can't Help It (2014)
2. Sugar Mama (2016)

Kindle/Paperback

http://www.johnnicholsonwriter.co.uk

Other John Nicholson Books
published by Biteback Publishing

We Ate All The Pies -
How Football Swallowed Britain Whole (2010)

The Meat Fix -
How 26 Years of Healthy Eating Nearly Killed Me (2012)